TALES OF KAIMERE

FOR MY LATE GRANDMOTHERS.

TO ELISI DARKWIND,

I CHERISH THE MEMORIES OF YOUR EXCITEMENT
FOR THE SEA, FOR ART,
AND RESOLUTE DEDICATION TO A JUST WORLD.
THANK YOU FOR MY NAME.

TO DR. ELIZABETH STRONG,

FOR YOUR UNENDING WONDER
AT THE NATURAL WORLD,
FOR NURTURING THE SAME IN ME,
AND LIVING A LIFE SO TRUE TO YOUR
PASSIONS AND CONVICTIONS
THAT I HAD NO CHOICE BUT TO DO THE SAME.

Tales of Kaimere

ANTHOLOGY 2
SONGS OF THE
INLAND SEA

Keenan Taylor

Contents

What is Kaimere?

Kaimere is a distant planet. It is defined by waves of life brought from Earth and set free to evolve independently in this new context. The indigenous life of the planet, swarms of microbes called 'magic' by the people who live there, are what harvest Earth organisms and make copies on Kaimere.

As the asteroid that ended the age of dinosaurs sixty six million years ago never struck Kaimere, dinosaurs carried on as the dominant terrestrial megafauna, continuing to evolve into a wide range of new groups and species. In addition to dinosaurs, more recent harvests have collected a range of animals much more familiar, including lions, horses, and humans.

Eleven thousand years ago, a now-extinct species of archaic human called the First Children domesticated many strains of Kaimeran magic. They used this ability to create homunculi, demons that were host to their tame magic that the First Children could control. After their culling of megafauna on Qajar, another harvest was triggered to repopulate their new home. With their knowledge of magic, they managed to trap the portal in a stasis, enabling them to not only close the portal, but also travel back to Earth.

The First Children are now gone. Subsequent civilizations rose and fell, all using different relics of the First Children's magic. In modern Kaimere, the peoples of the Known World have a strain of hereditary magic which grants them long lives and enhanced health as the magic bound to them takes great care to preserve their host. These peoples, called kaimerans, have a diverse range of cultures throughout the Known World. The regions beyond the known world are vast, each with their own distinct peoples, enormous monsters, and sinister demons. In some places, the land itself is enchanted by the indigenous organisms, making vast forests of magical flora and fauna.

Despite a history stained with many bloody conflicts, Kaimere is now a world of peace. Many of their long generations have gone by without war. However, rumors persist of massing dangers in the realms beyond. Peace has been hard won, and most would rather ignore these signs than address them, resulting in a state of tension that permeates the Known World.

This is a realm of wondrous adventure, dangers both natural and occult, wild magic, and monsters lost to time.

Welcome to Kaimere.

Good luck.

Map of Kaimere:

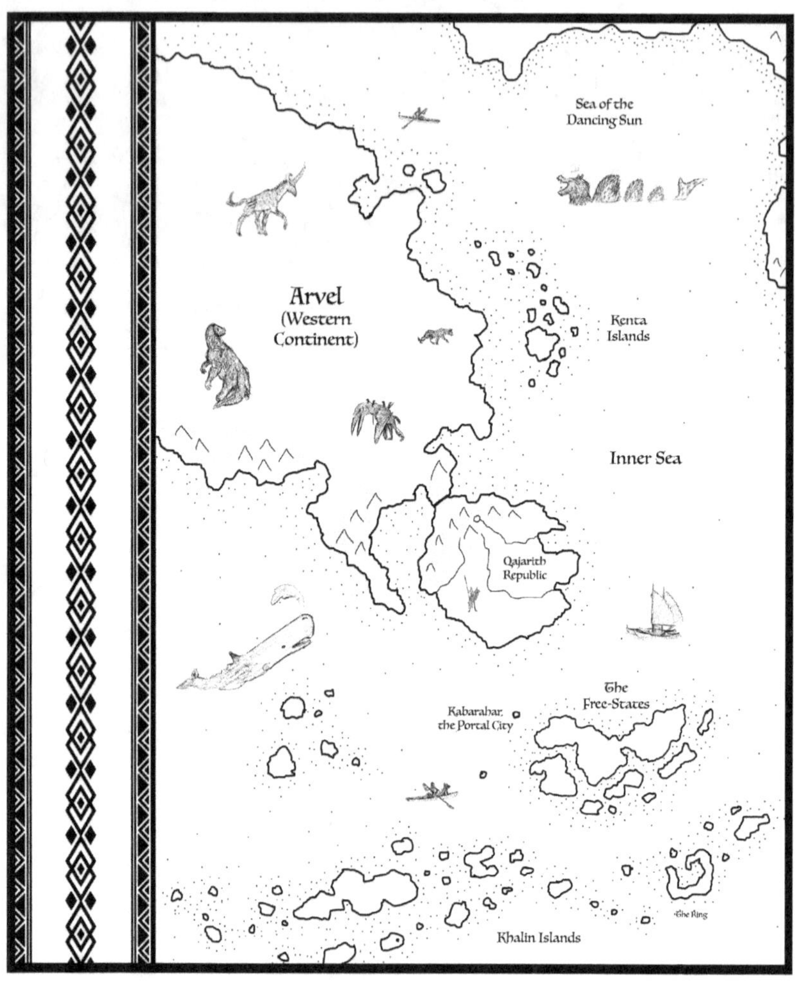

The Known World

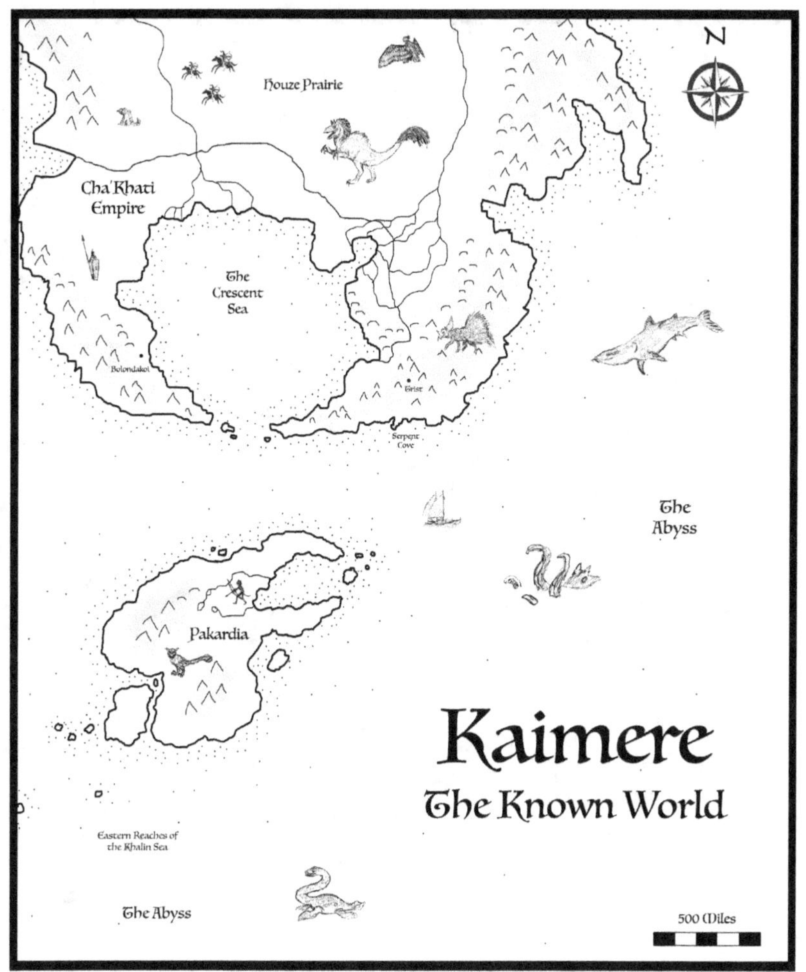

The White Coast

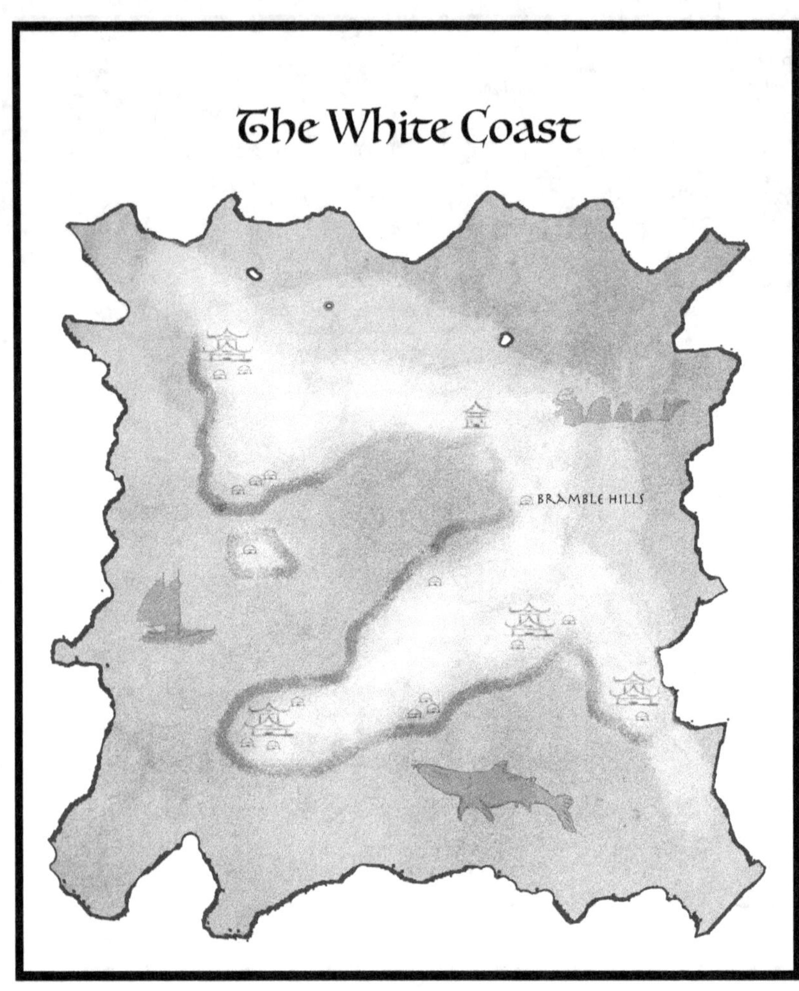

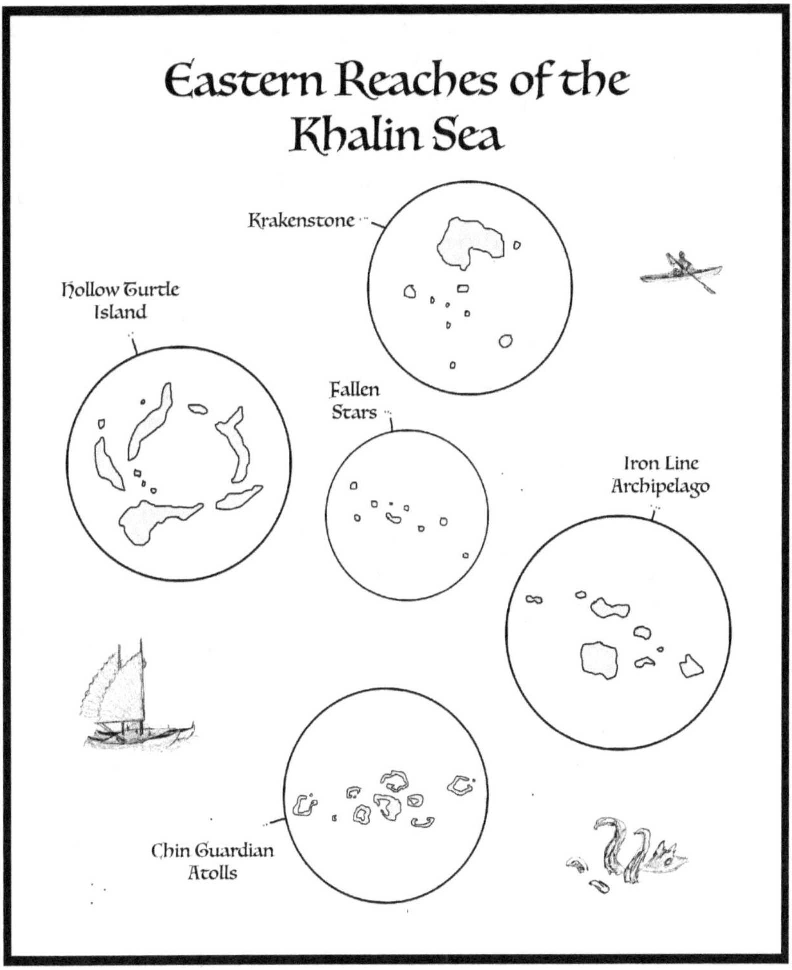
Eastern Reaches of the Khalin Sea
Krakenstone
Hollow Turtle Island
Fallen Stars
Iron Line Archipelago
Chin Guardian Atolls

Introduction

Without water, there can be no life.

Having grown up in more places than I could hope to count, I have always been a voyager. In all our travels, for most summers my family would return to the same camp in the Adirondacks. In addition to being my childhood sense of home, camp cultivated a love for the natural world, and it was on the nearby Beaver Lake that I learned how to navigate the water.

I first learned to paddle in a canoe; first in the front, then steering in the back. I also rowed on the lake, and sailed with mixed results a few times on the little sloop that camp owned. My favorite was the kayaks, and I couldn't tell you how many hours I've spent out on the waters near camp. I decided on Beaver Lake to write this next anthology centered around lakes, rivers, and vast oceans.

My love for open water was passed to me from both of my grandmothers.

Dr. Strong loved all creatures, but butterflies, elephants, and cetaceans held special places in her heart, and whale watching was a favorite way to pass time. She traveled to Alaska many times to boat with grey whales, and regularly visited Boston Harbor to see humpbacks dance and play. She and I took many whale watching trips together, and her wonder at their gentle majesty is something I am proud to have inherited.

For Elisi Darkwind, a life by the sea was of great importance. It was evident she cherished the connection in seeing her smile whenever her feet touched the sand. In the water she found truth and centering. The name she gave me, Duyugodvayosdi Truth-Seeker, is one I carry with pride.

Since the publication of my first anthology, Elisi and Grandma Strong both passed. My thoughts were on both as I went whale watching, kayaked the lake, and learned how to sail a larger craft on Lake Ontario. While I cannot say they directly inspired me to base my second anthology on seafaring, they were with me at every step of the process.

It was by no coincidence that Kaimere, the setting of my stories, features a great inland sea as its focal point. Most peoples of the known world rely upon the bounty of the sea for sustenance, and depend on seafaring for trade and travel. Each of these stories is set in the water. Some in freshwater, others from the perspective of creatures in the waters of Kaimere, but most are tales of the sea. Thrilling heists, narrow escapes, enduring the dangers of the natural world, honoring lost traditions, and struggles for vengeance await you in these songs of the inland sea. I hope you find excitement, joy, and wonder in these pages.

If you are able, I encourage you to seek water. Out on a lake, your feet in the sand, or dancing in the rain. All our human experiences are different, but I find little in this world makes me feel more alive and connected than when I am out on the water.

This song is my love letter to camp, to my grandmothers, and to the sea.

Disclaimer of Translation:

The following stories have been
translated from their original Kaimeran languages.

As is the nature of translation, it is not precise.

While great effort was made to preserve the
integrity of the original work, liberties were
taken for the sake of efficient comprehension
and conveying intended impact.

Keenan Taylor

Haunted Legacy

1

Haunted Legacy

Prologue

Nasiri's gaze locked on his target.

Some ten span out, a great lion was hunkered over its latest victim; a young man it had killed the day before. This lion's black and cream fur was a mark of having domesticated Nerotan war cat heritage. As the Nerotans insisted their lions were carefully monitored, it was likely this was descended from a stolen cub that later proved too much for the thieves who did not have the diligent training of the Nerotan lion tamers so abandoned it to the wilds, where it integrated into a wild pride. What resulted from this union was the hybrid before them had no fear of people, but the predatory instincts of its wild parent, a recipe for a man-eater.

The locals called him Aldakus: Blood in the Shadows. This far north in Republic territory, Nerotans had no authority so could not handle the situation, and Aldakus had become notorious. In his season of terror, presumably since being driven from his mother's pride, he had killed at least sixty-seven farmers, not all of which were eaten. For his great size, the cat had eluded locals.

As soon as Nasiri heard of the beast, he sought out Aldakus with his three apprentices.

While Zhehan, Borus, and Rukirha were behind him with their own weapons, Nasiri set an arrow to his bow.

The moment Nasiri raised his bow, his hand trembled.

With a deep breath, Nasiri fixed his attention on the blood-stained jaws, across the dark neck, over the rippling shoulders, settling on a notch in the shoulder muscles that marked the heart. As he focused on that point, the tremor in his hand eased.

Keeping his eyes on his mark, Nasiri raised his bow overhead, lowered it with the draw, and let the arrow fly.

As he released, the tremor returned, and the arrow went wide.

It sank into the grass just before Aldakus.

The lion turned, letting out a cutting roar so deep that Nasiri felt it in his joints. Rather than bolt as he anticipated, Aldakus returned the focused gaze. With centuries of experience hunting man-eaters, Nasiri had seen all the expressions a big cat could make. In those chilling blue eyes, Nasiri saw something he had never seen before, yet still clear in its understanding.

The great lion saw weakness. Vulnerability. A potential victim that would make any hunter press the advantage.

Nasiri's next shot missed by an even greater margin.

With a resonant snarl that made Nasiri freeze, Aldakus erupted toward him as a fire of strength and rage…

Chapter 1

Loregus had never taken a job on a ship, and indeed had no love for the sea, but he was bored and the pay was too good to turn down.

He was not pressed for finances. His mother's family paid well for her bastard to stay away and stay quiet. Although Loregus was happy to leech the coffers of House Derukov, he dared not press his grandfather, for the man obsessed with appearances and legacy would no doubt have him killed if he caused too much trouble. Baron Derukov ensured Loregus had enough to live comfortably.

Unfortunately, Loregus preferred to live a few ranks above comfort, and rapidly drained his allowances. Shortly after moving to the Free States and enduring an introductory career in a theater guild, he was approached by a man who not only saw his wasted potential, but had the funds for a lavish living, something Loregus quickly grew quite attached to.

The man was Jaran, and the means to this higher living was employment with a new guild: the Shards. Some called them a thieves guild. Jaran insisted they were merely a guild of freelance workers who valued discretion. Loregus was used to discretion, and so far all he had been asked to do was distract nobles so the real thieves could do their work, and Loregus not only was treated to many fine parties and costumes, he also had more than enough to turn his apartment into a suitable display of finery.

This appreciation for the finer things in life had landed him on a crowded dock. The smell of the sea around them was pleasant enough, but shrieking gulls soured the mood, as did the scent of their waste so abundant on the dock posts that they were more white than exposed wood. Even first class ticket holders like him still had to wait in line. Wasn't the purpose of spending extra to not have to do commoner things like wait aimlessly?

Although he had never much appreciated ships or the sea, Loregus had to admit the Imperial sunship cruiser was breathtaking to look upon. Easily seventy span in length and boasting more masts than he bothered to count. It dwarfed the other ships in Kabarahar's harbor, and this was the only pier it could dock at.

He looked ahead, taking note of one of the ledger staff at the end of the plank. The Kentarim girl with long gold coils who's crew uniform was two sizes too large for her petite frame. Toyate was her name, if he remembered correctly.

They met the night before in Jaran's 'office', a private dock owned by the Shards. Loregus had met the whole team. A banished Akanuk named Muluk who would be the muscle. A quirky old Imperial with a knack for tinkering named Shin. Toyate was the thief, supposedly a skilled acrobat. Jaran was the facilitator of the run. Loregus had been told his own talents in acting and impersonation would be required to distract those guarding the target until they were ready to abandon ship. If all went well, he might even be able to remain on the sunship for the whole voyage with none being the wiser.

The target was an object of... some sort. He probably shouldn't have gone to the meeting after visiting the Golden Belt, and the drinks he indulged in while at the great establishment were the source of the morning's headache he was still recovering from. Piecing together his fragmented memories, their anonymous client paid a lot of money for them to steal something off the ship. Jaran might not even have said what they were stealing. By the end of the meeting, Loregus was feeling the effects of his second bottle pretty strong.

No matter. If all he had to do was eat good food, draw attention, and flirt with anyone who caught his eye, Loregus was happy for the gig.

The other crewman with Toyate looked over her shoulder, standing quite close. Loregus presumed he was her supervisor of some sort. The man's leering gaze brought a frown to Loregus's face, especially noting her open discomfort. She was an infiltrator. Clearly playing the part of new hire on the ship wasn't to her liking, but Jaran had to do whatever he could to fit the group in. Loregus vaguely remembered Muluk was also added to the crew. Loregus didn't remember much about the towering man other than a full head of white coils, massive beard, and built like a mud bear.

Although they weren't standing together, Jaran and the tinkerer Shin were in the middle class dock further toward shore. Well, could it really be called shore if they were on a floating city in the middle of the inland sea? Loregus had lived here in Kabarahar for eight years but never considered the question until now.

As he looked back, Loregus spotted a pair of Imperial folk, western Imperials by their lighter tawny skin and coiled black hair. Both man and woman were strikingly attractive: the woman lean and wide eyed, the man broad and angular. Both wore a broadsword at their waist. Their silk dusters and boots were the same material, hers yellow and his a deep red, billowing below the waist in the crisp afternoon breeze, and they wore matching gold pins on their left breast.

Librarians.

A flood of information from the meeting last night came back to him.

The librarians had found some artifacts in Arvel, and were sailing back to the Great Library in Bolondakoi. This sunship had plenty of other passengers and luggage, but their artifacts were put in a secure vault, which was why Shin the tinkerer was so important. Would also help to have two members on staff. For the life of him, Loregus couldn't remember if he just forgot what they were hired to steal, or if Jaran hadn't mentioned. It was Loregus's job to distract the librarians and perhaps render them unconscious for the heist itself if the need arose.

Loregus had a keen eye for how people carried themselves. Was important to playing a convincing character. The librarians both walked with the erect posture of a trained combatant. The man had a relaxed confidence that made Loregus's chest flutter, and complimented a serious expression that spoke of a man in his prime who cut no corners and was used to getting what he wanted. The woman carried herself with similar training, but she was stiff and looked around with a nervous crease in her brow. She was young, barely in her first century, and if Loregus had to guess, probably a student of the older librarian.

These two would be the biggest obstacles to Loregus's team collecting their target, and it was his duty to distract them.

This was shaping up to be his easiest and most pleasant job yet!

***

Helana felt there were far too many eyes on them.

Ra Maslani walked with his usual relaxed gait, indifferent to everyone staring at them.

With what they now had below deck, they needed to draw as little attention as possible.

The crew of the ship had regarded them with no shortage of skepticism, but since the Captain was himself Bolondakir and this was an Imperial vessel, they at least hadn't voiced their worries. Loading their findings last night had been a tense affair. The captain had posted guards with the treasure hunter Kronan down below, but she was still nervous about leaving the ship. Ra Maslani said it would do them good to get something solid underfoot before the push to the Crescent Sea. Kabarahar was a floating city. She assumed he was making a joke about solid ground, but he sounded completely sincere. Even being Ra Maslani's apprentice for the past year, she still hadn't grasped his sense of humor, if he even had one.

Helana and Ra Maslani marched down the docks toward the Imperial sunship.

It was an astonishing vessel. Far larger than the sleek clipper they had taken from western Arvel. That had been a small craft and not terribly quick. This cruiser had four decks and nine masts. It would get them to the Great Library in half the time and would much better defend them from pirates or sea monsters. She knew she should feel safer, but she couldn't shake a sense of anxiety.

Maybe it was just worry about what they were transporting.

As they walked, a small group in the middle class dock caught her eye.

First was the tallest of the bunch, a handsome young Qajarith man with short-cut temples and a clean-shaven face. He was broad, much like the treasure hunter Kronan, only a lot younger. With his arms crossed while he was engaged in a heated discussion with one of his companions, his arms and chest flexed, and Helana had to suppress the next thought that came to mind.

The man he spoke to was a different sort of attractive. An Imperial, he was lean and his features sharp. He wore his hair long, now back in a horse tail, and his clothes were form-fitting. Normally it would make him look trim, but now it only showed he lacked the impressive build of the man to his left. His clothing wasn't too elaborate, but the silk and rich dyes made it clear he came from much finer means than his Qajarith companion.

The other pair of the quartet were Pakardiant. It wasn't often the inhabitants of the great jungle island left their home. The woman was young, around Helana's age, and her black hair was cropped short. She wore a leopard pelt as a skirt over trouser and chaps. Like her elder companion, she wore a holstered bow at her hip with a quiver at her lower back. She also had a pair of bandoliers filled with strange tinctures.

Helana at first only gave the older Pakardiant a quick glance, but when she saw the Trist spear and a long scar from his temple up into his grey knot of curls, she all but stopped in her tracks.

Nasiri the Hunter.

***

Nasiri wanted nothing more than to lie down.

There was no way for him to lean that didn't press into some ache. Some old broken bone or scarred wound that didn't heal quite right. He missed not having to think about taking care of himself. As long as he set the bone or cleaned the initial impact, his body would do the rest.

Ah, the innocent joys of youth.

This often happened with age, but in his youth, he never imagined it would happen to him. Zhehan explained that without hereditary magic, kaimerans would grow old and die by the time they were seventy, as happened with the humans of the plaguelands on the other side of the Whistling Door. Although magic let them live for centuries, it didn't last forever. Eventually the magic got old. Tired. Couldn't repair what it once could. Nasiri hadn't given it much thought at the time. Zhehan knew lots of interesting things Nasiri didn't pay much attention to. The notion now ate at him. His mind was sharp as ever, but now that he was approaching his fifth century, Nasiri felt his magic aging as much as his body. It seemed strange to think about, but that's what his own people said about spirits being distinct from bodies. Spirits don't age. When the body dies, they leave. Was the hereditary magic of Zhehan's university studies and the personal spirit of Pakardiant folklore two words for the same thing? Was his spirit aging? It made more sense by the day.

He hated the thought.

As he shifted, pain shot up Nasiri's left leg. He dared not lift his chaps to check the wound, which should have healed by now. The lion man-eater they had killed on the northwest coast of Qajar had scored a terrible bite. Nasiri should never have let it get that close.

He should have let Borus or Ru take the shot instead.

In his arrogance, Nasiri had shot despite a tremor in his arm. The arrow only injured the beast, causing it pain, and in its panic and rage, charged. Thankfully Borus and Ru had managed to kill the beast, but it was messy. Not the clean kill he usually made, and certainly not the lesson he wanted to teach his new apprentices.

A shrill cry overhead drew the attention of the other passengers around them. Many pointed up in excitement. Nasiri knew that cry anywhere, but looked up regardless.

Although he had seen plenty of titan crows since the Raven King, he still felt a chill at their presence all these centuries later. The wings were angled forward, which was the easiest way to distinguish bat-winged birds, or sky titans. The titan crow's black feathers seemed to absorb all light above, and only the sun shining through the membrane of its wings betrayed it was not a silhouette. It looked the size of a vulture, but it was surely a distortion of just how high above it flew: he knew its wings must span the height of seven men at least.

Vaskalamaldus the Raven King must have been twice the size of this natural beast, if not more. Nasiri thought back on the encounter, remembering how terribly unprepared he had been. Maybe the beast had been a demon, perhaps simply outsized, but he had ignored the warnings and rumors and proceeded as though it were a mundane beast. His arrogance had gotten good men killed that day. Must this flaw he thought he had grown out of be the death of his apprentices too?

Even as he chided his arrogance, he still thought back on how strong he had been in those days. How swift on his feet and accurate in his throws. There must have been a full two centuries where he missed a mark fewer times than he had fingers on one hand. Now his arrows hit with an increasingly generous radius, and the lion he missed altogether.

In his youth, the bite wound would have already healed. His body was repairing itself, but it was so slow. Five days later, he still felt the tenderness.

The titan crow continued its flight south. They always flew across the vast abyss in the spring and returned before winter began. The Akanuk whalers he spoke to during a hunt said the summer months of the mysterious polar continent were bountiful, and many birds and beasts traveled south to feast.

Despite the dark memories its presence inspired, Nasiri wished the great black bird a safe migration and a smorgasboard waiting for it across the southern ocean.

He had taken on apprentices to teach them how to kill man-eaters in a responsible and humane way. If they were messy and failed to kill it, or worse injure an innocent animal that would be then forced to kill people for sustenance, they would only make matters worse.

Was he making matters worse by insisting on accompanying them in these missions?

None of them said anything. Borus and Ru seemed indifferent. Sometimes you got hurt. Sometimes you miss. Mistakes happen. Zhehan might not have spoken up, but he had now been working with Nasiri for sixteen years. In that time he had no doubt seen a decline in Nasiri's strength, accuracy, and recovery.

Nasiri had taken on apprentices not just to lighten his burden, but to carry on his methods and learn from his mistakes after retirement. The reality was if he went on more missions, he was likely to die in the jaws of one of his targets. This was always a reality of hunting dangerous game, but now that he had more debilitating injuries than bones in his body, Nasiri knew his continued participation in these hunts was irresponsible. Hubris.

If he actually practiced what he taught, which was the importance of a quick, clean kill to remove dangerous animals from the known world so that animals living their natural ways could continue on, he needed to let those who could hold a steady bow take over.

As the known world became more populated and more settlements encroached on the wilds, it would become increasingly important for there to be experienced hunters like his apprentices who could handle the situation with minimal bloodshed.

Were his apprentices ready?

They would have to be.

****

Once the massive cruiser took to open water, Loregus bathed, left his spacious personal quarters in the rear of the sunship, and established himself in the lounge. For what ultimately was a room under the elevated deck at the front, it was quite accommodating. Well-padded to insulate outside noises, and he could barely hear commotion in what he assumed was a more spacious mess hall for the middle classes. The silk cushions were divine. They spared no expense with perfumes which complimented the fresh ocean air outside.

For a while he was one of only three patrons in the lounge, not including the few staff and four courtesans no doubt hired to make everyone present feel important. Loregus noted the men all seemed uninterested in socializing, so he kept himself busy with a foamed glass of whiskey with honey, ginger root, and citrus. His fellow patrons seemed miserable for all their wealth. Pathetic. Loregus loved the doting presence.

Although he quite liked this environment, and would happily chat up the male courtesan, he knew he had a job to do.

Loregus downed the cocktail, set the empty glass at the bar, and made his way downstairs to the middle class lounge. The doorman at the top of the stairway let him pass without question, no doubt being posted to prevent middle class clientele from entering the upper deck lounge, but Loregus was free to go where he pleased.

This lounge was the same size as the first class lounge above, but was a lot more crowded. Some thirty patrons were scattered throughout the many tables, and the bar staff were already busy ensuring everyone had a drink or some early dinner.

Jaran was seated alone in one of the corner tables, a meal before him and shrouded in smoke. Loregus respected Jaran for many things, not the least of which was his aesthetic and appreciation for the importance of presentation. Jaran should probably be blending in, and maybe he thought he was, but in trying to fade into the background, he only drew attention to himself when everyone else in the room was casual.

Even the two librarians, who had a table to themselves at the opposite end of the lounge, stood out less.

"What are you doing?" Jaran growled, his pipe still gripped between his teeth. "We don't know each other."

"No, we don't," said Loregus, sitting across from Jaran and crossing his legs. "I am a striking noble here to have a good time, and you are drawing some serious allure. I see no reason why my character wouldn't stop to see what all the intrigue is about. You are a brilliant man, but you are about as subtle as a titan in a dandelion meadow, and Raun of House Gradil would absolutely be drawn to you in this crowd. He is drawn to anything interesting."

"Are you just playing yourself with a different name, *Raun?*" said Jaran, his tone gruff as ever but a slight curl of his lip hinting at the lighthearted nature of the jab.

"Possibly," Loregus said, batting his eyes innocently. "Now I'm going to act deeply offended and go chat with the attractive librarian over there."

"Don't do anything rash. Earn their trust and keep them distracted. We're not moving until three nights from now. Keep a low profile."

"I'll take it under consideration."

After that, Loregus stood and turned to the bar. Fortunately it did not take long for the server to provide him with a cup of chilled red. Dry with spice hints from what the server said, but he didn't much care.

With cup in hand, he made his way to the table with the two librarians.

The man sat with a ceramic mug of dark liquid. Coffee, if Loregus's nose was correct. The young woman had tea. They had been sharing a hushed conversation, which died when Loregus arrived.

"Is this seat taken?" he asked, indicating the seat beside the woman.

"No," she said, although her companion said nothing, only gave a hard look to the woman then Loregus.

"Excellent."

Loregus sat beside her. Neither said anything. Loregus took a sip of the wine. It was soothing, enhanced by the chill, and the hint of clove was pleasant. He sighed involuntarily before smiling up at the male librarian.

"Apologies. This is good. Would you like some? I can have the bottle brought over."

"The servers are busy," said the man, his baritone smooth and chilling in the best way possible. "And my coffee is fine."

Loregus nodded. "Well and good. I couldn't help but notice the pair of you on your way to the ship. I was asking my friend over there," Loregus nodded to Jaran across the lounge. "If he had been introduced to you. He didn't say so."

"You're his friend?" asked the young woman. "He seemed confused when you sat down."

Loregus put his hands up while still holding the glass. "You've caught me in a lie, young beauty. I asked him because he seemed observant and, frankly, more approachable than the two of you. You librarians have a bit of an intimidating reputation. I am Raun of the Gradil Family. You may call me Raun. What names do you go by? Is it true the library assigns you names?"

"No, of course not!" said the young woman, suppressing a laugh. "I am Tra Helana Bolekari. Call me Helana. I'm an apprentice under Ra Doru Maslani here. You should call him Ra Maslani. Ra is the title of high scholar. We are part of the Acquisitions Department. Well, Ra Maslani is. I will be someday, though!"

"A pleasure to meet you both," Loregus said, placing a hand on his heart before nodding to Ra Maslani then his apprentice. "What is your specialization, Ra Doru Maslani?"

"Artifacts, primarily of the early First Age," Ra Maslani said reluctantly.

Loregus had to fight to not melt at his cadence. "First Age? Is that the Age of Witches?"

"That is the Third Age," said Helana, giving him a sympathetic shake of the head. "The First Age begins with the First Children conquering what is now Qajar around twelve thousand years ago, and ended with the collapse of their civilization a little over a thousand years later."

"I thought the First Children were, oh, I don't know. Some say they were magical insect or bat people. Others that they were swarms of magic that made tiny bodies for themselves. Lots of weird stories. I thought we didn't know much about them for sure."

"We don't," Helana admitted. "But recent discoveries are helping to give us a more comprehensive understanding. Although their settlements in Qajar are lost to time and destruction in their collapse, we've had a lot of luck with outlying settlements, which seem to not have been hit as hard in the collapse. In fact we're on our way back from a-"

Ra Maslani cut her off with a stern glare.

"Well, I'm actually not supposed to talk about it yet, but once the librarians have studied it, I'm sure the news will travel far and wide. Truly exciting developments. This is going to help understand the First Children not as fairies or gods, but as a complex civilization, and once we see them as people, it will help us understand what led to their collapse."

"Fascinating developments indeed," said Loregus, although his interest was not piqued. She was passionate and excited about the subject, which was endearing in no small part because she was pretty, but he had never cared much for history. Having known a few 'Great Men' in his time, Loregus was confident most if not all figures glorified in historical treatises were only made great by standing on the backs of others to catch the light. For all their accomplishments great and terrible, the First Children were surely no different. Not fairies, and certainly not gods. Anything mighty they created was surely done by a silent majority who would never be discussed in text or honored in a museum.

"Oh, that's Nasiri again!"

Loregus turned.

The name sounded familiar, and when he laid eyes on the figure at the front of the quartet now entering the lounge, he recognized the legendary hunter by his scar and Trist-point spear. If there was any doubt, the many trophies of pelt squares, claws, and teeth the Pakardiant man wore through his outfit cleared up the matter.

"See all kinds on a ship like this," he remarked as they took a seat at the only free table, the one which Jaran had just gotten up from. When Loregus saw how excited Helana looked, he smiled.

"Why don't you go talk to them?" said Ra Maslani. "Just remember to not talk too much about our work."

"Yes, Ra," she said.

Loregus barely stood in time for her to move past and start toward them, then veer off to get a drink at the bar beforehand. Helped his nerves too when going to speak to someone exciting.

When he turned back to take a sip, Ra Maslani was staring directly at him. Loregus froze with his cup at his lips. Once he overcame the initial intensity, he made a point to ease and enjoy his drink. "What is going on in that head of yours, Ra?"

Ra Maslani's eyes thinned. "You aren't subtle, Raun Gradil. Not nearly as subtle as you think you are."

Loregus's heart rate accelerated. He checked himself so as not to give away any concern with his breathing. Had he pushed too much with the questioning? Helana had thrown everything at him, he didn't exactly push, certainly not enough to raise suspicions. Stars, he didn't even care about the First Children. How had Ra Maslani possibly perceived anything to suggest the job they were running? Loregus did his best to appear calm as he thought through anything that could have given him away. Did the librarian perhaps recognize Jaran?

"For the past eight months, I've only had the company of a few laborers, an apprentice who I have begrudgingly grown to care for despite being assigned to me for no merit other than the high standing of her father, and the insufferable treasure hunter who originally found the site. I have a shift guarding our artifacts this evening. I'm going to go tell my apprentice to stay and enjoy the company at that table with the monster hunter. If you would like to join me in my room, I am in Suite Eleven. Knock three times. If you don't show, I don't care, but if you do, I assure you we will both reach our destination in much more pleasant dispositions."

Loregus was still in shock when Ra Maslani stood, straightened his earthy red coat, and finished the rest of his coffee in a long gulp. He set it down hard, making Loregus jump, and marched over to his apprentice, who was only just then getting her own drink. Loregus watched as Ra Maslani and Helana exchanged brief words, then he turned and strode out of the lounge with the presence and confidence of a lion patrolling his territory.

An entirely new rush made Loregus's heart drum against his chest. He slowly took a sip of his wine, letting it soothe him.

Before Helana had a chance to introduce herself to Nasiri and his group of misfits, one of them wandered to the bar beside her, looking ready to strike up a conversation. Always easier when someone else opens the conversation, especially when it was the cute if simple-looking Qajarith boy. Good for her.

This job was indeed proving to be delightful. Distracting and occupying the main librarian suddenly got a lot easier and a lot more enjoyable.

Loregus smiled. He took his time finishing the rest of his wine, set his glass down, and left to seek out Suite Eleven.

***

Helana could tell the bartender was getting impatient with her indecision.

She had barely had a few beers at university and wasn't terribly fond of them, Ra Maslani insisted on no alcohol at the dig site, so she was at a loss of what to get.

"Four drinks when you get a moment."

The voice over her right shoulder made Helana jump. She turned to see the tall Qajarith companion of Nasiri the Hunter looming behind her. When he noticed her reaction, he took a step back. "Sorry, miss. Tight space. Didn't mean to get so close."

"It's alright, I don't mind," she said quickly before wishing she hadn't said anything.

His brow creased at that before his expression shifted to a shy smile. "Good to know."

"What can I get you, big guy?" asked the bar tender.

"She was here first," the Qajarith said.

"I've asked her three times and she doesn't know. If you know what you want, I can at least get to work while she considers."

"What interests you?" asked the Qajarith. "Other drinks you like?"

"Get your drinks and maybe I'll get inspired."

He gave another one of those shy, gentle smiles and nodded. "Sure thing. I would like a pale lager, chilled please. Whiskey with stone, black coffee, and a rum and mint cocktail with a splash of blackcurrant wine."

Helana exclaimed. "That last one sounds excellent!"

"Two of the cocktails, please."

The bartender nodded and got to work after taking the eight silver coins the Qajarith set for him.

"Which one is yours?" Helana asked.

"Chilled lager for me. I like a drink that can fill me up. Whiskey is for my friend Zhehan, cocktail is for Ru, and Nasiri got the black coffee. He doesn't like fancy things."

"And what's your name? I'm Helana."

"Borus. A pleasure to meet you."

"Likewise. How did you meet Nasiri?"

"I sought him out," Borus replied. "My grandfather was a boy when Nasiri saved our village from a titan crow that turned man-eater. He's a bit of a folk hero where I'm from. I've always loved hunting. It's the only thing I'm good at. I heard Nasiri had taken an apprentice. Zhehan over there." Borus pointed over to the Imperial in their crew, who was looking over to the bar in confusion, likely wondering what was taking so long, but Borus ignored him and kept talking. "Soon as I came of age, I worked enough seasons as a logger to save up for a winged crossbow and kit, then went to find Nasiri."

"My father was working on a dig site in the southern mountains back when he was a student, and Nasiri killed a white cockatrice picking off shepherds in the foothills below. Said he got to see the kill shot. Clean and quick. Dead before it hit the ground."

"Sounds like Nasiri. He's one of the few times that the man lives up to the legend. If he thinks they can have a second chance, he'll put in the work. He's captured many man-eaters to live in menageries. When Zhehan first started working with Nasiri, he scared off a crocodile drake with an alarm that made it afraid to come around settlements. He's clever and I'm amazed by his knowledge and quick thinking, but you'd best not tell him I said that. Rukirha is from the Panther Clans of the Pakardiant. Her people are careful with hunting leopards, and she was like me where she came looking for Nasiri, wanting to extend the care she was raised with to all animals. He took Ru on as an apprentice shortly before accepting me. We've not been a crew for long. I've only been with them six years, but I've grown to care deeply for them and proud of the work we do."

The bartender set down the last of their drinks on a tray. Borus passed Helana one of the two cocktails. With mint leaves on top and swirls of purple currant wine swirling about, it was a beautiful sight.

"Let me know what you think!" he said, giving a nod. "Ru loves trying new things and mixing them. She will be excited to hear you wanted to try her creation."

Helana took a sip. The flavors danced, sending a rush of sweet and tart through her mouth. It was a moment before she realized she had closed her eyes. She laughed nervously. "Wow."

"Ru will be happy to hear it," said Borus with a deep chuckle. "I've talked a lot about me and my found family. Walk and tell me of you! What has you on this ship?"

"I'm a librarian apprentice. I was born and raised in Bolondakoi. Although I love research, I've always been drawn to the idea of finding the artifacts my people study. Getting to be the first person to touch history for the first time in ten thousand years! When Ra Maslani accepted me and one other student to work on the dig site, I was elated. It was a lot of work, but I loved every second, and I can't wait to see what we learn from the artifacts we collected."

This conversation brought them to the table. Although Helana had already seen them, it was useful to put names to faces.

"Whiskey with stone," said Borus, setting the glass before the lean Imperial man. "Coffee, black." He set the goblet in front of Nasiri. "And finally the blackcurrant cocktail! Helana here got one as well, and her review seemed positive."

"Fantastic!" said the Pakardiant woman, grinning as she raised her own glass to Helana. "I've had some that didn't land, but this has become a favorite."

"And who is this fine young woman?" asked Zhehan. "Helana, is it?"

"Indeed," she replied.

"I studied at the branch in Manu," he said, no doubt noting her uniform and pin. "I primarily studied natural history and botany. You work in acquisitions I presume? What field?"

"Archaeology. Did you graduate?"

Zhehan nodded. "Yes, but I never pursued the rank of Ra. I fell in with this lot before I could complete the track, and proved to be a great disappointment to the family." He grinned. "I have no regrets, of course."

"I still think you should finish your education," said Nasiri, and the jovial tone of the table fell silent. At first Helana assumed this was a sensitive topic, but there was no tension, just attention.

"This is the first I'm hearing of it," said Zhehan, clearly caught off guard.

"Having a member with the rank of Ra would open more doors to us in studying and accessing older accounts. Will be important in looking at trends of different animals."

Zhehan again nodded. "I can see the merit in that, but with your lived experience, I doubt it will be that important."

Nasiri took a sip of his wine, and the other three seemed to take that as a sign they could resume the casual tone of before, since they dived right back into banter.

One of the countless rumors was that Nasiri was born a girl and was acknowledged as a man when he came of age, a custom supposedly common amongst the Pakardiant. There was so much folklore surrounding the great hunter that Helana hadn't given it much thought, but she had heard of the practice, and seeing Nasiri in person she was fairly confident this was the case. In the Empire, there were so few legal distinctions between men and women that many cities had those who lived as a gender distinct from their sex. Some Imperial cultures did not accept this practice, like the Serid, but it had been the case in Bolondakoi since before Imperial consolidation. Her father once said the mind defines a person, not their spirit or body. Several of her fellow students identified as a gender opposite of their sex or even as neither, and it was given little consideration. She knew conceptually that other cultures saw notions of gender differently, and that it might not be so seamless for them, but she had met so few people outside the Great Library and the work site that Nasiri was the first person of another culture presenting as a different gender than their sex that Helana had met.

She realized she was still standing despite Borus having taken a seat a while ago, and at Borus's prompting, sat beside him and happily listened to the three apprentices banter, their fast-paced repartee reminding her of how her own family had been in her youth. Their humor and loving tones under the jokes and jabs warmed her heart to see.

***

Nasiri made a note to discuss with Zhehan privately when they next had a chance. He was serious about the young man becoming a full scholar. He would only need one more year of work, and once he had the title, there would be few academic doors closed to him. He was brilliant, hard-working, and well deserving of the title. He just needed the push.

Nasiri wouldn't always be there to offer his lived experience, but he didn't want to mention that at the table. Not now that his apprentices were so elated and having a good time. There had been many days of worry after the last hunt almost ended in disaster. He wanted more than anything to preserve this lighthearted mood. They would need to look back on this fondly if they were to be strong and united when establishing... whatever Nasiri's legacy would be.

Should he establish a guild? The idea had been proposed by a Free-States noble a century ago, and Nasiri had brushed it off, but now that he had to consider the logistics of how his traditions would be carried on, it seemed the wisest course of action. Nasiri had no notion of how to start much less manage a guild, but now that he had crossed the denial he had harbored for the past few years, he suddenly wanted to ensure everything was in place. A strong foundation for these three ambitious, kind, headstrong fools to continue his work.

A shift in his seat sent an unfamiliar pulse of agony up Nasiri's back, which he masked with a stretch.

Although most at the table carried on, Ru squinted slightly. While saying something teasing to Zhehan, her hands motioned to him in sign.

"Are you alright, Mentor?"

Once she looked back, Nasiri signed in reply: *"I am well. Just pain of age. Pain means your body still cares."*

Ru smiled to herself, but thankfully did not press the matter.

"What sort of archaeology do you do?" asked Zhehan. Nasiri noticed that the young scholar was being a lot more attentive to Helana than he usually was with strangers. He was a personable man, but usually more formal. Although he was flirting with the young woman, she had eyes for Borus, who seemed oblivious to Helana's attention. Borus had long harbored not-so-subtle feelings for Ru that he himself might not even be aware of, and Ru was happy to share a bed with strangers but, after she slept with Zhehan when she first joined and lead to confused feelings between the two for a while, drew the line at their family. A wise move in Nasiri's opinion. He was glad he had no such desires. They always seemed to complicate and hurt feelings, and the benefits never seemed worth the cost.

"We found a number of artifacts from the First Age that we are taking back to the Great Library for examination and detailed study."

"First Children artifacts?" said Zhehan, his flirting tone dropping and his shoulders hunching slightly as they always did when a topic captured his full attention. "What state of preservation?"

"I shouldn't be talking too much about it, since they're not yet researched and properly described, but I can tell you they are in excellent condition. There was an opening in the chamber that regularly illuminated the interior, so the preservation magic was sheltered by the roof but still powered despite the overall outpost having lost its magic to the elements. We took great care to regularly expose them to the sun before loading them."

"Wait, there are First Children artifacts on this ship?"

Helana nodded, barely able to contain herself. "We were worried about black market poachers so the Great Library didn't send us a robust staff that would draw attention, but once we verified the authenticity, we got to oversee a really exciting dig. I can't wait for the description."

"I'll say," said Zhehan. "The museum in Manu only had a handful of First Children artifacts, and all had lost their magic. Some of the pieces were barely recognizable as more than rusted or corroded slabs. They did have one piece, a little helmet with insectoid eyes, that was well preserved, but since it was in a dark tomb, the magic was long dead of course. It looked like it was made for a child. We also had a skeleton. Everyone in the class thought it was a young child, but our professor proved by the teeth and bone fusion that it was an adult."

"The Hall of Paleontology in the Great Library has a full wing of First Children skeletons, bog bodies, and three cave mummies. Those are unnerving. One of them looks like she has only been dead a few weeks. Amazing preservation."

"I've always wanted to visit that hall. My mother took me to the Great Library when I was a boy, but of course we were only permitted entry in the public wing. A small fraction of the collection and from what I understand, mostly replicas."

"Indeed. We have to keep the valuable specimens in the higher vaults or subterranean halls. There are a few exciting specimens in the main hall. The tyrant skeleton in the main hall for example is real, although we have dozens of better preserved specimens in the basement collections and restricted halls."

"That tyrant skeleton is partially responsible for my lingering interest in paleontology," said Zhehan, a wistful lilt in his voice. "What I would give to see one in the flesh."

"River drakes are bigger, and you can still find little tyrants in the Arvelith forests."

"Zhehan knows all about river drakes," said Borus, patting Zhehan on the back.

"Dozekanzho was only a subadult," he said, waving Borus off. "But you're right, I probably would run if I saw a tyrant in their prime in the flesh. A king of eight span would be quite a horror to behold."

"Only the queens got that large, and specimens over eight span are dubious," Helana noted. "But yes, they are astonishing. We have got a fossil femur from the Seridic foothills that might have reached just over nine span in length, but that would be an astonishing individual. The biggest a predatory drake could get on land, and even then, there's wear on her femoral head that suggests she probably weighed too much to walk efficiently."

"Means I could appreciate her size and trust I could probably get away," Zhehan offered.

"Probably, although considering at that size her stride length would be, what... three span? Four?" One step would carry her ridiculously far."

"Fair," said Zhehan, raising his glass. "Here's to living in a safer time in history."

Helana gently tapped her glass against his. "Especially since the First Children are gone. Their creations alone make me glad I live in modern times."

"We have fun stories about their demons," said Rukirha. "Monsters possessed by First Children magic."

"Vaskalamaldus was a demon, yes?" said Borus to Nasiri, before turning to Helana. "The titan crow I mentioned earlier."

Nasiri took a deep breath. "I think there was some magic in that beast. I pierced it with many harpoons, one of which is usually enough for a wyvern, and the loggers even felled a tree on it. Took your great uncle Tsingus crushing its skull with his axe."

"Even then, his body was gone when the loggers came back to the grove a few days later," said Borus, taking on a conspiratorial tone as he turned to Helana. "I imagine lions and cockatrices picked him over, but some of the loggers swear they still see trees moving in the night as the Raven King waits to get his revenge. I think I saw him at least once on my last logging season."

"I witnessed the last breath of Vaskalamaldus," said Nasiri, now all too familiar with the legend sparked by the quick disappearance of the Raven King's corpse. "Cockatrices can easily saw through and digest wyvern bones. But yes, I think there was some magic enhancing his size and strength."

"The demons made by the First Children, we call them homunculi, were a lot more potent than beasts which catch a strain of wild magic. A homunculus is a body made specifically for the hive, and that hive has been domesticated and bound only to the one body. A few homunculi still exist: harpies and ogres of the Houze Prairie, merfolk near the Kentarim Islands, and many giants and monsters in the Arvelith forests. These are all derived though, having spread to people as hosts in order to reproduce, had cloned offspring, or mated in the case of some merfolk and giants. Original homunculi are highly endangered, probably extinct, but they were almost impossible to kill without an enchanted artifact of some kind."

This conversation carried on for some time, but Nasiri found himself tired and struggling to focus. He had gotten the team a fine suite with appreciable bedding, and lying down after being on his feet with minimal respite since the hunt sounded entirely too appealing to wait any longer.

"I'm going to retire for the night," said Nasiri, holding his hand out to encourage them to remain at the table. "Please enjoy. Feel free to put anything you all and our new friend get on my tab."

"Gratitude," said Ru, raising her cocktail to Nasiri.

With a nod to her and the rest at the table, Nasiri left to get some much-anticipated rest.

Chapter 2

Loregus exhaled, preparing for the next step of the job.

The three days had passed in a pleasant bliss of intimacy, fine dining, and listening to Ra Maslani talk in his rugged, smoky baritone. That had all been part of the job, but this next part would be all the harder because, against his best judgement, he had become quite smitten with the librarian.

That night, Ra Maslani was on shift guarding the target along with one of the ship's crew named Tris. Loregus had yet to learn what exactly it was they were protecting, but all would be revealed tonight.

After pouring three cups of tea, he mixed in powder from his belt pouch into two of the cups. Tris had asked for honey in his tea the night before, so Loregus put that into one of the powdered cups. Ra Maslani didn't take anything in his tea, so Loregus would have to hope that the librarian didn't notice the difference in flavor. Kab powder was odorless, but it could have a slight metallic flavor if the base it was mixed in wasn't strong enough. To counter this, Loregus had brewed the tea a bit longer than usual.

Once the three cups were ready, Loregus loaded all three into a wooden holder and carried them down to the lower deck.

As there wasn't a special storage unit, their artifacts were kept in the same vault as all valuables. Not only did it have standard locks, the librarians had put a set of devices to seal it on top and bottom. Loregus didn't know what these devices did, but that was for Shin the Tinkerer to deal with.

As he walked down the stairs, Loregus spotted Muluk loading some crates at the bottom of the stairs. Busy work no doubt, but it was good to know their hitter was close.

Loregus rounded the corner to the vault, and his heart sank.

Ra Maslani and Tris were both present, both reading and seated at the table where Loregus expected them to be, but so was the treasure hunter Kronan.

This man was a brute in every sense of the word. A big man of ambiguous ancestry, raised in the Free-States based on his accent, Kronan seemed used to getting what he wanted by intimidation. Ra Maslani hadn't said it outright, but it seemed likely that Kronan hadn't actually discovered the dig site, instead taking the credit from someone else who had after threatening or killing them. After a few interactions and seeing how quick Kronan was to reflexively go for his knife, Loregus thought the latter fairly likely. Even though he was no doubt a brutal man, it seemed that the Great Library didn't care who got them their specimens, just that the specimens were in good condition. Ra Maslani had expressed nothing but distain for Kronan, but he worked with him out of obligation. Kronan notified the library about the artifacts, and once they were verified as authentic, Ra Maslani and a small crew came to dig them up and take them in. The rest of the crew remained behind to excavate any other relevant artifacts even if they lacked enchantment.

Loregus considered turning back, perhaps making up another cup with the poison, but Kronan looked up and spotted him through the man's wide-brimmed cap. Loregus knew there was no backing out now. The hallway back to the stairs was long. Wood creaked and waves struck the hull on either side. Hopefully Muluk was close enough to hear commotion.

Loregus put on a smile and closed the distance. Tris lit up, and Ra Maslani offered a slight nod of acknowledgement. Loregus knew that was the librarian's equivalent of an enthusiastic greeting.

"Made some tea to help keep you boys awake and alert. Sorry, Kronan, I didn't know you would be down here. I can go get you a cup if you like."

"Not interested," said Kronan with a squint. Loregus had at first assumed that Kronan was so short with him because he didn't like the idea of men with an intimate relationship. Such sentiments were more common in the Republic than the Free-States, but they were out there. As Loregus interacted with the treasure hunter more, he was now confident that Kronan was just suspicious of anyone that got close to his shot at fame and fortune, and a stranger showing up on the ship and always spending time with the leader of the operation no doubt raised his suspicions.

And, to be entirely fair, stealing from the vault was exactly why Loregus was there.

Loregus set their respective cups before Tris and Ra Maslani. He then took the remaining seat beside Ra Maslani. Loregus set his fingers into his belt pouch.

There was a slight chill in the air of these lower decks.

Absent any suspicion, Tris gulped fast, sighing and smiling as he drank. Ra Maslani took a sip. His brow creased.

"Apologies," said Loregus after taking a drink of his own, keeping his right hand at his pouch. "Brewed it a bit too long."

Ra Maslani shrugged ever so slightly before taking a longer drink. "No need, it is good. I like a strong brew."

The librarian and guard would be out soon, and as soon as Kronan put together what happened, he would no doubt attack. Loregus would need to time his throw carefully, for Kronan was quick with his knife. Kab powder wouldn't work quickly unless Loregus was precise. He had to be perfect.

"Tris, what's that you're reading?" Loregus asked after another sip. "Looks substantial."

"Witch Kings of the Third Age. Borrowed it from Ra here. I'm currently on an account of the Arvelith Witch-King Taurm. His realm was in the highlands. When his farmers were short on taxes, and he confronted them, they explained that emus were harassing their herds. Do you know what an emu is?"

"I do not," said Loregus truthfully.

"Flightless birds around the height of a man. Little heads but a vicious kick. We have some in Amentanoidiasia where I am from. Anyway, so Taurm says he will kill the birds, then his farmers would have no excuses for their late taxes. He quickly found that they were fast, and agile enough to evade his magic. His prized warriors aided with their bows, but the birds seemed to intuitively know the range of his archers, staying just out of reach." Tris paused to yawn. "Oh, sorry. Eventually he had to surrender to the birds, and the humiliation was carried far and wide..."

Tris yawned again. He blinked twice.

Ra Maslani was leaning back, his eyes already heavy.

"Hey!" shouted Kronan, shaking both to alertness. "If you two fools are just going to sleep through your shift, go get Helana. She may be lovestruck for that Qajarith oaf, but at least she pays attention."

"I am paying attention," said Ra Maslani, his voice still deep but a lot gentler than usual.

Tris yawned again. "I'll see if another guard is willing to switch. I'm suddenly quite tired."

"Careful, don't-" Loregus began.

As Tris stood, the last threads of his consciousness snapped, and he collapsed to the floor. Kronan turned to catch him, which is when Loregus stood, uncorked the vial, and flung Kab powder in Kronan's face.

Unfortunately, Kronan was turned away.

When he looked back, snorting to get the powder out of his face, his growl was nearly inhuman.

He threw Tris to the ground, pushed the table forward which knocked Ra Maslani aside, and kicked back his chair. Loregus backed away. There was a bit of powder left in his vial, but not enough for an immediate knockout.

"I knew you were a jackal," Kronan hissed, advancing on Loregus.

Loregus bowed low, keeping the vial at the ready. "Guilty."

"Going to enjoy killing you."

"You're so creative."

Kronan spat on the ground and drew his knife.

Loregus threw the entire vial. He didn't bother waiting to see if his throw was true. As he turned and fled, he heard a clatter that he could only assume was the vial missing its mark. Loregus rounded the corner, and nearly ran into the massive Muluk. He ducked low and slid to the side.

Loregus got a satisfying view of Muluk catching Kronan on the side of the head with his rubberhead axe.

Kronan collapsed in a messy pile at the turn of the hall.

"Splendid timing," Loregus whispered.

Muluk didn't acknowledge him.

Other figures filed in behind Muluk. Loregus recognized the rest of their motley crew. Toyate the thief and Shin the tinkerer. Jaran offered Loregus a hand.

"Well done," he said as he pulled Loregus to his feet.

"Thank you," Loregus replied, brushing the front of his coat. "That brute almost killed me and he wasn't even clever doing it. I would have been mortified if I perished in such a mundane way as a knife to the gut."

"I would ensure your funeral be ostentatious enough to compensate."

"Thank you, Jaran. You're a good man."

As they passed the table to the vault, Loregus's attention was drawn to Ra Maslani on the floor. He felt a pang of sympathy. He didn't know the man's story, not really, but it hurt to see him slumped and undignified.

He would awaken later, possibly near sunrise. At most he would have slight vertigo and would be short one less artifact. Loregus didn't expect forgiveness, but Ra Maslani didn't seem like the sort to let his guard down, and he had with Loregus. Hopefully he didn't lock himself away for good.

Already Shin was setting about addressing the strange devices just above and below the handle of the vault door. She was holding a metal compass of sorts that had a spinning crank on the side. The woman wasn't old by his reckoning, but she was greying and slightly hunched as she worked. Her hands, though, were steady as iron.

"What are those?"

"How much do you know about magic, boy?" asked the woman, a slight croak in her voice.

"Very little, I must confess."

"Right. Well, these little boxes on the door are home to magic. Think about them like a swarm of bees, and the boxes are their hive. Right now, the magic is spread throughout the door, and it would be impossible for us to break in. Our tools would bend and I expect it would be so hot that our fingers would burn off before we made any progress. However, with the right mix of sound from my *bathodani* here, sounds too high pitched for us to hear mind you, combined with the electricity that its interior sparks produce, I can tell the magic to go back home. Won't be permanent, but long enough for our friend Toyate to open the mechanical lock, then we can get inside, get the target, and get out."

A ringing began to pulse in Loregus's ears. He initially shook his head, then pressed a hand to his ear. After a quick glance, the others were also showing signs of irritation.

"Although our hereditary magic isn't immune, our strain doesn't seem as strongly impacted by sound. Also, it's already home, so where would it go? Feels a bit strange, but you get used to it."

Loregus felt a bit ill, and stepped aside despite her assurances. The others did so too.

Finally Shin made a satisfied hum and set a magnetized bead on each box. "That should do it! Toyate, your turn."

The young Kentarim took a deep breath, nodded, and got to work.

Loregus knew how to disable some common locks. Was a useful talent in his line of work. He knew this one, with three metal disks adjacent to the door handle, each with their own key hole, would be far beyond his capabilities.

Toyate, however, was up for the task.

Similar to Shin, she used a series of magnets along with a pronged tool to turn the gears. She also had a suction gadget that linked to a pair of ear buds, and she used sound to determine where she should turn. It was a lengthy process. Although Loregus didn't know about this particular locking system, he guessed she was trying to determine the wear pattern on the lock based on the sound of their scrape of tooth against base, since the gears would be worn down where they were usually set to.

After what felt like a lifetime, finally a series of clicks and shifts signaled that she had succeeded. Toyate broke her composure with a slight wobble of her head before resuming a stoic expression and nodding to Jaran.

"In we go," he said, stepping into the vault. Muluk remained on watch, but the rest followed Jaran inside.

***

Helana felt a rush sitting so close to Borus. So close, but unable to act.

They were playing Routing, a battlefield practice game. Zhehan and Rukirha were seated across from them, playing the opposing team. Nasiri was in a chair at the desk working on some documents.

"Ru, I really think we should try to flank them," said Zhehan. "That will push them to, well… I don't want to say it, but you know what I mean."

"No, I don't!" Rukirha snapped. "I think you're using all of our moves to set up some amazing thing that they aren't going to go for because they're also not strategizing. They're just reacting. You're playing like you're playing yourself, and I think we need to play like we're playing them. If we don't go on the offensive at some point, they're going to keep chipping away at our own flanks. How are we going to flank them if we don't have flanks, Han?"

Zhehan rubbed his temple. "So what do you propose?"

"I propose we charge! Straight down the middle. They've been focused on chipping our sides, and since you've already bulked up our middle, why don't we use it?"

"That's our defensive line!"

Rukirha threw her hands in the air. "What are we defending? In three moves we will only be left with that line, and with their scouts there, our back is completely open!"

"It wouldn't be open if you hadn't had our last knight rush their two pikemen."

"Sorry if I got a little bored and wanted to have some action in this action game!"

"It's not an action game, Ru, it's a strategy game!"

Borus shifted his knee against Helana's. He had leaned back at some point in the discussion, setting an arm on the couch behind her.

Over their three days spending most of their time together, he had made no motions of affection. She was used to the forwardness of boys at the university. Although she wasn't sure if Borus was interested in her the way she was with him, he seemed eager to be around her, always inviting her to join them for meals, or stay late.

She decided to test her theory.

Helana leaned back, resting her head on his arm. He tensed slightly, but didn't move.

"Sorry, is this alright?" he said under his breath. The other two were still engaged in a heated argument about strategy. Helana looked up, got a little lost in his dark brown eyes, and nodded.

He nodded back.

As Zhehan and Ru continued to bicker, Helana shifted so she was fully leaning against Borus's broad torso. He was warm and smelled a pleasant mix of cedar and salt. Although he went stiff again, he didn't move.

"Is this alright?" she whispered.

His jaw clenched, but he smiled. Two fingers brushed her left shoulder, easing her slightly closer. "Yes."

Shortly his tension eased. She hoped he just wasn't used to being around girls, at least not this close. From what she heard, the Republic was quite reserved with intimacy. The notion didn't make much sense to her. It seemed to build up a great deal of tension, but now that she had been building tension and excitement for a few days, she was starting to appreciate it.

"Fine."

"Fine!"

With that, their focus was brought back to the board. It seemed Ru and Zhehan had come to an accord. They advanced one of their vanguard down the center line.

"May I?" Helana asked.

Borus nodded.

She leaned forward, moved one of their scouts in an arc, and took the last catapult.

A long silence followed.

"Alright I didn't anticipate that," said Zhehan.

"I would never have guessed."

The two launched into another argument, and Helana leaned back against Borus, who proudly pulled her close.

***

The interior of the vault was, considering the effort to get inside, a bit underwhelming. Although the corners were lined with steel brackets, the back wall was primarily wood. The walls on either side were filled with cubbies, some of which had an additional lock. There were a number of luggage pieces, but most of the space was taken up by an ornate sarcophagus.

It was massive, easily three span wide. It appeared to be made of silver with green mineral highlights, although the material was so tarnished that it was difficult to tell. There was a basic embossing on the top of the coffin, appearing to be clawed hands, hooved feet protruding from the base, and a shark-like head sporting comically large ears.

For all this grandeur, it was one of the many small metal boxes that Jaran indicated. "Shin, if you would."

Shin nodded and knelt before the box, spinning her little anti-magic compass. The ringing pulsed through the room. Loregus felt a bit ill.

A series of clicks and hisses spread throughout the room. A dozen or so boxes split along some seam, starting with the box that Shin was working over. Some of the boxes seeped out a fine silvery mist.

A deep click made Loregus jump.

The Sarcophagus had split along its side, showing the raised embossed portion was a lid of some sort. A great deal of mist seeped out of the crack, followed by an unspeakably rank scent.

"Nothing to worry about," said Shin, setting aside her compass and lifting the lid of the box. "They will reset once the magic realizes it was falsely told to retreat. If the contents are organic, which it smells like something is, there may be some preservation issues back at the library, but I think they will manage."

Shin reached inside and withdrew another box, this one made of wood. Perhaps it was bamboo. Loregus didn't know for sure, but it was beautiful. Lined with threads of gold. On its surface was a series of odd circles in irregular shapes. He was about to ask what it meant, but movement on the sarcophagus out of the corner of his eye drew Loregus's attention. When he looked up, nothing had changed, but he still felt on high alert. Maybe he should have been wary anyway. They were inside a vault and there were hundreds of crew and staff on the ship that very well might discover them. It wasn't until he thought he saw movement in the sarcophagus that his heart began to hammer in his chest.

Shin passed the box up to Jaran, who took it gently.

"We're about to be astonishingly rich. Well done, team."

With that, he turned and led the way out. Toyate was right behind him, looking as shaken as Loregus felt.

He breathed a little easier once they stepped out of the vault, but that changed when a strained creak built up to a snap that echoed through the hall.

Something inside gasped. A deep, labored inhalation that sounded decidedly inhuman. A clang and clatter followed, leading to a series of cracks that sounded like a hundred joints popping.

The moment Shin was in the hall, Muluk threw his full weight against the door.

It stopped just before impact.

A tense moment of nothing followed.

Loregus moved to help Muluk close the door, when a long fleshy appendage lashed out of the crack in the door, punching Shin's torso with a sickening crunch as she tried to back away. She fell, and Loregus barely managed to catch her.

As soon as he set the woman down, he stood to-

A hand with long hooked claws reached through the crack in the door. It was naked, grey, and warty with a glossy sheen. The digits were long and gnarled, each joint a sore-looking bulge. The second and third digit ended in deer-like hooves instead of claws. After hovering a moment, it curled around, with the claws piercing through Muluk's arm like it was made of butter.

Muluk screamed, as much in terror and pain as anger, and drew his knife. Before it could be employed, however, the clawed hand raised his arm and thrashed him about, nearly colliding with the wall on the opposite side. Muluk braced his feet, one against the door and the other on the wall, and pulled back, dragging the arm out and slashing with his knife. The blade bounced off the creature's hide without evident injury.

"Not doing much!" he shouted. "Get something bigger!"

Loregus looked about. The Akanuk's rubberhead would do no good. Kronan had his arming sword at his waist. It might not be optimal for these enclosed spaces, but Muluk did say bigger.

He pulled the sword from the treasure hunter's scabbard. He turned it about and set the handle in Muluk's free hand.

With a triumphant yell, Muluk thrust the sword down into the vault. The sickening crunch and squelch of meat being pierced rolled up Loregus's spine.

Horror sank in Loregus's chest when he realized it wasn't the monster inside that had been pierced.

Another grey hand had reached through, plunged into Muluk's guts. The hand ripped back, withdrawing the fighter's entrails with

a long slurp. A deep croak followed and, with his entrails still interlaced in its digits, grabbed Muluk's face and pulled him into the vault.

Loregus and Jaran both threw their weight against the door. Before they could even ask, Toyate stabbed the door with one of her tools, and the gears shifted to lock it once more.

"Fuck," Jaran said, letting out a slow exhalation.

Inside, they heard a muffled scream cut short, and a hideous screech prelude the cracking and crunching of a monster feeding.

Jaran banged his head against the door. "Dung. Dung for days. Alright Shin, get these magic devices back running so we can seal that-"

Shin's eyes were wide open, but she seemed rigid from head to toe.

"What is it? Is she hurt?"

Loregus shrugged "The tongue or... tentacle thing got her. I didn't get a good look."

Toyate knelt before Shin. She checked her pulse and breathing. "She's alive. It's not a stroke and I don't think there's spine damage. Only injury is here on her abdomen, but-"

There was a bit of blood, but not enough to account for this level of shock. Loregus knelt before her, checking the wound by lifting her linen shirt. There was more slime than blood. The slime looked hard, but it trailed down her belly slightly.

"The appendage has some sort of venom, I think, but it's not venom I've ever seen before. Nothing that acts like this. It's... I don't even know how to describe it, but it's sludging up her blood?"

Shin strained, looking like she was trying to move. Her fingers twitched and her eyes rolled. Although her gaze seemed to be trying to lock on him, she couldn't focus. Repeatedly her jaw tightened and lips pursed, but no words were formed.

"We have to leave her," said Jaran.

"What?"

"Our contact is expecting us. We can maybe slip off a lifeboat without being noticed, but not with a woman who doesn't look like she's going to make it to the end of the hall. Also I would be shocked if they have not heard the commotion. If we're lucky, they will find her and the guards, which will draw their focus down here while we escape."

"We weren't supposed to… it shouldn't have gone like this."

"Well crack my cock Loregus, of course it wasn't supposed to go like this! But it did. Now do you want your damn cut or not? Let's go!"

Loregus took a deep breath and nodded. He checked on Toyate. She was staring at Shin, saying nothing. Clearly in shock.

A reasonable response, all things considered.

"Hey, kid," said Loregus, putting a hand on her shoulder. She jolted, but eased at his eye contact. "We're going. You good?"

Toyate nodded. "I'm good."

"Excellent," said Jaran. "Let's go."

Shin glared after Loregus.

Guilt sank in his gut as he turned away.

Steps echoed down the hall, back around the corner toward the stairs.

Jaran scowled and quietly set the box in Toyate's hand. He then took up Muluk's rubberhead.

A figure rounded the corner, and before they could utter a word, Jaran raised the weapon in a wide grip and brought it down, cracking bone as the stranger's hands were forced low. Jaran then struck the lump of gum at the side of the stranger's head.

The figure dropped.

Although he didn't recognize the features, Loregus knew the crew uniform.

Jaran took the box back, keeping the rubberhead in his other hand. "There will be more. Let's go."

Loregus and Toyate followed Jaran down the hall. Although he expected them to go to the upper deck, they actually veered off before the stairs. Down a short hallway, they reached a chamber along the hull, with several longboats lined up bow to stern disappearing into the darkness.

"Are we worried about more guards?" Loregus whispered.

"Yes, but there's only so much we can do," said Jaran. "Alright, that cable opens the side port, and we can lower the boat."

"This is a fast ship, yes?"

"Yes, now pull the cable!"

"We're just going to drop?"

Jaran took a deep breath. "Loregus, we're on a low deck. Will be quite easy to lower, and those beams are made to slide us out and away from the ship so we aren't caught in the bow waves. We haven't yet hit the northbound current, so we're just going on wind. It will be fine. Now help me with the damn cable!"

Loregus nodded, and took to pulling open the port by turning the gear beside it. Toyate helped Jaran set the boat on the ramp. Jaran then planted the box at the front of the boat and strapped it down. Once all was set, they assembled on the port side of the longboat.

Jaran looked to them on either side before nodding. "Alright. On my count, we push then all jump in together. One, two-"

"Wait!" said Toyate, stopping hard.

Jaran growled. "What?"

"That... that creature? It's in the vault. They don't know. They need to know. We need to warn them. If it gets out-"

"The librarians can handle it," he said, then turned to Loregus. "You didn't kill them, right?"

"No. They are asleep, and will awaken in the morning."

Jaran smiled. "See? The people who know how to handle it will wake up, and thanks to Muluk, the beast should remain in the vault with a full belly. Now can we go?"

"What if it gets out before they wake up?" said Toyate.

"Then we really don't want to be on the ship when it does."

Loregus raised a finger. "We could let Nasiri know. He can kill it."

"We caused this problem. We should help fix it. At least let us tell Nasiri."

Jaran closed his eyes. "I am… alright. Here's my offer. I will wait here for three rotations. If you are not back by then, I am leaving. Do we have an accord."

"Yes," both replied quickly.

"Excellent," said Jaran, taking up the rubberhead from the bed of the boat. "Time is precious. Go!"

***

Nasiri turned his thumb ring about in his hand, fingertips finding the familiar imperfections in the trickster's features. His fingers also found their way to his necklace which bore a claw. The claw of Amako, the first man-eater he killed. The beast that killed his brother. This he kept closest to his heart. It reminded him that the focus must always be on the just kill. Beasts could take loved ones, but that did not justify kills for vengeance. It was their nature. He enjoyed hunting, but when targeting a man-killer, it was critical to be as objective as possible.

His students were learning well. In their campaigns, he had seen their respect for his methods, even if now all he could hear was their bickering.

If he was going to retire, someday, they would retire too. If his lessons and methods were to endure, he would need to establish a firm code for their conduct that his students could teach their own students.

A bittersweet heaviness weighed his hand as he began to draft articles of his code. Putting structure to centuries of what felt like instinct at this point would be challenging. Some part of Nasiri knew that Zhehan should be writing these down. He had a good head for words and clarity. Zhehan would scribe the final draft, but first Nasiri needed at least an outline of-

A hard knock at the door shook Nasiri from his thoughts, and cut Zhehan and Ru from their latest argument.

They knocked again in rapid succession before anyone on the suite had a chance to respond.

"It's unlocked," said Borus.

Two strangers, a Kentarim girl in the uniform of one of the ship staff and a man of ambiguous heritage in a beautiful if disheveled silk robe, stumbled into the room. As Nasiri took him in, he recognized him as constantly being around Helana's mentor Ra Maslani. They both looked in a panic.

Blood stained the front of the man's maroon jacket.

"Nasiri, we…"

As the man took in the room, his eyes settled on Helana, and immediately his face fell.

"What is it, Raun?" she asked.

The man exhaled slowly. "My name is Loregus. This is Toyate. I lied about a lot of things. I have much to say and in little time."

The room turned to Nasiri.

He took a deep breath. "Go on."

"It's a long story," Loregus began.

"No time," Toyate reminded him.

"Fair. Sum it up: we are thieves hired to get an artifact that the librarians dug up. The operation went splendidly. Problem is we had to suppress magic to get the treasure, and when we did that, all the magic in the room was suppressed." At this, Helana gasped. "We accidentally opened a sarcophagus that had a monster inside. It ate two of our friends. Well, poisoned one and ate the other. It's locked inside the vault, now, but we felt bad leaving it to perhaps get out and kill more people. We are thieves and shall not be apologizing for that, but we aren't murderers or… whatever it would make us if we didn't say anything."

"No, I think murderer would be appropriate," said Nasiri.

The room went quiet.

Toyate cleared her throat. "That is fair. We deserve cold words, but we wish to make it right."

"Well, we wish for you to make it right." Loregus clarified. "We are unequipped for this sort of adventure. In simple truth, we desired to let you know before we leave."

"Your conscience has narrow limits."

"I just, apologies for the interruption, but I must clarify," said Helana as she stood. She took a slow breath. Borus stood with her, setting a reassuring hand on her shoulder. "Apologies, this is a lot to take in. We assumed the sarcophagus preserved it, but as a mummified corpse. That homunculus is over eleven thousand years old. Class Three homunculi can be brought out of stasis in that condition, but it was my understanding that this was a Class One, the most primitive, which are typically mundane creatures with minor enchantments or a slight hybrid modification. Nothing as sophisticated as later homunculi, and certainly lacking the heterothermic metabolism that allows such prolonged stasis. You're telling me it's alive?"

"Alive, hungry, and revolting."

"I… how? How was it not desiccated?"

"There was a lot of mist when it opened?" Toyate suggested.

"Can it be killed?" asked Nasiri. "You mentioned the other day that homunculi were almost impossible to kill without an enchanted weapon."

"That is consistent to what I have read, yes," said Helana. "I heard reports from Aznarith monster hunters that wild demon and thralls can also be killed with fire or sufficient conventional wounds, but a true homunculus is said to only be able to be killed by magic, typically a weapon with a swarm of magic bound to it, but witches and skin-changers can kill them too."

"Are we fortunate enough to have an enchanted weapon among our possessions?" asked Loregus.

"The Aznarith have forty-two enchanted blades, and there are around seventy in the Great Library, most made during the Age of Witches. I suppose there is an unknown number in private collections. But I don't have one, and nor do my fellow librarians."

"That legendary spear of yours," said Loregus to Nasiri. "I don't suppose it boasts enchantment?"

"No. It is of Trist: finest steel of mortal make, but still of a mundane forge."

"Might we steer to Pakardia?" Ru suggested. "My people have a number of enchanted artifacts."

"No time," said Helana. "Such would divert our course and be at least five days before we made land in Confederacy territory. This creature is strong, no doubt stronger now that it has fed, and who knows how long the vault can hold it. It's made of wood. Even with our enchantment wards up, that's meant to keep things out, not contain them. It's going to break out soon. Assuming it functions as Class Three homunculus, which I think we have to, given what you have described, the first kill was to revive it from stasis. Now that it's awake from a multi-millennia slumber, it will be ravenous, and must feed in order to remain conscious."

"Where is the vault?" asked Borus. "We should clear whatever area it is in."

"It's in the back," said Zhehan as he and Ru stood. "I took our payment there. The staff and lower class rooms toward the rear will be the first hit. We should start clearing there. Get everyone to the front and barricade zones in the upper deck."

Ru turned to Helana. "We cannot kill the demon, but we can wound it. Is this correct?" She gave a nod. "Good. If we injure it sufficiently, maybe we can put it back in its sarcophagus and seal it again?"

Helana nodded again. "That should work."

"What weapons would you recommend?"

"Later homunculi possessed a potent healing factor. I think we should assume this one does too. Slashing weapons will do you best. A pierce or crush will just heal, and quickly, so cutting it apart will likely serve you best. We don't yet know what creatures were used to make it, but usually their sarcophagi can give indication. The coffin had clawed hands with hooves, a shark head, and horns, so I would assume it has a lot of weapons. If it has venom, protecting your face, hands, and chest will be important."

"Good," said Zhehan. "Let's get as much armor as we can. It's going to be close quarters, but we need to hit hard, so favor swords and axes. Even so, you two should bring your crossbow and kara-toan bows. I know shots won't kill it, but anything we can do to weaken the homunculus before engagement will help. Toyate and Loregus, you clear out the lower decks. Get everyone to the dining halls and bar the doors. We will shut ourselves in the lower deck. Do not let anyone out until we tell you to."

"I will write a missive to the captain telling him to help our rogue friends in clearing the decks so there are no people when we go down there," said Helana. "If one of you two can run this to him, I will have time to run to our suite.

Loregus and Toyate looked reluctant, but agreed.

All eyes in the room then turned to Nasiri.

He realized they were waiting for his approval.

"Your plan is excellent. Do as Zhehan says. Let's get ready for a fight."

***

Loregus ran a hand through his hair as Helana drafted their note to the ship captain. The hunters were all busy arming themselves. Twice Loregus looked to the door.

"You know where the captain's office is?" asked Helana, holding out the missive.

"Yes, it's upstairs," said Toyate, taking the letter. "As far as he knows, I'm just part of the crew delivering your message."

She and Loregus left, heading toward the stairs, with Helana passing them on her way down the hall toward the librarian's suite.

Once she was out of range, Toyate looked up to Loregus. "Are… are we going with Jaran? I think it's now or not at all."

Loregus took a deep breath. He looked back up the stairs whence they came, then down the last flight toward the lower level, where their escape would not be waiting for them much longer.

"You do what you must. I'll deliver the letter if you wish, but I'm staying."

"No, I'm staying too," said Toyate. "I'm going to deliver this to the captain's secretary. If Jaran is still down there, let him know we aren't coming."

Loregus nodded. "You spread the word, and I'll clear out anyone down here I can find."

As she ran upstairs, Loregus jogged down.

It only occurred to him once he reached the bottom of the stairs that the creature might already have broken out.

There was nothing down the hallway ahead.

Nothing.

Kronan had been sprawled at the turn of the hall before. Now he was gone. The crewman Jaran had knocked unconscious was still there, his feet just in view if Loregus leaned to the right, but Kronan was nowhere to be seen. Loregus had assumed the powder combined with Muluk's strike had finished him off, but then again, he hadn't gotten much powder in the hit, and Kronan was a big man, so maybe he had recovered.

Kronan was the last person Loregus wanted to run into at the moment. At least the homunculus would kill him quick.

Although he half expected Jaran to be already gone, the boat was still there. No sign of the man, though.

He proceeded carefully, and almost shrieked when a figure stepped out of the shadows.

"It's alright," said Jaran, holding out his hands. "Apologies, just didn't want another crewman to see me."

"You are cold for that one," said Loregus, his hand on his hammering chest. He glanced where Jaran indicated, and saw another body, a bloody mark on his jaw. Loregus grimaced. Head wounds from a rubberhead usually healed, but the afflicted were often disoriented for several days.

Unsurprisingly, Jaran seemed indifferent. "Are we ready? Where's Toyate?"

"Upstairs imploring the captain to help clear the lower decks. Nasiri and his crew is going to kill the beast, but they don't want any bystanders."

Jaran nodded, then moved to the boat. "Fair enough. Let's go."

"I'm staying too."

"Truly?"

Loregus sighed. "I'll admit I don't fully believe it either, but it's something I want to see through."

"I'm not staying to watch you get eaten by that creature."

"I don't expect you to. I'm just here to help send you off."

Jaran cocked his head. Just when he looked about ready to argue, he deflated slightly. "You're a good man, Loregus. Or at least have some threads of moral composition. Never thought I'd say that."

"No one's more surprised than me. I guess I'm obligated to say send my cut to the foster houses or something. That's what heroes say, right?"

"Wouldn't know," said Jaran with a wry grin. "Never met one."

"Well now you have. Or at least someone dipping his toes in the pool of virtue. Stay safe, you scoundrel. Let's get you out to sea."

They both pushed, and just as the boat began to slide, Jaran hopped in.

Loregus watched the boat slide out along the ramp and impact with the waves generated by the sunship's advance. It nearly flipped. By the time Jaran stabilized, he was almost out of view. Loregus gripped the crank and lowered the port door, sealing it to the base.

The crewman groaned, reminding Loregus of his existence.

"You alright?"

"What happened?" the man said, his words slurred.

"What's your name?"

"Tsolus," he said.

"A fine Qajarith name. Northern Republic, right?"

"Yeah. You too?"

"My mother is, yes. Listen, Tsolus, there's something astonishingly dangerous here in the lower decks. Do you think you can walk?"

"I think so."

Loregus knew that was a lie. He could barely pull words together.

Something loud and heavy landed hard back down the hall toward the vault.

Loregus stood and poked his head down.

Still no sign of Kronan.

The lantern still illuminated the hall.

Not wanting to leave this concussed crewman to the mercy of whatever was down the hall, Loregus knelt before him again.

"I'm going to help you stand, Tsolus, and we're going to go upstairs together, alright?"

Tsolus nodded. "Alright."

Another bang echoed down toward the vault.

With a deep breath, Loregus ran as quickly as he dared up the stairs toward his chambers all the way up on the first class deck.

***

Helana sprinted through putting on her yellow uniform. The silk duster, boots, and gloves were padded and reinforced. Senior librarians of the Acquisitions Department like Ra Maslani had uniforms with a minor enchantment that offered additional protection and preservation. What had once seemed a costly, pointless extravagance just to save effort cleaning or absorbing a bump here and there now was something she would sacrifice a hand for.

Going against a homunculus, her backsword seemed decidedly inadequate.

Ra Maslani's spear in his personal chambers. She felt strange going in his room. He was a deeply private man, but she knew he would understand the invasion.

He was still unconscious right outside the vault. She had to help him with the best equipment possible.

Helana also dug through their medical kit. Kab powder wasn't something she had a direct antidote for, but it was a temporary respiratory sedative, so concentrated liver glue should revive him, although he would likely have a dry throat and cough after.

With a quick review that she had everything she meant to come for, Helana ran back to Nasiri's suite.

They were also geared up.

Zhehan had a fine silk brigandine over his padded robe. An open-faced Imperial helmet, also with silk over the metal, capped his head. She didn't know much about heraldry, but it looked consistent with northern Telmede he claimed to be from, so the black and gold with a sheaf of grain insignia was likely a family crest. He held a pump-setting crossbow with the same colors as his uniform, a dagger and curved sabre at his waist, and a broadhead spear slung over his shoulder.

Rukirha was next in view as Helana stepped into the room. She wore heavier armor than most engravings of Pakardiant warriors or their artifacts in the collections Helana had seen, but the style was consistent, being made of lamellar scales of baked leather between tree fiber padding on a cuirass, shoulder and wrist guards, helmet, and chaps. She was armed with a holstered bow, curved karatoan knife, and an oval shield with a spear head protruding from its top and bottom. A bandolier of vials rested across her chest.

Nasiri wore a lighter version of this kit. Instead of a shield, he held his spear in a relaxed grip. He had his holstered bow and knife. His helmet shielded most of his eyes, and had a menacing pantherine design.

"Zhehan, should I take my tower shield?"

Helana only recognized Borus by his frame as he entered the common room from his personal chambers.

His armor was a steel lamellar coat tied at the waist and at his boots. Solid plates protected his shoulders and forearms. Although he had a falchion at his waist, the crossbow in hand drew her attention. Rather than Imperial crossbows, which pumped then had to be manually loaded with each bolt, his was a Republic winged crossbow, which had a loading cartage spreading out under the bow arms, each holding a dozen bolts and giving the weapon its name. From what she understood, this weapon drew and loaded faster, but was considered not as accurate since the weight changed as it went through the shots and it was overall front heavy. In most of their line of work, a more accurate weapon seemed preferable, but perhaps it would be good to have an option of many bolts in rapid succession, especially since there were other archers in the team more focused on accuracy.

Also, they were going up against a homunculus, and their usual rules of precision didn't apply. This was an opponent they had to overkill if they wanted a chance of besting it.

"I would," said Zhehan. "Shooting from behind that monstrosity sounds rather appealing based on what little I know of homunculi."

Borus nodded and returned into his room. When he returned, it was with a towering sheet of steel backed by leather that looked more like a door frame than a shield. It had spiked feet at its base to plant into soil. Helana had never seen these shields outside of illustrations of a siege.

"Are we ready?" asked Nasiri.

Zhehan nodded. "Ready as we can be."

Ru grinned. "Let's go put that demon back in its coffin."

***

Nasiri had intended to lead the way, but agreed with Zhehan that Borus should take point with his tower shield. It was good for them to coordinate on their own. Hunting a demon wasn't what Nasiri would have chosen as the mission for them to step into leadership roles, but it certainly would test the limits of their ingenuity, cooperation, and efficiency.

They advanced in formation toward the stairs. Ru was in the rear with her own shield on her back in case the beast came at them from behind. Nasiri didn't see anyone about. It was the middle of the night, and the lack of people in the way was appreciated, but he did think it was odd that the staff weren't bustling to clear everyone out. There was a good deal of movement on the deck above.

Borus held up his hand, prompting the team to halt.

Loregus came up the stairs, helping a crewman who looked in a daze.

"Everything alright?" asked Zhehan.

Loregus shrugged. "Our friend here had a rough night."

"Are the lower decks clear?"

"More or less. Our librarian and treasure hunter friends are still by the door from what little I dared to investigate, which I confess was not much. No one in the immediate area at least."

"We'll have to go with it," said Zhehan. "Take him to the café, then go help Toyate clear the decks. We may handle this quickly, but if we're opening the vault, the homunculus might escape, so getting everyone out is critical."

Loregus nodded. "Will do. Good luck."

Once the thief and the crewman passed, Borus continued down the stairs.

The waves crashing against the side of the sunship were audible as they passed through the lower class deck, and all the more evident in the storage deck. The scent of fresh wood saturated with salt permeated the air. There was no creak in the steps. He wasn't sure how old the ship was, but it seemed new and sturdy. Well crafted, each plank snug. If they were going to fight a demon, doing so on a secure surface would be a boon.

They continued down the hall once they reached the storage deck.

At the turn of the hall, several bodies were sprawled about, just as Loregus said: two librarians, a civilian woman with a wound in her stomach, and a crewman. The door of the great vault was spattered with blood. There was no sound inside.

He wasn't yet certain if that was a good sign or not.

Helana pushed past Zhehan and Borus, producing her antidote and administering it to her mentor. He and the other student seemed unharmed.

Nasiri inspected the woman. Loregus had mentioned that she was paralyzed. Whatever venom the homunculus possessed, it had eventually proven fatal. Her dead eyes stared up at him. Her final expression was one of terror, not agony. There was no sign of spreading infection. The blood shed was minimal considering the size of the wound.

There were many injection points along her exposed abdomen. It looked like a bite, carrying in a long arch. Both thieves had insisted it was a tongue that struck her. Yet he was certain there were teeth marks. Perhaps the tongue brought her toward the bite? Such a thing would be consistent with the purpose of such an appendage, but then it surely would have dragged her in. Eyewitness accounts were not dependable in his experience; he lost count of the number of wild horses mistaken for drakes and wildcats for lions, but both Toyate and Loregus had insisted the tongue is what got her.

Strange.

"Where's the treasure hunter?" asked Borus. "Didn't Loregus mention him in the group?"

"No idea," said Zhehan. "Perhaps he recovered and left. Cold to leave the others here when the homunculus is right inside, but maybe he panicked and fled. Helana, how long until that takes effect?"

"Could be a few minutes, might be longer."

Something thumped in the vault.

Nasiri stood. "We should clear out the living. At least to the turn of the hall. We should be ready to go as soon as Toyate joins us."

They left the corpse. The crewman was in poor condition. Rubberheads weren't meant to be fatal, but the bruising on his temple looked potentially fatal. Nasiri still dragged him out of the way, careful to not pressure his spine in case the blow had damaged his neck.

The librarian, guard, and crewman were unconscious, but seemed unharmed save for the crewman with a rubberhead injury on his jaw. Ru and Borus got them into the hall without difficulty. Helana administered some herbs to the guard and Ra Maslani.

Footsteps marched down the stairs. Far more than would account for just Toyate.

Several members of the crew marched into view. Leading them was a bald man of unusual height and build enough to fill a door frame, with a brigandine jacket and rubberhead gripped in a meaty hands. His full white beard was impeccably groomed, and a curl tipped each side of his moustache.

"The fuck are you all doing down here?" he growled, his baritone filling out the hall. He was accompanied by around a dozen crewmen, all armed with nonlethal weapons.

"We are here to kill the creature in the vault," said Nasiri. "I presume our companion told you as much?"

"Your companion has been apprehended by my officers as a confessed thief. If you're trying to break into my vault, count on joining her."

Nasiri closed his eyes. He should have anticipated this.

"Captain Djuhan, my name is Helana," she said, stepping forward into the light. "I am a librarian of Bolondakoi, apprentice to Ra Maslani here. We met briefly while we were loading our artifacts onto the ship back in the Portal City. The rogues came to us for help. Apprehend them, such is your prerogative, but we need to get into that vault and put down the creature. If we wait too long, it may break out, and there is nothing we can do to contain it. At least now we have it trapped. If you can secure the door at the top of the stairs and fortify any doors, we may be able to deal with this before it kills any more people."

Captain Djuhan's scowl worsened. He had clearly come ready for conflict, but he appeared to have a great deal of respect for Helana as a librarian, even just an apprentice.

"You said them, Librarian. Are there more rogues?"

Helana paused. "She said she had allies, but it is my understanding that they had departed. As they took one of our artifacts, trust me when I say I want them caught, but putting down this homunculus in the vault is paramount, and I would ask for leniency and care for the rogue in your custody as it was of her good conscience that lead her to warn us."

"Very well. I will open this vault for you, but I'm not leaving the premises. Not that I don't trust you lot, but you can appreciate that our guests have entrusted me with their valuables, and I'll not be releasing the rogue so she can escape."

Helana nodded. "That's perfectly reasonable."

With a nod and standing a bit taller, he shouted back at one of the crewmen toward the back to relay the plan to the other boys in his office. Once he got confirmation from his subordinate, Captain Djuhan lead a march down the hall toward the vault.

From a ring of many keys in a belt pouch, Captain Djuhan set to unlocking each of the four segments of the vault door. Although he showed no fear in the face of whatever was behind the door, his men looked happy to let Nasiri's team assume formation: Borus at the front with his tower shield, Zhehan and Nasiri on either side, and Helana in the back with Rukirha, who downed one of her potions. Nasiri assumed it was her standard combat potions, confirmed when her brown eyes shifted to a pantherine golden green. They were the same eyes as many of the man-eater leopards Nasiri had killed. Even after working with her for the better part of a decade, he still got unnerved seeing them in the dim light. The protruding canines didn't help matters.

Captain Djuhan cast aside his rubberhead and drew the broad sabre at his waist. "Ready?"

Borus nodded. "You're going to want to step over there, Captain. This monster is supernatural."

"Thank you, son, but no. There's a demon on my ship, I'm going to help put it down."

"While I admire that," said Nasiri. "Your leadership would be better placed in maintaining order in clearing the decks. Let us do what we do best."

Captain Djuhan nodded and twisted the last lock. He and Borus pulled open the door.

"Fuck," growled the captain.

Nasiri peered around Borus's shield.

The vault might not have a monster inside, but it was a disaster.

A wall of cubbies had been torn off the wall. Personal items were scattered across the floor. A great silver artifact, which Nasiri guessed was the sarcophagus, had its lid open and bent at an unusual angle. Where the cubbies had been torn from, a hole had been broken into, leading out into a side chamber. Blood was spattered around the vault, and partial remains of a person were slumped beside the sarcophagus.

"Captain, where does that hole open into?" asked Zhehan.

"Storage," said Djehan. He turned to Helana. "Apologies for any doubt. Take these keys." He then looked down at Nasiri. "Please kill this beast, hunter. I will clear this third of the ship. Storage wraps around the vault and covers several floors. It could be anywhere. Watch your backs. Once I've got the zone cleared, I will fortify the entry points and have men on standby if you need assistance. Would you like me to send reinforcements?"

"Gratitude, but no," said Nasiri, clasping forearms with the captain. "From what Helana said, this creature requires experience, not numbers, and any you send may find themselves fuel in its rampage. Clear all people from these halls and fortify all ways in and out."

"You have my word."

With that, Captain Djehan marched down the hall, barking at his men to get Ra Maslani, and the other two men upstairs.

Chapter 3

Nasiri stepped into the room. He kept low, spear at the ready. As he advanced toward the hole, he did his best to listen, but he didn't know the sounds of a ship, much less one of this size, to know which to tune out and which was a sign of movement. The crashing waves and creaking wood was too disorienting.

Borus indicated a section of the hole. "These two planks here were infested with termites. You can see the holes. I still don't think that would weaken the wall enough to break easy, but this creature clearly has strength sufficient for the task. Looks like it used this artifact to break through." Borus nudged one of the shimmering boxes with his foot. "Clever."

"How did it know through the cubbies that section had been weakened?" Ru managed through her enlarged canines.

"Many animals that hunt termites can feel imperfections in wood," said Zhehan, turning to Helana. "I know you aren't certain what beasts make up this particular homunculus, but do you know of any others that have aspects of, oh, I don't know… anteater birds or woodpeckers?"

"We've found several specimens and illustrations with pangolins, but I'm not sure if they can feel through wood like anteater birds."

Zhehan nodded. He knelt before the remains. There was a time when he would have gotten squeamish about such things, but he had long since set that aside when he realized the value in looking over a body to learn how a creature killed their prey.

"What can you tell?"

"The bites are similar to those of sharks. Looks like the jaws are a pretty even crescent. Especially with these serrated teeth, it's a good shape for side to side cuts. A secondary set of teeth looks to be growing in behind the primaries, so it's not needing to be too careful with its teeth. That said, for all the jaw strength I'm seeing, it's only targeting meat that won't hit bone, and is precise despite looking like they are quick tearing bites. Where it does connect with bone, the bite strength is clearly capable of cutting through. For it to be both rapid and take this quantity with each bite all while showing precision is… odd for a homunculus that regenerates and has extra teeth anyway. I'm a little confused about the feet. The footprints in blood all show a sort of cloven hoof articulation, yet with pads like a camel, but it's also got clawed fingers. Both articulated fingers and hooves is not a combination I'm familiar with, but I suppose this is a homunculus."

Helana nodded. "I doubt a Class One homunculus is a skin changer, but shapeshifting was common in homunculi at the end of their reign. That would make this creature about a thousand years ahead of its time, but it might explain the inconsistencies we've seen with my understanding of what we're looking at. Do you think it is a skin-changer?"

"I don't think so," said Zhehan, indicating a print. "Here you see the knuckles of the last two digits beside the hooves, and the claw marks on this poor fellow are only in sets of two with a thumb."

"So we have something with shark jaws, hooves, and hands?" said Borus. "Looks like the sarcophagus."

"Don't forget the venomous tongue," said Nasiri. "It had barbs or teeth of some sort on the tongue to administer it. Is that something either of you have come across in your studies of the natural world?"

Zhehan looked up at Helana. She shrugged. "I suppose it could be any number of chameleon or frog? Xuono of Pakardia are amphibians that have paralyzing slime, but that is a projected spit, not a tongue. It was popular to use smaller animals in the later stages of homunculi development. Voles for example can shrink their skulls while in stasis and have disproportionally powerful bites. Class Three homunculi often had elements of vampire bat to thin the blood they consumed. Exoskeletons of insects were incorporated in their skin. That sort of thing."

"I think that's as much as we can glean," said Nasiri. "Borus, do you think you can fit through, or do we need to find the storage door?"

"I can manage."

True to his word, Borus stepped through, leading with his shield. It was tight, but once he was through, the rest could proceed with confidence. There was no lighting in this room. Zhehan took one of the closed lanterns from outside the vault to illuminate the interior.

A dark maze greeted them. Walls and shelves stacked with crates of goods and wares. One of the many paths looped around the vault to the other side, which from the outside looked quite fortified, save of course for the gaping termite hole. A set of stairs led up to the next deck, which cast more light into the room they now looked through. Beside the stairs was a set of doors. Up the stairway, by the flecks of light at the end of the lantern's reach, Nasiri followed their gaze to see what looked like a broken down door at the top.

Borus started left toward the stairs.

Zhehan made a click with his tongue, then nodded forward. "We should go around, then circle back. Clear the floor."

"It's not down here," said Borus, matching his quiet but urgent tone. "Already broke down the door."

"And what if it circled back? The last thing I want is a homunculus sneaking up behind us. Your shield is our best defense and you can't be on both sides of the group."

Helana bumped into Ru, yelping slightly. Nasiri assumed she was shaken when she saw the yellow glow in Ru's eyes by the light of the lantern.

Borus pointed up the stairs. "The longer we wait, the more doors it breaks through."

"You're being ridiculous," said Zhehan. "This is a homunculus we're talking about. We won't win by charging ahead."

"Win? Like this is a game?"

Ru snarled. "Borus, we could have already been halfway around if you just did what Zhehan said."

Borus cocked his head then scoffed. "Of all people, I expected you to be on my side in this."

"I am," said Ru, struggling a bit with some words through her elongated canines. "I just want to get to the fun part, and walking around the whole maze is ridiculous when we know it's up there, but I know Zhehan is good with plans and we're stronger with a plan."

Nasiri sighed. "Can we please focus?"

"Yes, sir," said Borus through his teeth.

The team advanced, keeping close behind Borus. Zhehan held his lantern high.

Save for the crashing of waves, creaking of wood, and muted breaths, there was no sound.

Nasiri kept the rear, spear pointed behind them. Although he should have his bow, with the tremor in his hand he didn't trust his accuracy, especially in the dark. In his youth, this challenge would have thrilled him. Now all Nasiri could think was how much of a mess this was. They had let their quarry set all terms. There was no control, no bait, no containment. His mind was aflame with all the ways this would surely go wrong. This was not at all how a hunt should be conducted.

Nasiri took a deep breath.

A light glowed from the door atop the stairs.

"Can we go upstairs now?" asked Borus. "That light wasn't there before."

Zhehan pursed his lips. "Yes."

Borus led the way, and Nasiri brought up the back.

***

Helana was in the middle of the group as they advanced up to the next floor of storage. Once the rest had passed, she saw the door to this level was caved in.

Between the dim light within and Zhehan's lantern, Helana saw through the group enough to tell that there was another maze ahead. They slowly advanced into the room toward the flickering light to the right, keeping close behind Borus's massive shield.

Everyone acted different under pressure, but he was not the collected young man she had gotten to know over the course of the past few days. She could hardly forgive that, but seeing him on edge made her all the more nervous, and Helana was already barely able to contain her building anxiety.

What she had assumed was another lantern was certainly producing a lot more light the closer they got…

Zhehan gasped. "Fire!"

Borus rushed forward, no longer leading with the great shield as he charged around the crates.

By the time Helana circled around, Zhehan and Borus were stamping the floor between two crates. Borus was particularly focused on the section nearest the crates to their left. The aisle lead down to an open door. A figure was sprawled out on the floor on their side of the flames near Helana, facing away toward one of the crate alleys. For all Helana's terror, the fire had not spread too far, but there were enough flames that it was clear their stamping wasn't going to contain it right away.

"Does anyone have water?" asked Rukirha, joining in the stomping.

"Yes, but no," said Zhehan. "That will just spatter the oil."

Nasiri drew a pouch from his belt and held it out for Zhehan. "Salt ash. Should help."

As Zhehan took it, Helana knelt down and checked the body.

A young woman with cropped dark hair, part of the crew based on her uniform. Still warm, but no pulse.

As Helana turned the woman over, she gasped.

Her ribcage was pried open. Most of the organs within had been eaten, just like the body in the vault. Unlike the body below, this one's limbs had not been consumed. Helana was struck by the woman's eyes, locked open and in terror, much like the other woman below who had succumbed to the homunculus's venom.

Although Borus and his companions had stamped out the worst of the flames, Helana still heard the sizzle of a fire. She looked about, trying to identify its source. It was missing some of the other sounds of flame, such as pops and sizzling, but the steady crackle remained. The company began to take formation again while Zhehan put out the last of the fire.

Helana heard Rukirha say something about blood down the hall. She ran forward, with Zhehan cursing and close behind.

A gloss caught Helana's attention further down her aisle, reflecting the final traces of light. It seemed to be the source of the muted crackling. As she focused and Zhehan stepped closer with his lantern, Helana realized the form was as a pair of enormous beetle wings from the back, with the same hard shine and general shape. Was it on a crate?

The fiery sounds accelerated, and as the form raised and eased closer, the back of the giant beetle split open to reveal the snaggled jaws of a shark, and the beetle wings opened to form a wide frill behind the pale ridges of a hideous brain.

Barely able to comprehend what was before her, Helana screamed.

***

Loregus was many things, but he did not think he would be a healer.

In the panicked evacuation, quarters were tight. Some elected to barricade themselves in their rooms when told that there was a dangerous creature on the ship, a few claiming to want to aid in the fight, but most had been ushered to the cafes and lounges toward the front of the mighty sunship.

Perhaps out of guilt since Jaran was the one who cudgeled him in the first place, Loregus treated the injury of the crewman who had been brought to the middle class lounge. Once his broken jaw was dressed and treated to the best of Loregus's abilities, he held ice to it for a moment.

One of the physicians on retainer relieved him, and Loregus stood and washed his hands behind the bar.

After helping himself to a glass of whiskey, he looked up at a familiar gravelly voice across the room.

"I am fine! You can unhand me, thank you. If you wish to be useful, get me some water."

Loregus took water from one of the pitchers, dropped in a few cubes of ice, and sauntered around the bar, making straight for Ra Maslani.

The librarian had been reclined on a makeshift cot of cushions of this makeshift infirmary. He had since stood, then had to take a seat, muttering something about his head. Loregus wasn't sure how he had missed him upon entry, but he was glad to see the man alive.

Based on the cold glare Loregus received, the feeling was not mutual.

"I heard you grumbling about wanting water, and thought I would make this peace offering."

Ra Maslani only glared.

Loregus held out the water.

"You must forgive my rudeness, but the last drink you gave me didn't exactly sit well, and is in fact the reason I need water instead of something far more aggressive."

With a sigh, Loregus took a sip, then set it in Ra Maslani's hand. "Delicious. Crisp and refreshing. Now drink up. Yes, I poisoned you, but that was just business. The pleasure was real so don't get that twisted up in that beautiful but entirely too overanalytical mind of yours. I am still on this plodding graveyard of trees because I acknowledge that there are dangerous consequences from my actions, and I am trying to make it right."

For a moment Ra Maslani continued his glower.

With pursed lips, he raised the goblet and took a sip, all while keeping his gaze fixed on Loregus.

Loregus sighed, speaking in a hushed tone despite there being so much activity in the room. "Listen to me; there is a dangerous creature down there. It could kill a lot of people. I may be a scoundrel and I will not pretend to be a good person, but will you please trust that I'm still here because I don't want more people to die?"

Although his face remained stern, the corner of Ra Maslani's mouth curled ever so slightly. "I would have thought my taking the sip showed I trust you." Ra Maslani tipped the cup back, gulping down the entirety of its contents then set it on the table. "Walk and talk."

"Can you walk?"

Ra Maslani stumbled a bit after his first step, and Loregus caught him. Loregus suppressed thoughts of how pleasant Ra Maslani's own scent danced with his nutmeg and hawthorn fragrance.

"Are you going to be alright?" said Loregus as Ra Maslani cleared his throat.

The librarian smirked. "Of course, I just need to walk it off. You aren't the first to poison me, and I doubt you will be the last."

"Pity. I thought we had something special."

With a hint of a smile, Ra Maslani stood on his own, straightened his uniform, and led the way to the door. The guard posted cocked his head.

Ra Maslani looked up. "We need to get through."

"Apologies, Ra, but the door is to remain locked."

"Because there's a threat outside. I do not wish to alarm, but this threat is almost certainly being underestimated, and I may be the only person on this boat equipped to resolve this conflict."

Although the guard looked torn, he nodded, and checked through the small window of the door. Once confirming there was nothing outside, he opened the door.

"Sun and stars guide you both," the man said. "To my knowledge it is contained in the rear third of the ship, and the front two sections have been quartered off. Guards will be posted at each section. Best of luck, Ra."

"Appreciated," said Ra Maslani, drawing the Trist backsword and buckler from his waist and stepping outside.

Loregus followed, drawing his own dagger. Though it felt hilariously inadequate, it was a comfort to be armed in any capacity.

As soon as the door closed, Ra Maslani backed against the wall. Loregus followed suit. "Raun, tell me everything you know about this creature."

"In the interest of honest disclosure, my name is Loregus."

Ra Maslani chuckled. "Your name means 'the deceiver' in old Qajarith? Your parents have strong opinions of you."

"Oh, far worse than simple deceiver: in this case egu means 'proof of', so is a compound meaning 'I am proof of deception'. My grandfather, Baron Derukov, named me, and is indeed a man of strong opinions, especially in the naming of bastards in his family."

"House Deruke? Well known for their hounds."

Loregus sighed. "Yes, you might surmise that my family is quite fond of pedigree, and on more than one occasion he threatened to throw me in the kennel to sustain the breed he was actually proud of. Less about the joys of my childhood, more about the creature I and my compatriots let out..."

"Apologies, yes. Start by telling me what you saw," said Ra Maslani. "As clear as you can remember."

***

Nasiri had just turned to tell Helana they were leaving when the young woman screamed.

He ran behind her, kneeling over the body as she was. He readied his spear where she was turning from.

A long-legged creature, around the size of a small horse, stepped into the light from the hall. The hooves with gnarled fingers alone told him this was the demon, not to mention the shark-like jaws stained dark crimson from feasting on the woman before Helana. It was a grey beast, warted like a toad, and the great frill surrounding its head like a shield drake revealed an alarming pale head.

"Go!"

As Helana scrambled to the side, Nasiri brought up his spear, guarding as he leaped over the body, lunged, and thrust forward.

Although the demon stepped back out of reach and closed the frill over its face, Nasiri's attack was passed under with a lashing of the tongue, striking his chest like a punch. The cuirass took the blow, but before Nasiri could suck air back into his lungs much less reposition, the tongue jerked him closer.

By luck or some old reflex, Nasiri managed to position his spear at the back of the creature's jaws. The serrated fangs gnashed as the demon pushed its full might down on him. Although the haft of his spear was not solid metal, Trist was braided over much of it, and the demon failed to chew through.

With a mighty shove, the creature pushed Nasiri back onto the floor. The breath was unspeakably foul, and red drool spattered on Nasiri's face.

Before the creature could throw off Nasiri's spear, someone shouted above and struck the demon's head with repeated blows.

After enduring several strikes with no sign of injury, the demon disengaged its bite on Nasiri's spear. Although it stamped on Nasiri's armored stomach, he landed a hard blow with the broad wing of his spear as soon as he was able to turn. The creature gargled and began to stand.

Twisting to gain distance, Nasiri thrust his spear hard into its chest.

With a reverberation that shot pain through Nasiri's wrists and elbows, he was knocked back.

It took a moment for Nasiri to realize his spear had bounced off the demon's hide.

As it took another step back, the creature reared on its hind legs like a bear, towering with such height that it nearly reached the ceiling two span high.

The tongue lashed forward, enveloping Nasiri's shoulder armor. The force of it shot pain through his shoulder. The end of the tongue was barbed with teeth like a lamprey, shifting to gain purchase. Each motion sent a fresh spasm of pain.

As the tongue disengaged, Nasiri tried to swing wildly with his spear in a gambit to slice the horrid appendage, but the retraction was blindingly swift, and his attack went wide.

Ru pressed the attack, her shield overhead as she closed in to use her knife. Although the shield endured a series of punishing kicks, Ru was forced to her knees before she could employ the iraku in hand.

Borus came from Nasiri's other side, his own shield high. He gave point with his halberd, but as Nasiri experienced, it glanced off the creature's leg. A crossbow bolt struck its chest, and was treated to the same fate.

Although Nasiri tried to stand, pain shot through his left shoulder with such agony that his eyes glossed over in white.

***

Helana was terrified, barely able to look around the crates at the homunculus as it cudgeled its hooves down on Ru and Borus. Nasiri looked unconscious, or at least immobile. Zhehan was pumping the lever on his crossbow and setting the next bolt, all while struggling to keep hold of the lantern.

"Hold this," he said, passing her the lantern before taking another shot.

His bolt again glanced off the closed frill, but he had been aiming for the mouth while it was briefly open. Helana wondered if that may have pierced.

The homunculus's hoofed hand struck Rukirha with such force that she buckled, collapsing onto the floor. It then grabbed Borus's shield and tried to pull it back. He held on, dropping his halberd so both hands might keep their grip. For a moment it worked, then the homunculus leaned forward, and the sudden change in force made both homunculus and man crumple down absent grace.

Another fiery crackle built up within the homunculus's barrel chest, and it pushed itself to its feet.

The tongue lashed out, striking Zhehan's lower leg with such force that it cracked. Although his feet were taken out from under him, the tongue kept its hold and flexed, beginning to-

Helana stood, swung the lantern about, and smashed it inside the creature's mouth.

As the glass shattered and oil caught aflame, the homunculus coughed to spit out the frame. It released Zhehan, and the great tongue recoiled. The motion must have drawn glass into its maw and throat, or perhaps it was simply the flame, but it sputtered and shook about, hissing in pain and fury.

While it staggered, the homunculus smashed its massive shoulder against the shelves nearest Helana. It struck the same shelf and shook its head. Helana stumbled to the side as a crate near the top fell and smashed where she had been a moment before, scattering the floor with triangular bags of sugar amidst straw.

At the noise, the homunculus's attention snapped to the floor. Again it crackled, the beetle-wing helmet folding up like ears. Its jaws were partially open, with smoke wafting out at each exhale.

As she finally saw its full form in the light, Helana realized that had seen engravings of this creature before.

Her hand clapped over her mouth, trying to stifle her breathing.

The creature must have heard the motion. It could surely hear her heart beat. As it turned, the ears opened, and as it crackled, a stream of clicks hit her. It wasn't with great force, but enough that she could feel where it was looking: up her arm, to her chest, then the hand over her mouth...

With a feral roar, Rukirha charged from back down the aisle, shield held high. She thrust one of the spear edges down hard on the creature's back, which promptly bounced off. Letting out a grunt, the creature kicked back like a mad stallion, impacting her chest and launching Ru back, where she skidded then collided with a shelf.

As it charged down the central aisle, leaping against more crates before galloping to the door, Helana backed up and tripped over the dead body. Although she managed to roll back, she still hit her elbow and tailbone in the fall.

By the time the painful stars left her vision, the creature was gone.

With a grimace, Helana pushed herself up. While she ached in many places, she knew she was the best off of anyone in the room.

At least Nasiri and Zhehan had been bitten. They both looked unconscious as far as Helana could tell. Slowing their blood and heartbeats might just save their lives. Borus was moving far outside of what Helana could see, but Ru was still. Hopefully she was alright. They would certainly both need attention, but for the moment, those bitten were her priority.

Helana looked through the crates, frantically reading the labels.

"What are you doing?" said Borus, his voice strained.

Helana didn't look over, scouring the shelves for a single word: "Salt!"

***

"And how do you plan to kill a demon, exactly?" asked Loregus as they rushed into the librarian's suite, and he shut and locked the door quickly behind them. "Sounded to me like they can only be killed by artifacts."

"We have a dozen artifacts in the vault," said Ra Maslani. "I just need a few things."

As Ra Maslani lit a lantern and prepared in his room, Loregus waited idle in the main suite, lighting a few more to pass the time. He wasn't certain what he was doing. He was not in any position to help, not in any way he could conceive as productive. He delivered the news as promised. Had he not fulfilled his obligation?

A rattle of the knob then knock at the door called his focus.

Were there still people in this section of the sunship?

Loregus opened the door, quick to let inside whoever might need shelter.

As Loregus recognized Kronan, the door was thrown open. Kronan grabbed Loregus's coat, and a flash of metal preluded a thrust to his throat.

***

"Why are you looking for salt?" asked Borus after confirming that Rukirha's injuries weren't debilitating.

"Salt is the only thing that can save Nasiri and Zhehan."

At this, Borus stood. He wrung his wrist and had a limp on his left leg, but overall seemed alright.

"I don't remember you mentioning salt as a counter to homunculi venom," said Borus as he scanned the crates on the other side.

"I was wrong," said Helana. "This isn't a homunculus. The viscosity of this creature's venom is inconsistent, and will become a solid when kinetic energy is applied."

"Common, please!"

"It makes their blood hard any time a muscle moves. A muscle like a heart."

"Oh."

"Would a blood thinner help?" asked Rukirha. She was holding her side with a grimace, but was conscious. Her fangs had retracted and her eyes no longer glowed.

"Yes! I imagine it would at least. You have one?"

Borus went to Ru at her gesture. He withdrew the vial on her bandolier she tapped. "Sloth bat venom. I make sure to take a few-"

"Easy, there," said Borus, holding out a hand to keep her calm. He then crossed over to Zhehan.

Helana spotted a crate with the label she was looking for. "Got it!" Upon sliding it out, Helana grabbed a sack of salt and rushed over to Nasiri.

Although his eyes were closed, his breathing was quite rapid. As she looked him over, his eyes fluttered open.

"Did the venom get you?"

"No," Nasiri replied. "My armor did its job. The strike dislocated my left shoulder, though. That was quite a tongue. I am of less concern. See to Zhehan."

While she wasn't convinced, she went to join Borus by Zhehan.

Right away she could tell his knee had been broken by the impact. The barbs of its tongue had torn through his silk trousers. He had a pulse, but it was sporadic: there wasn't much time.

Someone screamed down the hall through the door.

Helana closed her mind and focused on the task at hand.

With a gentle but firm hand, Helana dabbed salt in the many wounds left by the strike. Borus had put blood-thinner where he could, but Zhehan's entire leg was tensing.

Helana grimaced. "I think the venom has reached his thigh."

"What does that mean?" asked Borus as Helana took off her sash and readied it beside Zhehan's leg. She also grabbed a straw from the sugar crate then crossed back to Zhehan.

"It means I need you to hold him down and raise his leg so I can cut his femora- the vein in his leg. If I put a tourniquet on now, it might just push the venom to his heart. He needs to bleed it out, and he can only do that with an incision. I may need to spit saline water in through this straw if it doesn't flow on its own."

"You can't be serious," said Rukirha, who was already sound-ing astonishingly improved. Helana glanced back and saw that she was already looking greatly improved and was working on Nasiri's shoulder.

"If I don't do this, the beat of his heart will turn the organ into a solid and he will die."

Although Borus was openly skeptical, he held Zhehan's arms over his chest in a cross. Helana drew her knife. Willing herself calm, she slit open the inner thigh of his trousers and pulled it open. With Borus holding the arm up, Helana found the vein she was looking for.

"What are you doing?" Zhehan groaned. His tensing fully hardened the leg.

"Ru," said Helana. "I need you your help holding him down."

"Wait, wai-"

Between Borus and Rukirha, Zhehan was restrained.

With a deep breath, Helana made her incision.

***

Although Loregus recoiled, the knife didn't pierce his neck, although its point pressed just left of his throat.

"Kronan!" shouted Ra Maslani from deeper in the suite. "Unhand him! Now is not the time."

"Now is exactly the time," the treasure hunter growled, turning his gaze back to Loregus. "I've opened a lot of throats of men who crossed me. Now, I'm going to ask you a few questions, and you're going to give me answers that I believe. If I don't believe you, then your legacy will be a stain on my sleeve and these fine oak floors. Am I clear?"

"Clear as the autumn waters in the Sea of the Dancing Sun."

"Direct answers are appreciated."

"Apologies." Loregus gulped. "I embellish under pressure."

A scream echoed down the hall, back toward the back of the ship.

"Kronan!" said Ra Maslani. "That homunculus we found? The one you want to get paid for? Is out and killing people. It's come out of stasis, and must feed. It must feed far beyond the bounds of normal creatures: this thing isn't going to stop at a single meal."

"So let it feed," said Kronan, glaring over Loregus's shoulder. "Let it become fat and sluggish, then we can vanquish it with one of your trinkets and put it back in its cage. You want to contribute to your sacred library? Start documenting it's feeding patterns. Who does it target? Where does it strike for the kill? If you're right about its identity, then this creation is older than any of the demons out there today. Do you really want to pass upon this opportunity? 'Knowledge Above All' are the words of your order, are they not?"

"I am quite certain the Great Library would not condone letting everyone on this ship die for the sake of documentation," said Ra Maslani.

A dull series of clicks behind Kronan, like a fire with too much tinder, caught Loregus's attention.

Kronan shrugged. "You've sat back in every conflict, even when your knowledge and technology could save the numbers on this ship many times over. Don't pretend your order acts out of altruism. Not only would they condone your studies, I imagine nothing else could be more archetypical of a librarian, and could get you that promotion you were denied."

"We can debate the philosophical interpretations of my order another time. Please unhand my lover so I can put this homunculus down."

Kronan made some retort, but Loregus's focus was on the creature filling out the doorway. His first thought was a horrid offspring of a hyena and a toad with the size of a horse.

Although it looked ready to pounce, instead that hideous tongue that had killed Shin was shot out like an arrow, striking Kronan in the lower back with a dull crunch. Kronan's body arced, drawing

Loregus in as the treasure hunter's hand still gripped his shirt, although by some kiss of fortune the knife hand also drew back.

With the tongue adhered, the homunculus yanked Kronan in, pulling Loregus along by his still-gripped hand. Loregus grappled the knife aside as he and Kronan were thrown to the ground.

A gurgling grunt faded to a crunch as the creature bit down on Kronan. A hoofed and clawed hand slammed into the floorboards beside Loregus's head. Something wet spattered on his face, covering much of the right as Loregus turned to the side. The full weight of Kronan was pressed onto his chest, prompting Loregus to cough, then the body was lifted and slammed onto the floor closer to the door.

Tearing of clothing prefaced the revolting strain and crack of flesh and bone being ripped apart.

Although Loregus was tempted to lie still, out of his left eye, he saw Ra Maslani gesturing down with one hand and beckoning slowly with the other. The librarian was standing in the doorway of his personal room in the suite.

Behind him, Loregus heard the homunculus still feeding. With a deep breath, Loregus turned and crawled closer.

Ra Maslani held out his hand. Loregus stopped.

Another crackling sound sent a faint tapping along Loregus's leg up to his back.

The clicking stopped.

With further tears and crunches, the demon went back to its feast.

Loregus carefully crawled his way across the remaining distance. As soon as he was through, Ra Maslani carefully shut the door and barred it shut. Ra Maslani knelt before Loregus. After motioning to be quiet, he dabbed the cloth over Loregus's face. It was then that Loregus realized much of his face was numb.

After a moment, the room on the other side of the door went silent.

Ra Maslani stood and opened the door. Once he confirmed it was gone, he closed the door once more and slid down his desk to the floor across from Loregus.

"That demon is terrifying," Loregus whispered.

"It's not a demon," said Ra Maslani. "I was wrong."

"We're all allowed to be wrong sometimes."

Ra Maslani deadpanned.

After a moment, Loregus grinned. "You called me your lover."

Ra Maslani rolled his eyes. "How's your face?"

"Pretty as ever I imagine, although it's a bit numb on this side."

With a deep breath, Ra Maslani stood. "I'm going to go get some salt, track down that wretched creature, and kill it."

Loregus stood too. "I don't understand why we need to season it, but wherever we're going, I'm with you."

Ra Maslani looked like he was about to speak, but his retort died on his lips. He sighed, stepped in close, then kissed Loregus briefly. "Let's go then."

***

Helana felt like she didn't draw breath until Zhehan's blood finally flowed free.

He was unconscious and a few shades paler, but as far as she could tell, enough of the venom had been drawn out that any remaining toxins would be diluted by the salt naturally present in blood.

Once Helana finished her stitches and secured the bandage and tourniquet, she leaned back and let Ru step in. The Pakardiant gave him a potion. Although it was Helana's understanding that Pakardiant potions could only be used by someone who was attuned to the magic of the witch who made the potion, perhaps that included Zhehan. She had so many questions, but didn't press the matter.

Borus was kneeling over Nasiri. The hunter spoke quietly, but from what she overheard, it sounded like he was recovering well enough. If the worst of his problems was a dislocated shoulder, now that it was reset, he should be alright.

Helana saw movement down the hall. Although she rose to a crouch and readied Ra Maslani's spear, she lowered the blade when she saw it was two figures walking closer. One held a lantern. Once she realized it was Ra Maslani and Loregus, she wanted to rush into his arms. Exhaustion and knowing he wouldn't appreciate it given all the blood on her hands and chest kept her seated.

Ra Maslani took in the group of wounded hunters. He noted the bag of salt next to Zhehan and nodded, turning to Helana. "I take it you know what this creature is?"

"Yes," she replied.

"And what is it?" asked Nasiri, sitting up with Borus's aid.

"The southern islanders call them Moørkutlot: Through Death They Create Silence. Often called the Makers of Silence, or Silent Ones."

***

At this, the last of Nasiri's muddied focus seemed to fade away.

"That's not a demon?" asked Borus. "It is a natural beast?"

"I have heard many rumors of these creatures," said Zhehan, his tone groggy. "Predators on the polar continent of Kaishel which hunt by sound, like a bat or blackfish. I've heard they are related to both, depending on who tells the story, although I thought they were likely a demon or even a fictional creature in the folklore of the peoples of Kaishel."

Nasiri rolled his arm. He had endured many dislocations. There was a time when he could fix them himself, but this one had fully debilitated him. The quickness of recovery once Borus reset his shoulder was more embarrassing than anything else. His chest still strained, but as he moved his arm and chest, it began to improve.

"They are indeed poorly understood," Ra Maslani continued. "We at the library do have a fairly comprehensive understanding of their taxonomy, although I do not have time for such a lesson. What we need to know are three things: salt both defuses their venom and harms their skin, they are drawn to sound like moths to a flame, and it can be killed by mortal weapons. We can pierce its hide either by salting the skin, or by slowly attacking, as rapid strikes only harden its slime."

"Even my Trist spear could not penetrate on a quick thrust," said Nasiri.

"Indeed. I expect my sword would have no better success. Now, based on what I understand and what we saw in the hall on the way here, it has fed on a lot of people. Heterothermes like the Moørkut-lot require much food when they exit stasis, but the sheer amount that this creature is consuming is more consistent with demons, which leads me to believe it has a mild enchantment upon it, hence being in a sarcophagus, although the magic is not so potent that its form or conduct are dramatically altered. It is consistent with the appearance, size, and behavior of these creatures as I understand them, if a bit on the larger side and requiring far more food than usual. The halls of the sunship have been quarantined, so in theory, it is trapped in this section of the ship that Loregus here says has been mostly cleared. My proposal is we go down to the vault, draw it in for a fight, and if we can, trap it back in the sarcophagus so that it can be dealt with once we get to the Great Library."

Nasiri stood. "It can break through doors, so we should not anticipate it will be contained in this part of the ship indefinitely. If we-"

Ru took up her shield and went to the door. Nasiri held up a hand for silence. She listened, closing her eyes in focus. He hadn't noticed her drink one of her sensory enhancing potions. Although he thought to scold her for drinking too many at once, he held his tongue, for if ever they were to push themselves to their respective limits, it was in a fight such as this.

"The creature is on the upper deck of the ship," said Ru. "It's calling out. I hear screams. We should go."

Nasiri shook his head, wetting his spear then thrusting it into the bag of salt. "I do this alone."

"You cannot do this on your own," said Borus. "You took us on to help. Let us help."

"This is not a conventional hunt for man-eaters. I accepted you all as apprentices with the understanding that you would assist in the humane capture or killing of animals. This may be an animal, but it is far more dangerous, especially with any potential enchantment. The priority is to kill it."

"I am of the same mind," said Ra Maslani, as he thrust the tip of his sword into the bag of salt. "I will accompany you. I may lack your experience in hunting, yet I have slain many beasts and know much of this creature."

Nasiri nodded. "Very well. We go, you and I. The rest of you remain. Keep an eye on Zhehan." He pursed his lips to the door. Ra Maslani followed.

Ru didn't move to let him pass. Her features were hard. With a deep breath, she held out her shield.

"This is a beast, not a demon," she whispered in Pakardiant. "Make it quick."

Nasiri took the shield and led the way. He heard Ra Maslani keep pace behind him as he jogged down the hall then up the stairs.

As predicted, the door had been broken through.

"Draw it to us, then run it through?" said Ra Maslani.

Nasiri shrugged. "Presently, that is our option. Are you ready?"

"As ready as one can be."

Wind howled across the deck, and even some ten spans below, the sound of crashing waves on either side drowned out the creaking Nasiri had gotten used to in the hull. The moon was striking and nearly full, casting the deck in an eerie blue glow. Mist of salt was strong in the air. Although he knew he should not rely on such positivity, Nasiri wondered if the salt air might weaken the creature's hide.

Three bodies were in sight. All were crewmen from what he could tell. One was entangled in the rigging, and the other two strewn on deck. Each had horrid wounds in their torsos. The one closest to them actively bled. For all the carnage, it was quiet.

Nasiri took a deep breath.

Ra Maslani struck the hilt of his backsword against his buckler.

Nothing.

They kept close, moving along the deck and keeping their backs to the starboard rail.

A pained cry toward the port prow drove Nasiri and Ra Maslani to jog ahead.

As they ran, a long, mournful scream rang out at such a high pitch that Nasiri and Maslani slowed, grimacing through their continued motion towards the horrid source.

Around one of the forward masts, an older crewman crawled toward Nasiri and Ra Maslani. Red stained the deck behind him, and spasms rolled through him as he tried to raise a left arm that briefly solidified with each motion.

A dull crackle behind him was Nasiri's warning.

He spun about. The great grey beast closed in. Nasiri raised Ru's shield just as the tongue lashed forward.

The force of it pushed the shield back, but Nasiri turned with the force, thrusting his spear as his torso rotated. His salted spear bit into the base of its stocky neck, sinking in with familiar ease. The moørkutlot retracted its tongue, hissing as Nasiri withdrew his spear.

As the creature shook about, Ra Maslani raced in, his buckler guarding overhand as he gave point. The thrust penetrated without resistance. A swipe of its hoofed hand knocked aside Ra Maslani's buckler and grabbed hold of his sword arm. As the moørkutlot stood, it lifted Ra Maslani entirely off the ground then slammed him against the deck. It frantically stamped the deck, although Ra Maslani managed to weakly roll aside.

Nasiri's next thrust was a quick jab, and either by enough salt remaining on the spear or in the air that it penetrated, yet by the motions of the moørkutlot it was not a deep pierce. It was successful on catching the beast's focus, which gaped at Nasiri. Nasiri struck at the mouth, which snapped shut before his strike could land. It swiped wide with a long front leg, striking down Ru's shield with such force that Nasiri was forced to drop it.

Nasiri retreated a few paces, spear in a high guard as the moørkutlot stepped over Ru's shield.

The lashing of the tongue was swift. Although Nasiri tried to parry with the haft of his spear, it struck his left hand. The impact hit with a series of cracks as the barbed inversion of the tongue enveloped his grip.

As the tongue pulled him in, Nasiri swung up with his spear in a gambit to slice the horrid appendage. It disengaged from his hand, and while Nasiri's strike hit the tongue, it failed to sever. A spattering of ichor suggested he had at least done some damage.

A wide swipe from the moørkutlot struck Nasiri in the chest and cast him down onto the deck.

As it lunged forward, the creature stopped just above Nasiri, crying out.

Ra Maslani had thrust his sword into its side. At first the blade had not pierced, but leaning his weight into the sword made it slowly penetrate, and the librarian's blade pushed with ease once the hide was broken.

Before Ra Maslani could withdraw, the Moørkutlot's arm hooked back reflexively, and he had to let go.

Perhaps slowed from an earlier injury or simply not being fast enough, Ra Maslani was caught by a backward kick which sent him crashing back against the wall of the sunship. The moørkutlot turned and advanced upon the librarian, cudgeling with repeated stamps of its right foot.

Although Nasiri tried to stand, movement in his hand made it rapidly harden. He then relaxed and could move slightly, but the act of raising his arm flexed muscles which went rigid.

From the blurred edges of Nasiri's vision he saw the creature stand to its full height, tilt back its head, and let out another horrid scream.

Nasiri tightened his hand, knowing that was the only way to harden the venom and keep it from reaching his heart. Although his arm moved freely, based on what Zhehan experienced, it would be a matter of time before the venom spread. Yes, flexing his hand hardened it, but it also made the blood in his arm move faster.

He didn't know how long he had, but the moment the creature came back toward him, he would lose focus on his hand and likely perish.

***

Loregus wished he had come up with something clever to say before Ra Maslani left. Entertaining perhaps. Even a foolish thing that would put another smile on that ever-serious face.

Instead he had been frozen.

He was not the only one paralyzed with tension in the store room.

As Borus paced, limping off his left foot, his face was locked in a scowl. Rukirha drummed her heel on the floor as she sat on a crate by the door. Helana sat beside Zhehan, using more water to rinse hands still covered in his blood. Zhehan was conscious, if only just, yet looked more defeated than in pain. That he was conscious at all was astonishing.

Rukirha stood and drew her bow, flexing it a few times. She then poured oil into her quiver and a handful of salt.

"What are you doing?" Zhehan said quietly.

"I did not seek out Nasiri to teach me how to sit in a room."

Borus nodded, oiling and salting his sword. "Let's go."

"I'm going too," said Helana, grabbing a fresh bag of salt and oil.

"Wait," said Zhehan. "Just… slow down. Please, don't just run in. Do not fight this creature on its terms. Draw it to you, and stay on the starboard side of the deck. It can probably smell your salt, and you don't want it avoiding you because of it."

As she looked back to Zhehan, Rukirha opened her mouth as she looked about to say something, but turned in silence and left the room. Borus nodded to Zhehan, then he and Helana followed close behind.

Loregus had no interest in following the two young hunters and Helana to seek out an encounter with a creature that had nearly killed him twice, but he admired their dedication.

***

Helana followed the two hunters wordlessly upstairs.

With his shield held high, Borus kept his sword level. Rukirha warmed up her bow behind him.

They stepped out on the deck. Consistent with Zhehan's suggestion, the hunters kept along the wall. Helana's sabre remained in its scabbard as she held the bag of salt with a handful ready to throw. It seemed futile in hand, but she trusted this would be more effective.

Although at first they neither saw nor heard signs of the creature save for the bodies on deck, Rukirha pursed her lips port. There were only a few lanterns and the light of a half moon, but Helana couldn't see much. Movement at the edge of her visual range was all she could see.

With whatever potion enhanced her senses, it was evidently enough for Rukirha.

While keeping her focus on her target, Rukirha drew an oiled arrow free of her quiver. Helana held out the bag of salt, which Ru thrust her arrow into for a full coat.

A horrible scream rang out, the pitch so high Helana could barely hear it. The piercing noise was felt, much like its crackling echolocation, and Helana reflexively covered her ears.

Frowning through the cutting noise across the ship. Rukirha raised her bow overhead, drew it back as she lowered her arm horizontal to the movement on the port side, and took her shot.

***

An arrow sank into the Moørkutlot's shoulder, and it turned back whence Nasiri and Ra Maslani came. It hissed, a crackle at the base of its throat. Ra Maslani's sword was still embedded in its side, and the creature's left arm was curled up and immobile because of it. With a grunt the moørkutlot limped off in the direction of the arrow.

Nasiri's mind went blank as he thought of a functional tourniquet. There were thick ropes of nearby rigging, but the thought of slicing them up in time to tie one off struck him as impractical.

His forearm went solid with the next flex.

A nearby lantern caught his eye, the flames dancing high. Nasiri then turned to his spear.

Gritting his teeth, Nasiri took up his spear and pressed the tip into the gap of his elbow.

With a firm pull, the spear's blade slid into his elbow, and thanks to its width and diamond-dust edge, cleanly severed his arm.

***

Helana held out the salt for Rukirha's next arrow.

The creature paused briefly once it came into view, the great ears flaring out as a crackling fire of echolocation scanned the group. Even at this range, Helana felt it, although it may have simply been the grating pitch that was so high as to barely be audible.

After Borus set down his shield, propped on its feet, both he and Rukirha shot at the moørkutlot.

Their projectiles both found target. Although it cried out, the moørkutlot continued its limping charge. While Rukirha sent another arrow into the creature's shoulder, Borus switched to his sword and great shield, holding his falchion back for Helana to quickly salt. After one more shot, Rukirha joined Helana behind Borus's shield.

With a resonant clunk, Borus buckled. As his shield was pulled upon, he turned it slightly, advancing and swinging down with a great chop of his sword.

While he turned, Helana saw his falchion cleave through the tongue as it jerked against his shield. Once the horrid deed was done, Borus pressed the offense, slashing many cuts into the hide of the moørkutlot while Rukirha sank many arrows into its side. Borus's first few cuts left horrid wounds, but the salt wore off, making his blows deflected. Helana threw a handful of salt, which splashed on the back of its neck while it was hunkered down.

***

With the last fragments of consciousness, Nasiri held the remains of his arm over the flames of the lantern, gritting his teeth as the open wound was cauterized.

When the bleeding had slowed to a trickle, he drew his spear from where he had thrust into the deck of the ship, then turned to where he heard the moørkutlot continuing to fight.

Drawing upon any reserves, Nasiri pressed on to finish the hunt.

***

After enduring many strikes, the moørkutlot reared up and struck Borus with a swipe of its hoofed paw while his shield was aside to open for another cut. The strike knocked him back, staggering to the rail of the sunship. Following another throw of salt onto the standing beast's chest, Rukirha snapped an arrow which embedded to the fletching.

Helana cast the last of her salt onto the belly of the beast. While Rukirha put another arrow in its chest, Borus charged forward and hacked across with his falchion held in two hands, carving a mighty wound nearly to its spine.

Following a strained inhalation, the great beast collapsed.

Helana saw a figure behind the creature, a spear in one hand and missing the other. Once she realized it was Nasiri, the hunter had already started to fall. She, Borus, and Rukirha all rushed to his side.

***

Loregus paced, at a loss for what to do. Should he run? Would Ra Maslani need his help?

"I'm as well as can be expected," said Zhehan, taking a kit from his belt and tossing it to Loregus. "Don't remain on my account. They may be hurt. Go do what you can."

With a frown Loregus nodded. He raced down the hall and up the stairs, armed with more hope than he knew he deserved that there would be a man able to save.

***

Nasiri's focus was strained, but as Ru lifted him and demanded his attention in their native tongue, he pushed himself to not drift away with the strength bleeding from his severed arm.

"Hold out his arm!" shouted Helana.

As Borus did so, Helana began work on Nasiri's left arm, tying it off.

"You don't get to die," Ru snapped in Pakardiant, the growl at the back of her throat calling him back to focus. "Do you hear me, old man? You still have work to do."

"My apprentices finished what I could not," said Nasiri with a gentle smile. "I'm proud of you."

"I'm not proud! We are yet clumsy. That hunt was a disaster, only resolved through determination and luck, not skill, and you don't get to go until we are truly ready. Not until all three of us can complete this hunt on our own absent undue harm to our quarry. Now is not the time for rest. Now is when we review and determine where to each improve."

Nasiri winced as Helana cinched the tourniquet tighter. "That hurt."

"Good," said Ru. "Pain means your body still cares, right?"

Nasiri chuckled. "Yes, Ru. I still care."

"I know you do. Spare me your contemplations of surrender. There is much left to do, and I will be by your side through it all."

After a deep breath, Nasiri nodded. His next words were in the common tongue. "Ra Maslani was injured on the port side. I know not the extent of his injuries."

"I will see to him," said Helana. Borus went with her.

Nasiri leaned back.

He took a deep breath and closed his eyes. "I am going to retire, Ru."

Ru snorted. "I dare say so."

"What do you know about guilds?"

"I'm a hunter, Nasiri, not a woman of business. Speak to Zhehan of this."

Nasiri gave a tired smile. "I intend to."

After checking to make sure his hand wasn't still bleeding, that Helana had done well, Ru lay beside him.

***

Loregus saw Helana, Nasiri, and his apprentices by the mangled corpse of the moørkutlot. Although there were bodies, none were of Ra Maslani.

He carried on until he found more bodies, spotting Ra Maslani's crumpled form against the rail of the ship. There was no sign of movement. While part of Loregus wanted to remain in uncertainty, he mustered the fortitude to kneel over the body of his lover.

A still moment passed as Loregus set his fingers against Ra Maslani's neck.

A pulse.

Loregus exhaled a breath he hadn't realized he was holding in.

"Rogue?"

Loregus smiled. "Yes, Ra Maslani, it's me. I'm here."

"Is it dead?"

"Yes, the apprentices killed it. Splendidly, from what I could tell."

Ra Maslani took a deep breath. "Good. That's good."

"Where are you hurt?"

"Would be more efficient to describe where I am not."

Loregus brushed back a strand of hair that had escaped his topknot.

"Shouldn't you be trying to get off the boat?" Ra Maslani muttered.

"I was rather counting on you leaving my involvement in the heist out of your report."

Ra Maslani chuckled. "I could be persuaded."

"Luckily for me I'm quite proficient in the art of persuasion."

"Is that what we're calling it?"

Helana and Borus arrived from over by Nasiri.

"He's alright," said Loregus.

Ra Maslani coughed weakly. "I would not go so far."

"Fair. He will live."

Borus took Helana's hand and gave it a gentle but firm squeeze. "I will go see that the guards and captain are informed of the creature's demise."

Borus leaned down for a hesitant kiss to her forehead. Before he could pull back, Helana reached up, grabbed the back of his neck, and kissed him deeply on the lips. He took a moment of surprise before his hand found her waist.

***

Helana completely lost herself, and it was only after a heavy sigh from Ra Maslani that she remembered they weren't alone and disengaged.

"I thought you were going to speak with the captain?" said Loregus with a laugh. "You two can finish later. This voyage has another nine days at least."

"Right, yes," said Borus.

Helana calmed the blush no doubt spreading through her cheeks and knelt beside her mentor.

After a quick inspection she determined Ra Maslani had several ribs, right arm and shoulder, and left hand broken or at least with severe fractures. His breathing was strained. They laid him out so he might be more efficiently carried to the infirmary for proper care once the sunship was more under control.

Crew started to come out onto the deck, armed with a range of weaponry.

"Please ensure that our specimen is not mutilated further," said Ra Maslani.

Helana stood. "Of course, Ra."

"Helana?"

"Yes?"

"You performed spectacularly. I'm proud of you."

Helana smiled. "Gratitude, Ra."

Epilogue

Loregus had walked onto the sunship with ambivalence at best. Now, as they neared the conclusion of their eleven day voyage from the Portal City to the vast harbor of Tredakoi, he knew he would miss it.

Ra Maslani had not told the captain of Loregus's involvement, and indeed vouched for Toyate's release. She was to be the librarian's responsibility, and was content to relax in their suite. Loregus still didn't know her past, but she seemed quite content to avoid further trouble.

Although Ra Maslani's injuries were extensive, and he lacked the lover's passion he had upon their first encounter, he seemed comfortable with Loregus caring for him in his room. Loregus had never been a domestic man, but he found joy in the role, even if they both knew there was an expiration to their engagement.

"What is next for you?" asked Ra Maslani on their final morning, barely looking up from his book.

Loregus shrugged, thinking over a sip of tea. "I suppose I will return to Kabarahar."

"More criminal work in the portal city? You're far too interesting to fall back into such a predictable routine."

Loregus looked up, starting to feign offense but giving it a moment's thought.

Ra Maslani set down his book and met Loregus's gaze. "You are not a deception or mistake, Loregus. Even if your mother having a child out of wedlock were something to be ashamed of, which it is not, that has no reflection upon you. You have many talents and no shortage of ambition. Your legacy is your own, not his. Stop hiding behind the name assigned by one who distains you, and forge your own path. What would make you satisfied?"

After another drink, Loregus set down his cup. "Although I admit I played little role in the encounter, even the small part I played in this felt right. I don't know how I might replicate that."

"You are cunning, observant when engaged, and frustratingly good with words. You look like you could be from almost anywhere in the known world. I am quite well traveled, and your accent of the upper classes of the Free States was without flaw despite being raised in northern Qajar. I can think of many applications for those talents."

Loregus raised an eyebrow. "Are you suggesting espionage?"

Ra Maslani's lip curled slightly. "The Great Library trades in all sorts of information."

"How silly of me to think my criminal inclinations would close doors rather than open them."

"Give it some consideration," said Ra Maslani, opening his book once more.

Loregus looked out the window beside Ra Maslani's bed. His lover's proposal certainly promised no shortage of excitement. Certainly more than the Shards had offered him. Would he have the niceties of his work for Jaran? Not likely, but he had always enjoyed secrets, acting, and learning new things, and if nothing else, working for the Great Library would be an interesting next stage in his life.

"So if I were interested, where would I go to await instruction?"

"Contrary to our reputation, we do not actually live in the library itself." Still without looking up, Ra Maslani smiled. "I have an apartment."

"And you wouldn't mind me living with you for a time?"

"If our experience on this ship is any indication, cohabitation would be agreeable, so long as you forgive a degree of skepticism when you pass me strong drinks."

"I have no intentions of poisoning you a second time," said Loregus, taking another drink. "I'm far too interesting to do something so predictable."

"Good," said Ra Maslani. "That would be quite a damper on our relationship, and worse than that, predictability doesn't suit you."

Loregus smiled casually, but his mind was alight with thoughts of what might be ahead.

Boredom was behind him, and for the joys and dangers ahead, he could not imagine being more excited.

***

Helana had no interest in leaving the warmth of Borus's bed, nor his arms around her, but she knew they were closing in on the harbor. Even with the delays in docking such a massive sunship, she knew packing would take more time than she could spare if she stayed in bed any longer.

Although she started to slip out, Borus's arms caught around her waist and pulled her back in. Her lackluster attempt at escape was no match for him. "And just where do you think you're going?"

Helana pressed her body against his. "We will be docking soon."

"I know the ship will stay here for a few days, but I don't suppose you would be interested in remaining on the ship with us all the way to Manu?"

Helana giggled as he bit her ear. "With Ra Maslani's letter of recommendation, I'm certain he will get in, and you will be coming to visit soon enough."

"I look forward to it," Borus whispered, his hand trailing low.

After another round of play, Helana kissed his shoulder. When he didn't respond, being deep in slumber, she gave him a long, slow kiss before dressing herself and stepping into the suite.

Zhehan was reclined on the couch. His recovery was going quite well, although he still could not walk on his own. Ru had kept busy between his recovery and Nasiri's, and while she seemed ever ready to bicker with Zhehan, her touch was ever tender. For his part, he didn't have much energy for argument, but gave it what he could.

Nasiri was at the desk hard at work. He had wasted no time diving into study of guild management. Although it seemed he was enthusiastic about establishing a proper organization of hunters, and had devoted much time to the subject, Helana could tell the old hunter was in over his head.

"Sleep well?" said Ru, a mischievous smirk on her face as Helana quietly shut the door behind her.

Helana willed herself not to blush. "I am indeed well rested, and it sounds like Borus might slumber for the remaining days of your voyage."

"At least he gets to rest in bed," said Zhehan. "Meanwhile I must move around to recover. Make it make sense."

Ru scoffed. "You would give the same advice to someone else in recovery: if you do not tell your legs they need to walk, they will heal for rest, not for motion."

As they continued bickering, Helana made her way over to Nasiri.

His current focus was on land ownership. As he moved to turn the page on the book he was reviewing, he raised the bandages of his missing arm, sighing before turning with his remaining hand.

"What are you looking into now?" asked Helana.

"Looking into what it would require for me to own enough space to operate a guild out of. My estate in Muta is small but has a training pit and shooting range which has proven useful in training these three. If I am truly to expand this operation, I'm going to need more space."

"Would you consider establishing yourself as a freelance guild working with the library?"

Nasiri turned back, his brow raised. "Elaborate."

"Well, since Zhehan will likely be accepted into the Great Library, and his ultimate goal is to continue working for your guild, I expect that connection could continue in a more formal way. I'm certain that the zoological departments of the library would love to work with you as a consultant, and could provide a good amount of information that could better prepare your hunters for their assignments. I know they are trying to reach out and be less reclusive. I'm confident they would like working with a hunter of your reputation."

For a moment Nasiri's brow was knotted in thought, but he nodded. "I can certainly see how this would benefit both parties. So long as we still determine which cases to take, and are not beholden to the allies or subject to refusing enemies of the Empire, I think this could be a fine partnership indeed."

"I will propose it to Ra Maslani, and perhaps get you an audience with someone who can facilitate the process before the sunship departs?"

Nasiri smiled. "That would be splendid."

Helana bowed. "It would be my pleasure."

After bidding him, Ru, and Zhehan farewell, she left to pack, eager to report to the other librarians and hopefully set her sights on the next field mission.

Helana had tasted adventure, and she thrilled at the idea of what she might learn and experience next.

***

Nearly a year after losing his arm to the Moørkutlot's venom, Nasiri's gaze locked on his targets.

Seven new apprentices. Many were graduates of the Great Library, although one was a noblewoman of House Nerotok, another a Seridic archer, and last in line was Toyate the Kentarim rogue.

Zhehan was still at the Great Library, and would soon have earned his academic mastery. Ru and Borus flanked Nasiri as he took in his new apprentices, and each would train a pair of the new hunters.

Although he could no longer shoot, Nasiri kept the trickster ring his brother made for him when he came of age three centuries earlier. Turning the ivory thumb ring was a fidget which helped ease his mind.

Nasiri took a deep breath and addressed his new apprentices.

"Few beasts are natural predators of people. When an animal becomes a man-eater, they start a war. It is understandable that the loved ones of people slain seek justice, vengeance, and an end to suffering. However, so often this pursuit results in death of innocent animals, and also sees many predators harmed from failed hunts. Very often these wounded predators turn to people as prey when their natural game is impossible to hunt with their injuries. Thus we see the wheel of death spinning around the axis of the original man-eater, who may have themselves only walked this path following an injury. In removing these man-eaters, we stop the spinning of the wheel. While they are the axis of the wheel, it is imperative to remember that they are not villains. They are animals. When we kill these animals, it is to be done with precision, speed, and without pain, something the community impacted by their hunts cannot be expected to do as they are themselves victims. If we are able to remove them from the region without killing them, this is always an option that should be explored. Either by removal or a swift kill, it is our duty to remove the axis so the wheel of death can rest.

That the cycle of pain may end. This is our calling. Our honor. Our legacy. You have heard my words, now I must hear yours. Do you vow to uphold this mission? To follow this creed in our efforts to make the known world safe for both man and beast?"

His new apprentices nodded in unison. "We do!"

Nasiri smiled. "Splendid. Our first lesson will be in archery. The foundation of success is precision, and precision only comes with practice. Follow me to the range. I don't like being late."

When Sea Meets Shore

2

When Sea Meets Shore

When Sea Meets Shore

Argunite inhaled, drawing strength from the ocean breeze.

His grip was tight on his scallop necklace, his last connection to home. The sea goddess Melrahim was all around, and he couldn't express in words how refreshing it was to be in her embrace once more.

Commodore Yurai's shurugen frigate, the Brazen Mallard, was astonishingly fast. She was also beautiful. A ship this large should be slow on the turn, but extendable keels, side sails, and outriggers meant from the helm and the assistance of her crew she could utilize whichever features served her best in that moment. Argunite could make a dingy fly like an Eskaden clipper, but the adjustable features on this shurugen had so much utility! He felt the deck with his bare feet, spreading his toes over the waxed floor, imagining the control he could have if he could not only apply these sensations at a helm, but with the flexibility of the craft itself? As it was, they were making great speed, but he could feel the currents underfoot and waves around them. There was lost potential. Melrahim was offering boons of wind and water that they were missing.

If he could helm a craft like this, it would be the fastest ship in the known world.

They were two days out of Koban's cove. The highs and lows of Argunite's latest adventure were in the back of his mind, but it seemed with each passing moment, he could leave them further behind. He was only on this ship and eligible for being one of the Pirate-King's officers because Argunite killed the shield drake that escaped Koban's menagerie and killed many of his staff and threatened his son, but all that was behind him as they sailed south-ward. Argunite now had a chance to make a new future for himself. Being one of Pirate-King Koban's officers, or 'Blades', meant one day he might get a ship like the Brazen Mallard.

A chorus of familiar squeaks over the prow drew Argunite's attention.

He leaned over the rail to see a trio of yellow-sided dolphins. They were common where he grew up on the Kentarim islands, but rare in the colder southern seas. The sight of them playing in the bow waves and singing a familiar tune put a smile on his face.

As he leaned over, Fazid's note pressed against Argunite's chest from its safe place in his pocket.

He withdrew it and read the hastily-written letter for what must have been the hundredth time.

Argunite,

By the time you read this, I will be gone. In protecting the boy, I have earned Koban's attention. I have been given my first assignment. As it is a sensitive mission, I cannot outline the details here, but it is where I need to be. I hope you find happiness. Should we ever share port again, it would be my genuine pleasure to share your company.

Fazid.

They had separated before even taking their mission to collect Ukjali, the young drake that promptly escaped the Pirate-King's menagerie and caused so much trouble. Argunite had been in denial about the relationship ending, but Fazid had made his priorities clear throughout the voyage.

"*Should we ever share port again, it would be my genuine pleasure to share your company.*"

Argunite sighed. Did this just mean as friends, or did Fazid actually want to remain together? Maybe Argunite was overthinking what was meant to be a simple nicety. The Seridic people were known for placing high value on appearances and politeness. Perhaps that's all this was.

Fazid had all but saved Argunite from a life of poverty as a port city urchin, caring for him when everyone else had discarded him. He was a man of honor. Gentle. Kind. Argunite had known little kindness since his island home was destroyed, and Fazid was the first person to treat him as a man.

Fazid had joined the pirate's forces with ambitions to be a Blade all so he could get in favor with the pirate-king. To convince Pirate-King Koban to help liberate the Serid from the oppression of the Empire. It was a lofty goal. A noble ambition. Some part of Argunite felt guilty that he wasn't serving Koban for any goal more virtuous than his own self-interest. Well, he knew he should feel guilty. Fazid had made it clear that liberating his people was his singular goal, and to avoid distraction, he didn't want Argunite around for it.

Maybe Argunite should be enlisting Koban's aid in liberating his own people from the Republic, just as Fazid sought to free his from the Empire. Perhaps that should be his ambition over personal freedom.

Fazid had never known freedom. Had not seen the conquest of his people. He only heard about it in stories. Liberation was a fantasy. A thrilling idea that could never come to fruition given the might of the Cha'Khati Empire.

With a sigh, Argunite folded up the letter and returned it to his breast pocket.

Argunite witnessed the conquest of the Kentarim Islands. Seen the brutality. Smelled the stench of total defeat. It was real, visceral, and he knew there was no liberation that Koban could offer. Even with all his wealth, what could a pirate with a fleet of two hundred ships hope to do against the might of a nation, Republic or Empire? A single Republic division could wipe him out in an afternoon if they directly engaged. Koban had only lasted this long because he hadn't gotten involved. Even if he could intervene on behalf of Serid or Kentarim, he wouldn't. Why play his hand when patience had brought him such wealth and power?

No, liberation of a people by the Pirate-King was futile. A childish fantasy.

Now, personal liberation?

Argunite kissed his necklace and looked ahead.

Yes, the future looked bright indeed.

"What goes on in that stormy head of yours, Wave-Dancer?"

Argunite turned. Commodore Yurai's approach had been masked by his deep thoughts. Any focus he spared was on the sway of the sea and changes in the wind. Now that she had his attention, his excitement peaked while taking in her form leaning against the rail. The rich blue dye in her hair was striking even in the low light of the early evening sky. Thoughts of their shared pleasures by candlelight the night before were fresh in his mind. She crossed her arms over her eclectic silk jerkin and followed his original gaze out to sea.

"Thoughts of the future," Argunite replied, circling back to her question.

"Frightening thoughts," she said, a smile curling her cheek. "I prefer to keep my mind firmly in the moment."

"Normally that's my preference, but my fortunes just changed dramatically. What are we doing here exactly?"

"I am meeting with a contact on Teshoko. Possibly expanding Koban's operations in Pakardia. You are joining Eran outside Song of Greeting to pick up the latest shipment of furs from our contacts there. Eran has the payment. For now, you go with him. Straightforward pickup."

"Sounds good," said Argunite.

It was a bit less than good. The Gauridic officer had made no effort to hide his disdain of Argunite. He wasn't sure if the dislike was because Argunite wasn't Telmede, because he had gone from lowly pirate to Blade apprentice overnight, for his favor with Yurai, or some other objection. Whatever the big man's reasons, he was certainly not fond of Argunite.

Yurai freed her hair. With a playful grin she bit the clip. She shook her head as her fingers rolled through, letting the azure curls play in the wind. Melrahim's breeze encircled Yurai, making her curves all the more appealing. "Well, come to my cabin when you're done thinking. I have far more pressing matters than this mission that I want your attention on."

Argunite grinned. "Aye, Commodore."

***

Under cover of darkness, Argunite guided their sailed longboat to the rocky beach.

In the Empire and back on his home in the Kenta Islands, the beaches were made of sand. Here on Pakardia, most of the shores were walls of rock, with any beaches a collection of eroded stone and shells. He had long heard these rocky shores were part of why Pakardia had repelled so many invasions.

It also struck him as odd that Pakardia was called an island in the common tongue. The word 'island' lumped together a pile of sand the size of a ship with the imposing lands of rock and jungle before them. In Kentarim there were over a hundred words for every island size, shape, and origin. His people would much more likely translate Pakardia as a continent. It encompassed more terri-tory than the entire Republic, after all, which was a peninsula and therefore called the mainland. Yet another example of mainlanders getting to pick names for things they don't understand.

"Where are we parking, honey-skin?" Eran practically hissed in Argunite's ear. Melrahim blew the pirate's foul onion breath toward Argunite.

I don't like him either, Argunite thought to the wind.

"Looks like there's as close to a dock as we can expect up there. I feel a lot of coral though, so have to be careful."

"You can feel coral under the surface?" Eran said, leading the nearest pirates in a chorus of mirroring scoffs and chuckles. "Is that why you have raw feet on our deck?"

"It helps, yes," Argunite said, ignoring their whispered nothings as he guided the longboat to shore.

Eran had said they should row in, since their longboat was out-fitted for ten rowers and was why they fully staffed the craft in the first place, but Argunite insisted it would be easier to sail in. He was even more confident of that decision when he felt the sheer number of corals and rocks. A rowing team would be clumsy and no doubt strike underfoot. How they had used this site for the previous three pickups was beyond him.

Several gulls watched them from high rocks. As Argunite looked up, he spotted the silhouettes of several birds up in the conifers lining the coast high above. The more he looked, the more forms he thought he could see watching them from the gloom. Some must be his imagination, but it was unnerving to feel so watched. It was as if the forest itself was aware of their approach and in deep disapproval.

Once they were parked, one of Eran's men hopped onto shore and tethered them to a post.

At Eran's indication, Argunite was next on shore.

The strip of beach crunched underfoot. He sensed a dozen tiny creatures scurrying deeper. Sand was both more pleasant to walk on and reliable to live in. The shifting of these larger pebbles meant it must be impossible to make a stable burrow. How could a creature live in such constant fear of being crushed?

Argunite realized he was standing stiff as he assessed the condition of the tiny critters in the stones and only drew further attention from Eran's men.

Oh well. Let them think him strange. He had more important things to consider.

Eight large crates were set in the cave he only just then spotted. He could see the merits of this as a pickup point: a lot could fit with minimal exposure to the elements and chances of being spotted from both sea and shore.

Eran grasped the forearm in greeting with the Pakardiant man who came to meet them. Argunite had seen a few Pakardiant, some were pirates in Koban's employ, and indeed Yurai said her father was from this island. Their reddish skin and dark curls stood out amongst Kaimerans, but it was their impressive fitness said to be inherent to the people which was most striking. He had thought it a rumor, but the words held true. This man was in astonishing shape: broad and toned, his bare arms catching any light to feature his anatomy.

"Evening, Duriq," said Eran.

"I trust the sea treated you well."

"Well as she ever does," said Eran, passing off a small chest. "All yours."

The Pakardiant took it with a grin. Argunite raised a brow at the exquisite condition of his teeth. He had heard that they painted tree gum or some other resin to preserve their teeth, and that rumor seemed to hold up as well.

Although Argunite considered staying outside with Eran and the Pakardiant, he decided better to endear himself to the crew, and followed them inside to start gathering the crates.

Just as he knelt before one of the crates, cold steel was set against the base of his neck.

All around, sounds of surprised pirates and the crunch of boots on pebbles echoed throughout the cave.

Eran made a grunt of anger and surprise. "What is the meaning of this, Duriq?"

Argunite couldn't really hear the Pakardiant's reply, but it sounded mockingly apologetic. The cold blade against his neck pressed against his skin. Argunite slowly looked up.

A girl stood proud on the crate he was preparing to lift. How she managed to climb onto it without him hearing, he had no idea. Her spear was held firm in one hand, although she seemed more focused on the cave as a whole.

She called out something in Pakardiant. It sounded authoritative enough for one her age, although it was steeped in posturing. The other Pakardiant around the cave advanced, and the pirates were being guided outside.

Argunite had no intention of being taken prisoner.

At her slight push of the spear, he began to stand.

When he felt grounded, Argunite raised his arm and swatted aside the spear. Before she could draw it back for a thrust, Argunite shoved the crate with his foot. It slid back, tumbling over. The girl slipped off with what he could only assume was a curse in her native tongue.

Fighting erupted around them. Argunite check tackled one of the Pakardiant about to club one of his fellow pirates. The pirate scrambled off, and the Pakardiant regained his footing quicker than Argunite anticipated.

Argunite evaded the Pakardiant's strike with a rubber-headed axe. Another Pakardiant attacked behind him, which Argunite had to roll to the side to avoid. The tumble over pebbles was painful, and he nearly collided with a crate. He stumbled deeper into the cave as his assailants advanced.

An arrow struck the crate just above Argunite's head. He barely had time to process that it had a rubber ball for a head before needing to dodge the next attack.

A hand grabbed his arm and he turned with the pull, elbowing hard against the Pakardiant's temple.

He hopped up onto a crate. A quick scan confirmed that most of the pirates were out of the cave. Other Pakardiant were outside but the pirates managed to barrel past, probably toward the boat, but it was out of view.

Two other pirates had been restrained.

The Pakardiant were now gathered around Argunite.

If he hopped from crate to crate, he had a pretty confident line to the exit of the cave.

"This has been fun, but I've got a boat to catch."

Argunite leaped, kicking aside the hand that grabbed at his ankle. He landed poorly, crouching to avoid twisting his foot. Two more crates got him near the exit of the cave, and he leaped forwa-

The whistle of an arrow was his only warning.

An impact echoed through his head.

Argunite was unconscious before he hit the ground.

***

Awareness came back to Argunite in a jolt of agony.

His head throbbed. Restraints bound his wrists and ankles. He couldn't see, and for a moment he panicked. Finally clarity began to leak into his vision and the world fell into place.

They were still in the cave. Most of the crates were gone. Argunite was restrained with two other pirates. For the life of him he couldn't remember their names, but that wasn't unusual. At his left was the Pakardiant man who had met with Eran. Duriq, if Argunite's memory served.

He was usually bad with names, and really only remembered for sure if it was someone he wanted to sleep with, so the fact that he remembered the Pakardiant's name was reassuring that he hadn't suffered too bad a head injury.

"So I take it you aren't with them?" Argunite asked Duriq.

The Pakardiant glanced over Argunite. "Ah, good. You're awake. Was worried the arrow took you out for good. They say the rubber heads are nonlethal but there's nothing gentle about anything shot from a Karatoan bow."

"Karatoan?"

"Our noble warriors and hunters. Enforcers more like. Yeah, I'm not with them, but they jumped me and my boys, and made me play nice to get you lot too. Nice distraction you caused. Least you get to face the Three Days knowing your friends got away."

"Not exactly my friends," Argunite sighed. Two Pakardiant carried a crate past them, nearly hitting one of the restrained pirates. "Wait, Three Days?"

"Our justice system, if you can call it that. If someone doesn't confess to a crime that they are accused of, they must endure the judgement of the forest. Leave you restrained in the forest for three days. If you live, you're deemed innocent. If you're swallowed up by some beast, you are considered guilty. It's... a system."

A low, mournful wail echoed from deeper in the forest. It distinctly reminded him of the firebird he encountered in Koban's menagerie, but he decided to pretend it was an elk. He was fairly confident there were several types of deer in Pakardia. Surely some made those sounds too.

The call rang out again. It was farther off, but he was now confident it was a firebird.

"What if I confess?"

"To smuggling?" Duriq chuckled. "Not a good plan, kid. My people are extremely reserved about trade with outsiders. The beasts of the forest are more forgiving."

"What beasts are we talking?"

"Well fortunately there's not a lot of wetlands so you don't need to worry about hippos, and also not enough food to sustain the titans. There are panthers, wolves, firebirds, and giant monkeys that will all happily rip you apart while you're still alive. The monkeys are the worst. Seem to enjoy it, and know where the posts are usually set."

Argunite gulped. "I appreciate the reassurance."

A feminine voice called out. Argunite turned and spotted the young woman who had been holding the spear to his neck earlier.

Argunite spotted one of the Pakardiant, a Karatoan, with a recurve bow sheathed in fur. She wore rabbit fur over her shoulders and stood guard at the entrance of the cave. As she saw Argunite looking at her, she frowned and set a hand on her quiver.

Another Pakardiant tied a cord through their wrist bonds and untied their feet so they could walk. They were pulled roughly to their feet.

Argunite wasn't sure this archer was a woman the more he looked at them. The dress and hair style was consistent with the other female warriors, but Argunite couldn't tell if that was actually a reflection of male and female Pakardiant. Man or woman, the archer was easy to look at, and their intensity was much more attractive than intimidating.

Argunite should have been intimidated, as this archer almost certainly was the one who denied him his freedom, but he had never been drawn to wise partnerships.

"What are you looking at?" the archer said in rough Common after advancing a few steps.

"Something I like," Argunite replied.

The archer paused, taking a second look at Argunite. "You're not my type."

"Really? Thought I was everyone's type. First time for everything I suppose. I daresay you're mine."

A smile started to play across the archer's face, but they quickly resumed a stoic expression.

"Start walking, pirate."

Argunite and the others were marched out of the cave and up the winding steps of the cliff toward the land above. It wasn't a tall cliff, maybe five span, and the winds blew hard against them to keep them closer to the cliff. Argunite felt it as a protective breeze keeping them steady, but the other pirates and Duriq seemed to emit discomfort.

Up above, the crates were being loaded onto a pair of wagons, each drawn by a massive black beast. He had never seen water buffalo in person, but Argunite had seen these beasts in pictures. The young woman who had held him at spear point in the cave was speaking to one of the buffalo, petting its neck.

Although he entertained the idea of wriggling free of the restraints, they were tied too well, and Argunite climbed onto one of the wagons. Four other Pakardiant were on the wagon too, presumably Duriq's 'boys'. They all looked deeply ashamed and resigned.

The Karatoan archer checked all of their restraints, lingering on Argunite and looking almost disappointed that there was no sign of loosening. The archer smelled more like their furs than Argunite usually liked, but it complimented their fragrance, which had hints of clove and some sort of tree oil he had never encountered before.

Once everything was loaded, the back hatch of the wagon was secured.

The karatoan and young leader of the party were brought horses and mounted up. They rode at the back, quite close to Argunite.

The karatoan and leader were obviously close, but Argunite didn't sense any sensuality in the tender touches and reassurances from the archer or the smiles and whispers from the lead Pakardiant. Were they siblings? They looked similar enough, although perhaps that was simply Argunite not knowing many Pakardiant.

"What are your names?" Argunite asked in Common.

"You do not need our names," the Karatoan said just as the leader said "Emahari."

"Is Emahari your name or are you telling me to shut my pretty mouth? Apologies for not knowing your language. I'm not from around here."

The leader pursed her lips. She looked on the verge of smiling but looked around before composing herself. "Emahari is my name."

"You're a bold one," the karatoan remarked.

"In my experience, life has never rewarded discretion."

The two exchanged a quick glance. They sat taller on their horses.

"So you're Emahari. What is your name?"

He did not get a response.

"My name is Argunite."

"We don't care," said one of the Pakardiant marching beside the wagon, a warrior in his prime. The tone was harsh. In the man's defense, he had to deal with smugglers late at night. He probably would rather be in bed. Argunite couldn't hold a rough tone against him.

Looking back at Emahari and the karatoan, they seemed more reserved and stiff when the other Pakardiant were paying attention to them. This was not an operation lead by an experienced, respected commander. Emahari looked a few years from womanhood. Did Pakardiant have nobility? He had no idea.

Most of the Pakardiant had bows. They were in a forest, but he could feel the coast was near. Salt was strong in the air. Getting out of the restraints would be a chore, but probably doable. It would be a tall order to evade the archers, and the water here was a lot colder than he preferred, but if it meant he wouldn't be captive, Argunite resolved to try it.

A rumbling croak like the call of an alar drake shook Argunite from his thoughts.

The man astride the giant black-feathered bird was of a physique Argunite thought relegated to embellished illustration. His hair was a rich amber and flowed free as the mane of a lion. Despite the slight chill in the air, this man was shirtless, and there was no reason for him to flex as much as he did while holding the reins.

The carts came to a stop. The huge man pulled the bird to a halt and spoke urgently with Emahari. There was worry in his voice. Argunite noticed another rider was with him: a woman who's face seemed frozen in a scowl.

"What are they saying?" Argunite asked Duriq.

"Evidently a fisherman named Oniq from Song of Greeting and his grandnephew have been missing since last night and they're organizing a search and rescue party."

Argunite switched to a whisper. "Out on the ocean?"

"Indeed. Probably amongst the reefs."

"That's excellent!"

Duriq raised an eyebrow. "I can see you're in deep grief about this terrible situation."

"Yes, yes, it's tragic," Argunite waved off Duriq with his restrained wrists. "Hey, Emahari!"

The mounted god of a man scowled down at Argunite, again flexing far more than was necessary. Argunite felt a little faint taking him in but rallied to focus. "Apologies. What's your name?"

"Rolanix," the man replied, looking down with a mix of confusion and amusement. "Prince Rolanix in the common tongue. And you are?"

"Argunite. Yes, greetings Prince Rolanix. Thank you. You're just… lovely to look at, but I'm talking to the leader here."

The massive Rolanix balked. He looked between Argunite and Emahari, who was flush red and her attention was fixated on her hands. With eyes thinned, he urged his bird closer to better inspect Argunite.

He then looked back at Emahari, a smile growing on his face. Although Argunite braced for him to humiliate her in some way, the Rolanix's tone was surprisingly gentle.

"He's your prisoner, Emahari," he said in Common. "See what he wants."

Emahari frowned. She took a deep breath. "What do you want, Argunite?"

"Well, I, excuse me," Argunite shoved back against the pirate that leaned on him. "Apologies. Princess Emahari I presume? Yes, good. I couldn't help but overhear that you have missing people out on the reefs?"

"You speak our language?" Princess Emahari asked.

"No, but he does," Argunite nodded toward Duriq.

"So you couldn't help overhear words in a language you don't speak?" said Prince Rolanix. Again Argunite expected the tone and expression to be belittling, especially from a man so massive that he must certainly be used to getting his way, but more than anything he just seemed to be enjoying the banter.

The karatoan laughed at his comment before immediately falling silent. Argunite noticed the karatoan was as flushed as Emahari, but their nervousness seemed focused on Prince Rolanix.

If this man was the competition, no wonder the karatoan said Argunite wasn't their type.

Fair.

"You caught me. I asked, he told," said Argunite before turning back to Emahari. "It's worth mentioning that I happen to be an excellent sailor. If I find your missing fishermen, may I humbly request a trial that doesn't result in our executions or being left in the forest to have our guts ripped out by giant monkeys?"

Duriq muttered something next to him, but Argunite ignored him.

Emahari wore a confused expression for a moment, but quickly straightened herself. "How can I trust you to not attempt escape?"

"Right now I'm facing smuggling charges, which if I may humbly point out seem punished far beyond reason, but I'll save that conversation for another time. I imagine the consequences when you catch me stealing a rescue vessel would be far more severe, and I doubt I will get far. These are your waters, and you're using boats built for maneuverability, not seafaring."

"We have people proficient in sailing. Song of Greeting is a coastal town, after all."

"Not to disparage your sailors, but I am far more than proficient."

"He's very good," said one of the pirates.

"I am, thank you!"

The man was among those who laughed at Argunite when they docked and was never far from Eran on Yurai's ship, but it seemed he had the good sense to support Argunite reducing the sentence for all of them.

"How good is he?" asked Prince Rolanix. "Give us an example."

"He can feel reefs with his feet. That's why they're all naked and gnarly."

Argunite sighed and raised his feet, giving his toes a wiggle that elicited a disgusted expression from Emahari and the other Pakardiant. "He is correct: Melrahim is much more cooperative with me than other sailors. Mostly because I bother to listen. Listening means to be fully aware in this case. My bare feet on deck allow me to perceive all of her guidance and warnings."

Rolanix was openly grinning. He turned in his saddle to Emahari. "What say you, little sister?"

Although their hair was wildly different colors, Argunite suddenly realized the similarities in their faces. The karatoan still looked a bit like Emahari, but she and Rolanix had the same noses, dimples, eyes, and from what little she had shown, they had the same vibrant smile.

"You will take me and Utani in our fastest boat. You can ride with her. If your… feet really can guide us, you have my word that the sentences for smuggling will be greatly reduced. If you try to escape, the lives of these men may not be so secure."

Her words and posture were impressive, but her tone was still thick with posturing.

Not ideal, and Argunite didn't want these men's blood on his hands. Finding two people out on reefs should be easy enough.

"Sounds like an excellent deal." Argunite raised his wrists. "I don't suppose I can get out of these?"

***

Argunite was taken onto the karatoan's horse. He was seated in front. His restraints were kept on, although he had no illusions about trying to escape now. Earning their favor was a far more comfortable avenue out of the situation.

"Is your name Utani or Agakuaba?" Argunite asked as the karatoan adjusted in the saddle to get them both comfortable. "I've not been properly introduced, and both terms have been applied to you. Well, and Karatoan, but I've already been told that means you're a hunter and warrior."

"My name is Utani," she replied. "I am Agakuaba to Emahari. That means I'm her lifeguard. Her protector."

"Why does she need a protector?"

"She is a noble. A firebird clan princess, or *Dhandrakulu tehua* in our language. As children, nobles used to be assigned a karatoan of their father's clan to protect them. Now it's usually just a friend around the same age. She and I have been close friends since she was a little girl, and of course I said yes when she asked."

"So you are of her father's clan?"

"Yes," Utani indicated the serpent tattooed on her port arm. "Viper Clan."

"Why the father's family? Don't your people inherit through the mother?"

Utani made a grunt that Argunite interpreted as being begrudgingly impressed. "Yes. We are of our mother's clan, but the father's clan nominates a karatoan. All the warriors of the mother's clan fight for their nobles. One warrior from the father is a sign of commitment and connection. It's part of how the tribes remain united throughout the confederacy."

"That is clever."

"Gratitude. Now, stop talking. Looks like we're ready to go."

Utani kicked her horse, which charged forward. Emahari kept pace beside them. Argunite glanced back and saw Rolanix and the other rider on their great black birds. The birds kept pace with the horses at a leisurely jog.

"Are those birds dangerous?" Argunite asked over the sounds of huffing steeds and thundering hooves.

"U'ruekil are not dangerous as long as you are respectful."

"Is Rolanix and his scowling lady friend coming with us on the boat?"

"Johani is Rolanix's agakuaba. That won't be a problem for you, will it?"

Argunite shook his head. "Works for me. Wait, Johani is his lifeguard? Man looks like he could wrestle one of those buffalo back there and win."

"You may speak in exaggeration for humor, but when he became a karatoan, Prince Rolanix killed a hippopotamus with a knife and some javelins. Johani is more of an adviser, although I've seen her fight. She likes to be underestimated. I'm more frightened of her than him."

"I don't get the impression that you're afraid of him, but there are certainly other emotions I'm picking up."

Utani sighed but didn't disagree.

The ride down the road to Song of Greeting was brief. The gate nearest them on the wooden walls was drawn open before they had even reached it.

The village was active despite the early hour. Streaks of pink preluded the morning light, but Song of Greeting was already awake. Many were down toward the wharf. Several boats were being launched already. For an entire town to be so swift and invested in searching for two villagers was a level of kindness and community Argunite had forgotten about.

Or at least didn't like dwelling on.

Thoughts of his childhood sobered Argunite, and he was silent for the march down to the wharf. He was barely aware of Johani removing his restraints. As she wound up and tucked the cord into her belt, she gave him a stern look before idly resting a hand on her downward-curving knife. Argunite didn't avoid her gaze, but put his hands up after giving them a gentle rub after being freed.

Emahari split off and spoke with a muscular man wearing a red wolf pelt who many seemed deferential to. They spoke using hand signs. Argunite's distant cousin had lost his hearing as a boy. Argunite was never fluent, but knew enough signs to know Pakardiant sign language was entirely different. The wolf man and Emahari pressed foreheads, then she jogged back to the group. As she did, the man glared at Argunite with open suspicion, his eyes focused with the same predatory intensity as the beast whose pelt he wore.

"My father says they were looking for redfish in the western reefs," said Emahari, pulling Argunite's focus away from the wolf man. "Out by Braid Atolls. Should have been back by the afternoon. Others are going out now. There's a lot of reefs in the area, so let's see what you've got, Argunite."

Of the sixty or so boats still docked, most were double canoes connected by a platform and netting. He had never sailed one, but from what he understood they were quite similar to outriggers: extremely fast, proficient in both shallow waters and open ocean, but not terribly maneuverable. The four parked ships were upscaled double canoes, with the largest having two main masts and a pair of ferocious serpents rearing at the prows. They were beautiful, but far too large for their mission. There were a few outriggers, all of Eskadin design so Argunite presumed had been acquired by trade. Two Imperial-style keeled boats were at the far end of the pier.

"If we're going into reefs, we'll want a keel, not an outrigger or double boat. I'm not concerned about speed but I think there's going to be a lot of maneuvering."

Emahari nodded. She spoke to one of the nearby Pakardiant in their language, and the older man indicated the Imperial sailboat still docked on the pier. It was about five span in length and one wide. Small and maneuverable, but plenty of space for the five of them and the two they were rescuing.

Argunite stepped onto the still-tethered boat and shifted it side to side. The keel was metal, probably steel, which was perfect for their needs. It would tip more than an outrigger, especially on turns, but quickly right itself. Keeled boats in the Kentarim islands were rare and almost always wood. More stable in his opinion, but he had never sailed a steel keeled boat and so was curious to see. He would get a better sense of its length once they were sailing, but it was nothing he couldn't work with.

Once they were settled in the craft, Utani cast them off before hopping onto the outer rail. Although Utani seemed quite sure of her footing, Rolanix offered a tree-branch arm as a railing for her to hold before stepping into the hull. He also placed a reassuring hand on the small of her back, something he hadn't done for his sister or Johani.

Argunite leaned against the rudder. "Who knows roughly where they were headed? Braid Atolls?"

"I do!" said Utani, flushed and evidently quick to leave her current thoughts. "I grew up in Sunflower Grove. Not far from here, and I apprenticed with a local fisherman."

"Sit beside me then. We'll start there. Rolanix, you take the ropes of the headsail. Johani, you're on the mainsail. Emahari, how do you feel about watch?"

Emahari shrugged. "Utani has the best eyes of us. She should be on watch, but I can do it for now."

"Fantastic. You and Utani can switch once we get to Braid Atolls."

Johani continued to watch Argunite with open suspicion, but the noble siblings both went to their posts. Rolanix pulled on the ropes a few times of the still-wrapped headsail, clearly at a loss for what to do.

"Ever sailed, Rolanix?" Argunite said.

"Can't say I have. Only been a passenger," he said, although there was no embarrassment in his tone. Argunite could not recall having met anyone with such relaxed confidence as this walrus of a man. Utani looked on him with a bit of a sad smile. There was so much barely-contained melancholy that Argunite felt a swell of empathy.

"Alright, my prince. As we turn, especially if we're going against the wind, it will be your job to rotate the sails slowly from one side to the other so we keep whatever wind we can get. We will sail like a snake since it will mostly be against the wind. Johani, have you sailed before?"

Johani nodded.

"Alright. Excellent. You'll rotate with Rolanix. When I say ready rotate, you both say ready, and we'll turn. Once we cast off we'll do a few practice runs then be on our way."

Rolanix nodded and readied for his position.

Once they had coasted off the pier, Argunite hopped up onto the side rail and released both sails. With a bit of guidance Rolanix set the headsail to properly catch the wind. Johani indeed seemed confident in her task. Emahari was intensely focused up above, although they were still in harbor.

"Let's practice rotation," said Argunite. "Rolanix: pull on starboard, loosen port."

"What do those words mean?"

"Starboard is arrow, port is bow," said Johani before Argunite could think of a clarification.

"Got it."

Rolanix quickly picked up on the terminology, and after only two rotations had a good sense of not pulling too hard on the load or letting the lazy get too loose. By the time they left the small harbor, he applied it to the open air.

"I don't like sailing as a passenger," Rolanix said, his resonant baritone carrying over the wind and waves. "Having a hand in the control is much more comfortable."

"You're a natural, Prince," said Argunite. Utani pointed to starboard. "Let's rotate since the Braid Atolls are arrow side. Load bow, lazy arrow. Ready?"

"Ready to rotate!" said Rolanix.

As Rolanix and Johani switched the sides of the sails, the boat picked up in speed. Ropes tensed and wood creaked.

Argunite kissed his scallop necklace. He closed his eyes, getting to know the craft by feel.

She was an older boat, but well and lovingly cared for. Wood was sanded, ropes clean, and wax fresh. He hadn't sailed many keeled boats, and none steel, but quite liked how it moved and danced with the currents. It was far more sensitive to waves than he was used to, tipping about more dramatically, but having so much weight centered and low meant it always righted itself. It felt more authentic in a way. That the craft didn't fight the waves, rolling with them, but always finding its footing. He smiled at the sensation.

Feeling the boat reaching deeper waters and a stronger eastward current underfoot, Argunite called for a shift in sails so they would still remain close to the coast.

"So…" said Argunite, glancing over to Utani. There was enough ambient sound that he was confident Johani and Rolanix couldn't hear even though Johani was barely a span away. "I can see the appeal. What's holding you back?"

"Mind your business, pirate, and I'll mind mine."

"Fair enough. I only press because life offers only so much in my experience. Take the joys where they are. You have eyes for him, and he is tender with you in a way I don't see with anyone else. Not that he's brutish, in fact surprisingly gentle for a man with his… everything, but it's worth noting that he seems to care deeply for you."

Utani crossed her arms. "I can tell that he cares for me."

"So go for it! If you both want each other, why not take the chance?"

"There are many things you don't understand, pirate."

"You keep calling me pirate to push me away, but I think you're only doing that because you know I'm right."

"I should keep watch," said Utani. "Emahari is easily distracted. She knows these waters too and can guide you the rest of the way."

Before Argunite could say anything, Utani stood and walked to the mast. Rolanix offered another hand to help her, but she ignored it, climbing the rungs up the mast on her own.

They had already passed most of the boats that had left before them. Argunite spotted only one more up ahead. Normally he might find some glee in outpacing them, but guilt about driving Utani off sat poorly in his chest. Also these were fishermen out looking for their lost companion, not here to race.

Even so, it was important to his survival that he find this missing fisherman and his grandnephew, so he still called on Rolanix to loosen the headsail ever so slightly to catch a shift in the wind, and they picked up yet more speed despite generally going upwind. Angled as they were did help pick up the water currents, which generally followed their current course.

Emahari climbed down a moment later and meandered to sit next to Argunite. She seemed a lot younger now, hands between her knees and legs swaying because her feet couldn't plant on the hull boards. Her head bobbed slightly, and she hummed a soft tune under her breath as her toes tapped the floor. Now that she didn't have the eyes of her people upon her as a leader, she seemed younger by the moment. With her makeup, fitness, and hair tied up, he had thought she might be on the verge of womanhood. Now he guessed she was around seventy years old, and a good decade before she was an adult in the eyes of any culture he had encountered.

The boat was getting close to shore, so Argunite called for a rotation of the sails.

A spout of mist shot up in the distance, out in the deeper waters beyond the reefs. He recognized the double-plume shape and height as that of a young bilyuk whale. An arcing brown face followed, studded with sharp barnacles, sending a jet three span into the air. Argunite grinned. Although he knew not to get close, as bilyuk were one of Melrahim's fiercest warriors, their presence was still grounding and joyful to see. The sharp spout of the young whale blasted again before they both went tail-up and dived to sift through the sediment below to find the sorts of critters Argunite remembered feeling back on shore.

"Did you say something to Utani?" asked Emahari quietly. "She seemed really upset."

Argunite sighed. "Yes. I may have pressed too hard."

"About what?"

"Her romantic interests."

"For my brother?"

Argunite smiled. "If you didn't know, I didn't want to reveal it."

"I don't notice much, but I've seen the way they interact. They both really like each other. I'm glad he comes to visit my father's home so much. He's supportive and caring of me, but I know he also likes traveling with us. And her specifically."

"So why don't they act on it? Is your brother betrothed or something?"

"Not yet, although he will probably have a lot of wives over the years. Our duty is to have children with many different clans so that each clan has members of all the others. Helps keep the tribes united. He will be expected to have lots of children, and not only is Utani not a noble, she's not able to have children since she was born a boy, so will never be approved of as his wife by the elders."

"Your father, are he and your mother married?"

"Yes. Rolanix has a different father, if you couldn't tell by his hair. She married my father shortly after her first husband was killed in the latest Klaeg invasion. Rolanix's twin Katinari is the heir to the title of Queen, I think is the term in Common."

"Have they talked about that? Rolanix and Utani?"

"Not directly, but they both know it's the case."

Argunite blew out a slow exhale. "Well now I feel like a gull picking at a wound."

"You were trying to encourage budding love. I think it's sweet."

They passed the last boat on their port bow.

"It was my aim, yes. Too much sadness, disappointment, and malice in this world. I hate to see people not choose to be happy, but I appreciate that it's more complicated than that. I don't know. Life can get in the way of your happiness. Break up a good thing. Take the good when you can, I say."

"You lost someone."

Argunite clenched his jaw. He looked down at Emahari. Her wide eyes were locked on his.

"I thought you said you didn't notice much?"

Emahari shrugged. "I'm still figuring out what I notice. Isn't always consistent. My mother says I only notice exciting things. Pretty things. If I'm ever to be a good leader, I need to see the simple and mundane."

"Well, I suffer from missing the details too, if I'm being honest. I have sharp eyes for pretty things too, and so far it's worked out alright for me, but I don't have any responsibilities or expectations."

"I like you," said Emahari. "You're easy to talk to, and you say what you mean."

It was Argunite's turn to shrug. "I don't think I could be any other way. It's hard being someone you're not, and I tired of that life a long time ago."

Argunite called for them to turn to shore. Rolanix looked back for confirmation that it was done right, and beamed. Argunite grinned. He loved little more than seeing a newfound love for the sea.

"So who did you lose?"

Argunite thought back to the conversation at hand, and his expression fell. For a moment he sailed in silence, thinking about Fazid. He swallowed, steadying the wheel as his emotions made him blind to a series of passing waves and shifting winds from the west. "Someone dear to me. His life took a direction I couldn't follow, and he didn't want me there anymore, so the relationship ended. The love is still there, from me and I think from him, and I believe a part of it always will." Argunite felt warmth behind his eyes and a tightness in his chest. "I miss him. I really miss him. I'll cherish what we had, but don't spare me the pain if it means I'll have to pass on love."

"I'm sorry that happened," Emahari said quietly. The winds shifted again, and Argunite used any back draft he could to stay on course.

"I was, well… my point is that I don't want them to miss out on love because it might hurt. That said, I just stumbled out of love a short while ago. Our relationship ended before our last mission but we were still on the boat together, and it's only been six days since I last saw him. I'm not exactly in a position to be offering sound advice on love. You know, you're also easy to talk to. Haven't discussed this with anyone else."

"I like talking to people. I feel comfortable doing it. I wish I felt more comfortable with things that were important to being a princess."

"That seems like a pretty useful talent for diplomacy to me."

Emahari leaned back. "I suppose. My mother doesn't think so. She says I talk too much and don't pay attention to the things that actually matter."

"Like what things?"

Emahari grinned. "Well part of my problem is I don't know what things. I suppose knowing how to behave? Looking like I'm paying attention? I feel every time I do something I want to do, what seems right at the time, or excites me, it's what I'm not supposed to do. No matter what choice I make, there is some reason that my mother or one of the elders points out as to why it was the wrong decision. This rescue mission I think is something I'm supposed to do. I should be leading the mission to find one of my people, yes?

It seems correct, but there's some part of me that feels because this looks to me like the thing I should be doing naturally means I'm missing something important and it will of course be somehow wrong for reasons I can't think of now but after they explain how it was wrong I will feel foolish. The village elders said they heard reports of Duriq's smuggling plans and told me to lead the counter attack. They said I should just catch Duriq. I decided we should also capture the pirates that were smuggling with him. That would be you I suppose."

Argunite called for another rotation of the sails, and they turned back out to sea. Wood and ropes creaked as wind filled the sails anew. A small flock of gulls was disrupted by a wide-winged elk tern on his way out to open water.

"If it's any consolation, I think your instincts were right about that. If you hadn't set that trap, you wouldn't have captured the best sailor in the known world, and you then might not find this missing fisherman and his grandnephew. When you do, you get to tell those smug elders that it worked because of your leadership and choosing to trust a stranger."

Emahari giggled. "Let's not get ahead of ourselves. We're not even at the atolls yet."

"It sounds like other people are making you doubt yourself and what you can do. Don't help them by denying your own accomplishments."

"You're probably right, I–"

"Braided Atolls up ahead!" Utani called down from the nest.

Argunite closed his eyes.

Wind curled slightly, and he guessed the rough direction of the islands. Disturbances in the water flow underfoot attested to the nearby reefs. There was enough light that when he opened his eyes, Argunite could see the islands ahead.

It was a long string of atolls. He could see through the scattering of trees on the few larger ones, and it appeared that the islands were all closely connected.

Argunite felt a great variety of reefs up ahead. His uncle, with whom he sailed the most, often said uneven reefs were the most dangerous. Low reefs didn't show much on the surface but could still damage a keel, while high reefs could shred a hull but usually came with a lot of wave warnings. Uneven reefs had the worst of both, looking to have safe passages but often tricking sailors and serving as a trap, which would then shred you against a tall reef. His uncle had lost an arm after a wave sent him into a familiar reef just before their island was made a protectorate. Argunite was wary as they approached.

"We're going to rotate back out toward shore, then draw in the sails. Reefs here are close, but not regular enough for waves." Once the task was done, helped by Emahari angling out the headsail as Rolanix drew it in, Argunite turned the boat so it would stall. Now with the wind mostly coming from the northeast, but the water currents still coming west, they were steady enough that the boat barely moved.

"See any sign of them?" Rolanix called up.

"None. No boat, no gear, no wreckage. If they got to shore they would have surely started a warning fire by now. Can we move further east? The trees are tallest there and I can't see the north shore from here."

Argunite made the requested adjustments. The main sail was still out, and at Argunite's request, Johani wordlessly shifted it to be completely flat to the wind so the water currents could take them east.

"Hard to tell what it is, but there's something on the north shore. Most fishermen harvest on this side since the waters are calmer here, but the channels beyond do bring cold waters and draw in a lot more fish. Maybe they gambled out there?"

"Draw out the headsail again," Argunite relayed to Emahari. "From what I can tell the wind is mostly eastward on the open waters. Let's go back west and circle around to whatever Utani spotted. I don't want to try and fight more open currents and stronger winds in this boat."

The crew nodded, and set to task. They turned about, now with the wind at their backs. In short order Argunite felt minimal obstructions. The reefs here were low. Since the winds changed direction out in the open water, he had them keep the sails out to port, and arced about. The change in winds was strong, and they rapidly picked up speed.

"Netting! Up ahead!"

Argunite called on Rolanix and Emahari to draw in the headsail. Rolanix effortlessly held both ropes in place so Emahari could draw it in, a task Argunite was used to taking two people or a lot of back and forth. Having someone with his strength would be a blessing to any ship.

Rolanix and Johani drew in the mainsail next, and Argunite turned the boat in a spin to slow it to a stall. The water currents still carried them east, but at least they slowed enough that Argunite was confident Utani could get a good look.

"There are nets there! Of our designs, not Imperial or Eskadin," Utani shouted.

"Do you see anything between us?"

"There's a pretty open path straight ahead. Arcs slightly to the west but gets us within pole range."

Argunite closed his eyes. He spread his toes, trying to get a sense of what was in the area.

All he felt from the waves and wind was the basic sense of the island before something splashed heavy in the water.

Argunite opened his eyes. Just as Rolanix shouted after Emahari, Argunite saw she had jumped in.

"Fuck," Argunite muttered.

It was a roughly fifty span swim from their point on the edge of the reef to where Argunite spotted a mass near shore of what he assumed was Utani's netting, but at this angle he couldn't really tell. Although he initially prepared to jump in after her, Emahari swam with impressive form, and was halfway across the distance by the time he readied himself. At least the space between the boat and netting looked clear of reefs, but there were extensions on either side that could pose a threat if she veered off the arc.

Utani shouted something from the nest that Argunite didn't understand. She shouted it again: "Kaligogu!"

Argunite didn't know the word, but he heard terror behind the shouts. He looked out to Emahari, who was nearly to the net and not slowing her pace despite the screamed warnings of her lifeguard.

Argunite cursed again when Utani leaped off the nest and plummeted three span to the surf below. Like Emahari she swam confidently, and was closing the distance faster.

"What is kaligogu?" Argunite asked.

"A sea serpent!"

"Alright, Rolanix, release the-"

Before Argunite could finish, Rolanix launched himself off the boat and into the sea.

"WE ARE ON A BOAT!" Argunite shouted. "If you could just-"

"Stop complaining," said Johani, clapping her hands to draw Argunite's focus. "Tell me how to get us closer. It might not attack the swimmers if the boat is there."

"Yes, good," Argunite said. "Draw out the main sail."

After turning the wheel so the rudder at least spun and stalled, Argunite helped her draw it out so they could catch a cross-breeze sent as a blessing by Melrahim. With that tethered, Argunite returned to the helm and turned to send them in.

A wave he barely registered sent them much further to port than he anticipated. Argunite compensated with a sharp turn of the rudder. Johani quickly flipped over the mainsail, catching another blessed surge of wind that righted their course.

Argunite glanced up. Emahari had clambered onto a rock and was holding some of the netting. She was pulling a shouting Utani onto the rock with her.

He saw no sign of Rolanix.

"Where is the prince?" Argunite asked.

"Get us closer," Johani snapped.

"Can he swim?"

Johani didn't respond.

Argunite turned the wheel to avoid the reef he felt a swell bounce off of. Johani again shifted the mainsail without instruction.

Emahari and Utani both screamed. They pointed. Argunite followed their frantic gestures to the port side of the boat.

Red filled the water near the eastern reef. Argunite's heart sank.

"Rotate the sail!"

Johani did so, and the boat jolted starboard so they were parallel with the spot of crimson.

A massive form erupted from the surf, and a low thud struck the opposite side of the boat. At first Argunite feared there were two creatures, but it was all a single coiling form.

As the swaying boat shifted back to port, Argunite got a clear view of the creature:

Serpentine coils of bright yellow spotted with black. The entire body was elongated muscle dotted with tiny scales. Argunite immediately recognized it as the Reef King, or katabo in Kentarim, the colossal son of serpents and sea lizards. By its size and vibrant coloration he guessed it was a subadult, but at easily five span, plenty large enough to be dangerous. Its head was long and shaped like a pair of shears. In those cutting jaws was the arm of Rolanix, blood saturating the waves with red.

Far from being a limp form, Rolanix had the creature caught in a grip of his massive legs, all while he cudgeled its snout with his free arm.

And he was laughing.

Argunite turned the boat and, thanks to a prompt rotation of the mainsail by Johani, sent their craft hard against the creature's back. The reef king thrashed about, undulating and curling itself around so it was fully on the port side. Twice it fully lifted Rolanix out of the water and struck him against the surface, but on he cudgeled.

The third rise struck him onto the deck of the boat. Several planks bent and something crunched. As the reef king curled back off the boat, Rolanix punched where its throat met its jaw. The bite released just enough for him to withdraw his arm, although he was still flung back into the waves.

Argunite prepared to turn the boat again, but he spotted a swell of yellow and black bolt away from them.

"He's not coming up!"

"Get the hook!" Argunite pointed to the pole hook on the side of the boat. Johani quickly took it in hand and thrust it into the surf. She obviously strained, and Argunite rushed to assist.

When it was clear they weren't getting him out, Argunite dived in.

Impacting the water quickly sent a clear image of the scene. Rolanix was still in the water. Several reefs were nearby, and any could have hit him in a disabling way. He was a massive man and all muscle. Argunite knew getting him out was a fool's ambition without some help.

Johani's hook was under his arm, but it wasn't at a good angle for leverage. Argunite rolled with the next wave, positioning himself under Rolanix.

Red stained the water around the prince. It was impossible to tell where his injury had been. If it was to the neck or spine, lifting him could be disastrous.

So would leaving him in the waves, especially with so many reefs around.

Some might have seen the reefs as threats closing in all around, but Argunite saw opportunity.

A wave from behind the boat turned it port, just as another tilted it to the starboard side. This sent the keel toward them, which lifted Rolanix. As the keel swung back and the boat tipped, Argunite felt another wave behind him.

He crouched against the nearest reef, and with the wave at his back, pounced forward.

He hooked his arms under Rolanix and twisted. The force combined with the wave sent them straight up onto the deck of the boat.

Argunite's plan was flawless until the trajectory resulted in a man over twice his size landing on top of him.

"Slowly remove your prince, please," Argunite managed as the boat settled.

Johani carefully did as requested. As soon as he was free, Argunite crawled free and looked over Rolanix.

Although most of the blood came from his arm, his chest was scraped something fierce. Argunite guessed it had struck a coral. He explained as much to Johani.

"You have a good sense of steering. Keep us from the worst of the reefs and I will do what I can for him."

Johani looked like she was about to argue, but another wave tipped them more than was comfortable, and she scrambled to the wheel.

Argunite closed his eyes and set a hand on Rolanix's chest.

He wasn't breathing, but he had a pulse. No sign of neck or back injury. His arm bled heavily, a typical symptom of reef king venom. It would need to be bandaged, but its toxins only thinned blood, something that wouldn't matter if he were drowned. The wound on his chest was shallow, and hadn't pierced any organs. Treating it would be painful, but the water in his lungs was the source of his unconsciousness.

After waiting for the next wave, Argunite put his full upper body weight into compressions into Rolanix's chest. He kept a shred of awareness on the waves, keen to maintain most of his force when the boat was at its most stable.

Following the compressions after the fifth wave, Rolanix coughed up a surge of sea water. Argunite helped turn him over. As Rolanix caught his breath, Argunite took off his sash and traded places with Johani, telling her to bandage Rolanix's arm with it to slow the bleeding. "The venom isn't potent enough to kill, but it will make any open wounds bleed out quick."

Argunite felt at least one large creature nearby. He glanced over his shoulder and spotted a pink form in the more open waters. A rose shark, based on the shape and color. Larger here than on the Kenta islands, a trend he was noticing in these colder waters, but he assumed they were of the same temperament: curious but not aggressive. He had never known them to hunt Kaimerans, but there was blood in the water, and she seemed curious.

As Johani attended to Rolanix's injuries, Argunite steered with only the keel to get them a bit closer to the reef Utani and Emahari were on. He then used the starboard pole to give Utani a hand back on deck. Emahari was quick to follow, then used the hook to pull the net on deck.

The shark continued to circle them, never getting too close. Argunite didn't point her out to the others. Some acted rashly around sharks, and as far as he could tell, she was just investigating all the new commotion in her home.

With Emahari and Utani's help, they navigated out of the reefs. The rose shark remained behind. The faster winds of the open water carried them rapidly around the braided atolls. Once they were in calmer waters, Argunite had Emahari and Utani draw up the sails and slow to a stall.

Argunite dropped anchor, which was a ring of bronze tethered to the prow, and slumped against the wheel, taking in his messy crew.

As far as he could tell, none were in terrible condition. The nobles and Johani were keen on catching their breath, but Utani was frantically making sure each rope was secure.

"Sit down, Utani," said Rolanix after Johani helped him sit up.

"Why, so you can jump off the boat and drown again?" she then turned to Emahari. "It is my duty to protect you. Must you make that harder by leaping into the surf?"

Emahari pursed her lips, pulling the blanked she just wrapped on closer. "I thought it would be a quick and easy swim."

"You know all the dangers of the reef! Why would you jump in? Also, we have hooks on board. Getting the net from the safety of the boat would have been so easy!"

"Everything worked out fine," said Rolanix, who was a shade lighter from bleeding out the katabo venom.

"It won't always be fine!" snapped Utani, rounding on him. "You two are too important to be so reckless."

"I refuse to live carefully," said Rolanix with a shrug. "A cautious life is barely living."

"You can have an exciting life without jumping on the back of every monster you encounter."

"I'm sorry I caused you concern." Rolanix pushed himself to his feet. "I'll always be drawn to the excitement, Utani, although in this particular instance I had to engage the beast or it would have attacked you and Emahari."

"Sit down," said Utani. "You're just going to hurt yourself."

Rolanix grinned. "I look forward to the day you choose excitement."

"When I do, will you choose the simple but wiser path?"

"I could find such a compromise agreeable."

Utani stepped forward, put a gentle hand on his cheek, and kissed him carefully on the lips. Emahari looked on in open delight, and Johani went deadpan before a long sigh. The kiss was quick, but it was enough to make Utani blush and Rolanix stand a little taller, a smile drawing attention to the dimple on his left cheek.

"There, I chose excitement," said Utani with a deep breath. "Now take the wise path and sit down."

"As you wish." Rolanix beamed as he took a seat.

"Splendid. Now, we do have fishermen to rescue. Shall we depart, my friends?"

"We don't know you," said Johani.

"After today, he's a friend in my eyes," said Rolanix, waving her off.

"Friend enough to not tie me up in the woods for three days and leave me to be eaten by monkeys?"

All but Johani laughed. The mood dropped when they at once realized Argunite wasn't being humorous.

"Who told you we were going to do that?" asked Rolanix, raising an eyebrow.

"Doriq said that's what you did to people accused who don't confess."

Johani gave a heavy sigh.

Emahari shook her head. "The trial of the forest is reserved for a particular situation: when there are no living witnesses, there is good evidence of guilt, but the accused will not confess. Many don't like it these days. I think the last Three Days trial was before my mother was born. Your original punishment would be your name and description taken down, and banishment from the island after either a fine or a brief period of labor. Consider your record clean after helping us here. I think Doriq was making jest with you."

Argunite let out a slow whistle. "Well, that is a relief. I won't lie to you, that was hanging heavy over me. Alright, is there anything helpful in that net?"

Emahari lit up, clearly having forgotten about it. She lifted the net, turning it about twice. "It wasn't open."

"What does that mean?" asked Rolanix.

"Means it wasn't lost while they were fishing," Argunite said. "Means it fell overboard, yes?"

"Most likely," said Utani. "It's saturated but has no growths. I think it is safe to say this was lost last night. Can't promise it was from our missing boat, but it's a safe bet. We're careful with our equipment, and this is a good net."

"If we're in a condition to carry on, I say we go. Utani, keep a sharp eye for any more debris. I don't think we need to collect any more, but if this boat was tipped, we might be able to see further signs."

Utani nodded, and the team took to their stations.

***

After another ring around the atolls, Utani spotted several other things amongst the reefs. Nothing significant, just a few bobbers, spare rope, and what she guessed was the remains of a bait barrel, although it wasn't at a good angle and they elected to all remain on the boat this time.

It was enough to assume something happened, but there was no sign of a wreck.

Argunite noticed the rose shark following them for a time, but after a while, it seemed she got bored and returned to her reefs.

Utani spotted some other boats on the horizon, finally making their way to the scene. Their crafts were built for speed, but like most sailors, they didn't seem able to accept all of Melrahim's gifts. Most of his people couldn't either.

"Should we wait for them?" Argunite asked.

"Yes. We need to let them know what we've found, and see if they have any advice for the next steps," said Emahari.

With that, Argunite turned them toward the boats. With the wind at their backs, they closed the distance rapidly. Emahari pointed out the craft of Raniq, a fisherman with centuries of experience.

Argunite pulled alongside them. Anchors were lowered, and he joined Emahari in crossing to Raniq's boat. Raniq listened closely as they explained what had been found so far.

"Taking a full bait barrel makes sense. Impossible to catch redfish without some sort of lure." Raniq scratched his grey braided beard, and Argunite's attention was drawn to his missing right thumb. "I agree: an open net of our people means they weren't actively fishing. Oniq is brave and a fool at times, but he takes care of his kit, and his grandnephew Jemiq is sound of mind and body. They wouldn't lose that overboard, much less their bobbers, unless something happened."

Argunite glanced out to the reef before looking back to Raniq. "Might a... what did you call that sea serpent?"

"Kaligogu," Emahari clarified.

"Thank you. Might a kaligogu attack the boat? We have them where I'm from, call them katabo, and they will grab swimmers, but I've never known a katabo to attack people on boats."

"That would be new to me, and there's not much around here new to me."

"I thought as much. Any ideas?"

Raniq thought for a moment. "No storms last night. Fishing too close to the reef always has its dangers. I prefer reef fishing closer to Song of Greeting, but they aren't as productive since the reefs are smaller. A lot safer though. Some of those reefs catch you by surprise, and it only takes one good hit to scull a canoe."

Emahari nodded. "If they took a hit, where would they go?"

"Depends on the hit. If it was a scratch, and they didn't want to risk the reefs of the atolls, I imagine they might try to get to land. If it was bad and they took water, I expect they would just brave the reefs to get to the atolls. We've been scanning so far and seen no sign of them on the shore behind us."

"We'll go on ahead and keep looking," said Emahari.

***

Argunite was thankful for the keen eyes of Utani. Not only did she see with clarity, she also could quickly deduce what was important to look for.

She noted a shift in the current before Argunite even felt it.

Sweeping along the lower reefs out to sea.

With a fit boat and full sail, it would barely register. If they were in any way damaged and took on water, this could wash them away from their intentions to reach shore.

Argunite closed his eyes, called for a shift in sails, and turned out to sea.

∗∗∗

The open waters were thankfully calm. Even so, the winds were swift, and most waves nearly as tall as the boat. At several points after a large wave, the entire boat creaked from nest to rudder. The merits of the keel kept them righted as they sailed, much more stable as they rolled with the waves, but he found the speed of the craft lacking. They were making good time, but it could be much better in a sleeker craft.

As they picked up the pace following a surge of wind, Argunite felt his frustrations fade as though the accelerating winds blew them like a storm against sand.

Argunite closed his eyes, his hand barely touching the wheel, and let Melrahim push the boat to its limits. He smiled as the sails and rigging groaned from the strain, the mast in a slight arc as it pushed.

"The wind will shift ahead. Rotate the sails, please."

Argunite heard his request followed through. Just as they completed the shift, the winds came at them hard from rear port, launching them along the same trajectory.

On they went, tearing across the sea at Melrahim's acquiescence. Time lost meaning. Argunite's eyes were closed, letting the crew know when the winds or water currents would change. If there were waves, which some part of him knew there were, they only assisted and didn't break against their hull or stern. The winds were perfect: cool but not cold, swift but not harsh, and carrying a delectable swell of salt, earthy surface algae, and hints of driftwood.

Argunite could not recall feeling more at ease.

More in control.

Free.

"I see something! Quarter turn to port!"

Argunite called for a shift in the sails, and the boat launched ahead.

It took a moment for Argunite to feel he had settled back in his body. Although still feeling weightless, he was present enough to spot a dark speck just starboard of the prow.

Argunite smiled as the winds seemed to pick up with even greater speed. Although he was vaguely aware of Emahari and Johani looking concerned and uncomfortable, some part of him knew their quarry was just ahead, and a sense of urgency that he couldn't identify urged him forward.

In short order, Argunite had a clear picture of the target.

It was an outrigger fishing craft. They had their sail drawn. The boat sat low on the water, and two figures frantically waved them down.

Argunite still felt a bit out of body as Rolanix and the fishermen used hooks to draw the crafts together. With Emahari and Johani's help, they brought the men aboard, along with some of their supplies. The boat was definitely going under. Argunite tried to center himself enough to understand their words, but realized his inability to understand them wasn't the haze of the sea: they spoke in their native language. Emahari spoke with them gently, made sure they had water, and gathered everything she could from the boat before returning to their craft.

"Are we ready?" Argunite asked.

"Yes," said Emahari, patting the younger fisherman on the shoulder before joining him at the helm. "I got most of their kit. At least this way they only need a new boat."

"Is it something we can salvage?"

Emahari shook her head. "Oniq said they took a bad hit on the reef from a rogue wave and lost a lot of their kit. Managed to seal the holes, but the planks along the starboard side were hit really hard and would all need replacement, and it also loosened the foundation of the mast to the point that he's amazed it hasn't fallen over yet. Their focus was on patching holes, but by the time they realized the rudder was hit, they were too far out to turn around, and were basically adrift. Any further and they would be in the azure current which empties into open ocean."

"Fair enough."

Argunite turned the boat toward shore. Rolanix and Johani shifted the sails, and they picked up speed. It would be some time before they were past the reefs and again in the winds that would take them home.

"How does it feel, leading a successful rescue mission?" asked Argunite.

Emahari smiled and raised a black eyebrow, bearing a striking expressive similarity to her brother. "Let's get back to Song of Greeting before congratulating ourselves. You did all the work. I just jumped in the water and nearly got everyone killed."

"We all make the wrong call now and then. I won't pretend that was your wisest plan. However, you recognized when we needed to ask for advice. Don't know if I would have considered searching in the open water if the old man with a missing thumb hadn't suggested it, and that's exactly what we needed to do. You knew Utani had better eyes so had her on the nest, which has consistently proven to be the right move, I'm glad to say your brother and his stoic and grouchy bodyguard should come along since they've more than proven their value on this mission. Most importantly, you accepted my offer to come along, and since I'm the most vital thread in this quilt of success, I say give yourself a healthy serving of credit there too."

Emahari laughed before her face softened. "Gratitude, Argunite."

"It's easy to see your missteps, kid. Sounds like they're pointed out to you a lot. Don't need to help them by dwelling on them yourself. People will always underscore your mistakes. Take it from a chronic disappointment: own your losses, but don't dismiss your wins. If I was humble, I would never have asked to help, and these two men would be lost to sea and their families would never see them again."

Emahari cocked her head, looking up at him from her seat. "I've never met someone who sees the world as you do."

Argunite shrugged. "I'm a lost pirate in love with the sea. Not much to it."

"I thought you weren't humble."

Argunite smirked.

He guided the ship over a low point of the reef, and at his request, Johani and Rolanix adjusted the sails. With the wind now in their favor, travel was expeditious, aided by an occasional change in currents. The fisherman and his grandnephew made several comments in their native tongue, their words saturated with wonder, and Argunite couldn't help but smile.

"Are you a witch?"

Argunite blinked twice before looking down to Emahari.

"I meant no offense. Sometimes I forget that other peoples do not share our views on magic. My sister is a witch, as is my mother, and my father's grandmother is also blessed with a lot of magic, not to mention Xangogao, founder of our clan. Many others have a bit of magic they can do. I'm not a witch or anything, but I have a sense for it. I can feel magic, I think. It seems like there is magic when you sail, especially when you were on the open water."

Argunite exhaled, releasing tension throughout his body he hadn't realized was there. "I don't think so. Witches of my islands were... we were lead by those blessed by Melrahim for a long time. The Qajarith Republic has always been afraid of witches. When they forced us to join them, most blessed by the sea goddess went into hiding. I was a boy when they first came, and saw how they treated witches. I had just become a man when my island was taken.

They never said I had magic, but Melrahim has always spoken in a way I can listen. I don't know if that makes me a witch. I'd like to think I speak the language of the sea, and that's the end of it."

"Apologies. Well I'm glad you can hear her. It sounds like a lovely relationship."

Argunite smiled, pushing down the swell of emotion. "It is indeed. I don't know where I would be without her guidance and company."

It wasn't long before they met up with the other fishermen. Cheers spread through the small fleet of boats still searching around the atolls. Argunite expected them to want to return to the village, but Raniq said most of them wanted to get the day's catch while they were out. He respected their diligence. Oniq and his grand-nephew Jemiq were in no condition to keep working though, so they continued on toward Song of Greeting.

Once they reached the village, Argunite docked as Emahari's father in the red wolf pelt took the line. Oniq and his grandnephew were taken into the excited arms of a small crowd, who Argunite assumed was their family. The tenderness of their touch and joy on their faces was overwhelming.

After gathering some of the fishermen's supplies, Rolanix hopped off the boat. He offered a hand to Utani, who took it with a shy smile and stepped onto the pier.

Argunite glanced to Johani and Emahari. "Is this the part where you restrain me again?"

Johani turned to Emahari. "Say the word, and it will be done."

"Of course not! You helped save Oniq and Jemiq. You are our guest!"

Johani raised a finger. "The elders will not approve of him wandering about with a pending charge."

Emahari sighed. "She's right. You are technically still being held on pending charges. The elders will pass sentences, but I promise they won't be harsh. We'll vouch for you, and as word spreads throughout the town, you'll surely have everyone on your side."

"Do what you must," said Argunite. "Tell me where to stay, and I'll stay there. No sense in running if it sounds like it could be resolved soon. A window to the sea would be my only request."

"One of the rooms at the inn should do," said Emahari.

"I'll see it done," said Johani.

After bidding Emahari farewell, Argunite accompanied Johani to a large longhouse. After a conversation in their native tongue, in which Argunite gave his food and drink preferences, Johani walked with him upstairs. She opened a door at the end of the left hall. The room inside was at the corner of the building, with a window to the town and another out to sea. Gulls cried and the surf sang. The smells of the sea filled the room. He barely noticed the desk and bed.

"By far my most pleasant holding cell."

Johani snorted, offering what must be her closest capacity for a smile. "The innkeeper will bring your food soon. Please don't try to leave. I like you, but will put you down if you make my job difficult."

Argunite nodded. "Noted."

Johani left, and at first he assumed she would just leave his door open. A moment later Johani returned, passing him a worn grey book.

"If you like to read, I recommend this one. I got it from the library downstairs. Poems about the sea from authors throughout the known world. I read it the first night we were here. Many of them are beautiful. Emotional. Good humor in there too."

"Thank you, Johani," said Argunite, turning the book over in his hands. It looked quite well loved.

"My room is three doors down if you need anything. Food will be up shortly."

Before he could thank her again, Johani closed the door and left him with the book.

At a loss of knowing what was ahead, he sat in the sill of the sea-facing window and tucked into the book of poetry.

As Johani promised, it was an excellent book. The opening poem was from an Eskadin poet about the duality of the sea: comfort and danger, allure and fear, give and take. Some spoke of the ocean's malice, others as if it was a caring parent. He was on the seventh poem, this one from a Pakardiant poet, when a worker at the inn brought him a tray of oysters with a side of fried yam strips, red pepper sauce, and baked seaweed. A cold pint of dark corn stout was also provided. Argunite had them set on the desk beside him so he could remain on the sill, and tucked in.

He was mostly finished with his meal when someone knocked on the door.

"Come in," he said, feeling a bit silly considering he was a prisoner.

The door opened. At first he spotted Johani, but she stepped aside to let another person in, who spoke to Johani in their native tongue before stepping inside. Johani gave him a stern look before departing.

Right away, Argunite saw Emahari and Rolanix in this young woman's features. This must be Rolanix's twin, since she looked around the same age and shared his fiery amber curls. Her tree-fiber dress was decorated with floral motifs, and clung to her alluring figure. The smell of honey and lily followed her in the room.

"Katinari, is it?" Argunite asked, setting down the oyster knife.

"Indeed, and I am told you are Argunite, our smuggler and savior," she said, her Common bearing the hard consonants of someone diligently schooled but having little real world practice. "Please continue your meal. Don't stop on my account."

"As you wish, Princess," he said, nodding before taking up another oyster and the knife. "How can I help you?"

"I suppose I just wanted to meet the handsome stranger everyone's talking about," she said, stepping into the room and taking a seat on the chair beside the desk. He was surprised at how comfortable she was, considering she was heir to, from what he understood, the entire island of Pakardia.

"What are they saying?" Argunite asked before downing the oyster and chewing slow. It was a smaller oyster, this one rich with salt.

"That the tides brought us a powerful witch to save our lost fishermen, and he saved them just before they washed out to the Abyss."

"I'm not a witch," Argunite clarified after swallowing.

A swell of wind picked up outside, nearly unseating him into the room. The breeze carried the aroma of pine, turned soil, and fresh rain.

Argunite adjusted his seating then turned to see Katinari smiling, an expression beautiful and a bit frightening.

"Of course. No witches here."

Argunite took a deep breath and opened his next oyster, this one quite a bit bigger, and cut the muscle free. "Besides, they were on the verge of an ocean-bound current, not the ocean itself. Can't say I mind that embellishment, though."

The wind calmed and Katinari's expression became a lot more mild. "I didn't imagine you would." She gestured to his platter. "May I?"

"Of course."

She took the knife he passed and opened an oyster before returning it. "How long have you been working for Doriq?"

Argunite scoffed. "I don't. I work fo-" he paused, deciding to take a long drink of corn stout as he collected his thoughts. "I am a freelance smuggler."

Katinari took him in with open skepticism. Finally she rested an elbow on the desk and tilted her oyster back slowly. Part of the allure of oysters was the intimacy involved in their consumption. It was difficult to not be sensual, and Katinari made no effort to compose herself on that front.

"Do you want something from me, Princess?"

Katinari missed a bit in her tilt, quickly dabbing with a napkin, an act which helped dispel some of her mystique. "Apologies. I've been shown how to eat oyster, but I must confess I've not had much experience. My sister has the coastal father. All my blood is from inland. We're only here to visit her father's family."

"Kind of you to support her that way."

"Of course. I love Emahari dearly, I'm just not much used to the ocean and its bounties, though they are quite delicious."

Argunite picked up another oyster, pierced and twisted it open, and readied another bite. "Takes some getting used to, and can be a bit strange at first, but once understood, they have no equal."

"So I'm told. To answer your question, yes: I want something from you. You are a man who has seen much of the world, yes? Emahari implied as much."

Argunite raised an eyebrow. "Indeed."

"My people are reserved. Secluded. Proud. The world is changing. The Empire and Republic grow in power and influence by the day, while my people remain the same. I don't wish to change my people, but I do need to know what is happening in the world so we are not caught by surprise. I have plenty of people telling me of great men and mighty nations throughout the known world, but my tutors often say the condition of the forest cannot be discerned from the giant drakes alone. One must also look to the spiders, hares, trout, and frogs to truly know the forest."

"You want me to tell you what my fellow spiders and frogs are saying?" Argunite said with a grin. "You really know how to charm a man, Princess."

Katinari pursed her lips, holding back a laugh. "I meant no offense, and apologies for any given. I shouldn't be so flowery in my speech."

"I'm enjoying it, for what it's worth."

"I appreciate that. I do mean it though: I want to know what is happening in this world. And what is really happening, not what the elders decide I should be told."

"Everyone has their own truth, Princess. My truth may not be the real truth any more than your elders and heralds."

"Please, call me Katinari. And yes, your view of the world may not be the entire picture, but it is a piece of the puzzle that I am being denied, which will hinder my ability to one day lead. When I am queen of Pakardia, I wish to rule with as much of the puzzle complete as possible."

Argunite nodded after a slight pause. "That is an ambitious goal. How would it work?"

"For now, I would give you a seal ring to permit sending letters through noble rookeries. It would permit you to send letters from most ports of the known world, and eventually would get to me. You will remain in contact, giving me an overview of the world as you see it. I would like to meet you now and then, preferably in port cities of Pakardia."

"I take it you are confident my sentence won't be debilitating."

Katinari shook her head. "Emahari and Rolanix has already vouched for you, and the elders now debate if anything more than marking your names need be done. Needless to say, yours will not be on the list and you will not be banished."

"So all I have to do is tell you what I see in the world, and you will give me access to royal rookeries to do it?"

"That's the deal."

Argunite smiled. "I think we have an accord."

"Excellent," said Katinari, taking the oyster knife and opening one. "Oh, pearls!"

She lifted the top shell to show Argunite. Both were tiny white beads grown side by side.

"You should eat them. It's good luck, at least where I'm from."

"Really?" Katinari said. "Plenty of our people on the coast wear them as jewelry. Wearing them brings luck."

"I think the Eskadin do too," said Argunite. "Maybe my folk are a bit strange."

Katinari tilted her head to the side, then shrugged. She picked them both up, stood, and held out a hand to Argunite. "I don't mind strange."

Argunite smiled, taking the offered pearl. "May the luck of Melrahim bless this partnership."

Katinari and Argunite each swallowed the pearls. He had swallowed much larger pearls, and this one barely registered. Based on Katinari's expression, it went down strange for her at first, but she locked eyes with him and gulped, looking quite proud once it was complete.

"I look forward to our partnership, Argunite," said Katinari.

Argunite stood and bowed. "As do I, Princess Katinari."

Katinari stepped closer, and took his hand. Argunite tensed. The aroma of honey and flowers was overwhelming, especially mixed with the salt of the oysters and her own natural scent. Her fingers, softer than any he had touched in a long time, lifted his hand and delicately traced around the base of one of his fingers. A swell of desire coursed through him. She looked up after circling his finger a second time, brown eyes wide, a mischievous smile dancing across her lips.

"Just taking measurements for your signet ring," she whispered. "So you can contact me."

"Ah, of course."

With a slight lean toward him, pressing him gently against the wall, Katinari turned and left in a few quick strides.

Argunite barely felt his feet on the ground as she closed the door behind her.

***

The following day, Argunite and his fellow prisoners were released. He wished his new friends all the best, getting a hug from Emahari, a suffocating embrace from Rolanix, a reluctant but eventually sincere hug from Utani, and a curt nod from Johani. Katinari passed him a parcel.

"Write to me," she said, her smile shy but excited.

Argunite nodded. "You have my word."

With that, they departed on a double canoe owned by Doriq, one of the few possessions of his the elders allowed him to keep.

Doriq and his men were banished from Pakardia and had, evidently in their imprisonment, negotiated joining Commodore Yurai's crew. Argunite wasn't sure how Yurai would feel about low-ranking crewmen hiring old contacts onto her ship, but he would let her address the matter.

As Doriq insisted on sailing his boat, Argunite opened the parcel.

First he produced a signet ring of silver with a firebird as its crest. Next was a short letter.

Argunite,

Argunite couldn't help but smile as he read the letter again.

He folded it up and put it in his pocket beside Fazid's. It felt odd, having both letters in the same pocket, but he wasn't quite ready to let go of Fazid.

Up ahead, the Brazen Mallard was anchored just where Commodore Yurai said they would be.

They came aboard as the crew tossed down a rope ladder. Eran was there helping the crew aboard. He brought Argunite up with a firm hand and a nod that might have a hint of begrudging respect. This was probably as close to an apology for abandoning him as Eran could muster, and Argunite chose to take what he could get.

Not waiting to offer explanation to Eran and the rest, Argunite marched straight for Yurai's cabin.

After two knocks, she called him in.

"Ah, wave-dancer!" she said, looking up from her glass of gold liquor and grinning. "Welcome back."

"Glad you stayed anchored," he said, closing the door behind him. "I was afraid you would flee once Eran said we were captured."

Yurai shrugged. "Call me optimistic, but I had a feeling you would get them out of that mess. Cabinet's open. Help yourself."

Argunite nodded, pouring himself a small glass of yam whiskey and taking the seat opposite her. "Turns out that was a good bet."

"Excellent. Any exciting tales of escape?"

"Not particularly. One of their fishermen got lost at sea, I helped bring him home, and they pardoned us. Well, the others are banished from Pakardia, but I'll be given a hero's welcome at any Pakardiant port."

"Splendid news," said Yurai with a grin.

"Evidently our contact Doriq and his boys were offered roles on your ship. I want it known that I had no part in that."

"If they prove useful on the voyage home I'll consider it. Not every local smuggler has it in him to turn pirate." Yurai pointed her pinky at Argunite's hand. "What's that?"

Argunite looked down at the ring on his finger. Although it might prove a useful connection for any number of things, he realized he didn't want to disclose the nature of his connection to Katinari. At least for now, he wanted to do exactly what they agreed upon, and that meant not using her as leverage. "Ah. Gift of one of the Pakardiant. The firebird is sacred to them."

Yurai raised a blue-dyed brow. Argunite suddenly remembered her father was Pakardiant. She also was rumored to have noble heritage of some sort, but he never knew from which side. She might well know exactly what the ring was.

If she did, she gave no further indication, and the moment passed with her taking another sip. "Well, I'm glad to hear you not only escaped, but did so as a folk hero. Needless to say that will reflect well in your ambitions to become a Blade. Not all pirates need be brutes, and making a name for yourself as a man of the people certainly has its values."

Argunite took another sip. "I won't lie, it does make piracy and smuggling taste a lot better if I can go from that angle. I'm sure I'll have to make compromises, but helping people where I'm able, well... I didn't take the quest for anything more than selfish reasons, but it felt good all the same."

"Lean into those inclinations, and I think you will find a lot of opportunities come your way."

They tapped their glasses together before another sip.

"Well," said Yurai, standing and rounding the desk to refill her glass. "Would you like to stay for supper? Beru is making a fine supper from some of the ingredients we got at Teshoko: elk tenderloin with baked horsetail and corn bread."

"Yes, but I would love to step out for a moment first."

"Of course," said Yurai after finishing her pour. As he passed, Argunite stepped in for a kiss. She held up a finger to his lips. "For the record, I know your heart is conflicted. You were closer to Fazid than you've told me, and you looked at that ring like a forlorn seal pup. If you want to be alone, know that there is no pressure from me, and that won't influence my recommendations for you. But if you want me, I'm right here, and I want you, even if we're just ships passing in the night."

Argunite put a firm hand on her waist, pulling her closer. "There are many things in my life I don't know. Things I want but know are out of reach. Things I know I should do but am afraid to take the first steps. Wanting you is among the few things I'm sure of."

Yurai grinned and pressed her full body against his. "I was hoping you'd say that. Go think and maybe we can reconnect before dinner."

"I like the sound of that," Argunite whispered.

After a long kiss, he left her cabin and found his way to the prow.

The anchor had already been lifted, and they were making good time out to open water. Argunite took out Fazid's letter.

He wasn't sure how much longer he wanted to carry it with him. The separation was so raw, and he wasn't sure how the wound would heal. Before he showed any potential or any beauty could shine through the grime, Fazid saw him as a man who needed help. He learned of Argunite's potential at sea and urged him onto

Hanau's ship. His motives were to be favored by Koban, but Argunite never felt Fazid was taking advantage of his talents. If anything, he ended the relationship when Argunite began showing the most potential.

Maybe Fazid ended things because he didn't want Argunite to feel beholden to his cause.

Tears came hot, and Argunite returned the letter to his pocket.

Fazid was driven by his ambitions to help his people.

That wasn't childish. That was inspirational and heroic.

Argunite kissed his necklace. "Maybe I'm not ready to liberate my people, but I can help others as I prepare, and someday I'll follow his example. I'll make him proud."

After kissing his necklace once more, Argunite exhaled.

His breath stirred with the wind and filled the headsail, pushing the Brazen Mallard surging forward to their next destination.

Grandmother's Roots

3

Grandmother's Roots

Grandmother's Roots

Wild Heart turned away from the wind as she worked.

She held the stem firm and drew her sickle across its base, hearing the satisfying drum of a dozen snail nuts into the rest of her nearly-full basket. As she worked, she hummed the song of Dead Tree Grandmother:

When demons crawled into our homes
And cast us into the sea,
Grandmother wept, and tears she cried
Drew from gods, sympathy.

As boats rolled in the currents,
Grandmother, she proclaimed
Her form and soul would sacrifice
If safety were assured.

Her wish was taken by the gods,
And on these shores, new home at last!
When foot she set upon the shore,
Grandmother became a tree!

Her roots dug deep our wells.
Her blood made hard the clay.
In the marsh she still stands tall,

Behind her, Cherry Blossom was reminding Reed Whistle of the proper technique for what must have been the third time. The boy meant well, but Reed Whistle's mind was often far from his chores, and he lost focus halfway through his mother's explanations. Some thought him dim or indifferent, but Wild Heart saw how hard her grandson tried to focus.

Her own brother Tide Maker had been the same. He was always easily distracted, but when there was a single task, none did it better. His nets were ever the strongest, his harpoons most precise, his knives the sharpest. Reed Whistle showed much of the same potential. At first Cherry Blossom had been worried her son would be ostracized, but Wild Heart reassured her that Tide Maker's spirit was in the boy, and sure enough, with patience and clear instruction, Reed Whistle showed a lot of promise as a craftsman.

They were still working on gathering.

Wild Heart continued up the hill, periodically kneeling down to clip a line of snail nuts. Many weren't ready to harvest after the last gathering, and she left them to recover.

The top of the hill looked to have many stems ready for collection, so she advanced to the top.

Wild Heart had barely crested the hill when a sight stopped her heart in her chest, and she nearly dropped her basket.

Rumors had come to their village of Bramble Hills months ago that another warlord was assembling for another Ocean March.

Wild Heart hadn't really given it much thought. She assumed it would be another failure. When the last rumors came some ten years ago, the conscriptions didn't even reach the peninsula, much less round to their villages on the north shore.

Three ships sailing upriver proved her wrong.

Wild Heart turned and clapped twice to get the attention of her daughter and grandson. Once they looked up, she spoke and signed quickly. "Take what you have. We're going back to the village."

"What is it?" Cherry Blossom signed, her brow furrowed as she touched a thumb to her ear then jaw. She clawed a hand at her chin. "Boar-camels?"

"Nuboku," said Wild Heart before putting a thumb to her chest. Cherry Blossom's face fell.

She rushed Reed Whistle, who was focused on a length of snail nuts and meticulously cutting so as not to damage the stem and let future nuts grow. He looked up confused.

"Back to the village," said Cherry Blossom, bringing one arm down as the other carried her basket. "Nuboku. Don't worry. Stay calm."

Reed Whistle did as he was told, but his demeanor quickly tensed.

Wild Heart led them home, turning back to speak and sign as she walked. "We go in, gather any supplies we can, get Nettle Top and Owl Eyes, and go."

"Mother, where are we going?" signed Cherry Blossom.

"Into the marshes until they leave."

Wild Heart's mind was racing. She panted on her march down the hill, and was already sweating. Memories of the Nuboku coming and taking her three brothers to die, either on the voyage across the sea or when they made land on foreign soil, dominated her thoughts. How her mother had watched them take her boys, scolding Wild Heart for crying as they were taken. "This is why we have sons, Wild Heart. They go to retake our home, and we stay to make more sons. You don't want to live in this swamp forever, do you?" Tide Maker had been an invaluable member of the village even though he showed no competence in battle. He was too unfocused for war, but they took him all the same. Sent him to die as millions of other scared boys were taken every time a southern warlord decided he would be the one to bring their people home.

It had been more years than stars in a clear night sky since her people were banished from their homeland across the Abyss. Countless attempts had been made to return. None succeeded. The voyage alone took half the fleet, most of the survivors died on enemy shores, and the few who returned were either executed, castrated, or rewarded with siring the next generation of voyagers depending on the opinions of the current southern kings.

Cherry Blossom grabbed her mother's wrist. "If we go into the marsh and they find out we did so to escape conscription, we will be cast out as fodder for the crocodiles."

Wild Heart's jaw clenched. She looked back at Reed Whistle, whose shaking hand betrayed his resolved expression.

"We will say we're going to fish, and want to let the children get some air. None should be suspicious. The ships are on the horizon. We have some time."

Before waiting for Cherry Blossom to reply, Wild Heart carried on.

Normally the walls of Bramble Hills felt welcoming and protective. A structure of wood twice her height with a brick base surrounded by a ditch. Now that she advanced toward it with plans to sneak inside, it felt a bit imposing.

The gates were open as most people were out foraging or fishing. Although she was on edge, the young warrior Star Finder who was on watch today didn't even acknowledge them when Wild Heart gave him a slight wave. He didn't seem to have noticed the ships, even though his position on the tower should give him a fairly clear view. It was morning though, so perhaps he hadn't looked to the east with the sun rising from the same direction.

It would be a matter of time, though. They had to hurry.

A trio of small peccaries scurried in front of them, followed by a frantic boy trying to corral them. A marsh camel, shoulders at Wild Heart's hip height, kept pace behind the boy.

Although Wild Heart sometimes complained that their hut was so far back into the settlement that it was tedious to get to the main gate, and this walk through Bramble Hills made her feel countless eyes on them, they were close to the west gate which lead to the boats. A small blessing, but it would surely be a blessing once they were packed. No one said anything to them. Most of the villagers were engrossed in their tasks around the village, be it washing clothes, weaving, tanning hides, or preparing meals. Wild Heart knew it was paranoia that made her feel they were being watched. No one gave any indication otherwise. Even so, she felt a touch of relief when they stepped inside the main hut.

The structure was typical of the other huts in Bramble Hills: red mud threaded with reeds for stability, a circular main hut for their lounge, stove, and dining space, with several smaller huts built around for each person to have individual rooms connected to the main space by short halls. The floor was dug around waist height into the floor, again with red clay floor and walls. It was cool inside, which was a life saver in the heat of summer.

Owl Eyes was seated with young Nettle Top in the lounge. There were toys about, and it looked like the girl had been telling her brother a story. Owl Eyes was, like Reed Whistle, a bit oblivious, but even she sensed the tension as the others walked inside.

"Is everything alright?" she asked, setting down her toddler brother and passing him a wooden toy.

"We're going fishing!" signed Cherry Blossom before lifting her youngest and twirling him about. At this, Nettle Top looked excited. He started mumbling excitedly about fish.

Owl Eyes looked between her mother, grandmother, and older brother, openly skeptical. "Grandmother, you said today was for gathering nuts."

"It's so nice out today," said Cherry Blossom with an arc of hand after setting Nettle Top on her hip. "We decided to change the schedule."

"We don't change schedules," signed Owl Eyes with a frown. "Grandmother doesn't like it."

"Sometimes we have to do things even if they make us uncomfortable," signed Wild Heart.

Although she looked unconvinced, Owl Eyes stood.

"Get all the dried produce we have in here," said Wild Heart, passing Owl Eyes a basket. She turned to her grandson. "Reed Whistle, we might be gone for a day or two so bring some blankets and mosquito salve, please."

As they all took to their tasks, Wild Heart put their well water in a few canteens, set aside a few torches, and made sure they had all their fishing supplies. Even if fishing wasn't the real goal, it would be important to keep up the façade, and they might need to fish for food so being prepared wasn't a bad thing.

Cherry Blossom ensured everyone was slathered in insect repellant. Reed Whistle tied their collective kits in travel blankets while the other two children occupied themselves with packing toys or whatever food was handed to them.

Wild Heart reached up to the rafters and took her obsidian knife. She kept this out of reach of the children. After securing it to her belt, Wild Heart also grabbed her sword and scabbard.

She originally traded a traveling merchant five pelts for the blade when rumors of the last Ocean March came. Even though that

Ocean March never happened, she still felt better with the blade in the house. It was made to be used with a shield, but she didn't own one. Although she had been inclined to purchase an iron weapon, the merchant said a bronze blade like this would be as capable of piercing gaps in armor as even a steel weapon, and require a lot less maintenance. She hadn't planned for it to be for emergency use only, the merchant was indeed right. He had added that it would darken with age, but would retain its function. Dusting it with her sash, she found that to be the case. A test draw on her sash cut cleanly. Surprised and satisfied with its sharpness, Wild Heart returned the sword to its scabbard, wrapped it, and set the blade with the fishing gear and oars.

If Reed Whistle noticed, he didn't give any indication.

Once they all applied mosquito balm and gathered the packs, Wild Heart took up a blanket of supplies and led the way outside.

***

Canoes were stored in stacks, overturned so critters would not nest inside. Most of the canoes were out, as anyone planning to fish was already out, but Wild Heart's boat was still on shore. There was a tower near the west gate, but Wild Heart hadn't spotted anyone inside while they left. Not strange to not have someone stationed, but this would be part of the rotation, so they would have to be quick.

Reed Whistle and Cherry Blossom set down their packs and began to pull down their canoe. Wild Heart stood with the children, setting her own bag down to hold each of their hands. It was unusual for crocodiles or river seals to bask or lurk when there was activity around the boats, but it had been long enough since the canoes all cast off that she wanted to be sure the little ones stayed close.

"Decided it is a fishing day?"

At recognizing the voice, Wild Heart closed her eyes. Willing herself to look relaxed, Wild Heart turned to see Petrel standing in the western gate. They had been girls at the same time. While young, Petrel was called Dove for her striking white hair and beauty. This beauty got her a doting husband, one of Little King Red Moon's younger brothers, who made sure she got everything she wanted. Once her beauty faded, her name changed to better reflect her nature as a scavenger of gossip. Petrel hated the name at first. However, dire petrels were imposing birds after all, and eventually she embraced it. Her smile now was full of performed sincerity, yet it exposed her notably long canines with no effort to hide a threat.

"The wind seemed too pleasant to pass up," said Wild Heart, releasing Owl Eye's hand to circle her hand about and touch her chest before tapping a knuckle beside her eye and wriggling her fingers. "Will mean we might have trouble seeing the fish, but at least there won't be many flies."

Petrel nodded, but her focus was on their gear. "Lot of food. Planning to be out for a while?"

"Good to be prepared."

"It is indeed." Petrel nodded to the hilt of Wild Heart's sword, protruding out of Reed Whistle's pack after he had to set it down. "Very prepared. I heard you bought a sword all those years ago. I've never seen you bring it with you to a fishing trip."

Cherry Blossom and Reed Whistle set the canoe in the water, sliding it carefully so as not to scrape the bottom on the sandy shore. Wild Heart forced a smile to Petrel. "Like you said. I like to be prepared."

Before Petrel could make another prying comment, Wild Heart ushered the children toward the boat.

The bronze gong rang through the air. The sequence of three beats called everyone home from any chores they partook in outside the settlement.

Star Finder must have spotted the ships.

Wild Heart looked back. Petrel had a quizzical expression, taking in that Wild Heart's family wasn't moving to return the boat, which melted into a honey-sweet smile as a realization crossed her face. "Well, aren't you coming inside? I expect that will be the Nuboku conscriptors my husband was warned about."

With that, Petrel turned and started to go inside the west gate. She might not know it was the Nuboku for sure, but she knew Wild Heart's family was trying to go somewhere, and she would be the first to point them out when the Nuboku arrived.

There was no one else around. Petrel hadn't opened the gate yet, there still weren't sentries on the west gate tower, and all the boats that were going out were long gone.

Wild Heart rushed Petrel and tackled her to the ground.

Before Petrel could recover her winded breath to scream, Wild Heart grabbed her by the throat with both hands.

Petrel snarled up at her. Gone was the sickly sweet demeanor. The fangs she usually hid were bared in a grimace. Her nails – grown long as her status did not require chores – slashed at Wild Heart's arms and face.

Wild Heart snarled back, biting at the clawed hand that raked along her jaw. The bite didn't land, but Petrel drew back and hissed. Her other hand went for Wild Heart's eye. Wild Heart kept her position, gripping on Petrel's wind pipe and repeatedly pressing down with her full weight and enduring the injuries Petrel kept delivering. Although Wild Heart had never done anything like this, she knew her best chance was to keep hold of Petrel's throat.

Petrel continued to gasp, wheezing and straining. With a push of her leg, she flipped both over and they tumbled through the reeds. Wild Heart was on top, but her feet slid in the mud and she didn't feel secure in her position. They weren't in the water yet, but they were close.

If Wild Heart could only hold Petrel under...

A swipe of Petrel's hands raked across Wild Heart's left eye. Wild Heart reflexively covered the wound. Following another wheezing gasp, Petrel landed a flurry of bludgeoning strikes.

While Wild Heart was stronger from more work, Petrel was taller, younger, and enjoyed more rations from her station. Wild Heart found herself holding up her arms to block the blows. With a growl, Wild Heart rushed forward, tackling Petrel to the ground once more.

"Your boys will walk across the ocean with the rest," Petrel said through a snarl. "Your daughter and hers will be bred for more, and you will be flayed and impaled on a spike to warn others against desertion. You have never been one of us, and you will die in a way that nourishes nothing!"

As Petrel swiped up at Wild Heart's face, Wild Heart grabbed the hand on impact and bit hard at the wrist.

This earned Wild Heart a scream.

Before the cry could finish, it was silenced by an object out of Wild Heart's line of sight striking her neck. The scream ended in a gurgle.

Petrel's body went limp.

Wild Heart slumped back, spat blood from her mouth, and inhaled deeply. It took a moment of blinking her good eye and slow breaths to process what had happened.

Cherry Blossom stood over Petrel, shock on her face as she held the bronze sword pierced in Petrel's throat.

Knowing there was no time to spare, Wild Heart urged her daughter to withdraw the blade. As soon as it was free, she rolled Petrel to the edge of the water. If they put the body in, blood would spread fast and perhaps be seen sooner. On the shore hidden in some of the reeds as it now was, she might be mistaken for a crocodile attack. Such an assumption would not hold up to close scrutiny, but any moments they could spare were a blessing.

Wild Heart took the sword from a still stunned Cherry Blossom and ran it through the water to clean it off.

"You did well, daughter," she said quietly. "We must go."

Cherry Blossom nodded.

Wild Heart glanced up at the west gate tower. It still didn't have a sentry, but that would surely change soon. The other fishing boats would also be coming back any moment.

The children were piled into the canoe with their belongings. Cherry Blossom steered, since Wild Heart now only had one good eye, and Reed Whistle took the front. Wild Heart rowed opposite whatever side Reed Whistle was on to help power the canoe, keeping the little ones in front of her. All in the boat were deadly silent. In short order they had built up momentum. Cherry Blossom had the good sense to take them along the north channel, further from the wallows where most went to fish.

There was shouting back toward Bramble Hills. Someone screamed.

They had found Petrel's body. Would they come searching?

Probably.

"Mother?"

Wild Heart glanced back. Cherry Blossom had her oar out of the water. Reed Whistle looked back after making sure they didn't hit anything as the channel was tight ahead.

"Yes, Cherry Blossom?"

"Do we hide or flee?"

Wild Heart looked toward their home. The place she lived her whole life. She could still make out the tower, which now had someone inside. It was a silhouette, but they were moving frantically.

It might be paranoia, but they seemed to be pointing toward their canoe.

Wild Heart looked out ahead. The reeds were tall on either side, but she could just make out the maze of trees and grasses all around.

To the east was the sea.

The west brought them further into the marshes.

"They know what we did. They will come for us and take Reed Whistle. We cannot allow this to happen. Our fate is now in the hands of Dead Tree Grandmother. We go west."

***

If the village sent boats in pursuit, Wild Heart didn't see them. They continued fast, cutting through the maze of channels deeper into the marshes.

Owl Eyes was usually so full of questions. She said nothing as they rowed. Nettle Top also sat in uncharacteristic silence, ignoring the toys Wild Heart set down for him.

Wild Heart washed out her bad eye. She could see out of it, and guessed the impairment was because the lid or under her eye was swollen, but the eye itself was fine. A minor blessing considering it was so swollen and in pain that she couldn't really see, but she would take any blessing she could get.

None of the scratches were deep, but Petrel had landed countless strikes. Wild Heart's face stung in many places. Her arms had several longer cuts as well. Nothing serious now, but Wild Heart had seen lesser injuries get terribly infected even with bedrest, and they were out in the marshes. A dip in slower water could be lethal. Owl Eyes still didn't speak, but did help clean the blood with well water and dab honey on the wounds.

Plenty of biting flies and mosquitoes flew about, but their citrus balm combined with the open jar of black onion oil meant that none of the insects bothered them. Wild Heart felt a bit ill around the black onion oil, but considering the alternative, she counted the rancid smell amongst her fortunes.

Their peninsula didn't have much in the way of large beasts, but these wetlands were an exception. River seals and crocodiles were the most dangerous, but she was still wary of the trio of stilt-legged boar-camels gorging themselves on reeds some ten span away. These long-jawed beasts mostly ate foliage, but she had heard plenty of fishermen claim that they would charge and flip boats without provocation. River seals and crocodiles tormented fishermen out of hunger. Boar-camels hurt for boredom or pleasure. Fear of the Nuboku back in their village drove them onward, but Wild Heart breathed much easier when she looked back and all three beasts remained about their trough of reeds, paying their canoe no mind.

A branch horn flew overhead. These enormous birds flew on wings of skin stretched from their longest finger to their heel. It was said that there were many other types of these skin-winged birds out on the coasts and on the prairies to the north, but this was the only bird like it in the marshes. Most called them poor omens, especially when all white like this one, but Wild Heart had always felt at ease in their presence. To her, they had always heralded good fortune. There was a certain majesty in their imposing size, but they only had an interest in fish or small critters. Perhaps not something she would trust around her baby, but his shadow passing overhead felt more protective than threatening.

At the takeoff of several toothed pheasants, perhaps frightened by the branch horn's shadow, countless yellow butterflies swarmed about the boat. One landed briefly in Nettle Top's hair before following the rest of its kin. Two signs of luck right after each other? Wild Heart felt some of the tension leave her shoulders.

Rather than go toward the main river, which would only wash them back toward Bramble Hills, Cherry Blossom continued steering them through the marshes.

"Who is coming for Reed Whistle?" asked Owl Eyes with words and signs. "Why did we have to leave? How come we couldn't just stay home? Why did you fight Petrel? She was just talking and you attacked? I know you always say she was annoying and lazy, and I know she's mean sometimes and pretends to be nice, but you also said it is most important to support each other. That the world is dangerous so our village shouldn't fight. I don't understand and it's very frustrating."

Wild Heart tried to answer the first few questions, but gave a sad smile and let her granddaughter finish. "Thank you for listening to us. The plan changed quickly and I know it was stressful. We didn't have time to tell you, and I appreciate you doing what we said. It is important for you both to be quiet if we tell you to. There are many dangers, but now is a fine time for questions. Just know that we may need to be very quiet without warning or explanation, okay?" Both children nodded. "Good. Now, what question would you like me to answer first?"

Owl Eyes took a deep breath. "Who is coming for our brother? You told mother they would come for us and take him. Who is them?"

Wild Heart kissed her granddaughter's forehead. She thought she had been speaking quietly at the time, but clearly not.

"The Nuboku are coming for your brother."

"Who are the Nuboku and what do they want?"

"The Nuboku are warriors of our people. You remember the story of where our ancestors are from?"

Owl Eyes nodded. "Our people, the Maku, lived across the sea. Demons attacked us many years ago, and we had to flee. The grandmother of the people promised the gods she would sacrifice herself if we got a home. The gods honored this, and the current brought our ancestors to Bramble Hills. The grandmother went into the marshes and became a tree. Her roots dug wells for freshwater, wood for the wall, and her blood made the clay good for bricks."

Wild Heart pet Owl Eye's head. "Yes. That is our story. It is important to our village, but we are not the only Maku village descended from our ancestors across the sea. Not every village was made by a grandmother who made such a sacrifice. There are hundreds of Maku villages along the White Coast, north to the fire sands and south to the realms of the kings, and thousands more of other peoples who already lived in these lands. Some of the peoples who lived here before welcomed the Maku. There is so much land here. However, many do not like the Maku, and think we should return home. I like it here. It is now our home, but there are those of our people who think we should go back across the water to the lands we are from and take it back from the demons. This morning, three large boats came down the river. I saw them while we were gathering snail nuts. These boats want to take Reed Whistle away and make him fight to take back our land."

"Why don't we want to go back home?"

"Because Dead Tree Grandmother made this our home. There were no people here before her sacrifice. It was a desert. This is our home. We didn't take it away from anybody. It is ours. Why should we send Reed Whistle and thousands of other boys to die trying to get back our home from the demons when we have a perfect home here?"

Owl Eyes nodded. "That makes sense. But now we ran away from our home. It's not our home anymore because you and mom killed Petrel. They won't let us back. That's why we took all our food and blankets, right?"

"Yes."

"Where is our new home going to be?"

Wild Eyes sighed. "I don't know yet, baby girl. Right now we need to get away from the Nuboku. Once we are confident that we have escaped, we will find a new home. Just the five of us. Maybe we'll find someone else's home and we can share it if they are willing."

Reed Whistle indicated to the left with a firm hand.

On a nearby mound of mud, around ten span away, the distinctive sleek body with dark fur and honey-gold stripes of a river seal drew her attention. It was massive; at three span, it was nearly as long as their canoe. Unlike ocean seals, it's front fins were long and articulated like arms as they were predators hunting much larger prey than fish.

The river seal yawned, flashing a chilling row of shearing teeth culminating in tusk-like fangs. At the end of the display it shook its head and looked to the canoe, its forward-facing eyes black voids of focus.

Wild Heart picked up her sword. Peripherally she spotted Reed Whistle raise his oar with both hands.

Although she feared a challenge would only provoke an attack, the river seal instead lowered its head onto its mud bank and ignored them.

"I don't think we should share a home with him," Owl Eyes whispered.

Wild Heart laughed, releasing tension in the grip of her sword as she set it back behind her, facing away from the children.

They rowed on, continuing deeper into the marshes.

***

By midday, Cherry Blossom and Reed Whistle were exhausted, and the sun beat down furiously. They found a still stretch of bank on an islet and parked the canoe, got out to stretch, but remained beside the boat to eat. Cherry Blossom set up a canvas blanket to shield them from the sun.

Wild Heart was still in pain, but from what she could tell, the honey was helping minimize any potential infection and inflammation. Once the wound was cleaned and treated, it seemed the wound was shallow and she could see well enough that she trusted it would heal soon. A persistent fly kept approaching her forehead, likely drawn to the honey, but the repellant she wore kept it from landing. Even so, the critter was infuriating, but Wild Heart was in no condition to do more than wave it off.

Reed Whistle prepared a fire. Although Wild Heart was worried about smoke, he insisted that Old Man Flint showed him how to make one without smoke. True to his word, with dry wood from a dead tree on the islet, he nested branches over it and slowly brought it to a burn. While they were seated, Cherry Blossom set a frame to hang a pot to boil river water. Once it had heated to her satisfaction, she put it in a jar that they hadn't had time to fill.

Once they were ready to depart, Reed Whistle covered the majority of the fire with a domed rock he found on the islet. Again true to his word, the fire barely let out any smoke, all trapped under the stone. Wild Heart whispered thanks to Old Man Flint into the air. Few people had patience with an unfocused boy like Reed Whistle, but clearly the effort had paid off. She would miss the old man. Much about their home. Much of it she would not miss, but there had been truly kind neighbors, and she hoped they would be well in the future.

Through the maze they traveled, continuing upstream. Wild Heart didn't have a destination in mind, nor did her daughter she assumed, but it still felt important to put more distance between them and Bramble Hills. She wouldn't feel ready to slow down until they had put at least another day of travel behind them.

Behind them, Cherry Blossom clicked urgently.

She slowed her steering. Reed Whistle brought them to a stop. Wild Heart signed for the children to be quiet, and they both nodded. Nettle Top looked deeply nervous, his lip trembling. Owl Eyes offered him a consoling embrace, looking up to reassure her grandmother that she had the little one taken care of.

After nodding to Owl Eyes approvingly, Wild Heart followed Cherry Blossom's pointed finger.

Out toward the main river, the mast and sail of a boat passed over the line of grass atop an islet between them. There were many channels between their canoe and the sailboat, and its sail and mast a tiny strip of red and wood, but it was still far too close to comfort.

"How did they find us?" signed Cherry Blossom using only her hands. Wild Heart shrugged, wondering the same thing. There were many main channels. For the boat to be on the very main branch closest to them seemed highly unlikely unless many boats were sent out, a daunting task for a fleet of ships only present to conscript young men. Surely they would be made example of if found by chance by a fishing boat or if they were ever foolish enough to return, but the notion of the Nuboku investing all the boats on their ships to hunting down one boy was ridiculous.

They did have a reputation for making a brutal example of any who defied them.

Perhaps she shouldn't have underestimated them…

The sail carried on, making no change in speed or direction. It wasn't until the mast was out of sight that Wild Heart even realized she had been holding her breath.

"Deeper into the maze," Wild Heart signed. Her daughter and grandson nodded.

Without speaking, they rowed to the right, winding through the channels as they went.

***

Maybe she was focusing more on dangers above water, but considering they were the makers of the channels, Wild Heart was surprised it took so long to spot a crocodile.

It was a small one, about as long as Owl Eyes was tall. The stripes of emerald and gold were still vibrant. It was said that they were made of gems in the egg, and shed these precious materials into the sediment as they grew, just another way that they shaped the bounty of these wetlands. Local crocodiles could grow massive. Many of the residents could reach five span. Seven in extreme specimens, especially in the tusked species.

The largest horned crocodile she had ever seen was the god River Maker, a behemoth fifteen span in length. He spent a summer near Bramble Hills, eating all the camels, rhinos, and other large beasts and fish. Many of the channels they now paddled through had been dug by the river god as he carved his way through the marshes, too large to crawl on land. She only spotted him a handful of times. All the gems and gold had been shed from his hide years before his arrival: he was a dull green and grey, with dense vegetation growing on his sailed back, and great branches sprouting from his wooden head. It was the first time she had ever seen a god, and even looking upon him from the towers, he was a marvel to behold. Although River Maker initially depleted the land, the years after saw unprecedented returns in fish, regions that had been dry since she was a girl now flooded and verdant, and it was safe to venture into many places once saturated with dangers. The god left to bring new lands destruction and a fresh start, never to be seen again. Wild Heart always looked upon crocodiles with fondness after his visit. She imagined if this little creature still studded with emeralds beside them might one day become a god of desolation and rebirth.

Reed Whistle looked to the left as they passed a gap in the channel and tensed.

The sailboat was back. It was navigating the channels, coming fast with the wind at their backs. They were following the flow of the river, so must have circled back after passing them earlier.

How did they know where to find them?

Wild Heart only caught a glimpse of the Nuboku at the front of the boat.

In some ways, he was completely different than the men who came to take her brothers. This man had darker skin than Wild Heart, while the Nuboku she met as a girl had the typical lighter skin of the peoples of the southern forests. His hair was a light amber, while most southerners had black hair. He looked forward with a predatory focus of a beast, not a man, made all the more frightening by the flash of yellow where most eyes were brown or blue. Like the men she remembered, however, he wore thumbs and ears around his neck. It was said that Nuboku took the thumbs of their defeated foes so they could not carry weapons anymore, and ears so that when they collected the pointed ears of demons over-seas, this would signify their might in contrast with their rounded ears. Old Man Flint had, like most men of the village, lost his right thumb and ear when he returned from his Ocean March a failure. This man wore nothing but his necklace of mummified thumbs and ears, grinning at her as they closed the distance. The image of his fangs, far larger than on any man she had ever seen, locked in her mind and sent a chill down her spine.

"Move!" she said, plunging her oar into the water. Their sail-boat was certainly faster with the wind, but they were much less maneuverable, especially since the sailboat was around twice the size of their canoe. "Keep right! Stay in the maze."

Owl Eyes held her brother once more, staying low so Wild Heart could easily switch sides to row where she was needed.

She glanced back as they turned. Although the reeds were tall on either side, she could spot the top half of their sail. It was close.

Too close. Fortunately it seemed to have come to a halt. When she spared another look after a few more strokes, the sailboat was moving again, but having to stay in more open water for its size. Now that it lost the wind, they were putting distance between them once more.

After her third glimpse, only the tip of the sail could be seen, and it was moving out further toward the main river.

"Did we lose them?" asked Owl Eyes.

Her heart was racing, and her hands too occupied to offer a full explanation, but Wild Heart nodded. "I think so. At least for now."

***

Twice they spotted the sail in the distance. Never quite close, but ever in sight. At one point it was far ahead, next lagging behind. Wild Heart didn't know how the Nuboku were keeping such focus on them, since there was no line of sight and all they could spot was the tip of the mast, but however they were tracking them, it was working successfully. The waters were slow, which was a blessing, but even then, consistent padding at full speed was exhausting.

Wild Heart called for a rest. She hadn't spotted the sail in a while and they needed rest, drink, and to relieve themselves. They dared not beach, but they came to shallows enough to stand in and hastened through a stretch and anything else they could think of. She was endlessly grateful that she boiled as much water as she did, for they would be almost out otherwise.

Perhaps they should be rationing. She hadn't imagined this escape as a sprint with pursuers. She knew there would be dangers, but this was unlike anything she had expected. Enduring was what she had in mind. There was plenty of food, enough for a week and more if they fished or foraged. However, at this rate they would be out of water by tomorrow, especially drinking as much as they needed to with such rigorous movement. They would have to start another fire to boil more water.

Wild Heart was in good shape, and she would be fine were it not for her minor injuries and their pace. Several of her bandages on her arm showed fresh red seeping through the cloth. She would be on her way to recovery if she sat idle, but regular motion was taking its toll.

She took stock of her family. Cherry Blossom was holding Nettle Top close. Her arms trembled with the child. Her eyes were heavy and breathing uneven. Reed Whistle was sweaty and a bit out of breath but physically fine. His arm tapped urgently on the prow of the boat and he couldn't focus his eyes on any one thing. Owl Eyes had relieved herself, drank only a bit of water after making sure everyone rowing had what they needed, and was sitting in the boat quiet and ready for whatever happened next. More than anything, this diligent obedience from a girl ever full of contrary inclinations and curiosity threatened to break Wild Heart, and she held back the tears hot behind her eyes.

Reed Whistle climbed onto the nearby islet and looked about. He didn't spot any sign of the sailboat.

Although she wanted peace of mind and to perhaps settle down for the night, Wild Heart knew they had to press on. There was still enough daylight that they could make good time.

After one last stretch all around, they piled back in.

They rowed on until the sun began to lower and pink lined the horizon. It was still fully light out, but by now on a normal day they would have long since settled in for the night, telling stories, singing, and playing games. Wild Heart missed home. Missed their routine. She was thankful that they had been able to leave. That they didn't let Reed Whistle sacrifice himself was a victory, but it didn't mean she didn't miss home.

At their next stop, they had calmed enough that they felt safe actually getting out of the boat. After drinking their fill, Reed Whistle lit another of his smokeless fires and Wild Heart boiled enough water to refill all their containers, along with anything they could find that was watertight.

At their first stop, Reed Whistle had seemed so proud of his fire. Now he seemed indifferent. Worn down.

He drummed his fingers against his knee as he stared into the flames.

"What troubles you?" Wild Heart signed.

"This is because of me," he replied quietly. Cherry Blossom held Nettle Top and both seemed on the verge of sleep. Owl Eyes was on the lookout on the top of the islet.

"Yes," Wild Heart said after considering rebuking his thoughts. He was a man. Usually he would have another year or two before he truly came of age, but the expectations of him going forward were those of adulthood, and he needn't be coddled. Certainly not if she was going to be forthright with Owl Eyes about the realities ahead.

"You all would be safe if I had gone with them, yes?"

"Yes, we would be home, but we would not be happy."

"You are afraid because you think if I went with the Nuboku, I would be killed? That I am not brave or strong enough to survive?"

Wild Heart's jaw tensed. She pursed her lips, weighing her response to be honest but not hurtful. "Most do not survive. My fears for you are born of the situation being set up for failure and death, not because you are weak. You are clever and resourceful. You are a boy- no, a man, with many talents. Unfortunately the Nuboku are not looking for people to be clever or resourceful. They don't care if you can make a fire like this that does not smoke, or that you do tasks better than anyone but you need much longer to learn. They aren't looking for talent. They are here for bodies. They need boys that can hold a spear and be thrown against an army of demons with metal skin and arrows of fire. They will be upset that you need time to learn, and they don't care how many skills you have. If you go with them, you will be sent to die at the hands of demons all so that a southern king can say he tried. That is not a fate I wish for any of our boys. I cannot save them all, but I can save you, and I can save Nettle Top from the same fate when he becomes a man too."

Reed Whistle looked to his mother and little brother, who were now both asleep. The hum of insects came to a crescendo around them.

"I do not wish to be weak. I hate how my mind works. How it does not. Why can't I think like normal boys? Boys who just want to fight? If I wanted to fight, I would join the Nuboku, and my family would be safe."

"It is easy to assume the worst. It is easy to think any anxiety or insecurity must be correct simply because it makes you afraid. To think that you are weak because you are interested in things other than fighting. That is not true. Fear is not reality. It is not weak to die against enemies that live for centuries and spend their every waking moment training how to kill. They are not people. They need not sleep, eat, or seek pleasure. Demons are creatures who exist only to harm. Dying at their hands is not a sign of weakness. Fighting them is an act of futility. Running with us is not weakness, Reed Whistle. You have already faced many dangers here, and I am confident there are more threats to come. You have saved us with these smokeless fires. We now have water when we would certainly be out, and if I made the fire, there would be smoke and the Nuboku would see. I am proud of the way your mind works, Reed Whistle. It is different, and in that difference, you give us a chance at surviving. Please don't mistake difference that gives us a fighting chance for weakness."

Reed Whistle nodded, although his focus remained on the fire.

Wild Heart stood. She lifted her sword from the boat and returned, setting it in his hands.

"Draw it," she said.

Reed Whistle did as commanded. He pulled the bronze blade from its horn and leather scabbard, marveling at its feel in his hands. The curved hilt fit snugly in his larger hand in a way that it always had at least another finger of room in hers. The pommel, a lump of ivory riveted between horns, curled around his last finger. The guard was simple, being two pieces of polished horn riveted to a spike of ivory which curved out away from his hand. The Merchant said it's shape would help catch enemy swords. Reed Whistle turned it about, eyes captivated by how it played with the light. While it wasn't the striking gold coloration it was when she bought it, Wild Heart preferred it as its current brown patina. It looked more honest. No posturing, just a weapon with a honed edge and strong core.

The longer he held it, the straighter he sat.

"How does it feel?"

"It fits perfectly," he whispered.

"Then it's yours. Don't throw your life away for a southern king who will never risk anything himself. Fight for your family, Reed Whistle. Fight for us."

He took his eyes off the sword for the first time since holding it. He lowered the blade, setting it beside him, before taking Wild Heart's hand. "I will, grandmother. I promise."

"Something's coming," said Owl Eyes from up on watch.

"The sailboat?" signed Reed Whistle, raising the sword once more.

"No. Boar-camels. Many of them, maybe two hands, and they're coming this way."

***

A foul stench hung in the air. A primal musk blended with urine and vomit. Despite wanting nothing more than to rest a moment before, Wild Heart was quick to lead them in packing up. The last thing she wanted to do was share space with boar-camels.

Reed Whistle couldn't find an ideal rock to put out the fire, but working together, he and Wild Heart smothered it with enough mud and rocks that he was confident it wouldn't leave much smoke. Certainly not enough to give them away in the early evening light.

They backed up the canoe, doing as best as they could to keep an eye on the boar-camels and maintain as many islets and channels between them and the herd as possible. The beasts meandered, ripping up vegetation as they went.

Wild Heart had never gotten close to these beasts. Any time they were spotted by others fishing, they made haste back to shore. She had never gotten a good look at them. As they rowed, keeping the pace slow to minimize any sound, Wild Heart got a more clear view of the beasts than she had ever hoped to.

It was difficult to tell since they were partially submerged, but Wild Heart was confident the smallest one would be around her height at the shoulder when accounting for their long legs, and the larger bulls half again as tall and much more than double the mass. Their heads, far longer and larger than they had any right to be, were usually slung low, but when elevated, the similarities to the small marsh camels some villagers kept for meat was much more evident. They grunted and belched as they walked through the shallows. Wild Heart was thankful their canoe was downwind so the beasts didn't smell them, but the scent of the small herd was ripe, overpowering, and threatened to make her sick.

One of the bulls inflated his tongue, letting it roll in the wind for a moment before drawing it back in.

Wild Heart had never seen a creature so horrid.

The wind blew strongest from the southwest. To avoid their scent getting back to the herd, they rowed to the northwest much more than Wild Heart preferred. It meant taking them back toward the main river, but she wanted as much distance between them and the boar-camels as possible before circling back around, and rowing deeper into the maze to the south would put them directly upwind of the beasts. She had been wary of them before, but now that she saw their size, that the bulls were easily as wide if not wider than the canoe, Wild Heart wanted to be as far away from them as possible.

Once the excitement was over, Wild Heart was overtaken by a wave of exhaustion. Her head hung low. She just wanted to stop. To rest. Even a quick nap would be ideal, but she kept rowing. Kept moving.

Mosquitoes were out in force in the early evening air, even with the eastbound breeze. Wild Heart realized with all the in and out of water, they might have lost some of their balm. She reapplied the repellant to the children, dabbed some of the wretched black onion oil to her wrists, and made sure Reed Whistle and Cherry Blossom had some too.

Owl Eyes let out a scream and pointed back.

Wild Heart turned to where she pointed.

Barreling toward them was the Nuboku boat. Their mast had been somehow lowered, perhaps to mask their approach. Again the amber-haired man stood on the prow, beckoning his men and grinning with a reviling intensity. They were still around fifty span away, only spotted because Owl Eyes happened to be facing them, but closing fast. With four strong men paddling, it would be a matter of time before they caught up.

Cherry Blossom and Reed Whistle paddled hard, but when Wild Heart glanced back, it was clear that this was going to end poorly for them. Quickly.

"Turn right!" said Wild Heart, paddling hard on the left side.

Her daughter did as requested, but called out "They're closing in!" as she completed a turn. "Should we be winding like this?"

"We're a lot more agile and I think their boat is deeper."

"Aren't the boar-camels back this way?" asked Reed Whistle between strokes.

"I hope so," said Wild Heart.

As they moved, Wild Heart kept the Nuboku in her sights. They did struggle in the winding paths, having to take longer routes, but they were much faster, making up for any lost time. Wild Heart's arms strained from the effort and rising tension.

The Nuboku were gaining ground.

At Reed Whistle's indication, they passed through a gap that was quite shallow. Their boat barely cleared it, and there was no other passage on either side that Wild Heart could see.

After further rowing, with Cherry Blossom keeping an excellent sense of their position, they came near the islet they rested at before. At first Wild Heart didn't recognize it since they came at it from the opposite side, but the small trail of smoke confirmed. Although she knew she should be glad the beasts had moved on, a part of her was disappointed.

Splashes behind them drew Wild Heart's attention. The Nuboku must have somehow cleared the path. Not long after, they came around another islet.

Now there was only open water between them.

The leader screamed in primal delight, cutting over the water. The Nuboku raised both arms as his men launched their boat forward.

A guttural bellow cut off his scream, and the Nuboku's face melted from glee to horror.

Wild Heart barely managed to raise her oar in deterrence as a boar-camel surged past them from behind an islet. It snapped up at her, the jaws wider than her torso clamping shut with a jolting clap, but continued on toward the Nuboku.

Others barreled out from behind a nearby islet. It seemed they hadn't gotten as far as Wild Heart feared. Although most raced toward the Nuboku, that relief was quickly replaced by one of the bulls charging their canoe.

Cherry Blossom harried it with her oar. The bull grunted as she struck his snout. She landed another blow, but before she could withdraw, it bit the oar. The wood cracked, and Wild Heart recoiled like it was one of their bones. The beast tossed the oar aside.

It lunged.

Cherry Blossom leaped off the back of the canoe, diving into the water on the opposite side as the boar-camel. He roared, flashing tusks longer than Wild Heart's hand. Although she considered the obsidian knife sheathed at her belt, she kept hold of her oar. There was no killing this beast in her future, but the reach of the oar might keep it away from the children.

Not that it had worked for Cherry Blossom, but the premise made sense in the moment.

Cherry Blossom was on the opposite side of the canoe, keeping it between her and the beast.

Nettle Top started to cry, but Owl Eyes urged him to be quiet. Her tone was gentle. Trusting that Owl Eyes could keep them hushed, Wild Heart covered them with a flick of the nearest blanket and aimed her oar at the boar-camel.

The beast was thrashing about, posturing with a wide-gape display. His movements had knocked the canoe's rear away, and they now had their full length facing him. The water was shallow enough for Cherry Blossom to stand, and she stopped the boat from spinning further. At first she thought Cherry Blossom was trying to get back on the boat, but quickly realized her daughter's intentions.

With its full length opposing the boar-camel, it looked like they were much larger. Far more imposing.

He took a step back and yawned, then backed up another pace.

Wild Heart was thankful that the apparent size of the boat was intimidating, but she didn't want to yell. The rest of the herd was otherwise occupied, but she didn't want to draw their attention.

Another bull and many cows had mobbed the Nuboku boat. One of the men had been pulled off, and three of the cows were actively dismembering him. One cow had a massive spear in her side, and tried to get away, but the bull on that side attacked her as she fled, leading to another cow joining in mauling the injured beast. As she watched, another cow lunged at the rear Nuboku who had his attention forward, grabbing him by the leg and dragging him behind the boat and out of view. His scream of fear and fury cut over the din of the assault, but was quickly silenced. Two other cows abandoned the boat, quick to participate in the attack against the man most recently dragged off.

A series of cracks rang out as one of the cows had bitten the side of their boat and was chewing through the rim.

The lead Nuboku let out another scream, this one full of rage. Wild Heart tried to see if he had been grabbed, but before she could process, their bull charged the canoe.

Wild Heart swung at its snout with her full strength, but it just bounced off. The beast didn't land his initial bite, but did impact the canoe with his face then shoulder, shoving them forward.

After stabilizing, Wild Heart noticed Reed Whistle had drawn the bronze sword. With the beast now facing him, any attack would result in it lunging at him.

With a yell, Wild Heart hit the beast's shoulder with the butt of her paddle. It wouldn't do much, but at least she could pull the boar-camel's attention back to her.

The plan worked. He stepped back and groaned, snarling to expose his fangs, and swung his head about.

As soon as there was an opening, Reed Whistle lunged and thrust the sword into the base of the boar-camel's neck.

He bellowed furiously, twisting about. Reed Whistle let go of the blade.

Smart boy.

The boar-camel backed off, shaking back and forth. The blade was lodged in halfway to the hilt where its meaty neck met its shoulder. Blood seeped into the water, staining the marshes around it red.

Still the beast would not die.

While the beast struggled, Wild Heart and Reed Whistle leaned left, and Wild Heart offered her daughter a hand to get back into the boat.

"Are you hurt?" asked Wild Heart.

Cherry Blossom shook her head. "Pass me your oar. We're getting out of here."

Wild Heart nodded. She passed off the oar, then checked on the children. Nettle Top had silent tears on his cheeks, but when asked if they were hurt, both said they were fine. She reassured them that their mother and brother were well, then covered them up again.

The bull continued to bleed into the water, repeatedly trying to turn and bite the sword impaled in its neck. Although it just tried to kill everyone she loved and still posed a significant threat, she couldn't help but feel a pang of sympathy as it looked about, confused and in pain.

A harrowing scream called her focus back to the Nuboku.

Another creature was in the fray: a strange giant hare. It had fangs on either side of its pointed incisors, culminating in a ferocious snarl. It was perched where the leader stood before and was hissing down at the nearest cow. Only one Nuboku remained, and although this creature was on his boat, he seemed more concerned with the beats that had bitten off several chunks of their boat and started to sink it.

With another scream, which sounded entirely too human for Wild Heart's liking, the giant hare leaped on top of the nearest cow and bit at the base of its neck. She cried out, but couldn't shake the creature chewing into her. Finally she fled, and the hare leaped back onto the boat.

At the cries of his herd, the bull that had attacked their canoe turned and roared. Ignoring the sword in his neck, he charged.

They were around eight span away, but his charge was swift, and he closed the distance quickly.

Not wasting the opening, Cherry Blossom and Reed Whistle turned their canoe to loop around the islet they stayed at before so they could continue on. It would mean a bit of back tracking, but if it got them away from the scene, it would be worth it.

Wild Heart looked back in time to see the bull impact the Nuboku boat.

Rather than avoid, the hare creature hopped over the bite range of the bull and landed on its back. With a paw it grasped the hilt of the sword. While the boar-camel thrashed about, trying to shake it off, the hare creature began to stand. Wild Heart struggled to comprehend what she was seeing in the movement, but it looked like the creature was losing its fur.

The creature grabbed the boar-camel bull by its mane and withdrew the sword. It thrust down, then repeated the process. With a heartbreaking bellow, the bull slumped into the water. The other members of its herd began to scatter, leaving the bull to his fate.

Just before they passed out of view, Wild Heart saw the creature fully stand on the corpse of the boar-camel.

The creature was now a man.

The leader of the Nuboku.

He looked directly at her with the same yellow eyes he had as a beast.

Although he grinned once more, flashing those fangs that would forever haunt her, his scowling eyes and claw-curled fingers spoke of raw fury.

***

No words were spoken as they paddled.

They looped around the melee and rowed north. Although she wasn't positive, Wild Heart was increasingly certain that the Nuboku had been tracking them by scent. If their leader was a skin-changer, sniffing them out was surely an ability he possessed.

She tried to remember all she could about skin-changers.

A traveler told them of warriors in the forests who could take the form of saber-toothed panthers. The men who went out to gather fish on the coast said there were dolphins and seals that could take off their skin to reveal that they were beautiful women underneath, and that they were always excited to make love, but Wild Heart had until this time assumed that was a story told to make their wives jealous. There were also stories of witches who could turn into any number of creatures, or turn those who wronged them into pigs.

There were no stories about men who could turn into giant marsh hares.

Also, and more importantly, none of the stories talked about how to kill skin-changers.

She had to assume that they could be killed conventionally. If they were impossible to kill, surely that would be part of the lore.

All they had now was her obsidian knife.

It was said that obsidian was a ward of malevolent spells. That it was so sharp it could cut magic, whatever that meant. Maybe the magic that allowed him to switch between two bodies would also be vulnerable to the material.

If so, she was thankful that she invested in the obsidian blade rather than bronze or iron.

They crossed the main river and continued into the marshes of the north. She wished she had a map of some kind, but would just have to go off of memories. From what the other villagers said, the swamp carried on all the way inland toward the mountains, which would take months to reach. She had no intention of leading her family that far. No, they just needed to get two or three days deeper into the marshes. Maybe five to be confident they wouldn't be stumbled upon. From there, they would need to find a solid islet on which to build an elevated hut. She didn't know how to make a hut, but between the five of them, she was confident they could put together a good home.

It was getting dark. The sun had fallen under the horizon, and most of the sky was pink. Soon they wouldn't be able to see at all.

A large island with a fairly steep bank showed promise. Three trees, one of which was dead, stood tall amongst the low brush. It would be difficult for anything to climb up and reach them. There was a sloped bank on the north shore, which enabled them to park the canoe.

From there, they unloaded everything. They were too exhausted to fully drag the canoe up, but brought the front up most of the way and flipped it to keep any critters out. It was a clumsy process, but at least it would dry out. Reed Whistle tethered their food baskets to the branch of one of the three mahogany trees, whose roots seemed to be holding up most of the island in its elevated state. Wild Heart and Cherry Blossom lay their blankets down over the ferns and grasses dominating the small islands interior, establishing as close to a comfortable bed as they could hope for. Although the sky showed no sign of rain, Reed Whistle still set up their canvas blanket overhead, pointing out that it would collect dew overnight which would be safe to drink. After making sure everyone had another round of insect repellant, and leaving the wretched jar on the upwind side of their camp site, Wild Heart urged her family to sleep.

For all her exhaustion earlier, Wild Heart felt alert. She volunteered to take the first watch at the highest point of the island, especially since her daughter and grandson had done most of the rowing. Cherry Blossom kissed Wild Heart on the cheek, thanking her for saving her babies.

"Of course," Wild Heart said, holding her daughter's hand tightly. "They're my babies too. As are you. Now get some rest."

With her two youngest wrapped in an embrace, Cherry Blossom was asleep after three deep breaths. The excitement had caught up to the little ones, and both were asleep soon after.

"I'm sorry I lost your sword, Grandmother," signed Reed Whistle as he sat beside her.

Wild Heart shook her head. "You didn't lose my sword. You chose to give up your sword. If you hadn't done that, it might have damaged our canoe to the point that it couldn't float, and if you had held on, it would have taken you with it. You were wise to let go. That was a good instinct. I would choose you over a sword, young man. I'm glad you chose the same."

Reed Whistle sat with her for a time, silently pondering what she signed. He may not have the sword, but he still sat taller than she was used to. It warmed her heart to see. More than anything, that inspired her to carry on.

"Now get some rest, young man. We only have two oars now, so you're going to need your strength."

Reed Whistle smiled and kissed her on the forehead. "Yes, Grandmother. Get me up when you're ready to sleep. I want Mother to get as much sleep as possible."

Wild Heart nodded in agreement.

She was glad to hear his breathing level quickly.

Time trailed along without any sense of grounding. The elevated position she was in helped Wild Heart see clearly in every direction. The three mahogany were the only large foliage, and they were so tall that their branches didn't obscure much, although there were two shorter trees thick with leaves that made the southwest a bit hard to see. She leaned against one of the trees, scanning about and making sure to check behind her tree and on the other side of the two mahogany saplings.

The cast of creatures was entirely different at night. By the light of the half moon and countless stars, she spotted many forms moving about. In the village, night was a time of quiet, but she could always hear birds and insects singing over the wall. Now, it was vibrant. Maybe she was just paying closer attention, but it seemed the creatures at night were even louder than during the day.

A dire heron meandered about to the south. These toothed birds only hunted small fish, so she wasn't concerned despite its length exceeding their canoe. As it walked, it either looked down with wide eyes or felt with its long snout. At several points it lunged forward, and a few times it came up with something, although fish or crustacean she couldn't tell.

At first a bellow frightened her, but Wild Heart relaxed when she spotted the crocodile. The reptile lounged on an islet to the east. It was much larger than the one she spotted before, maybe three span long. It didn't stay for long, and after a few more bellows, crawled back into the water. Wild Heart heard more calls further west. A congregation of crocodiles. They didn't sound angry or frightened, just calling to each other. What did crocodiles talk about? Her thoughts ruminated on the subject for a while.

A nauseating pulse rumbled from the north took Wild Heart from her thoughts.

By the generous light of the moon, a truly massive form caught Wild Heart's attention. Around forty span away; close enough to see clearly but not so close as to be an immediate threat, was a lumbering creature. At first it was still, and she mistook it for a stand of small trees, but as it moved and turned slightly east, she saw it with greater clarity.

In basic form it resembled a boar-camel, with high shoulders, long yet sturdy limbs, and an enormous head sporting broad cheek horns and a long snout. In size, however, a boar-camel might come to this creature's knee. Although it waded through the shallows, the beast must stand nearly three span at its bulky shoulder hump.

She had heard stories of these creatures: Bokodu. They were gods of the hoofed beasts; great fortresses of muscle and rage. Settlements had been leveled and entire families consumed in moments. For all that reputation, the bokodu meandered about with the disposition of a gentle giant. Although she could barely hear its bellows, the deep noise echoed in her joints and turned her stomach.

A great yawn flashed great fangs in the moonlight, and its gape was so wide it looked ready to swallow the moon.

The bokodu paused in its steady trek, turning to Wild Heart and their island.

Wild Heart tensed. The frogs and insects that hummed before were silent as death. Her heart beat rapidly in her chest. Her hand shifted to the hilt of her obsidian knife, for all the good it would do her.

With a rumbling snort the god of beasts turned and continued its southward march.

Wild Heart's breathing didn't slow until it was far out of sight.

For all her terror, seeing a god felt like a blessing. A reminder that the wilderness was stronger than any witch or army that might threaten her family. Out here, all were at the mercy of the gods.

Movement from the southwest, where the saplings obstructed her view, called her attention. Wild Heart stood and looked, beginning to draw her knife.

A spur rat crawled through the ferns toward her. Although at the size of an infant they weren't terribly dangerous, their bites could hurt and the spurs on their feet had a painful venom. She mock charged it and the creature scurried off, hopping off the island and swimming away.

She looked about, getting a full view with the advantage of standing.

It took a moment to spot the dire heron: it had meandered far to the east by that point. There were several small marsh camels grazing on an islet to the far north that she hadn't noticed before. Frog songs came to a crescendo but of course she couldn't spot any.

With a deep breath she returned to her vantage point. She was beginning to tire, but wanted to carry on, at least a while longer.

The tree she leaned against was the dead mahogany. Its trunk felt like two smaller trees growing into one another, so the surface was flat and comfortable to sit against. In its state of affairs, with no leaves on the gnarled branches, she could easily see the stars overhead. A memory of sitting under the sky with her brothers came to mind. Tide Maker said there were pictures that you could make with the star patterns, and they each came up with a few characters. It was around the same time of year, and she spotted all of them up ahead.

A fish leaping out of the water. A hand. A dancer with long hair. The marsh panther leaping, if you were generous about how long a marsh panther's body was. She smiled as she thought back on them joking with each other. It wasn't long after that night that all three brothers were taken by the Nuboku and none returned. Emerald Finder was so young when they took him away. Five or six years before anyone could call him a man, but the Nuboku didn't care. They put a spear in his hand and threw him to the demons all the same.

Wild Heart wished she could have saved them. Taken them away. Her mother just looked on coldly.

"Stop crying," she had said. "This is why we have sons, Wild Heart. They go to retake our home, and we stay to make more sons. You don't want to live in this swamp forever, do you?"

Wild Heart did not miss her mother when she died, but she did now. Was she afraid, when they took away her babies? Did she cry when Wild Heart wasn't around? Did she hate the Nuboku?

Maybe she did. She was always hard as stone, but Wild Heart remembered the relief on her mother's face when Wild Heart had a girl, and when Reed Whistle was born, she hadn't looked proud. She looked sad. Wild Heart never forgave her mother for letting the Nuboku take her brothers, but perhaps she had been too cruel to her mother. After all, her mother made sure Wild Heart knew how to fight. She made her strong, always making her stay and finish extra chores after the other children got to go home. Made sure she could power and steer a canoe, that she inherited one and could care for it, and that she could teach her daughter and her own grandchildren these skills too.

Her mother couldn't save her sons, but as Wild Heart looked to the sky, hot tears clouded her vision as she realized every act she thought cruel was her mother preparing her for this journey.

Giving her every tool she needed for this moment.

Even after all these years, an old woman herself now, Wild Heart had much to learn.

"I'm sorry, mother," she whispered into the wind.

When she looked down, the grinning visage of the Nuboku skin-changer stopped her heart. Before she could inhale to scream, he planted a firm hand over her mouth. His eyes flashed red in the light of the stars above.

Agony punched through her abdomen. A hollow thunk marked his weapon passing through her and sinking into the dead wood she leaned against.

His grin widened. The hand over her mouth was too strong to draw breath from mouth or nose. Although she tried to struggle, to make some sound, all strength leaked from her wound, and she couldn't even raise her hand to reach for her obsidian knife.

The Nuboku leaned in close.

"This is an excellent sword."

Hatred burned through the pain. It was her last thought before the world faded to black.

Then nothing.

***

Cherry Blossom awakened with a start as a hand covered her mouth.

Before she could scream, her eyes adjusted to see Reed Whistle's face, an expression of urgency on his face.

He pointed out the side of their makeshift tent.

A figure crouched before her mother, the moon perfectly silhouetting the sword in Wild Heart's gut.

Although she wanted to scream, to charge, Cherry Blossom knew they had to be careful. It was paramount to protect Owl Eyes and Nettle Top. As Reed Whistle moved, she got the children awake, urging them to be silent.

Before she could stop him, Cherry Blossom saw her son step out of the tent, his motion silent as a marsh panther, an oar in hand.

With both hands on the oar, Reed Whistle slunk forward.

The figure turned, his eyes catching the bright starlight in a flash of red. He stood tall, his form imposing and rippling in silhouette as he loomed over Reed Whistle from the high ground and what must be another full head of height and far more broad.

Undaunted, Reed Whistle choked up on the oar's haft and swung it like a blade at the torso of his grandmother's killer. A quick hand from the skin-changer caught the oar just below the paddle, but Reed Whistle didn't slow his advance, bringing the butt of the oar across the skin-changer's knee with a satisfying crack.

The skin-changer screamed in shock and pain. Reed Whistle twisted the grip of his left hand and shoved it up toward the skin-changer's jaw. The man grabbed Reed Whistle's hand, stopping the impact even as his knee was buckled.

Cherry Blossom was torn. A part of her wanted to get the children away, but she couldn't abandon Reed Whistle against a much larger and more experienced foe.

"Hide," she said to Owl Eyes. Without waiting for confirmation, she turned back to help her son.

Reed Whistle and the Nuboku grappled with the oar. Although he was hurt, the skin-changer pressed down on the oar. Rather than seeking to kill him outright, the Nuboku seemed more interested in dominating. He had an opening twice to reach over the oar and strike her son's unguarded face, but he didn't take it.

He was testing her son, and he seemed increasingly impressed.

At least his focus seemed direct.

After a moment of searching the ground, Cherry Blossom found a suitable rock that filled her hand. The way they now stood, she didn't have a clear shot at the Nuboku's knee, but if their grapple could only shift to the left...

Movement behind them drew Cherry Blossom's attention. With her son and his attacker in front of her, it was difficult to see for sure, but it looked like her mother's body was moving.

Rising.

If there was another of these vile brutes, she and Reed Whistle would have to end the skin-changer immediately.

Just as Cherry Blossom looked to see where she might get an opening against the Nuboku, he spun the oar about, which twisted Reed Whistle's hands. He grabbed both wrists with a quick grab, tossed the oar aside, and spun her son about, wrapping an arm tight around his throat in a full hold.

The Nuboku looked down at Cherry Blossom, wearing that harrowing grin of his.

"I was sent to kill all of you and bring your bodies back to be mutilated and displayed as an example of what happens when people flee conscription. Your trick with the camels lost me all four of my men. Well, Kagu was alive, but I left him. He was only slowing me down. I came here ready to kill you all, but I've had a change of opinion. Your boy here shows true potential. And you," he grinned down at Cherry Blossom. "I expect there could be many more fighters in you yet. If you agree to come back with me, I will ensure the boy is given good rank in Gurdatemik's Ocean March, and as long as you carry the child I give you before we depart, you will have good standing in your wretched little village."

The Nuboku kept talking, his drawl assertive and smug, but Cherry Blossom's focus was entirely on her mother behind him.

Wild Heart's body was jerking up the trunk of the dead mahogany she was impaled against. It was as though she were crawling using her shoulders. The sword was still embedded in her torso. A dark line trailed along the trunk.

Her body settled where the trunk branched. Fingers of bark began to draw her into its form, raising her arms to be absorbed into the two main branches. Although her head was limp, it was drawn back against the central branch, which flared out from her skull like the antlers of stags on every illustration of the motherland.

Wild Heart's branching head turned down, suddenly looking very much alive.

The Nuboku had stopped talking. Although the light was low, he looked annoyed that Cherry Blossom wasn't paying attention to him. He turned back while still holding Reed Whistle.

Both bodies slacked when they took in the sight behind them.

Dead Tree Grandmother's trunk split, and one section stepped out, bending like a clawed foot. The other followed, and she reached forward with a gnarled branch hand.

The Nuboku threw Reed Whistle to the ground.

Before he could dodge, Cherry Blossom struck his knee in the same spot as her son hit before, throwing her full weight into the blow.

He howled in agony and buckled just before the branch grabbed him.

Cherry Blossom crawled to Reed Whistle. He gasped for air, but as soon as she confirmed he was alright, he was already guiding her back and away from the fight.

The Nuboku struggled. As he fought, his body changed into that of a long-eared creature, using powerful legs to scrape at the branch. His paws also clawed at the hand lifting him off the ground. Her wooden form creaked and groaned as it acclimated to movement.

Just when it seemed the creature might wriggle free, he unleashed a harrowing scream: one of the branches had pierced his leg and grew further, wrapping him in a lock. Another impaled his gut, punching out his spine to reveal Wild Heart's obsidian knife. The creature cried out and bit the branch. He continued to struggle through the torture, even as his legs became immobile from a broken spine.

Cherry Blossom and Reed Whistle got to the other side of the tent. She couldn't see Owl Eyes or Nettle Top. Panic made it hard to draw breath.

When it appeared she deemed his torment sufficient, Dead Tree Grandmother grasped his torso with her other arm and tore the Nuboku in half. Viscera spilled onto the island below. Both branches gripped tight, crackling the bones of both halves for good measure. When the horrid ordeal was over, she extended each arm on opposite sides of the island, opening the branches to let his remains slump into the marsh.

Although this was at least partially her mother, and it had obviously acted in their aid and defense, Cherry Blossom was still cautious around the being standing before her. The form creaked and swayed as if not quite comfortable in its body.

"Is it safe?"

Cherry Blossom's heart melted when she heart Owl Eye's voice from just outside the tent. She looked up at Dead Tree Grandmother, taking a deep breath. "Yes, baby. It's safe."

A pile of blankets flipped, and Owl Eyes and Nettle Top rushed out into Cherry Blossom's arms. She covered them in kisses.

"Whoa."

Owl Eyes stared up at Dead Tree Grandmother. Still standing on the highest part of their little island, she stood easily three span in height before her antlers were accounted for. Although Cherry Blossom couldn't be sure, it seemed more of her mother's body had been absorbed by the tree, and only the vague outline of her body pressed against the bark now encasing her. Her face was obscured by height and shadow. The sword was still deep in her chest, with a trail of blood down to her roots.

Although Cherry Blossom was afraid, Nettle Top barely able to look, and Reed Whistle looking on edge, Owl Eyes advanced without hesitation.

She waved up at the being.

"Hello, Grandmother."

One trunk raised from the soil, roots curling in like bird toes before planting a pace away from Owl Eyes. Both trunks bent, again articulating like the legs of a bird, lowering Dead Tree Grandmother to be close to Owl Eyes.

"Hello, little one. You hid well."

Her voice was dry and strained, but definitely belonged to Cherry Blossom's mother. She couldn't sign with her hands in branches, but her words were articulate enough. This confirmation welled tears in Cherry Blossom's eyes.

"Are you hurt, Mother?" Cherry Blossom asked, picking up Nettle Top and closing the distance. Reed Whistle followed close behind. As she closed in she saw her mother's face clearly despite thin sun-bleached bark growing over it.

"I don't feel much of anything," Wild Heart replied. There was no emotion or inflection in her voice, and Cherry Blossom couldn't tell if her mother was sparing them any painful details, or if she really felt nothing. The bloody sword in her chest and contorted way her body was consumed by the tree certainly looked agonizing.

"Are you dead?" asked Owl Eyes. "Did you sacrifice yourself?"

Wild Heart smiled. "I suppose. I didn't mean to, but it seems to have worked out that way."

"Are you still you? You seem like you."

"I feel like me. At least my thoughts are my own. This body feels strange, and I feel... many others. I don't think I'm alone in this form, or at least not the only one to inhabit one like it in the marsh. I can also feel many of the plants around us, or at least they are communicating with me. I am both me, but also Dead Tree Grandmother. It's all very confusing."

Owl Eyes lifted her feet off the ferns she was currently standing on. "It sounds confusing."

Wild Heart chuckled before looking up to Nettle Top. The boy looked frightened, but at least was looking at his grandmother, taking her in.

"Good job listening to your sister, little one. You were wise to hide. I'm proud of you."

He nodded, still looking upon her with confusion and disbelief.

Wild Heart turned to Reed Whistle. Confusion then recollection crossed her face. At first Cherry Blossom feared she might be losing her awareness, but she instead reached a branch toward her chest and withdrew the bronze sword. Fresh blood trailed down her chest, but she paid it no mind. The branches turned the hilt toward him.

Reed Whistle wordlessly took the sword, replying with a resolved nod.

Finally Wild Heart looked to Cherry Blossom. She produced the obsidian knife and sheath, and set it in Cherry Blossom's hand.

"I love you, my child. Thank you for trusting me."

"Always, mother."

Wild Heart smiled, then addressed her family at large. "I can feel where a haven is. It's like another being in my mind remembers. I can't truly explain it, but I know where it is." A branch reached over and flipped their canoe, setting it beside the tent. "Get everything and everyone inside. I will take us there."

Cherry Blossom did as her mother asked, directing the children in packing everything up. The canvas was rolled, food gathered, and onion oil sealed. Soon the boat was set, they all sat in the hull, and Cherry Blossom nodded up to her mother.

"Ready."

The sensation of branches wrapping around the bow and stern was strange.

Being lifted off the ground was stranger.

Owl Eyes cried out in delight. Nettle Top nestled close to Cherry Blossom, and Reed Whistle laughed nervously. It was odd enough to be lifted, but the rocking of the boat was particularly unnerving as Dead Tree Grandmother carried them east, deeper into the marshes.

***

Being in this new body was a confounding blend of peculiar and making perfect sense.

She was still herself, but it was as though she had to ask to move her legs each time she took a step. The body always responded, but it was an odd feeling. By morning it felt natural, but she was still aware that it should be strange.

For the most part, they were ignored by the fauna. Creatures gave them a wide berth, and a herd of marsh-rhinos cleared out of her path, but mostly they were just treated as another beast. Just another creature in the marsh. Owl Eyes was enamored with all she could see from the boat. For much of the following day she sat on Wild Heart's shoulder, secured by branches that twisted and bent to form a seat and strap around her waist.

After two days of steady walking, with occasional breaks to boil water or get their feet under them, Wild Heart brought her family to the place she felt called to.

A haven.

It was an elevated platform supported on posts with a surrounding wall around a span high. A dock was built outside a small gate. All the wood was overgrown with moss and vegetation.

Wild Heart was tall enough to peer inside.

There was no sign of any recent occupation, even though the settlement looked like it could house several families. A well was at its center, but surely it would no longer be safe to drink without maintenance. Several birds nested inside, and a pair of herons hissed up at Wild Heart and her family before taking off.

"What happened to the people?" asked Reed Whistle. "I don't see any sign of a struggle."

"Maybe disease?" Cherry Blossom said, nodding toward the well.

"Possibly," said Wild Heart. "I feel many have lived here, but it has been many generations since this was called a home. My memory of other Dead Tree Grandmothers are weak. Blurred, but I think this is meant to be a place of rest. A haven, not a home. We need community. I do not think we will be safe back in Bramble Hills, but there are many other villages, and those deeper inland are not likely to face conscription for Ocean Walks. But if we want this to be our home, at least for a time, it will need to be maintained. First step will be clean water. Termites will have compromised much of the wood, so we will likely need to make repairs."

Wild Heart set the canoe inside the outer wall. Her family piled out, stepping carefully on the floorboards. Reed Whistle led the way, sword out in case any beasts lived in the huts, paying close attention to the path ahead. His vision scanned, and Wild Heart imagined he was already assessing where the worst damage was and where his repairs would have to begin. Cherry Blossom held a child's hand in each of hers as they followed Reed Whistle.

Some part of her mind remembered that there were axes in the settlement. In a chest near where Reed Whistle now explored. Their hafts would be weathered, but the heads in good condition, and could be used to cut planks from the nearby mahogany stands.

Everything they needed, at least for now, was here.

As the wind picked up, Wild Heart turned east.

Her family was safe, at least for now, and they were equipped to endure whatever came their way. From this foundation they could build a happy life. It wouldn't be as easy as living in Bramble Hills, but their lives were their own.

The next step she took was strained. Difficult to move as her joints were hardened. Feeling her roots extend and spread through the soil.

Some part of Wild Heart knew she wouldn't have this body forever.

It pained her to acknowledge what was happening, but at least she had it long enough to bring her family here.

Her own mother had made her strong, and that strength had prepared her family to make a life here.

"Thank you," she said to the wind, to both her mother, and to Dead Tree Grandmother for loaning her form so Wild Heart's family could be given their best chance at survival.

With a smile on her face, Wild Heart exhaled and closed her eyes.

A moment passed, and as she faced the wind, the great tree became still.

Tides of Restoration

4

Tides of Restoration

Tides of Restoration

Yesi took a deep breath and dived off her canoe.

The impact of the water was cold. Waves rolled her about, throwing off her sense of direction. She tasted salt that slipped through her lips, and wished she could relish the sensation, but there was work to be done.

A few kicks pulled her below the surf, and she spotted her target: the cable of her crab trap.

She took hold of the rope and pulled. Something caught, and the trap didn't move.

Another wave rolled overhead, and Yesi felt the undertow draw her down. She struggled to right herself, but the next wave was soon after. With a snarl, Yesi pulled once more. Again, nothing.

Her chest began to strain. Twice more she pulled. No progress was made. She knew she should go up for air, but her focus now locked on completing the task.

Tension built to pain. Yesi released the cable and shot up for-

Another wave barreled overhead, and she was sent tumbling. In a panic, Yesi raised an arm and kicked hard.

Her hand struck something hard. Reef! The cut darkened the water around. By the time she realized she had dived down instead of up, Yesi's chest felt fit to burst. As she planted a foot on the reef, hoping to use it to launch up, the undertow took her feet out from under her, and she was again sent spiraling.

A silhouette passed overhead as Yesi opened her eyes.

The shock clipped her last threads of control, and Yesi took a deep breath.

The world went dark.

***

Force on her chest forced consciousness back to Yesi, and she gasped. Cold water lapped at her feet. After an agonizing fit of coughs, her vision came into blurred focus.

A backlit figure with a face white as rubber, dark brow, and striking blue eyes shook her to attention. Although the hair was loosely tied back, locks of copper curls escaped to frame a beautiful face. The expression was tender. Cautious.

The stranger raised a hand with webbing up to the last joint and brushed aside a strand of Yesi's own hair. The gesture was done with such care. Yesi's emotions had quickly shifted from panic to attraction, but she knew part of it was simply the rush of terror and embarrassment after nearly making herself drown to pull in a trap that at best had a dozen crabs.

"Are you alright?" asked the stranger, her voice smooth with few lilts.

Yesi noticed the sharp teeth behind pale lips, recalled the webbed fingers, and now that she was aware, a hard rubbery body pressed against her left leg. "You're a Khalorim," she whispered. "A mermaid."

"Yes," said the stranger with a slight laugh. "Of the Sunrise Reef clan. My lineage has the aspect of dolphin."

Sunrise Reef Clan, lead by Storm Eater, a sea goddess said to be ten thousand years old, and one of the first daughters of Melrahim. The Sunrise Reef clan were the merfolk who lived in these waters before the Night of Last Song, when they and all other Khalorim fled north.

"Who are you? What is... what is your name? I am Yesi."

She smiled, tilting her head to the side. "I do not think you can say it fully. Not with how your voice works. Coral Under Moon in your tongue will suffice. Coral if that is too much."

"What do you mean with how my voice works?" Yesi said, clearing her throat. "Is there something wrong with my voice? I promise I don't usually sound this coarse I... I did just drown. Gratitude for saving me, I should say. Apologies for that not being my first- the first thing I-" her next words were lost in a cough.

"Your voice is lovely, Yesi. I apologize if I offended. My people talk with our minds as much as our voices, as some of us cannot speak due to the anatomy of our aspects. There are components of my name in our language that you will not hear and cannot say."

Yesi enjoyed being under this beautiful stranger, but realized it might seem a bit forward. She also wanted to be closer. Her scent, which was of salt and sand, was strong with a pungent allure. Each inhalation made Yesi feel closer to the sea.

"I think your boat is still out there," said Coral. "I should retrieve it before Melrahim makes a claim."

Coral raised the hand that supported her body being over Yesi's. The force of it planting into the sand on the other side of her sent another rush through Yesi, and with surprising aptitude given her form, Coral crawled back toward the surf. They were at the edge of tide, and Yesi got only a quick look at her savior's full body before she dived into the waves.

From the waist up, she was built much like a woman of a strong, voluptuous figure. From the hips down, she resembled the yellow-sided dolphins which often played in the waves, with a smooth form tapering to broad flukes and a dorsal fin where a woman's tailbone would be. Her skin throughout her body resembled that of a dolphin, sleek with the look of wet rubber, and colored dark on her back, white on her belly, with streaks of grey and gold on her sides.

On land, she was powerful if a bit clumsy.

Once she was in the water, Coral Under Moon erupted out toward the canoe like an arrow from a mighty bow.

Amidst the turmoil, her boat must have flipped despite the outrigger. Coral gathered everything floating on the surface, and dived to gather any kit which sank. She even set the crab trap in Yesi's hull.

Although attraction was perhaps at the front of Yesi's mind, there was a deeper and far greater yearning than simple carnal desire.

She had always loved the sea. Found peace in the waves. Any time she was upset, she needed only to set foot in the water, and her mind, body, and spirit would center. Her people lived on the islands and were never far from the scent of the surf, but even a few feet onto shore felt too far. The idea of living in the waves, not just visiting from time to time, filled Yesi's heart with fiery desire.

Once all was accounted for by her reckoning, the mermaid took hold of the docking rope at the prow and surged back to shore.

"I think I gathered everything," said Coral as she pushed the canoe onto the beach. She then crawled up the sand to where the furthest wave met shore and arched up so she was facing Yesi. Her breasts pressed between her arms again drew Yesi's thoughts away from the moment.

"Oh, yes… I believe so," said Yesi, quickly standing. She suddenly felt embarrassed having done nothing but watch as Coral rescued her from what would have been a long afternoon of trying to collect all her belongings and possibly even losing the boat that was her only reliable way back home several islands away. "Thank you."

"You're welcome," said Coral, grinning proudly. Her sharp teeth probably should be intimidating, but all Yesi felt was charmed. "Happy to help. Where are you from?"

"Pinkfoot Archipelago," said Yesi, raising her foot. "Sand and soil is pink so it dyes our feet. I don't know why the sand is pink.

My uncle says it is because our ancestors gave their blood to the sand so it would give us gum trees and turtlenuts, but he says a lot of strange things. I think it's probably just because we have so many pink corals on the barrier reef. Lots of pink sand critters too."

"You're amusing. I like you."

"I like you too," said Yesi. Her throat was dry, but she didn't want to pause the conversation and get a drink. Khalorim were always quite skittish in the stories her grandmother told, yet Coral showed no sign of wanting to leave.

Another story of the Khalorim came to Yesi's mind. The thought burned at the back of her mind.

No, that would be rude.

Setting her question aside, Yesi nodded toward the trap in her boat. "Want some crab? You caught them, after all."

Coral peered over the canoe. She pursed her lips and nodded. "I would. My people eat food raw, but from what I hear, yours usually cook your food. Is this true?"

"It is indeed," said Yesi. "I don't have everything with me that I would usually cook them with, I think you'd love it dipped in turtlenut butter, but I've got some citrus and parsley that will be really great. Let me just get a fire going and I'll have us with a nice meal in no time."

"It would be my pleasure."

Yesi didn't have firewood with her, but the island had a stand of turtlenut trees that should give her what she needed. Indeed a tree had been felled, and she found a particularly dry portion of the wood riddled with termites that she was able to portion off with her axe. From there she set up a small fire near the waves. With onshore winds it took some time to light, but the wood was ready to catch.

"That is fascinating," said Coral, sapphire eyes wide as she crawled forward to watch the flames dance.

"Have you ever seen fire?"

"Only at a distance. We are told that it is not safe to get too close."

Yesi nodded. It was said that before she was born, the merfolk and her mother's people often traded and were quite friendly, especially amongst the northern islands like these. All that changed when the mainland soldiers came in the Night of the Last Song, brought all the queens to heel and killed those who would not submit, and took control of the larger islands. Many things changed after the Last Song, especially as witch hunters came and killed all those they found with magic under the authority of the surrendered queens. For fear of the witch hunters, the merfolk retreated further north to the Sea of the Dancing Sun. Few had seen them since.

Although Yesi was born after Last Song, her father was a southern noble who had lived through it, and was one of the few to escape. He was dead now, returned to Melrahim when he joined other warriors to liberate the southern islands and they failed, but she remembered how broken he was, especially whenever anyone discussed his home and family.

"It is interesting that you have all this with you," remarked Coral as Yesi set her stand over the fire.

"We have to be able to cook food while we're out foraging, especially since we can be gone for many days at a time. Usually we're in groups and a bigger canoe will have most of the cooking, but I like being on my own. My cousins are further down in the atolls to the west. I like crabs, and these reefs always have a lot of them. I'm just sorry my turtlenut butter got emptied when my boat flipped. I think you'd really like it."

"Another time, perhaps," said Coral.

Yesi felt herself blush. "I hope so, but let me know what you think of this, first."

Once the fire was steady, Yesi filled her pot with sea water. She then set it on the stand hook. "How hungry are you? How many crabs do you want?"

Coral's brow furrowed. "I am sorry, I must confess I do not know an appropriate answer."

"Don't worry about etiquette," said Yesi, waving dismissively. "These are elk crabs. Really common here and easy to trap. I set the trap to only let in ones around this size, and the smaller ones get out. Too big and it can be hard to cook, and too small are mostly shell. I usually eat just one in a meal with other stuff, but I'm so hungry after that scare and I don't have much to go with it, so I think I'll make two for me. If you're hungry, I'll cook up all six here."

"I would appreciate that, thank you."

With her pair of tongs, which felt like her own pincers, Yesi lifted the trap, set it beside the fire, and opened it. She then lifted and dropped each crab into the pot.

"How long do they take to cook?" said Coral, looking at the pot in fascination, then looking a bit bashful herself. "Apologies if I'm being intrusive. We just eat them raw, so I don't know much about the process. It is quite new and fascinating to me."

Coral crawled back into the water briefly, citing a need to wet her skin again. Yesi wondered if it would be rude to ask how long she could be on land. She didn't seem to be able to breathe water as merfolk were said to do in the stories, instead breathing in much the same way as Yesi, although she evidently still had to spend some time in the water now and then.

After dropping in the last crab, Yesi stepped back. She turned to Coral, who had crawled back on shore, cocking her head to the side. "Do you mind if I ask you a personal question?"

"Please do," said Coral, giving a shift of her shoulder and a suggestive smile.

Yesi gulped. "You do not seem familiar with the ways of my people."

Coral nodded. "That is true. I remember when our peoples were closer. Distant memories. I was very little when we moved north."

"So you were, and I hope this is not rude to ask… you were born a mermaid, yes?"

Again Coral gave a nod.

"I have heard that mermaids were once Kentarim Islanders like me. Is that not true?"

Coral's next nod was slow, as she looked to understand this was the question Yesi was leading up to. "Some of us are. My lineage are born from our mothers, and we look exactly like them. All the mermaids of my lineage are of this coloration and features, although our hair does come in different shades. Others can mate and make unique children much like you islanders do. Still others cannot have children, and must reproduce by kissing a Child of the Land and making them into a being in our likeness."

Being called a child of the land was odd to Yesi, since her people called themselves Children of the Sea, especially in contrast with the mainlanders, but it made sense that a mermaid would not see the distinction.

After it had been sufficient time, Yesi took to drawing out the crabs. She set them on a platter to cool.

"Are you out here hunting?" Yesi asked as she cut up citrus and parsley, not wanting to pry but curiosity was getting the best of her. "The stories only say your people went north, but not how far or if any of you live here still."

Coral smiled. "We live in the north. I confess I have come out of curiosity about your people. I tell my family that I'm fishing at new reefs, but really I like to come here and watch your people work sometimes. You're the first Child of the Land I've spoken to."

"How do you know my language if you were not born of our people and yours no longer communicate with us?"

"I was taught the words, like all our children are. I asked the same thing of my mother, who told me this was what the elders decided. I think they hope one day our peoples can feel safe to reconnect, although they have not said so. It is the only thing that makes sense to me."

Once the crabs had cooled, Yesi set a platter and cracker for each of them, then drizzled the citrus and parsley over it. "Do you need help with the crackers? It might be difficult with your hands, although your thumb is fully mobile."

"I was just going to bite into it."

"If that is what you want to do, but let me just show you how this works. When you cook them the shells get more brittle and you can get little pieces of shell. It's a lot more tender this way. Here, I'll show you."

Yesi guided Coral's hands, showing her where to crack the shell and how to extract the best parts. Although it was clear that she had eaten crab before, and knew which parts to avoid, she seemed delighted by the warmth of cooked crab and differences in texture. Dipping in the citrus and parsley quickly depleted it, and Yesi happily made more before getting Coral the next crab.

After both had their fill, and indeed Coral ate all four as she said she would, the pair leaned back on the sands. The sun above them was steadily getting low, and a pinkish hue began to overtake the sky.

"What do you think of cooked crab?" Yesi asked, looking over. Coral couldn't lie on her back because of her fin, so she lay on her side facing Yesi.

Coral grinned. "You were right, that was really good. I'm excited to try it with your... what did you call it? Turtlenut butter?"

"Yes, from turtlenuts like are in those trees. Inside is a milk that when you beat it and treat it turns into a soft spread that's sweet and a bit tangy. Really smooth. I think you will enjoy it. I would have made it for this meal but it can take a while without the right tools."

"Gives me something to look forward to."

Yesi couldn't hold back a smile. "So can I count on meeting you again?"

"Yes."

They sat together for a while, chatting about nothing as the sun continued to set.

A splashing and other voices dimly caught Yesi's attention. Coral's too. She tensed, her easygoing confidence shown in the rest of the evening shattered.

"I think I recognize my cousin Byama's voice," said Yesi. "Sounds like my cousins are coming around the island over there. Do you want to meet them, or maybe another time? They can be a bit loud, but they're really nice."

"I do want to meet them," she said, her voice catching slightly. "I admit I'm a bit nervous, but I want to."

Yesi nodded. As the first canoe rowed into the low lit view, she spotted the twins Jash and Meian. Next was Hemi. Byama was last, his weight lifting the front of his canoe out of the water. As Yesi waved them over, she reassured Coral.

Hemi's canoe was the first to strike the shore. He steered so he wouldn't be too close. Right away her eldest cousin spotted the stranger and realized he shouldn't make sudden movements. He held up his hand as the others rowed in.

"Hello!" said Yesi, not leaving Coral's side. "This is Coral Under Moon. She saved me when I got trapped underwater trying to get my trap. Coral, these are my cousins! Hemi is the tall one. Meian is the girl twin, Jash is the boy, and Byama is the big fellow back there."

"I'm not a boy," said Jash puffing out his chest. "I'm a man!"

"They both came of age in the spring," said Byama with a grin, thumping Jash's back as he walked past. "He says as much any chance he gets."

"Are you alright?" asked Meian, looking Yesi over with a mix of caring and judgement. "You said you got trapped underwater. Mother said we shouldn't be alone."

"Well good that your friend here was able to help out," said Hemi, his tone gentle as always. "A pleasure to meet you, Coral Under Moon. Thank you for helping my cousin."

"Of course, happy to help," said Coral, looking a delightful mix of nervous and excitement.

"We should head back," said Byama. "Skies are clear, but it is storm season, and we don't want to be here if one shows in the night."

Hemi nodded. "We'll give you some space, then help you pack."

"Gratitude," said Yesi.

Hemi rounded up the twins, who looked like they wanted nothing more than to bombard Coral with queries, and guided them back a bit.

Yesi helped Coral back into the surf. The water chilled a bit, but any nervousness Yesi had felt before washed away.

"When will I see you again?" she asked as Coral resurfaced after wetting her hair.

"I live far away, but we often travel while foraging. Shall we meet back here the day of the next full moon?"

"Yes please," said Yesi with a grin. "I'll bring turtlenut butter next time."

"Good."

Coral closed the distance, raising a cautious hand to Yesi's shoulder so she was level. Yesi took Coral's other hand in her own. The waves gave Yesi further confidence, and she pulled Coral close.

Their first kiss was brief, but sent a rush through Yesi. She had kissed boys and girls before, but this was entirely different. There was more than fun. Much more. It was thrill, hunger, but mostly she felt grounded. This simple gesture, surrounded by water with someone born of the waves, was overwhelming in its sense of authenticity.

Coral was grinning as she eased away. With a quick squeeze of Yesi's hand, Coral turned and dived into the waves.

Yesi barely heard her cousins cheering behind her.

All she wanted was to be able to dive into the waves.

Partly to follow Coral, but mostly to be one with the sea.

***

A year had passed.

Yesi and Coral, whose spoken name in her mother tongue was Kirino accompanied by a click at the back of the throat and squeaks that Yesi could not manage despite her best efforts, indeed met at least once every full moon. Typically Yesi made dinner, while Coral brought the ingredients. She had been nervous about the reception from her village, but everyone seemed excited. Matron Nabilya said their relationship was a sign that the world was healing, that the Sea of the Dancing Sun was returning to the old ways before the Night of the Last Song.

That all felt strange. Monumental. Grand beyond her understanding.

What she actually felt was happy. Authentic. Comfortable when she was with Coral, and most true to herself when they swam and made love in the sea.

"I think you're getting better at holding your breath," said Coral as they surfaced from a swim through the rocks of their favorite cove.

"It doesn't feel that way," Yesi said with a halfhearted laugh. The tide was rolling out, and already they could sit with the water up to their chests.

Coral kissed her deeply before taking a deep breath. "Well, it was long enough to do the trick."

"I'm glad. All I can think is wishing I could remain down there for longer."

Coral grinned as she closed her eyes and leaned back against the stone they liked to be intimate against. "A bit of a break now and then will do us both good. Do you want to keep playing?"

"No, thank you," said Yesi, slouching back.

Coral rested her head on Yesi's shoulder and settled in close. "What's on your mind? You seem troubled, but you weren't like this when we started. Did something happen?"

Yesi ran her fingers through Coral's copper curls, taking a deep breath.

"It's okay if you don't want to talk about it. We can just relax. I only want you to know that I'm here if you need to say anything. I'm here for you in all ways, not just for fun."

Yesi took a deep breath. She had spent the past days feeling nothing but yearning and excitement for these moments, but now she was ill at ease. It felt deeply disrespectful to want more. To want anything but what they shared, which was more delightful and satisfying than any intimacy she had experienced before, felt selfish and shameful to even consider.

Coral kissed her gently on the cheek.

Her fingers trailed slowly over Yesi's hand underwater, following the tendons of her fingers up to her knuckles, then fully covering her hand. For a moment they sat together, Coral's hand over Yesi's. Yesi clenched her jaw and turned her hand over, gently touching Coral's palm.

Coral set another careful kiss on Yesi's cheek then the side of her neck, sending a thrill with each touch. Finally she softly kissed Yesi's ear, giving it a gentle bite. "Whatever you want, you only need ask."

"I want to be like you."

Coral pulled back.

Yesi's eyes went wide. She hadn't meant to say it out loud. Or... had she? She must have. It's what she wanted, even though she knew she shouldn't.

Although she was afraid to even look at Coral, her lover set a knuckle on Yesi's jaw and gently but firmly turned Yesi to face her. She looked into Yesi's eyes. Yesi never liked eye contact, but felt more at ease than usual, drawn to look at Coral now.

"You wish to be Khalorim," Coral whispered, realization in her voice as she scrutinized Yesi.

"I'm sorry, that was- I don't know. I don't... I'm so sorry Coral, I'll-"

Yesi began to stand, but Coral took her hand, again tender but secure. "Sit. Please. You can sit quiet if you need to collect your thoughts, but do not run where you know I cannot follow just because you're afraid of offending me. I know you didn't kiss me last year just to get to this moment. I know there is distinction between your attraction to me and the call of the sea. They are different songs you wish to sing."

Yesi slumped back down, emotion swelling and burning her eyes, threatening to bring tears she couldn't bear to shed. Not like this. Not in front of Coral.

"There are two different ways you look at me," said Coral. "I do not presume to know your thoughts, but I have seen both and know the difference: one is a lustful desire, and trust me, I love when you look at me that way. To know the very sight of me excites you is deeply attractive and I won't pretend otherwise. But there is

another look you give. A yearning. A desire I've never quite understood. This realization does not offend me. I did not anticipate it,
but I must confess, it makes sense. If this is true, I will not see you
judged, least of all by yourself. I love you, Yesi, and that love is in
all ways."

Again Yesi frowned, trying to find words. She should thank
Coral for her compassion. Affirm that the longing she felt for the
sea wasn't why she fell for Coral. Say something. Anything.

She opened her lips to speak, took a deep breath.

And wept.

Crying completely took over. She doubled over, gasping for
breath. As her arms crossed over her stomach, Yesi lost herself in
cries. She felt carved open. Clawed raw inside.

Coral lifted her up with strong arms, keeping her face above the
rolling waters in the receding tide. Coral kissed the top of her head
and held her. Yesi leaned into the embrace, trying to get out words,
but every effort ended in mumbled sobs.

The tide was to their waists by the time Yesi had cried herself
to a vague feeling of release. Her breathing was still strained, each
gasp barely sufficient, but feeling Coral's arms around her helped
Yesi gain a sense of grounding.

"I'm here," said Coral for what must have been the hundredth
time. "I'm here, Yesi."

***

Yesi put a fresh cut at the trunk of the rubber tree, watching pale
liquid begin to swell from the wound and seep down toward the
vessel where this new wound and the earlier gash intersected.

Coral had left to speak with her elders about how to help Yesi
become Khalorim. Yesi had told her mother about her wishes too.

"I think some part of me will mourn never being a grandmother," she had said after they spoke. "If you disappear and never return, I will be sad of course, but I know this is what you want. You sound afraid, but also with a burning hope I've never heard before. The stories say not all survive the change, and I will not lie to you and say that doesn't worry me, but I must have faith that Melrahim will guide you to what you feel is right. There is no greater honor than hearing the call of the sea, and I will give you anything short of my joy and blessing. All I ask is that you please be careful."

Was she being reckless? It was difficult to know. She had forgotten the stories of those who did not survive the kiss. Tragic stories of beings whose body died halfway through the transformation. In some stories it was due to some fault of the being bitten. A southern trader sang a song of merfolk who intentionally killed beings and used their corpses to reproduce, but Yesi always dismissed that as a twisted nightmare of a story. Now some part of her wondered if it was true. Her memory was of the thrilling tales of a sailor who fell in love with the sea, who was kissed by a mermaid, and the act transferred Melrahim's blessing and they were able to swim with their fellow children of the sea. These were the tales that stuck in her mind. That made sense to her. It was these stories that had made her wish, even back when she was a little girl, that she could swim free and never have to walk again.

Was she being naïve? Was this just a wishful fantasy, and the truth was far more dangerous or even sinister?

No. Coral would have given warning. She had said it could be dangerous, but that was why she was speaking with her own elders. Coral would not encourage her to do something likely to be her end.

The building anxiety made her heart race.

She was so lost in thoughts that she shrieked when she turned and nearly ran into Hemi.

"Apologies!" she cried, dropping her machete as she nearly cut him. "I'm so sorry, I didn't see you."

"I don't think you're seeing anything right now," said Hemi with a laugh. He held out a skin. "Here, have some water."

Once Yesi's heart stopped threatening to burst from her chest, she gulped down half the water skin. "Sorry about that. What's on your mind?"

"More coming to see what's on yours," said Hemi. "You've been working these trees since before sunrise and it's not an urgent task. We have enough rubber to trade with plenty to spare when the southern islanders pass through. You should relax."

"Because I might be in danger? Mom warned me about that too. All those stories of people not surviving the kiss? Or is it a bite? Now I'm digging through the sands of my memory trying to remember all the details. I don't want to disappoint her either. She wants grandchildren, and I cannot give her that if I go to the sea."

"Let's sit down."

Hemi guided her to one of the felled trees a few paces away that had yet to be dragged to the boathouse for materials. As they sat, Hemi rubbed her back, encouraging her to take another sip of water.

"Our ancestors had many traditions which we set aside after Last Song. Someone like me, born male in the body of a girl, would have had no difficulty with the ceremonies of transition. Now I was only able to do it because the witch hunters did not come this far north so Matron Nabilya was not killed. She guided me through the transition, but many in the village were not in support, saying I should instead have children to make up for the warriors we lost and traders who were slaughtered. Our fellow children didn't know why the elders did not approve of me, but they sensed it. If you and Byama hadn't supported me, him always being my sparring partner and you taking me as your man in dances, I would have been lost.

Our ancestors had these traditions, of celebrating becoming our true selves regardless of the bodies we were born into, because they knew how important it is to be your most authentic self. This is who I am, and I am so grateful to the ancestors for having these traditions, and to the matriarch for preserving them. We all know that the water calls to you, Yesi. More than any of us you are a child of the sea. In the days before Last Song the discussions would have long been underway. It can be intimidating, using herbs and magic to change your body, but our ancestors had these traditions and passed down this wisdom because it works and those who do them find themselves fulfilled. Our ancestors would not have kept the tradition alive if it were too dangerous. Of course I will not tell you what to do, but I wanted to reassure you."

Yesi took a deep breath. At some point her and her cousin's fingers had become interlocked. She squeezed his hand tightly.

"Thank you, Hemi. I didn't know how much I needed to hear that."

"You're in your head. I understand. Had a feeling you might want to hear it. You can do this, and know that your family is here for you. Every step of the way."

***

Yesi waited in the cove.

The tide was coming in, but she was still able to sit on their favorite rock.

No wait ever seemed so long.

What if the Khalorim were still wary of mainland witch hunters and declined? What if they decided she was not worthy? Coral had said that a merfolk would need to volunteer to help her transformation. At first she had assumed that merely voicing her desire was the hardest part. Now she had overcome that anxiety, it was quickly becoming apparent that there were a wide range of unforeseen complications. She might get the approval of all mortal beings, only for Melrahim's luck to turn against her, and the ceremony itself might kill her.

Each moment passed in agony.

Yesi had almost given up for the afternoon to go have a meal on shore when she spotted several shapes moving just under the surface. The tide was now low enough that she could stand, so she climbed off the rock to greet them.

Right away she recognized Coral as her lover broke the surface with an excited grin.

Next was a woman with quite similar features. In fact the face was so much the same that Yesi had to check again. No, she had been correct about which was Yesi, but she had not been exaggerating when she said she had no father and was born a copy of her mother. This woman was slightly leaner, had ever so slightly harder features, and her hair was a darker shade of gold, although that might just be the water.

Her attention was quickly captured by a highly elongated figure, who she had at first mistaken for at least two merfolk if not three.

This being's aspect was quite familiar and immediately sparked a rush of fear.

Katabo, the Reef King, a long sea serpent.

His form was so long that he encircled the rest. This being's features were that of a man in his prime, at least from the front. When he angled slightly to the side between strokes, she saw his features were elongated to account for long jaws. He had neither hair nor beard, and the fangs which drew Yesi's attention as he inhaled through cheekless jaws were quite menacing. Katabo on the reefs were venomous creatures. Many fishermen had been killed by them. She wondered if he was venomous like the creatures he resembled. As he seemed to stand in the water amongst his coiled form, Yesi noted a bandolier of sorts, coated in rubber, upon which he had many vials and tiny bottles. Yesi had to suppress a chill of equal parts fear and excitement as he scrutinized her, even though he was some five span away.

Next was a being who moved with slow, deliberate gestures, never a motion wasted. Her face looked more fish than woman, with hard gills under her jaw, segmented plates on her cheeks, and diamond-shaped eyes set in deep sockets. A common grouper was her aspect, Yesi was sure of it. Yesi could only assume this woman was equally ancient. The hair atop her head was thick and stiff, looking to be somewhere between locks and spines. Her skin had a radiant iridescence to it, contributing to a captivating beauty.

She spoke with a steady, even tone with an accent Yesi could not begin to place.

"Greetings, Yesi Pinkfoot. I am Storm Eater, matriarch of the Sunrise Reef clan." Yesi's knees buckled beneath her. Storm Eater, daughter of the creator. "I have known your family for a long time. I remember when Nabilya first brought your people here. I am glad that we might now begin to reunite our peoples."

Yesi tried to speak, but could only muster a feeble exhale.

"In order to determine which aspect and lineage you might acclimate with, we will need to taste your blood. If you are bitten by an aspect who you are incompatible with, your body may reject the kiss like a disease and you will die. May I send Binds the Fighting Whale to collect? He is best at determining these things. He only needs a drop."

"Uh, yes, of course," said Yesi, tensing under the hollow gaze of the sea serpent.

Fortunately, Coral closed the distance first and offered a gentle hand. Yesi clasped it firmly. Yesi knew her lover had no more experience with this than she did, and also seemed a bit nervous as the serpent man approached, but gave Yesi a reassuring smile.

Binds the Fighting Whale looked hard at Coral. At first Yesi wondered what the expression meant, then barely heard a faint hiss under the serpent man's breath and remembered Coral telling her that the merfolk spoke with more than just words. Perhaps Binds the Fighting Whale could not use words. His snout-like jaws certainly implied as much, with scaled lips and long fangs.

From his rubber-coated belt, Binds the Fighting Whale unsheathed a wicked knife of bronze, coated in a rich green patina.

Keeping a firm grip on Coral's hand with her left, Yesi pricked the meat of her forearm with the tip of the knife. Red promptly welled up. "Is that enough?"

"Like I said, he only needs a drop."

Yesi nodded. After squeezing Coral's hand, she let go and held her arm out to Binds the Fighting Whale, keeping it well above the shifting waves now at her waist.

Although she was afraid he might attack given the focus with which he inspected the wound, Binds the Fighting Whale simply reached out a pale finger, pressed a rough fingertip against it, then touched it to his tongue. For a moment he sat in silence. After shifting back a full span with a simple bend of his elongated form, Binds the Fighting Whale turned back to Storm Eater.

She gave him a nod, then looked to Yesi. "Your blood is most compatible with the rose shark lineage. We will speak with those of our clan of this aspect, and return with one who shall be your mentor for the transformation. Tell Nabilya to be ready in seven days."

"Yes, Storm Eater."

With that, the merfolk turned and submerged without further word or acknowledgement. All except Coral.

Yesi paused a moment, then pulled Coral close. Coral barely got out an 'oh' before Yesi kissed her long and deeply. Coral quickly caught up to the mood, kissing her back.

"How do you feel?" Coral whispered. "What's on your mind?"

"I'm elated! I can't feel my feet. This is something I've wanted since before I knew any words. I feel like I'm finally able to see a picture that's been ever at the edge of my vision. Now the reality is setting in. It's tangible. I can feel it. "

Abandoning all composure, Yesi let out a whooping cry of joy. Tears and laughter came out in equal measure. Both consumed her, and she could barely breathe. It all culminating to reality felt like shedding great stones strapped to her back. Although she still struggled to inhale from her undignified cries, cackles, and coughs, she still felt it was easier to breathe than ever before.

With a deep breath, Yesi took Coral's face in her hands.

"I love you," Yesi managed between gasps. "Thank you for being my friend. My guide. My lover. I'm so happy."

Coral beamed, a stroke of her tail raising her to Yesi's level. "I love you too."

They kissed again.

Yesi could not recall being happier.

***

Seven days had passed, and Yesi sat by the sea.

A hammock had been posted on the water line of low tide, so when tide was at its height at sunrise, the hammock would be partly submerged. Yesi had taken several potions meant to relax her body and fortify it for the coming change. Her focus had been hazy at first, but now that the potions had settled, she felt a great sense of clarity.

It seemed the entire village was there waiting. Watching. She was grateful for her mother, Byama and Hemi, and for Matron Nabilya. They were all present to support her. The rest seemed more there for spectacle, or to celebrate a return to a tradition many feared had perished.

Yesi took a deep breath, exhaling and releasing any lingering bitterness. If they were inspired by her decision, if this made them feel hope when so much hope had been lost, Yesi knew it was selfish to judge them.

Besides, there might be another child watching this ceremony who, like her, has always felt the call of the sea.

The thought put a smile on her face.

As the sun began to set, casting pink across the sky, Yesi saw many forms cutting through the waves out on the barrier reef.

Coral was at the front, accompanied by easily a hundred other merfolk of at least a dozen aspects. Possibly more. Although Coral had never said how many were in the Sunrise Reef clan, Yesi had assumed it would be a small group. Now she wondered if this might not even be all of them.

The waters where her hammock had been set, out near the docks where the sands were deepest, the Khalorim could all look as though they were standing in the low-rolling waves.

Although Yesi wanted to greet Coral, the assembled crowd and hundreds of eyes upon her was overwhelming and kept her planted.

Matron Nabilya came forward. She and Storm Eater exchanged respectful bows. Nabilya spoke out to both clans.

"A thousand and one generations ago, both of our people were born of the sea. Some came onto land and became people, but we have always had salt in our blood. The sea calls to us all. To some, that call is louder. Stronger. More final. For a thousand generations, those who heard this strongest call would be welcomed back to the sea, taking on aspects of Melrahim's children. We have known much loss and pain in this generation. Blood was shed, lives lost, and fear spread like a disease. I cannot begin to express my gratitude that we now live at a time when these wounds to our people, this damage to the way our lives are supposed to be, can begin to heal. Yesi, daughter of Jaya, is our first to hear this call. She is one of many signifiers of hope. Of healing. She is a promise that we are still Kentarim. Yesi answering the call of the sea is proof that yes: we have been hurt. We have been insulted. We have suffered, but we are not broken. We are still the Children of the Sea."

Yesi's grip tightened on the hammock's netting. Tears pressed behind her eyes. Although this was still a deeply personal choice, she hadn't realized just how important it was to her people. She felt suddenly selfish for having wished to skip this ceremony. A fool for thinking she and her immediate family would be the only ones involved.

She looked back to the crowd on the shore.

All faces beamed. More than a few wept.

These were her people. She would join the waves, become who she felt to her core she was meant to be, but she would ever be of this village, and she vowed to herself that she would always look after and defend them.

Nabilya gestured for Yesi to stand. She did so.

The water of the incoming tide immediately rolled around her feet. The chill was welcome. Soothing. It felt like a reassuring embrace.

She was ready.

Byama and Hemi appeared on either side. She embraced each. Byama was firm, ever bursting with warm energy, and told her he was proud. Hemi was tender. He kissed her on the forehead.

With hands locked, the trio advanced.

As they reached the deeper waters, now at their waists before the slide to deeper waters, one of the merfolk moved forward to meet them.

She had rough-looking skin the same pink as common coral. Like Storm Eater, a hint of iridescence danced across her face. Her irises were a striking bronze, demanding Yesi's attention. Copper curls danced in the light as she freed and retied her hair. Her aspect was a rose shark, a common sight on the reefs, driven home by many small, sharp fangs.

She was beautiful, frightening, and perfect.

"Hello, Yesi," she said, her tone a bit rough but smile gentle and reassuring. "I am Clarity In Fog. I will be your mentor. I was kissed many years ago, and have been mentor to three others in our lineage. It is a pleasure to meet you, and an honor to be your guide. Coral Under Moon has told me much about you. I look forward to our friendship. Are you ready?"

Yesi suppressed her building emotions. "Yes."

Clarity in Fog swam closer.

Yesi knelt. "Will it hurt?"

"No. When I was kissed, I immediately fell asleep. My mentor said my experience was normal, it was consistent with those I mentored over the years, and I have no reason to think yours won't be too. When you awaken, it will be once the tide has reached your hammock. You will have a form like mine, and be able to breathe both air and the salt sea."

Yesi looked back to her family. To her mother, who waved out to her with a smile both sad and beaming with pride. To her cousins, who both reassured her with nods and tight grips. Then to Coral, who she had never seen happier.

Yesi took a deep breath and nodded.

"I'm ready."

Clarity in Fog took Yesi's face in her hands. Her palms were coarse, like sand against stone. Like Coral, her fingers were partly webbed save for the thumb. She smelled of brine and a vaguely floral scent that Yesi couldn't quite place.

Although her face was rough, looking to be covered in tiny sharp scales, her lips were surprisingly soft.

The kiss was slow. There was intimacy, but not of a romantic or sensual nature. It was another feeling entirely. A prolonged, calm expression of understanding. Of vulnerability. Yesi's tongue gently brushed across one of Clarity's fangs, its edges honed to slicing points, although she was not cut from the simple touch. She found herself a bit lost in the connection. Numbness spread from Clarity's lips, and soon Yesi's eyes felt heavy.

As Clarity in Fog disengaged, her cousins lifted her up, and Yesi's world went black.

***

Cold water against her back brought Yesi to consciousness.

Her eyes snapped open, and she was greeted by the sight of Coral settled beside her.

Coral's eyes fluttered open, and she smiled. "Good morning, beautiful."

As she inhaled, Yesi was overwhelmed with a host of new scents she could never place before. So much that she picked up was new that she was forced to shut her eyes to avoid overstimulation.

She could suddenly identify great distinctions between things once lumped together. The mist of the waves smelled more of sand and more salt on the way out, and a musty organic blend of various fish, serpents, and beasts on the way in. The hammock on which they sat mostly smelled of its rubber coated straps, but she could also detect the tree fiber cloth through any abrasions in the coating. Coral's scent was a fascinating blend that was also of a single entity, both being and a scent she occasionally sensed around Nabilya but could never put a word to until now: magic. Curiously, she did not smell at all like what some part of Yesi knew was the dolphin she resembled. It seemed the similarity was only in appearance.

Once the scents around her were a bit less overwhelming, Yesi opened her eyes once more.

Colors were still present, but muted. To make up for it, she saw with far greater clarity. It was as though she was perceiving far closer than she actually was. She would have assumed that touch would be muted by her now rough skin, but especially along her sides, she felt with the sensitivity of lips and raw fingertips.

Yesi only then began to take stock of her altered form.

Her hands were webbed, like Coral's up to the last joint. Unlike her former golden brown skin, Yesi's hands were a radiant white on the palm and rose gold that glistened in the light. She wondered if she had rainbow iridescence too. Maybe her hand needed to be wet for it, or perhaps her eyes now couldn't pick up that level of color. Any disappointment she felt at that loss was far outpaced by the excitement at taking in the form of her hand. It was strong. Firm. Her palms were generally soft, but the back of her hand was clad in armor of interlocking scales shaped like teeth.

As teeth crossed her mind, she noted the many rows of teeth in her own mouth. Along her palate they were coated in some sort of... it seemed to be enamel, which made the edges dull. The outermost layer, however, were just as sharp as in Clarity's mouth, and she tried to commit that to memory when she tried to speak to be careful around the many blades now lining her jaws.

She still had hair. As she shook it out, it appeared that rather than grow reddish copper hair, Yesi's hair was the same dark blond coils it had always been.

As expected, her legs were gone. Where legs had been was now a pair of fins, and moving them used the same muscles as her legs. What perhaps should feel strange was instead natural. Validating.

Pulling entirely unfamiliar sets of muscles, Yesi turned to see a pair of dorsal fins, one large where her tailbone used to be and a smaller further down. She also noted the great flukes at the end of her tail, true to form of a reef shark, with the top fin far longer and clipped just before the tip.

"*Can you hear me?*"

Yesi started, then realized it was Coral's voice in her mind.

"*I think so. Can you hear me?*"

"*Yes!*" Coral switched to words. "I'm sure it will take time, so don't try to strain it too much. Let Clarity in Fog guide you through that. I just wanted to know if it would work this time."

"What do you mean this time?" Yesi asked.

"Oh, I've tried to say some things to you before. You know, nice things. Cute things. Romantic things." Coral grinned. "Plenty of vulgar things."

Yesi laughed. She leaned in for a kiss, then paused, not sure how to navigate her new form with regards to intimacy. Thankfully Coral took the lead. It was a gentle, careful kiss, but having the familiarity in this body which felt vastly more comfortable was greatly reassuring.

"Let's get you in the water, my love."

Yesi nodded. Coral was able to crawl out into the waves, which were now level with the hammock, quite easily. Yesi needed much more effort, although with Coral's assistance she managed to get free.

Right away, the legs which were now fins spread to give balance. It felt awkward at first to try and swim. She couldn't tell if she was moving her hips too much or not enough. Swimming with her hands as she had done in human form did seem to help.

Coral was by her side the whole time. They kept to the shallows for a while, remaining amongst the pink sands where Yesi could reach down to touch the bottom or sort of brace herself against her tail. Finding a good position to do so would definitely take time.

They continued to swim out into deeper waters. Soon they were out past the furthest docks and the pink sands were deeper than the tip of Yesi's tail could reach.

Again they kissed, this time with more confidence. Although her back and sides were armored, Yesi's underparts were soft, and every part of her more sensitive than before. She could barely contain her excitement at the thought of all she could feel being intimate now.

"There is one thing you can do that I cannot," said Coral after another long kiss. "You can breathe water."

The notion had not even crossed her mind before. Suddenly it was all she desired.

"I'm right here," said Coral, laughing when she saw Yesi's delight. "Try it!"

They kissed once more, and Yesi took a deep breath of air.

She exhaled, feeling suddenly stiff and nervous, but excitement was far stronger. As she let the air out of her lungs, Yesi sank below the waves. She closed her eyes, knowing she had to focus.

Although she wanted to inhale, Yesi couldn't shake the instinct that had been with her all her life. A reminder that she was bound to land. That she would only ever be a visitor to the sea.

As her chest started to burn, worry set in. What if she wasn't ready?

Overhead, a wave rolled just as she felt the beginnings of surrender. Undertow pulled her down. Fear escalated to panic, and-

As she opened her eyes, Yesi saw Coral. Her lover was smiling. Their fingers intertwined. As another wave crossed above, Yesi felt it was not the dangers of the sea. Not wrath or punishment. She had been embraced by Melrahim, and the goddess knew she just needed a push.

She chose to trust in the sea, in Coral, and herself.

Yesi drew breath.

The Reaper's Choice

5

The Reaper's Choice

Chapter 1

After finishing the waterskin he brought outside with him, Kirut returned to the frame on which he exercised.

His hounds Guppik and Tam were nearby. Guppik was happy to relax beside the arch as Kirut went through his drills, but Tam was eager to participate. This pup was of a litter one of the guardian dogs had with one of the tame wolves. The others of the litter looked and acted enough like the guardians that they had been well trained for the task. Young Tam might have the appaloosa coat of a guardian, but in muzzle and obedience he took after the wolf, and training him over the past year had been an arduous undertaking.

Kirut enjoyed the challenge, and although young Tam still struggled to focus, he was responsive to commands as long as he wasn't distracted.

As Kirut kept elevated on the arch and switched to a leg lift routine, Tam hopped up with each lift. Although he wasn't trying to bite Kirut's feet like he used to, it added a complication of trying to avoid kicking as he exercised.

"Do you even sleep?"

At the sound of his aunt's voice, Kirut dropped from the arch and turned.

Shaku held little Arlu close to fend off the morning chill. The girl was only a year old but already open eyed and curious. Kirut smiled and offered a finger, which his cousin took in a fierce grip.

Guppik gave a tired sigh as Tam stumbled over him trying to lick Arlu's face. It took three commands to get the pup to settle down. He had more growing to do, but already was tall enough to reach Kirut's face when he reared up.

Although Kirut was still warm from his exercise, Shaku and Arlu were still cold, and sat beside Guppik. The great whale hound was in his prime, twice Kirut's weight, and radiated heat like a furnace. Kirut sat on her other side, scratching Tam's side before he wandered about to lick Guppik's face. After two commands and a 'tsch', Tam finally settled beside Guppik.

Shaku nudged her shoulder against Kirut's. "We're home for the season. Your mother will permit you to visit Huu Taukit. I'm sure Mia misses you, and you should see your sons again."

Kirut's hand brushed the necklace he wore. Mia had given him a pearl she found before the attack. Although she said it had no special properties, he certainly felt warmer when he wore it, and made it into a necklace shortly after he returned home.

Tam started to get up, but Guppik put a massive arm over the pup's back. The wolfdog slumped down in resignation. Tam might be big for his age, but he was less than half Guppik's size, and there was no use in trying to get out now.

"Go to her," Shaku repeated. "I'm sure Guppik misses her too."

Kirut smiled and nodded. "I'm sure he does."

Kirut looked out to sea. It had been seven years since that cold night in Huu Taukit when he and Shaku helped defend the villagers from demons. When her son Tamuk and so many others were killed. Kirut had gotten used to seeing with one eye, and cold was much easier to endure, but he still felt he could not rest. Could not sleep. Could not justify closing his eye until the hezuki was vanquished.

Kirut knew he was obsessed. He knew hunger for vengeance had rooted and rotted his chest. He pretended he was happy, and sometimes it was true, but the need to feel the demon suffer and extinguish consumed him.

Everyone said they secured a victory that day, but when he was alone with his thoughts, Kirut considered it ultimately a loss.

The hezuki was still out there, and since he had failed to kill her, she was no doubt still hunting.

Kirut was ashamed that he still held on. That he still hated. That he still kept watch. The demon may have retreated, never to be seen in the known world again, but in possessing Kirut's every anxiety, the hezuki still defined him.

The hezuki lost that day, but so did Kirut.

"You're right, Shaku," said Kirut, leaning forward and kissing little Arlu on the forehead then repeating the gesture to his aunt. "I will visit Mia."

✳✳✳

As always, Yumichin was the first to complete her transformation.

While she had to train rigorously for easier skin-changing, barely gaining or losing mass in the shift was instrumental. Yanochin more than doubled in mass when he became a golden sea badger, substantially adding to his time needed to take fur, and resuming skin still took a while despite the fact that he was shedding mass. Yumi always wondered where they drew their additional size. Her cousin Jadhe said they took it from the sea. It was certainly easier and faster transforming near water, but surely there was more to it than just borrowing from the sea. Any time she asked that, the elders brushed her off with some platitude.

Sea Badger was the spirit which blessed their lineage with His form. Although she and her company knew it was a type of walrus, many thought they were sea lions or fur seals owing to a more doglike head and lack of tusks. In her mind they were more like walruses in how they swam and crawled, but now that she had met more outsiders, the similarity lead to a common misconception.

Yumi took one of the robes left for them on a nearby stone and tied it loose around her waist. While the other shifters continued retracting their snouts, growing fingers from flippers, and stretching their legs, Yumi marched over to the general.

Tikah might be on the eve of her fourth century, but the Imperial woman stood resolute, her posture that of a soldier half her age. She wore the dusting of grey on her temples with pride. A tactician, warrior, and mother of seven brilliant scholars, bards, and warriors, Tikah was everything Yumi admired and more.

Tikah offered a slight bow, hands still clasped behind her back. "Back earlier than I expected. Any sign of them?"

Yumi returned the gesture before shaking her head. "Argunite insisted on pursuing, and my brother sent Aro, Gota, and Omu to accompany him, but we encountered no further signs of the Klaeg. They appear to have some means of masking their scent, and were faster on the water than we anticipated. Apologies, General."

"No apologies necessary, Yumichin. None of us expected Klaeg raiders to outmaneuver a Pakardiant scouting party, much less one led by Am'Elosi. What little mental capacity the Klaeg possess is devoted to direct violence. I have to assume it was some accident that favored their assault. Was there any evidence of a storm that far out?"

"There are many strong upwells from the abyss this time of year. It's possible that they used one to strike the Pakardiant, gather the survivors, and continue along the current north. That doesn't explain how they could mask their scent. We should have at least gotten some traces, especially since the attack on the reef looked quite bloody. The Pakardiant weren't taken without a fight. I did smell magic, faint though it was. Might they have a witch?"

Tikah frowned. "There has never been a Klaeg witch. Mastery of magic is exclusive to our people. Currents often come with wind. It could be as simple as a breeze hindering your tracking, a breeze brought on by the very current that by the cruel favors of fortune brought their ambush and assisted them in capturing and killing Am'Elosi and her party. I would withhold the assignment of clever plotting to such simple opponents. Sometimes you lose, and there's no conspiracy involved to cushion the blow to our pride. It does not serve our campaign to build a fantastic explanation for the mundane. Even against such simple foes, we aren't going to win every encounter."

"Yes, General," said Yumi, still skeptical. Tikah smiled and raised an eyebrow, clearly noticing Yumi's doubt. She looked like she might inquire further, but Yanochin and the rest had resumed human form, dressed, and were approaching.

"Your sister enlightened me on your progress, Captain," said Tikah.

"Fair enough," said Yano after finishing the large pint of ale the general had been left for him beside the robes. His deep, resonant voice projected far despite a calm tone. "We should collect what we all saw and give a comprehensive report, but I'm sure she covered what was important."

Yumi pursed her lips and looked down: her brother was their captain, and it was his duty to report. His tone lacked any malice, but this wasn't the first time she had accidently undermined him, and although all present knew there was deep admiration between Yano and Tikah, Yumi didn't want to disrespect either of them.

"Regardless of procedure, this letter came for you in your absence, Captain."

Yano passed off his pint, dried his hand on his robe, and unfurled the scroll comically small in his massive hands. Blue eyes skimmed the parchment. His brow furrowed more with each line of tiny script.

"What is it, Captain?" asked Tikah, openly concerned.

"The missive is from our matron," Yano said. "There have been several disappearances in nearby villages, and one of our fishing boats went missing while at sea. Jadhe, Uru, and Ogao, her daughter, son, and nephew who are both skin-changers, went to investigate and have not yet returned."

Bruhe, young son of the matron who joined the company with Yumi three years earlier, had closed in at the mention of his elder sister's name. "Jadhe? They're missing?"

"No, they just haven't returned from a scouting trip," said Yano, although his bass was less level than usual.

"If you and your scouts need to return home, I understand," said Tikah. "Some of your numbers remaining behind would be most appreciated, however. Your talents in marine scouting are unmatched, and the Klaeg are still out there."

"Jadhe, Uru, and Ogao have only gone a day as of this letter. It was sent three days ago. They may have returned by now. There are many in our village trained for combat, and Uncle Jaka has twelve skin-changers to protect the village. She does not speculate what might be taking our people, but there are many beasts in our waters that turn man-eater, and plenty of hunters who know them and are surely assembling to track whatever it is and kill it. I would not wish to break contract so hastily. She is not requesting our return, merely keeping us informed. She knows this is important. If the Klaeg establish a base in Pakardia, all peoples of the known world will suffer."

"I do not disagree."

"What if just I go?" asked Yumi. "I shift faster and am more agile in the water than the rest of you. If she just needs more skin-changers tracking and guiding our hunters, not warriors, maybe I would be enough?" Yano's jaw visibly clenched. She knew he was protective, but didn't want to say it out loud. "It's not as if looking for a man-eater at home is more dangerous than tracking the Klaeg. I can do this."

"I wish to go as well, with your permission," said Bruhe. "We will sail faster if we do not pause for rest."

"I do want to support our village." He turned to Tikah. "Have you a boat that could get them home quickly? We all came on the same craft, and would take at least eight to properly crew."

"Argunite's shurugen would be fastest of course, but if that fool ever returns from his chase, I'll need him here."

"I can sail," said Yumi. "We both can."

Tikah nodded. "One of our sloops will be at your disposal." The general jotted down a note and passed it to one of Yumi's cousins. "Give that to Admiral Hirah. My brother will see them outfitted with our fastest shurugen, and show her how it operates. Go pack, Yumi and Bruhe, and may your gods carry you both safe and swift."

"Thank you, General."

Yano pulled Yumi and Bruhe aside.

"Please be careful," he whispered, worry heavy on his features. "Bruhe, your mother is reserved. Proud. She never asks for anything. Although she did not express worry, she would not send for aid were she not truly concerned. Have Niri send word of your safe arrival as soon as you arrive. Yumi, promise me you will ensure I am informed."

"You have my word."

After a quick embrace with her brother, a wave to her kin, and bow to Tikah, Yumi and Bruhe ran up the ravine and through camp to the officer's tents to pack.

Yumi gathered all her belongings, which on campaign consisted of a variety of clothes, gloves, a hat, and sun balm. She tied her bedroll onto her pack. Rubber-coated boots weren't her usual preference, but it would no doubt be preferable to sealskin if she were steering. Once she had everything in order, Yumi filled her waterskin from the camp pump and jogged back down to the docks with her cousin.

A dwarf in a black and white suit waited for her at the far end of the wharf. Admiral Hirah, Badger of the Crescent, was impatient by reputation, and his current scowl suggested she was no exception. The two bodyguards behind him stood stoic as ever. His nephew, Captain Sobah, at least had a somewhat jovial expression. The umber-skinned captain towered over most men, all but Yano from what Yumi had seen, from a father of Shu ancestry.

A few deck hands were loading a gorgeous Shurugen sloop behind them. It was a single-mast craft, with rigging for many large sails fore and aft. All cables traced back to the helm. The wood was carved intricately, painted in silver, black, and white, and culminated in a bowsprit with the pouncing form of a snarling honey badger.

Yumi's heart sank, and his deepening frown showed that Admiral Hirah noted her realization:

This was the admiral's personal shurugen sloop.

"You are Yumichin and Bruhechin, yes?" said the admiral, his jaw tightening.

Both nodded quickly.

"Have you ever sailed a shurugen?"

Both shook their heads.

"You can speak," said Sobah, flashing that winning smile that made him talk of the camp and the company of Yumi's prettiest cousin Amyi. "He won't bite,"

"I appreciate those who do not waste words," said Admiral Hirah before looking back up to Yumi, a dynamic she was not used to at her stature. "Come."

Both nodded, following the admiral across the plank. Sobah brought up the rear.

"It has three sails, each unfurled by these levers. Black is the main sail, white the headsail, and striped the spinnaker. Do you know what a spinnaker is?" Yumi nodded, having used these great balloon sails on the voyage east while the wind was at their back. Bruhe wasn't much of a sailor, although he seemed to be following well enough so far. "Good. Only unfurl when the wind is within a thumb of the rudder. The gears throughout these chambers will take care of drawing, you need only raise or lower to these markers. This lever will drop the keel, these extend the outriggers, and this lowers the rudder. Steering with this wheel is quite intuitive. When you need to tack, this bar need only face the side you wish the cables settle on. I have a manual in the wheel cabinet that I made for teaching my daughter. She is an artist, not a sailor, and she comprehended the mechanics within a day. I trust you will have no trouble. I have filled the hull with supplies sufficient to last you for twelve days, although with conventional winds this time of year and the speed of this craft I trust you will find yourself home in eight. seven if winds prove more favorable. Not as fast as a shurugan clipper, but for a boat that can be sailed with a crew of one, you will find none faster in the inland sea. Now, if you will excuse me, there are other matters I must attend to, and I understand you have a schedule to keep as well. I know this craft as though it were a third hand. I presume I need not stress her inherent value, but also her value to me." Again Yumi nodded. "Excellent. Sobah, answer any queries she may have, then see them off. I wish you speed and good fortune, Yumichin and Bruhechin."

Yumi bowed quickly, then stood stiff as Admiral Hirah departed. Bruhe followed suit.

Once he, the deck hands, and his two guards were partway down the docks, Sobah chuckled. Yumi let out a slow breath. Bruhe still looked on nervously.

"He addressed you both by name," said Sobah. "That means he likes you."

Bruhe raised an eyebrow. "He did the same for you."

Sobah shrugged. "Most people like me. Now, let's see what of that you two need translating."

Yumi listened closely as Sobah talked through the mechanics once more, taking out the manual to explain each lever. It was indeed quite thorough. Although it could comfortably hold ten passengers, one person could do everything. She was glad she was not alone, though. While she would have preferred to be on watch, she knew Bruhe came along out of worry for his sister and was not himself a noteworthy sailor. If nothing else, he was a proficient enough sailor to keep the sloop going while she slept.

"Seems like you two have the basics." Sobah pointed out to water. Yumi spotted the familiar golden blond head of her brother in fur, along with a white, a spotted, and a dark brown walrus all bobbing in the middle of the harbor. "Looks like some of your kin have come to see you off. Don't worry about the boat. I assure you; he can afford to fix any damages, and if gods forbid something does damage it, I imagine he's got a list of improvements already planned if this one takes a beating." Again he showed that winning smile that, if Yumi had any interest in men, would have long since melted her heart. "Besides, you're skin-changers who turns into sea badgers. This boat's name is the Sea Badger. I daresay that strikes me as good fortune."

Sobah helped Yumi and Bruhe cast off. Yumi took the wheel. Thankfully, being on its own small pier at the end of the wharf, they needed little maneuvering to get to the main harbor. Yano in fur took the headline and, with his own might alone, drew them out to more open waters. Having swum these channels dozens of times now, Yumi knew where each large stone or submerged tree was that might obstruct her path. Once they were clear of the mangroves, Bruhe took the headline from Yano. After making sure all other lines and buoys were in, Yumi drew down the head and main sails with the simple shifting of a few levers. Bruhe crawled up to the nest so he might keep a keen view of their surroundings.

The wind was fully at her starboard. She lowered the keel and felt the boat steady. With the rudder slightly off her aim, she quickly built up speed.

Admiral Hirah was absolutely correct: the Sea Badger cut through the waves like a marlin.

Yano and the rest sang a farewell song, their voices filling Yumi's heart with confidence for the path ahead.

***

A chorus of barking signaled something approaching from the sea. The wall of the village kept them contained. Kirut was focused on ensuring his oar had a full coat of wax. Although Tam barreled toward the sound, Guppik remained by Kirut's side.

The gate was opened by his cousin Mauk who was on watch.

The man who stepped through was greeted by an onslaught of hounds immediately switching from barks to licks and wagging tails. Tam launched himself atop the pile with no effort to make successful contact, only wanting to be part of the fun.

"Off, you mangy beasts!"

Kirut grinned as he recognized the voice. He stood and crossed the clearing, waded through the hounds, and pulled the newcomer to his feet.

"Where I'm from, dogs are half this size, and for good reason!"

"At ease!" Kirut called. The guard hounds promptly acknowledged his command and fell back, although they lingered in the area rather than fully returning to their huts. It wasn't often that a new person came to Modegk, although Haruin was hardly a stranger. Tam in particular sat close, around a span away, a distance where he was technically obeying, but close enough to join any excitement before the adult guardians did.

Haruin straightened his seal fur coat and brushed back the black straight locks that had escaped his topknot in the brawl. "Relentless beasts, you know that? I've been here more times than I have fingers but they still pin me like they did the first time."

"The first time was to make sure you were safe. The others are to show their affection."

"I prefer that form of affection from large women, thank you."

Kirut chuckled. "Fair enough. What other than the tide and a resignation to being tackled by a dozen hounds brings you to Modegk?"

The Eskadin's features softened. "There was another attack."

A weight sank in Kirut's chest. His grip reflexively tightened on Haruin's shoulder. Kirut muttered an apology and withdrew his hand.

"At least six Eskadin settlements were hit. Scattered throughout the eastern sea, south of the Ring. Seemed random enough but all were the same: small villages with most of their warriors abroad. In every case there were too few to fight back. I'm not aware of any with survivors, but this is just me piecing together over a dozen rumors, so I could be missing details, but it certainly seems like your Great White Death is back."

"What was the most recent settlement hit?"

"An island southeast of the Ring," Haruin replied. "Might be best for us to just go to the Ring and ask around. That news was a few days old when it reached me nine days ago, so there have certainly been new attacks since then."

"Are you coming with me?"

"I won't pretend to be excited by the prospect of sharing land with a demon, certainly not intentionally, but yes. You'll want an Eskadin from the east to vouch for you with the villagers as we try to narrow down where this monster is. My folk are wary of strangers, especially with the spike in slavers from the Free States, and call me soft, but I feel what you might say is a righteous fury at the thought of a demon picking off innocent villagers while the fighting men are out fishing or trading. If nothing else I can lend my sailing expertise to the cause."

Kirut nodded. "It's good to have you on the crew."

"The crew?" Haruin snorted. "We have a crew?"

"Yes. You, me, and two dogs."

"That's what I thought."

"I'll need to get permission to leave from my mother, but I expect I'll be with you shortly. Are we taking your outrigger?"

Haruin tipped his head to the nearest pair of dogs wrestling over frayed rigging. "Sure not leaving it here to be a chew toy."

Kirut nodded and jogged toward the lodge. Although his mother and aunt wouldn't be thrilled that he was choosing the hunt over visiting Mia, he hoped they would understand the importance of taking this opportunity.

His mother, Shaku, and Chief Koda were having lunch inside. None were presently eating. When they looked to him, all three wore an expression of resignation.

His mother spoke first. "We are told your Easterner friend, the pirate Haruin, is here."

"He is," said Kirut. "He says there are reports of attack that resemble the pattern leading up to the assault on Huu Taukit. The hezuki is back in these waters."

"Son, to slay this creature is not your duty. Your duties are here. If there is anything beyond our waters that should have your attention, it is your sons."

"I must do this, mother."

"This obsession is going to be your doom."

"I cannot sit idle while this threat remains in our world. Not when I know it can be vanquished and I have the means to do so."

"You have hardly sat idle!" said his mother. "This demon has consumed your every thought for seven years. By the first song, Kirut; it took your eye. Must it take your life?"

Chief Koda took a deep breath. Shaku leaned forward, tapping her prong against her plate.

"I would like to have your blessings for this voyage, as both matron and my mother," said Kirut. "This conflict has consumed my every thought these seven years because it is my duty. I failed. I did not kill it. Had I been stronger or better prepared, I might have slayed the demon. Now, many settlements have been struck. Six at least, each with many families. They may not be sons and daughters of the whale, but they are still children of the sea. Our kin. Our blood. This demon slaughters and gorges itself on the bodies of our people because I wasn't ready. I am stronger now. I am better prepared and, thanks to Haruin, I have an enchanted artifact with which to slay it. The knife may be a poor substitute for the Lance of the Corpse Whale, but it will kill the demon I hunt. Please, mother; send me on this quest. Let me right my failure."

Matron Kaya looked to her brother, then sister.

Finally Shaku spoke. "I will not deny that our failure has haunted me too. I lost my son. How many more mothers must lose their children?" She looked up to meet his gaze. "I cannot accompany you, Kirut. Arlu needs me, and her birth has helped to heal my wounds. I wish that were the case for you too. I would much rather lose you to a happy life in Huu Taukit, but I will not pretend I do not understand your need. You have my full blessing. Go."

Kirut's mother sighed. She stood, and Kirut met her in an embrace. "As you have mine. Please have care. You have so much life ahead of you. Someday you will be chief. If slaying this beast is to be your trial, your song, your legacy? So be it. Just know that there is no failure. Should it evade you, you will be welcomed home and the fire will be kept warm."

Kirut kissed his mother's forehead, then crossed around the table to do the same for Shaku.

When he looked up, Chief Koda had stood and crossed to the mantle of the hearth.

He lifted Nyrannuk, Lance of the Corpse Whale, from its hook display.

"Nyrannuk is the spirit of Clan Modekesh. It is passed down to the eldest son of our matron. Since my mother died three years ago and Kaya became our matron, I may yet be chief, but this is your birthright." Chief Koda planted it in Kirut's hand, but did not break focus nor let go. "Your eldest sister is with child. Dimwu says it will be a boy. If this is so, Nyrannuk will be his birthright. Your duty to this family as chief will be to prepare him to be the man he must become in order to carry this spear and all it represents. In order to uphold that duty, you must bring this back."

Kirut could not find the words to speak.

He could only nod.

Koda pulled him into a brief yet strong embrace. In all his life, Kirut had never had this gesture.

He said his farewells, then gathered his kit from his cabin.

Over the years, he had refined his armor. It was primarily made of baleen lamellar, along with a quilted wool gambeson, with the aim of as thorough and reinforced protection as he could find without using metal, which had proven generally ineffective at protecting from the freezing bites and breath of the hezuki. His shield was also thick and had many layers of baleen, with the steel boss, rivets on the edge, and grip core being its only metal component. The helmet he had made himself, again with minimal metallic components. He had also made a gambeson with lamellar for Guppik that would protect much of his body while still allowing him to move. He had not yet made one for Tam, but set the necessary supplies aside that he might make it on Haruin's outrigger.

Kirut lifted the throwing knife and bracer that Haruin had found and purchased for him. Kirut of course reimbursed him handsomely. It was of Pakardiant make: a throwing knife made of bronze, forged and enchanted thousands of years ago during the Age of Witches. The bracer that was purchased with it was blessed with the same enchantment and enabled the knife to be summoned back after a throw. Kirut had become quite proficient with it in the four years since Haruin brought it, but in truth, it took little skill. From what Kirut had learned, enchanted weapons of sufficient potency had memories of their own, and once attuned, could aid their wielder in combat.

Holding both weapons together, the Pakardiant knife in one hand and Nyrannuk in the other, felt uncomfortably warm and a bit prickly.

One of his cousins stopped by to gather some things and start loading Haruin's outrigger. With his pack filled and all accounted for, Kirut passed through the village and wished all his kin goodbye. He lingered in his sister's cabin for longer than he would have had Koda not left him with the wisdom he had. Once he felt his obligations of departure were complete, Kirut met with Haruin at the docks, gathering up Guppik and Tam on his way.

Shaku and two of his distant cousins were loading Haruin's boat with four barrels of whale oil.

"Are you certain?" Kirut asked.

Shaku nodded. "Of course. Half barrels proved invaluable before. That will no doubt be of service."

Kirut and his aunt embraced once more. Once she promised to let Arlu know he said goodbye once more, Kirut set down the dog plank and urged his hounds on board. Guppik promptly settled down under the canvas on the larger bed Kirut had asked his cousin to load. Tam busied himself looking overboard on either side. Although Guppik was a veteran of the sea, born and bred for voyages, Kirut wasn't sure how the more energetic guardian wolfdog would take it all. The pup had only been on day trips. He handled it fine, but preferred shallower waters where he could hop out and trot along shore to explore. As they would be in more open waters, Kirut set aside a lot of toys and hoped he wouldn't be too uncomfortable.

"Four barrels and two hounds, one as big as two barrels," said Haruin. "My outrigger has seen more smuggled, but this is quite near the limit."

"I'll make it worth your efforts," said Kirut, setting the throwing knife and bracer in Haruin's hand.

"Are you certain? You gave me your share for what... five voyages for this?"

"And we both know you paid more than double the worth I could provide. You did so because you knew how important it was to have a weapon with enchantment. Well, as it happens, I've been honored with Nyrannuk to finish what I started, and not only did I feel the two weapons did not enjoy sharing a body, I think if you're going to risk your life in hunting demons, you should be properly armed."

Haruin drew the weapon and turned it about in his hand. It was a beautiful blade, turning down sharply for most of its length before curving up, with several projections along the way. The enchantment kept it polished as though fresh from the forge. Although

Kirut typically liked the look of patina, he could not deny the beauty in this knife.

After sheathing the blade and securing the oval scabbard to his weapon belt, Haruin pulled on the bracer onto his wrist. One of Kirut's cousins had tried it and suffered a terrible rash. Kirut later learned that not all people could attune to magic or at least not to all artifacts or spells, with Skald Boli comparing it to how some in the settlement were allergic to eggs or grass pollen. Haruin had brought him the knife, so Kirut wasn't too concerned, and was re-assured once Haruin strapped on the bracer that he would attune quickly enough.

Kirut freed the lines. He waved to Shaku and his assembled cousins. Once he and Haruin had rowed out, they opened the sails and promptly caught an easterly wind.

Kirut kissed Mia's pearl set in the small bronze medallion he had made. The warmth it gave him certainly felt like magic. Perhaps not as potent as Nyrannuk, but it was more than simple comfort.

After making sure all was set and accounted for, Kirut took a seat behind the helm. Tam immediately hopped up so his elbows were on Kirut's lap. Kirut ruffled the wolfdog's fur and leaned back. "So our plan is to sail to your home back on the Ring and, what? Ask about and hope to find the most recent attack?"

"That's where we begin, my friend," said Haruin, a grin on his face as they picked up speed. "Better a mad plan than no plan. The Great White Death has returned to our waters. Let's show her how mortals too can bite."

Chapter 2

During the final two days of their voyage, Yumi was able to draw the spinnaker sail as the wind was at their backs. Their speed was unprecedented. Although Bruhe disliked the pace, Yumi relished it.

As they reached familiar waters, she drew in the spinnaker with a simple shift and push of a lever, then drew out the headsail. The complex mechanics compared to the manual work she was used to was endlessly fascinating.

As they drew close, with the islands distant flecks, Bruhe stood rapidly. He sniffed the air. Yumi followed suit, taking a deep breath to calmly shift the interior of her nose to smell with the acuity of Sea Badger spirit.

Death permeated the air. It was faint, downwind of them now, but had so filled the region that it had pressed north.

Bruhe spotted the first body of their kin bobbing on the northbound current, signaled by a group of gulls and pair of buck terns. Yumi couldn't possibly identify the corpse by sight, and the rot was so strong s scent couldn't be narrowed to an individual.

As they drew closer, she saw countless birds above the islands.

For most of their journey, Bruhe had foregone a shirt and Yumi relished the cooling of the winds against the warm air. At first she assumed the cold was from her building terror, but Bruhe drew on his coat, and Yumi shivered at the wheel.

They drew closer toward the outer reefs. Even with her mortal nose, she could smell death heavy in the air, overpowering the familiar salt and foliage of the interior.

Circles of gulls marked what must be dozens of bodies scattered throughout the reefs. Sharks and sea lizards splashed about. Yumi dared not look too close at any of the forms, but even in death, she now recognized many scents. She had seen snow now and then in winter, but frost on the sand and foliage was an odd sight at the height of summer, even when upwells brought in cold water.

The maze of reefs would deter outsiders, but she knew every coral and stone. The central island, where most of their village was consolidated, was surrounded by a stand of cabbage gum and olive trees that protected Guardian Atolls from storms.

It was from this central island that the strongest scent of death hit her.

Yumi guided Admiral Hirah's shurugen around the last atoll to the dock of the central island. Bruhe stopped the craft with a pike and hopped off to secure the lines. Several boats were still tethered: the attack had been too swift for many, if any, to escape.

Yumi passed off their packs and spears, making sure both she and her cousin were armed.

"My shield too," said Bruhe. Yumi passed it over.

As she took Bruhe's hand and stepped off the boat, Yumi pulled her fiber jacket close. She was dressed to endure wind and sea foam, not frost. She walked low to steady herself on the docks.

Amidst the scents of her family, she noticed the smells of birds. At first she had assumed it was the scavenger birds. Indeed a crawling gull screeched at her and took off from the steps leading up to the boathouse. However, this scent was stronger. Unfamiliar. It was everywhere, especially near the first body they found.

It was her aunt Eyna.

Even in death, her grip was tight on her glass-bladed club. Yumi's eyes were drawn there because the rest of her body was too mangled to take in. Frost had corroded whatever hadn't been eaten.

The bites were sawed. She saw marks of teeth. Now that she was closer, she recognized the scent of this bird.

The Akanuk called them Xuul. They were much more common to the southwest, where the whalers encountered them. Occasionally these toothed birds, which looked like the mutant offspring of penguins and seals, came to their reefs with summer upwells or when winter was coldest. They were dangerous, but generally seemed to prefer fish and seals to hunting people.

Did upwells bring them north? There were so many of them she couldn't imagine this was the usual group of one to three. Now that she was paying attention, at least a dozen individual scents were around the boathouse. By their scent, the attack had been three days earlier.

"We must send word to Yano," said Bruhe.

Yumi nodded, following Bruhe through the boathouse.

Three other bodies were strewn about inside, both frosted over and feasted upon. A marine otter continued gnawing on one of their legs, ignoring Bruhe and Yumi as she passed by. Yumi didn't know otters were scavengers, mostly hunting fish and the occasional crab in the reefs, but evidently they weren't above a free meal.

As they walked, Yumi stopped to grab a heavier sealskin coat hanging up in the boathouse and pulled it on instead of her jacket. She then took Bruhe's shield and spear so he could take one too. Whoever made the coats wouldn't need them anymore.

Both chill and stench of death grew stronger with every step. Yumi couldn't bring herself to look. Couldn't process. It was enough to recognize the scents of everyone she had grown up with.

The lodge, their destination, was just ahead.

A body to their left demanded Yumi's attention.

It was their uncle Jaka. Although dead for what seemed to confirm her suspicion of three days, he remained in his walrus form. He was frozen over in a grapple with the decaying corpse of a xuul.

Right away Yumi could tell this was no ordinary bird.

It was emaciated down to skeletal features. Ice had encased both it and Jaka, although her uncle held the bird's neck in its jaws.

The stink of strange magic, ripe and briny, wafted from the corpse.

This must have been a demon.

It was said that her ancestors were given the gift of skin-changing by the guardian spirit Sea Badger to protect the sea from demons. Although many spoke of demons, they did the same when talking about the skin-changers of Guardian Atolls, as ferocious supernatural beings. Yumi should have known there was truth to tales of demons, but she had always assumed if there was, they were just beings with some bond with the wild magic of Kaimere, same as witches and skin-changers.

This monster seemed far more powerful. There had been others in its pack, at least forty by her scent count, but they had slaughtered a village with several hundred people. Jaka was one of the few skin-changers in the settlement. She had seen him fight off a dozen men in skin and best a sea serpent in fur. It was said that in his youth he slew a milaq, or merfolk, singlehandedly. Even in his prime and almost as big as Yano, her uncle had been slain by the ice of this demon and its clawed feet imbedded in his throat.

At least he had taken it with him.

Knowledge that the creatures could be slain did bring some comfort, although this was the only slain demon she had come across by scent or sight so far.

Bruhe walked without expression, wordlessly taking in the devastation.

Yumi knew she should be terrified or sick. Broken or furious. She had cried over breakups with girlfriends from nearby villages and feeling left out of celebrations when she was too young to participate. This should have her shattered, but she was numb.

"We must continue," said Bruhe, his voice cracking slightly.

The entrance to the lodge was just ahead.

Yumi smelled her mother's corpse before she even opened the door.

Her mother and the matron of the village were both skin-changers.

The matron, Jirhe, was in skin and guarding the prayer room. Like so many, she had died with a weapon and shield in hand, although most of her flesh was frozen off and consumed. Bruhe stood before the body of his mother. Yumi's mother's form was iced over like Uncle Jakachin. Also like her uncle, Yumi's mother was in fur and frozen in a grapple with the corpse of a demon. Another skin-changer, her distant cousin Ari, was slain but no sign of her having taken another demon with her. The girl had only just awakened. Seeing the young walrus torn open before she even had a chance to fight…

The door that Matron Jirhe had died before was ajar. Inside Yumi smelled a dozen scents. Children who must have been fortified.

All dead.

Yumi braced herself on one of the chairs lined along the outer wall of the lodge. She gripped the back of the chair.

After a deep breath, Yumi carried on. Bruhe was frozen before his mother. Yumi couldn't blame him, and wanted to break down herself, but Yano and the others needed to know.

The pigeon rookery was in the back of the lodge. It had been three days. She had never worked with the pigeons much. Could they go three days without food?

Thankfully, sounds of hooting pigeons greeted her as she rounded the hall to their isolated hut.

A corpse was sprawled and frosted over. Niri had tended the birds as long as Yumi had been alive. The woman wasn't a skin-changer, but a witch of some talent. Evidently her magic had not been enough to fend off her attacker. She spent most of her magic on fortifying her birds, which did not leave energy for combative spells.

The pigeon linked to Tikah's camp, a red and white bird, was still present. That meant Niri had not gotten word out about the attack.

Yumi gathered seed and ensured all birds were fed. The pump ran filtered water down the tube trough so they could drink as well. As the birds fed, Yumi sat at Niri's desk and took a pen to parchment.

Yano,

We arrived at Guardian Atolls. The voyage took us seven days. Ice demons have attacked. No survivors. I will await your reply and further orders.

Yumi.

Yumi rolled up the scroll, tucked it in a case, and went to put it on the red pigeon. She had never done this before, only seen Niri and her apprentice do it, but thankfully the clever bird helped slip on the tiny padded vest and scroll case. With that, she pulled the lever that opened the back of its cage, and the pigeon dutifully flew into the hut and out the window.

Yumi shut the windows and let the rest of the birds out to stretch their wings and interact on Niri's shelves.

With the birds cared for as best Yumi could, and word sent to her brother that would take three days to arrive and three more to respond, Yumi finally collapsed onto the chair before the desk.

She let out a broken scream before doubling over in sobs.

***

With the winds at their back for much of the journey, it took nine days for Kirut and Haruin on the Eskadin outrigger to reach the Ring.

Kirut was elated that they now sailed out of its interior sea.

Enthusiastic at the prow, Tam also seemed happy to be back on open water. Guppik seemed as content as ever to relax in the middle of the boat, his great weight keeping it stable along with the barrels of whale oil under the canvas.

The Ring was disputed territory. It was a crescent shaped island. Both Free States and Eskadin Coalition claimed its governance, but ultimately it was a hub of trade and chaos that neither party controlled.

The port cities on the interior of the Ring were busy and loud. The smell lingered. It was here that most of the oil that Kirut and his kin harvested in their voyages was ultimately sold, although they never came this far east, usually trading to Eskadin merchants like Haruin and letting them deal with the bartering, chaos, and stench of large towns and cities.

Along with being a hub of trade, it was a hub of rumor. Kirut had planned on asking fishing villages what word they had of ice demons, but Haruin was wise to take them to the Ring. Kirut hated the place, but he couldn't argue with the results. Over the course of a meal and a few drinks, Haruin got three independent rumors about the latest attack.

A village on the eastern atolls. Said to be the home of skin-changers. Kirut had grown so used to people falsely assuming his people were skin-changing hounds that he forgot that skin-changers were real. It felt strange doubting their existence after he watched his cousin and half a village slaughtered by toothed penguins infected by ice magic.

Once they got coordinates, the pair departed. Haruin wanted to spend the night in port, recommending several brothels before they went off chasing demons, but Kirut was of a single mind.

"It seems strange that the hezuki would attack a skin-changer village," Kirut said as Haruin turned starboard to account for a shift in the wind. "Are they not capable of killing demons with their magic?"

"That's what the stories say, at least. The skin-changers of the Guardian Atolls were blessed with magic and mighty forms to slay demons. Similar story to your lance there, from what I have heard." At Haruin's request, Kirut filled a horn with ale and passed it over before filling one of his own. The spiced ale they had picked up in port wasn't his usual preference, but the kick shivered out any lingering exhaustion.

Haruin downed the rest of his horn then refilled it. "Didn't you say these demons were cowards?"

"They were. Had they been bold, killing them would have been a lot easier. The Blackfish who set up Huu Taukit as a trap was quite clear that they would only come if they thought we were easy prey. For them to intentionally seek out a village with perhaps the only beings in the eastern sea that can do them harm perplexes me."

"Maybe you're not the only one who's been taking these past seven years readying for a fight."

Kirut frowned. "I don't like the idea of the demon adapting."

"You're the one who said the Great White Death seemed a lot more clever, and the rest acted as her puppets. Maybe we should be prepared for her to act different than she did last time."

"Perhaps." Kirut took a long sip. "The other attacks you heard about all followed the old pattern though, yes?"

"Was a copy to the stitch. Striking settlements with no defenses. Easy kills and no survivors. Didn't raise much suspicion. The accompanying frost made many think it was a beast brought by a storm from the polar continent, and everything's more deadly down south. As we heard in this city that's the prevailing assumption here too, but the pattern was so exact to your description I knew to find you as soon as I heard. Striking the most famous village with skin-changers is strange, but can't have been a coincidence. A much larger village than her usual targets. From what I hear, the Guardian Atolls are a fortress of reefs, each one a ship killer. Suppose that's not a problem for swimming demons. Point is: Hezuki must have attacked them knowing there were skin-changers and that's why she did it: eliminate the threat before it had time to prepare."

Kirut wanted to disagree, but some part of him knew Haruin was right.

"With the wind at our back, it's a three day sail. I'll take first shift. You get some rest, my friend. You're going to need it."

Kirut nodded, finished his ale, and laid himself to rest against Guppik. Tam joined the pile and was out before Kirut even settled in. Kirut held Mia's necklace close.

***

Over the next two days, Yumi and Bruhe took it upon themselves to care for the dead.

There were countless in the village alone. Yumi cried so much that she felt a husk of a person. Some part of her knew she had to drink lots of water to compensate. She kept fed from the elevated store huts. Hate and the hunger for vengeance wouldn't sustain her: she needed real food for that.

Each body she carried to water she saw as strengthening her body and resolve.

Her family was dead. She knew their scents and what remained of their faces, but the bodies empty. Their spirits departed. They returned each body they found to the sea whence they came.

Forty or so giant banshee gulls had gathered and feasted on the bodies of their kin that she and Bruhe brought out from the lodge. These crawling birds once disgusted her, but they made no aggression toward her and Bruhe nor their usual squabbling calls. Maybe the truth is there was plenty of meat for all and no need to fight, but some part of her felt their solemn feeding was their way of helping her return her family to the sea.

By the second day, most of the cold had passed, and the regular summer heat returned. The frost encasing the bodies still trapped out on the reef was in thaw. The stench that morning was horrid.

It hadn't taken long to realize there were far more bodies than had lived on the atolls before she and Bruhe left to join the company three years earlier. Many of the bodies were briny and far more decayed than the timeline allowed for, and she wasn't certain they were from the village. Since many of her people had wounds of axes, clubs, and spears, she wondered if these corpses had been minions of the demons that led the assault. Although her initial assumption was that the entire village was slain, there were a few missing boats.

"We should see if we can find survivors," said Bruhe over breakfast in the lodge. "We should seek them out and let them know it is safe to return."

"Where would we assume they might go?"

"I would guess Gathering Island. If they were fishing the night of the attack, they might not feel safe in returning."

Yumi shook her head. "We should be here in case word comes back from Yano."

"Yumi, a pigeon will take three days to reach Tikah's camp. They probably got your missive this morning. We will not hear back for at least three more."

Yumi frowned and picked at her plate. "I do not think we should leave."

"I cannot stay here doing nothing for another moment," said Bruhe, standing from the table. "You can stay if you must. I'm taking the Sea Badger out to Gathering Island."

"Fine. be back before nightfall," said Yumi, more bite in her tone than she intended. "I'll have dinner ready."

Once he was gone, Yumi felt ashamed of how relieved she felt in his absence. Although his mood was worsening her own, she didn't begrudge his sour demeanor. They had no choice but to sit in the remains of their home.

After gathering some food for her and Bruhe's dinner, movement under a hut stopped Yumi in her tracks.

She caught a vaguely familiar scent underneath.

Yumi didn't know this distant relative well. He was young, near but not at adolescence. His scent smelled living, bur also rotted. Brine stank the air, mixing with his scent. Bari was the name which came to mind after she leaned down to get a stronger smell.

A guttural hiss met her inspection, and Yumi scrambled back.

Yumi cursed under her breath. She didn't bring her aunt's club, and there was no time to shift.

A chill in the air fogged her accelerating breath.

After getting some distance and arming herself with a nearby oar, Yumi knelt to get a better look under the hut.

A small figure was definitely moving under the hut. Red eyes glowed in the setting sun behind Yumi. Although she couldn't see all the colors of most people because she was a skin-changer, Yumi knew Bari's eyes would glow yellowish if he were also a skin-changer. Red was not an uncommon eyeshine amongst other creatures, but these were certainly the glow of the child, not something scavenging him.

"Bari?" she whispered. "Bari, it's me, Yumi. Are you trapped?"

Another gurgled hiss was his reply.

The more she took in his scent, the more confident she was that the boy was dead.

Grinding her teeth, Yumi jogged off toward the boathouse. It was only after she got some distance that the temperature increased considerably.

At the boathouse, Yumi found a pair of rubber-coated gloves that fit her. She returned to the hut with a rope and crescent spade. These were used to catch and redirect seals and sea badgers without hurting them. Whatever was under the hut, Yumi didn't want to jump to harm, especially if there might be some way to save what remained of Bari.

Once she got close, Yumi could see in the low light that something stored under the hut had toppled onto Bari, trapping him. Tethered logs for firewood by the looks of it. He was about as deep into the underside of the hut as Yumi was tall.

Now that she got a better look, Bari was clearly dead. A horrid wound was on his arm. An infected animal bite by the looks of it. His appendages were blackened with frostbite and skin overall frosted and pale. The scent of death was mixed with a ripe salt and rot she now associated with the magic of whatever demons had slaughtered her family.

Bari contorted slightly, setting off several cracks from his stiffened and frosted body as he struck the ground and clawed with far greater speed and strength than his initial movements suggested. Yumi stepped back, but he was still lodged under the tethered wood.

After taking in his situation, Yumi fell back and grabbed the oar. It was a long steering oar that probably should be in the boathouse, but she was grateful for whoever was too lazy to return it on the day of the attack.

Holding her crescent spade and rope in her shield hand, Yumi took the oar at its handle and extended it to its furthest reach. Bari shifted and snarled, but was still restrained. Once the oar was jabbed under the tethered logs, Yumi rolled a large stone closer with her foot and set the oar on top.

With a deep breath, and staying crouched so she could see Bari, Yumi pressed most of her weight onto the oar.

The aid of her oar combined with his superhuman strength, Bari wriggled free. With the blinding speed she now anticipated, Bari scrambled out from under the hut and pounced.

Yumi struck him in the chest with the butt of the crescent spade. He stumbled aside. Although fast and strong for such a young frame, his leg seemed to have been critically damaged by the logs. Yumi retracted the crescent spade against his good leg before he could recover, sending him face first onto the ground. From there she thrust, catching the base of his neck with the crook of her spade.

As he struggled, Yumi planted her foot on the crescent and began to restrain him. It felt cruel when one hand was so ruined by the bite and an entire leg below the knee crushed by the logs, but she couldn't risk him biting her and spreading whatever infection he might carry.

He was dead. That much she was confident of. He smelled freshly dead though, within the last few hours. Was whatever magic animating him also preserving his body in a freshly-dead state? She hoped that was the case. The alternative was he was there for two days and she could have saved him.

Once he was tied with a thoroughness that would make her uncle who had taught her such restraints proud, Yumi rolled out a cart, put him inside, and pushed him back to the lodge.

Yumi further secured Bari outside the lodge under a low awning that at one point stored more firewood but only had a few logs and tinder. Yumi didn't know if rain would be bad for the living dead. Aside from them being featured in a few campfire stories, she didn't know anything about them, and this was her first time thinking they might even be real. Although she was fairly certain she could destroy it, since the demons that made it had been vanquished by the bite of a skin-changer, she further restrained the frigid body just in case. No need to tempt fate, and Yano would surely want to see it. She put it under the awning to protect it from the elements. Did the living dead need food? She wasn't sure, and wasn't about to risk removing the gag she now had in place. The heat of the day probably wouldn't be good for the body and preserving it in the shade seemed the best choice at the time.

Yumi carefully removed her gloves and threw them in the sea.

Wanting a new pair in case Bari had to be dealt with further, Yumi meandered to the boathouse.

She was walking up the back steps when she spotted an outrigger at sea.

Not any of their sloops, so it was not Bruhe returning early. Of Eskadin design, but she didn't recognize the pattern on its sails. A pair of naked dancers was not a sigil Yumi encountered. Too small to be a raiding or slaver vessel. Likely scavengers.

Yumi cursed under her breath.

She should have anticipated this. Usually people were afraid both of the reefs and from the rumors of witches and skin-changers in the Guardian Atolls. She assumed they would keep their distance. Although Yumi had never seen a stranger's boat this close to the atolls, it was practically hugging the outer reef. This close, the signs of her home's destruction was surely evident. Scavenger birds would see to that. From there, of course word would travel. It had now been four days since the attack.

Plenty of time for the gulls to gather.

They were still a fair way off. She could trade skin for fur. Toppling their boat as they're in the atoll maze would almost certainly kill them. However, she knew Yano would want to question them.

Her brother would want *her* to question them. There was no notion of when he would be back, and although Bruhe was son of the matron and chief by default, he was gone too.

This was up to her.

Yumi sprinted to the lodge. The 'armory' which was just a long closet with a few dozen weapons, presented many options. Although Yumi had come for a bow, she grabbed and loaded the Republic winged crossbow. The weapon had cost a small fortune, but after several campaigns of mercenary work with Tikah, they had more funds than they needed. She had been shown its use once and shot a few times. Much different than a bow, but it packed astonishing power, and all it took to reload was the pull of a lever.

With the cumbersome weapon in hand, Yumi sprinted back to the boathouse to wait for the scavengers.

***

"Port load!"

"Are you sure?" Kirut shouted over the crashing waves. "I think we can make it through the cut of the channel. Turning gets us tied up with the reefs."

"We're in an outrigger!" Haruin said, steadying the rudder. "Not exactly built for navigating mazes!"

"Also not good at turns."

"I know that! Just try!"

Kirut did so, even though the walls of the atolls on either side were too close for his liking. Guppik whined at his feet. Tam wagged his tail, no doubt thinking this another game. While Kirut was glad he had acclimated so well to seafaring, he wished the pup would sit still.

The boat turned hard to starboard, and as the headsail filled with wind, Haruin's craft launched forward. Spray showered Kirut. The outrigger lifted from the water in the hard turn, clearing the nearest reefs. Both men cheered, although the cry was cut off as the barrel of ale tumbled into the surf. They passed it swiftly, and a surge smashed the barrel against a nearby coral. Haruin cursed under his breath but kept onward.

"Alright we're going to have to tack ahead. Starboard load!"

Kirut pulled the port side ropes while easing out the starboard. Haruin eased them through the channel. Although the turn was clean, a low grind made Kirut cringe.

"Did we take water?"

"Can't tell," said Kirut. "Felt something, though."

"Let's see how far she'll take us."

Kirut tried to see what was ahead, but the channels swelled with such chaos that it was difficult to determine where other hidden corals might be.

"Think this one ahead will take us in?"

"Should be. I think we took the long way but it's all we could manage in this mess. Steady. We're turning hard to port."

Kirut nodded to a tower coral jutting from the surf. "See the-"

"I see it! Shift the sails. It will be tight but I think we can manage."

Kirut held the cables firm, waiting for Haruin's command.

"Tack!"

Kirut shifted the cables. The gap ahead looked to shrink as they approached. Gulls cried out overhead, as if mocking their efforts. Tam barked up at them, though his tone was playful.

"Kirut, the port cable!"

With his focus on the starboard side, Kirut didn't realize how quickly the rope was sliding around the hook since the section in his hand was still taut. He cursed his missing left eye and grabbed both ropes.

Although Kirut tried to ease the rotation of the front sail, the turn snapped it starboard with greater force than he anticipated. To make matters worse, the outrigger hooked against the tower coral. It spun the boat about, a low strain building to a crack as the outrigger snapped free.

"We lost the-"

"I know!"

Kirut looked to see if they took on water from where the outrigger was torn away, but didn't see a sign of damage to the interior. There was a good amount of water underfoot, although he couldn't tell if it was from waves splashing in, the loss of the outrigger, or some earlier impact.

The boathouse was just ahead. Although the wind was at their backs and they should have peaked in speed, the boat was slowing.

Tam hopped off the front of the boat and swam toward the docks.

When Kirut glanced down, the water in their hull had doubled in depth.

"I'll steer, you gather our things," Haruin shouted. "We can hook out the barrels, don't worry for those."

Kirut nodded. He started with the lance and armor, then grabbed their pack of rations and Haruin's satchel.

The water was now up to his knees. At his command, Guppik hopped off the boat, sending it careening right.

"To the front! Get ready to hop on the dock."

Kirut was already making his way. Haruin locked the rudder and sloshed through the hull to the front.

They leaped onto the pier just as Haruin's sinking boat collided with the craft already in the docking spot. Wind still filled its sails, but water finished its conquest of the hull, it's rails were now barely above the waves, only kept afloat by virtue of being made of wood.

"Haruin, I apologize," said Kirut. "I thought I had the cable. With my eye-"

Haruin wordlessly passed over his weapon belt, hopped back onto the boat, and grumbled as he drew in the sails. Guppik had climbed out onto one of the many ramps and shook out his shaggy coat a few piers down. Although he was still in the water, Tam started barking angrily.

"If either of you move, I'll send this bolt through you both. It's a winged crossbow, so I can reload faster than you can sprint down the docks."

The voice was feminine. She sounded exhausted and frightened, a terrible combination for someone armed with a mainlander crossbow. He had heard terrible stories about their ease of use and lethality.

He clicked twice to Tam and Guppik to stay and be calm. Tam was still in the water, but complied once he reached the ramp Guppik had used to get to one of the piers.

"May I turn around?" Kirut asked.

"Disarm yourselves first."

Kirut nodded. He set the lance down and unclipped the sheathed knife too, followed by his axe. "We're not looking for a fight. We're just here to talk. May I turn around?"

"Yes."

Kirut turned down the dock and looked up at the stairs leading to the boathouse.

Their captor was young, barely a woman. Her hair was straight and thick like Haruin's, but a sandy blond with a patch of umber brown on her left temple. Dark circles under blue eyes hinted at lack of recent sleep, and a slight tremble in her hands added up to a traumatized sight. She was indeed armed with a winged crossbow: a bulky weapon with a steel bow. It was aimed at their feet and her finger beside the trigger rather than on it, but he didn't imagine he could do much before she repositioned and shot. Even in the hands of someone on the edge of consciousness, a weapon like that could be lethal.

***

Yumi held the crossbow steady as she could. The run to the lodge and back had been more exhausting than she had anticipated, and she felt a little lightheaded. She couldn't remember the last time she drank water. She was in no position to defend her village.

Shaking her head, Yumi took in the two men.

The older of the two was an Eskadin man. His black hair was knotted back and he let his moustache grow long. Although they looked worn from travel, he must have recently shaved, for his cheeks were clean, and his overall demeanor was put together in spite of the less than graceful arrival. The fine embroidery on his shirt and several pieces of silver and gold jewelry suggested a wealthy profession or inheritance.

The younger man truly caught her eye. She had never met an Akanuk in person, but the whalers and hound breeders were known by reputation. He wore only trousers and a tunic in spite of the strong winds, speaking to what must be quite hot compared to his home to the southwest. He wore his curls long and in braids, and had shaved recently too. A patch over his port eye drew attention to a scar across the entire left side of his face. She had never thought much of men, but for one of that persuasion, he was handsome.

Their two dogs were quite different beasts: a great black and white monster of a whale hound, nearly as large as Yano in fur, and a creature that looked small by comparison but came nearly to her hip and had the snout, ears, and hackles of a wolf. The whale hound looked at ease, if a bit nervous. The wolfhound glared at her, ready to spring.

A strong scent hit her nose: a metallic scent with hints of fruit, and she traced it to both weapons at the Akanuk's feet. The witch Niri had several small artifacts, and that magic had a similar aroma, although these weapons smelled much more potent.

Yumi realized that the Akanuk had been talking. She took a deep breath and focused.

"Sorry; start again?"

"My name is Kirut Modekesh. This is Haruin of the Ring. Those two are Tam and Guppik. Hey, Tam! Tsch. Be nice." After scolding the wolfdog, Kirut turned back to Yumi. "Apologies. We heard that your village was attacked. Many other villages in the area have been attacked in a similar way. I'm from… quite far away, and have been tracking an ice demon for many years. We came here to see what else we might learn since it was their most recent target."

"I am Yumichin. I arrived three days ago, which was five days after the demons attacked. You know what they are? Have you fought them?"

Kirut nodded, slowly tapping the scar on his face. "I've killed several, with help of course. They are called hezuki, Bringers of Frost and Famine, by the villagers I fought beside. We bring two weapons with sufficient enchantment to end them. I was unable to vanquish the greater demon that created the thralls. That is a failure I intend to correct."

Yumi lowered the crossbow. "Welcome to the Guardian Atolls. I don't know when they left, but the hezuki killed every living being on the islands. Every warrior, every elder, every child. If it's revenge you're looking for, Kirut Modekesh, you've come to the right place."

***

After helping Haruin draw his outrigger from the water and leaving him to its repairs in a seething silence, Kirut and Yumichin exchanged all the details they could about their respective encounters with the demons. That skin-changers could kill the demons, Yumi was a shifter herself, and had a warband of almost thirty others that she was waiting to hear from. Finding that as many as forty hezuki were part of the attack was daunting, but having nearly as many skin-changers in the Chin warband was an optimistic counter. Suddenly killing the hezuki seemed a tangible goal.

After a meal, shave, and shower, Kirut walked outside to clear his head. With Tam at his heels, he passed his idle thoughts with throws of sticks, letting Tam tire himself out after so many days on a boat.

They didn't know where the hezuki were, but this was the closest he had felt in years. This was real. He might finally end this horrid story.

Kirut's wandering brought him to the undead child restrained outside the lodge.

It hissed up at him, which trailed off in a low gurgle. The area around it was cold, a striking contrast to the hot summer air in the rest of the village. Tam snarled, looking eager for the kill, but Kirut firmly told him to leave it alone.

"You said they made these creatures when they attacked Huu Taukit?"

Kirut turned to Yumi. She had eaten too, and was already looking in better condition. No doubt being around other living beings helped too. It was good to see.

They would have to all be at their best for what came ahead.

"One of the first things they did was slaughter the single huts inland. Some they killed and ate, but they turned a lot of children into these creatures. I assumed it was for the elements of horror, but it could be that they just wanted to eat the adults since we have more meat, or perhaps their venom can't turn adults as easily."

"I didn't find many children aside from a few in the lodge. Many of our warriors are also missing. I assumed they were the first to be carried off by scavengers. Do you think they followed the demons? Some of the dead were killed with mortal weapons, and I found a many bodies I did not know. It may be that the hezuki bring some of the dead with them from each attack? Your friend Haruin said the rumors were that other islands to the southwest were struck first. My mother mentioned the same. Perhaps Bari here was supposed to join the other living dead and was left behind?"

Kirut hated the casual tone of the conversation, but both were numb to what they discussed. Had he started to heal before this? Some part of him always knew he would try to finish the hezuki. Prevent it from slaughtering more. Thinking about his twin sons made him both want to forget and cherish these new lives, but also hunt down the monster so no one else lost their family.

"It's possible. Those the demon infected almost immediately at-tacked Huu Taukit. I don't believe they were considered part of the pack, just tools. The dead that attacked were all of the residences outside of Huu Taukit on the same islands, not the neighboring settlements attacked beforehand. Then again, many elements of this situation are different. Perhaps they brought the dead along this time for a larger force."

"If they took that larger force with them, two skin-changers, a pair of hounds, and you and Haruin with your enchanted weapons aren't going to be enough."

"I agree. Do you think your brother will come home to help?"

"My brothers and the rest of our company are fighting the Klaeg in the east. They are cruel beings, said to eat kaimerans, but they have no magic. Klaeg are not demons. They're dangerous, and our company are valuable as scouts in tracking them, but this is an entirely different threat. I think at least some will come, but at best we have two more days to wait for a reply, and if they left as soon as they got our letter, even with favorable winds a fast clipper won't make it anytime soon."

Kirut crossed his arms. "As you said, we don't have the numbers to defeat this foe. Are there any large settlements we could go to and convince them to take in refugees? We must clear these waters of easy targets. If we can starve them out, we may be able to force the hezuki to attack a place with the resources to fend off the dead."

"There are four other island chains in the area: Fallen Stars is to the north, Krakenstone north of that, Iron Line Archipelago is a large chain to the east, and Hollow Turtle Island to the west. Hollow Turtle is the largest and best fortified. Our center of trade with each other and to The Ring. Matron Jonka is a kind and practical woman, and Chief Tonko is honorable. They have taken in refugees during storms and slaver raids. I expect most who are already aware of threats will sail there, but I do not know much. Guardian Atolls is generally avoided by outsiders, so they would not come here, and I don't know who all must be warned. I should send word to Matron Jonka and let her know of what happened here." Yumi went red. "I should have done so right away."

"You can be forgiven all things considered, but yes; it would be good to be in communication with any potential allies."

Haruin called from the boathouse. Kirut and Yumi turned as he jogged over, and stopped as Tam nearly took his legs out in an excited charge.

"Is your boat alright?" asked Kirut, feeling no shortage of guilt.

"What? Oh, yes. It will be fine. A shurugen sloop approaches from the west."

Yumi nodded. "That will be my cousin Bruhe."

Haruin squinted. "You and your cousin have a *shurugen?*"

Yumi grinned. "We're borrowing it from our employer's brother, but yes, and she sails with speed and grace far greater than any craft I have helmed."

"What is a shurugen sloop?" asked Kirut, raising an eyebrow. He had never seen Haruin so animated, and Yumi smiled for the first time since they had met her.

Haruin looked to Kirut, openly flabbergasted. "How have you sailed… a shurugen is an Imperial boat which, through cables and levers, can be fully operated from the helm. Sails extended and drawn. Outrigger and keel adjustable to suit whatever your needs. The shipwrights of Bolondakoi coat the hull in a secret lacquer that not only protects it from damage and parasites but actively repels water such that it may cut through the sea as a knife. They are dry as they sail! One of the greatest feats of engineering in the modern age. A paragon of the sea, the most sophisticated ships in the known world. Also the fastest! A shurugen clipper once sailed from Kabarahar to the Imperial Capitol in five days and four nights. Five days, Kirut! How have you never…"

"So it is a fast boat," he said with a nod. "This is good. That means we can quickly sail to, what was it, Yumi?"

"Hollow Turtle Island."

"Yes, that. I assume by your reaction that you don't mind if we use their boat for the journey, Haruin?"

Haruin's brown eyes went wide. "A fast boat? Kirut, I have a fast boat. Or, I might have a fast boat if I can sort out the impact to her hull. But I would burn my fast boat for a chance to sail a shurugen for a single morning. Yes, we can use their boat."

Yumi nodded her head toward the boat house. "Come meet Bruhe."

Kirut and Haruin followed.

The boat was indeed beautiful, with striking black and white paint coated in a shining lacquer. The brawny young man at the helm, who Kirut inferred was Bruhe, had reddish brown hair with a streak of white down the center. Yumi took the prow in a forked staff to slow it to a stop. Although Bruhe looked upon Kirut and Haruin with open suspicion, he tossed them the lines without hesitation.

"Bruhe, this is Kirut and Haruin. Kirut here has slain these creatures before, and says he can help. Was there anyone at Gathering Island?"

Bruhe shook his head before taking Kirut's hand and hopping onto the pier. "No. There was no sign of anyone present. Nor at Southwatch. If there were survivors, they're not in these waters."

As Haruin made dinner in the lodge and Yumi wrote to the matron of Hollow Turtle, Kirut explained the situation as best he could to Bruhe. Haruin brought out a dinner of sweet potatoes, bottle gourd, and smoked shark tail that Yumi had gathered from their supplies and baked together in flax oil and parsley. Haruin made sure there was plenty for Tam and Guppik on either side of Kirut.

Once they were finished, Kirut addressed the table. "Here is my proposal: tonight we rest. Eat. Fortify. We wait for a response from Matron Jonka of Hollow Turtle Island. If she does not send word by the following morning, we start with Iron Line Archipelago, the closest island, and continue west toward Hollow Turtle."

***

Yumi waited impatiently in the rookery all the following afternoon with no sign of the blue and white bird she had sent the night before. Hollow Turtle was nearly two days away by sail, but a pigeon should have reached it by sundown, and be back by midday. As evening approached, Kirut stopped in with a gourd of taro and more shark tail that Haruin had made and set it on Niri's desk in front of her.

"Still no word?" he asked, leaning against the wall and tucking into his own gourd.

Yumi frowned. "Thank you, and no. None. It's possible it may have been attacked. Ospreys, buck terns, and eagles are all predators of messenger pigeons, and it's not unusual for jackal birds to wait for them near rookeries, which is why they have armor. Should I send another?"

"No. I think we should wait for the rest of the evening, then be ready to sail before dawn. I've already loaded all of our things in the boathouse, next to where Bruhe packed his and yours."

"Should we begin at Fallen Stars?" Yumi said, laying out Niri's map. "With the winds coming from up here, we might be best suited to just arc around then sail north rather than going all the way to Iron Line Archipelago. I do think we should head to Hollow Turtle, but we may as well pass through Fallen Stars anyway."

Kirut nodded. "You know these winds and waters. I defer."

"I'll write a note and leave it here for my brother in case they do come. Seems foolish for them to come here then go back north, but since we don't even know if he's coming, and I cannot wait around any longer. If I'm here one more day-"

Kirut put a hand on her shoulder. "You are not alone in that impatience. I waited for seven years, and now it feels another moment is too long. No more waiting. We leave in the morning. Now, regarding your cousin, the living dead... would you like me to take care of him? Bruhe said yes, but I wanted to hear your thoughts on the matter."

Yumi thought a moment then shook her head. "No. He is restrained, and the dead cannot spread the venom from what you say, so he will be of no danger to any surviving family of mine. He may prove useful in understanding them should my brother come back and wish to learn more of their strengths and weaknesses. He likes to understand his foes."

"A wise man," said Kirut, patting her shoulder once more. "Get some rest if you can. We leave at first light."

Chapter 3

Yumi awoke before the dawn, her every muscle tensed and ready for a fight. Knowing she wouldn't get any further sleep, she got up and moving.

Kirut and Bruhe were also up, as were the hounds. Once Haruin was awakened, the crew piled into the Sea Badger. They rowed out of the atolls, reaching open waters as the first rays of pink danced along their starboard rail.

Although he had been a bit groggy to start, Haruin's expression of glee when Yumi asked if he wanted to open the sails was a delight to cut the steeping tension in her. For a little while, it was nice to see his elation at its mechanics. True, the boat was made to be intuitive, but he rapidly got control of the craft, laughing like a madman as the easterly winds shot them northeast so they could loop around to Fallen Stars.

Part of the appeal of Guardian Atolls was its isolation. Fallen Stars, a chain of thirteen tiny islands, was their closest neighbor and would normally take a day and night to reach.

In Hirah's shurugen, they arrived by late afternoon.

The desolation of Fallen Stars was absolute. Few bodies remained from what they could see from the surf, with any remains having been picked at by scavengers. They could see nothing but death on the little islands. Toward Morning Star, the largest island where the living huts and lodge were constructed, more bodies were scattered about. All were frozen and desiccated.

At first, Tam refused to get out of the boat. It was only once Kirut was most of the way down the pier that the wolfdog hopped out and sprinted to close the distance. He remained fixed by Kirut's side, whining with each step. Guppik kept pace, his ears forward and suddenly looking quite unlike the easygoing whale hound she had gotten used to.

The stop to search for survivors was brief: none were to be found. She had been here often in her childhood, and nine large families had called Morning Star Island their home. Several of these people had been her friends. Her first lover, Kay, was from this settlement.

Yumi forced herself to check Kay's family huts.

There were several bodies inside. One frozen form, fed to the bones, had Kay's favorite bracelet on the wrist.

Yumi felt hollow.

After whispering a prayer, she left the hut.

Like Guardian Atolls, it seemed all boats and their two ships were still docked. The attack had been at night. Most signs of conflict were in the family huts. The lodge and boathouse were untouched. No possessions had been taken. Skeletons were strewn about, although many bones had been chewed into so the marrow could be eaten.

"Two nights ago?" Kirut asked. He was knelt over the skeleton of a man. A warrior by the looks of the skeleton's tree-fiber armor and the spear in hand. Gripped tight, for all the good it had done him.

Bruhe nodded. "My sense of smell isn't as strong in skin, but it's fresh enough that I can tell."

"They attacked here, what… six nights after your home was hit?" said Haruin, then turned to Kirut. "That sounds like a long gap, yes? The attacks we heard about in the islands to the southwest were more frequent. Every few nights."

"Those settlements were smaller," said Kirut. "Looks like there may have been a few hundred people here based on the huts, yes?"

"Near two hundred I would guess," said Bruhe

Haruin looked out to the west. "You said Iron Line was the next nearest settlement?"

"Iron Line and Hollow Turtle are about the same in either direction. Normally a full day and night's sail from here, but in the Sea Badger I think we can make it by nightfall. Both have far greater populations, well over a thousand."

Haruin frowned. "You said two hundred people lived here, yes?"

Bruhe nodded.

"I would estimate there's only around forty bodies here that they ate. Assuming most were present, that means over a hundred more bodies in their armies of the living dead."

Yumi reflexively hugged her chest. She hadn't allowed herself to consider the notion of her family being among the living dead, but if Bari was any indication, it was something she should prepare for.

"So where do we go?" asked Bruhe. "Hollow Turtle is better fortified and I expect that's where most are going, but we should not abandon the people of Iron Line. They must be warned."

Kirut stood and took a deep breath. "We should have anticipated this back at Guardian Atolls. I saw their rookery. If there are any birds to the nearby islands, will you send word?"

Yumi couldn't bring herself to speak, but nodded before going. Perhaps sensing her grief and shock, Guppik ambled alongside Yumi toward the rookery and waited by her side as she wrote letters to each of the neighboring islands and let the rest of the pigeons out so they would not starve in their cages.

Once she was finished, Yumi and Guppik returned to the fallen older man. The others were loading onto the boat, but she forced herself to look him over.

Yumi looked back down at the warrior. An older fellow based on his wisps of white hair. As she took in his scent and what remained of his features, the memory of a face came to the back of her mind. Gentle grey eyes. A wide smile and greeting as she and Kay walked past. She remembered this man from a brief greeting. He seemed so frail in her memory. Aged and tired but still going through life with kindness and a smile. The skeletal grip on his blood-stained spear was a testament to his vigor when it mattered. What remained of his desiccated features was a snarl and scowl.

When death came for his home, this man who was gentle in life faced it with strength and fury.

With a deep breath, Yumi marched to the docks.

***

Although Kirut knew Haruin must be exhausted from not relinquishing the helm since morning, the delight on his face as he opened the sails and outriggers to maximize their speed, even as they sailed within a thumb of the prow, warmed Kirut's heart.

Bruhe was on watch, and Yumi lay back on the opposite bed as Kirut, although she stared up with no sign of restful thoughts. Knowing he might need to take a watch or sail rotation before the night was done, Kirut leaned back between his hounds and closed his eyes.

Kirut was almost asleep when Guppik shifted under him. The great hound's tail wagged frantically. Although the whale hound was silent as trained, his ears were perked, and Tam whined while staying low.

Both dogs pointed starboard.

As Kirut stood, a chilling gust brought him to focus.

Amidst an evening sky, cold fog hung low over the water as if wafting up from the surf. It was a great distance away, easily a few hundred longboats in distance, but Kirut felt the chill downwind. Kirut made his way beside Haruin at the helm. Haruin and Yumi both shivered, holding their coats close. Kirut knew he should be cold, but if anything he felt warm as anticipation built.

Although fog billowed southeast with the wind, the chilling source was moving steadily westward. The Sea Badger was outpacing them, but even at this distance, Kirut could tell that the submerged origin of the cloud moved in the same direction as them.

Straight toward Hollow Turtle Island.

"That's the hezuki, yes?" Haruin whispered.

Kirut nodded. "A cold storm was their prelude before. Sensible to expect the same now."

"Lot of them by the looks of it. Reckon they're swimming below?"

"I don't know how many thralls she has this time, but from what we saw at Fallen Stars, they have at least forty dead with them. Probably a lot more considering how many settlements they hit before, and I have no notion of how many dead. A few hundred if we are correct about them taking some from each attack."

"Demons are bad enough. How can we expect to fight an army of the dead?"

"The dead had supernatural strength, but not so much that they could not be overpowered and vanquished. We killed some with javelins."

"That does bring comfort," said Haruin, though his expression as he looked out to the fog now behind them was devoid of confidence.

The frigid cloud was a distant blight by the time the sun had set.

Kirut took over steering around midnight, when Haruin was ready to fall unconscious at the wheel. Yumi had finally fallen asleep, and since Bruhe also needed rest, Kirut told him to sleep. Kirut wasn't concerned about watch with Guppik at the helm. Although he lacked Haruin's passion for sailing, seeing it as more a way to get between locations than something he enjoyed on its own, he could not deny that the shurugen was quite satisfying to sail. He was used to rudder steering, but the wheel was highly responsive, and rotating the sails took no effort at all. He found it far more calming than sailing usually was. With his missing left eye he was thankful they were on open waters so he didn't need to worry too much about obstacles.

By the light of a full moon and hearing familiar spouts, Kirut spotted a small pod of common whales swimming near the shurugen. Guppik pointed and wagged his tail, but the hound didn't seem surprised when Kirut shook his head. They were not here to hunt whales. The proximity made him assume these whales were not used to being hunted in these waters. Given their notorious speed, common whales normally didn't need to worry about ships if they weren't trapped or surprised, but the Sea Badger sailed at such a clip that they weren't notably quicker than his craft. Seeing a familiar face on the other side of the Khalin Sea was reassuring.

It was shortly after sunrise that they reached Hollow Turtle Island.

A vast stretch of foliage was their first sighting. The trees here looked sharp and brittle, same as on the other Eskadin islands and quite unlike the wetter climate he was used to back home. The beach arced in either direction.

Haruin came to take over the helm as Yumi climbed up to guide them in. After passing off the wheel, Kirut pulled on his lamellar, checked his shield, and secured his weapon belt. If they were to meet with and impress the warriors of this village, going in full kit would send the right message.

As they closed the distance, Haruin veered south, adjusting the headsail accordingly.

The island proved to be a massive atoll, with its interior being a vast shallow lagoon. Many huts were built out on the water, with several large boathouses. There were more boats than Kirut could possibly count, including a few ships anchored further out in the middle of the lagoon.

"Where are we docking?" asked Haruin, glancing back to Bruhe.

"I've never seen it this busy," he said, his brow furrowed. "I suppose you can try to dock on that side…"

Haruin pulled a few more levers, drew in the outriggers, and steered them around the main boathouse to one on the side. There was no prime docking space on the secondary boathouse either. The piers that many houses were built on had their own docks built off the houses, but were clearly for personal use.

Yumi tapped the rail and pointed back to the main boathouse. "There! Between the keeled boat and that strange blue outrigger."

Haruin nodded and steered into the space Yumi spotted. They slowed enough that Kirut and Bruhe were able to make the craft stable with pikes. The pier was at least as high above the waterline as Kirut was tall. Yumi climbed down and tied the waist to a side post, and with Kirut's aid, Bruhe hopped out and tied off the headline.

As Kirut set his dog ladder onto the pier, a young man jogged down to greet them. His black curls had mostly escaped his bun, his rubber-tipped staff held loose, and the bags under brown eyes made him look twice his age.

"What is the docking fee?" said Bruhe, clasping the young man's shoulder as he caught his breath.

"What? No, I mean… there is, but I am here to tell you that we have no lodging. All the rooms in our inns are full, as are the spare rooms in the lower lodge." He nodded to the four barrels of whale oil in their hull. "If you are merchants, now may not be the best time for bartering, although whatever you have I expect the elders will pay handsomely for."

"We are not traders. I am Kirut Modekesh. I'm here to speak with your matron. I have come to kill the creature."

The young man looked dazed for a moment. At first he looked like he might laugh, but as he took in their collective armaments, the two large dogs, and the humorless tone of the quartette, he swallowed. Finally his eyes settled on Bruhe.

Bruhe stood tall, looking to have aged considerably from the youth barely composing himself Kirut met not two days earlier. "I am Chief Bruhechin of the Guardian Atolls. Tell Matron Jonka and Chief Tonko we are here to speak with them."

The guard nodded. "I'll see if I can get you an audience right away."

***

Fear was thick in the air. So saturated Yumi could taste it.

The young guard guided them through Hollow Turtle Island toward the great lodge. When Yumi came here in years past, the main pier was often busy as most of the trade was done there. It was still packed, but no one traded goods. They all waited in huddled corners. She wanted to ask their escort why these people hadn't been moved inland, but maybe they couldn't support so many people?

Armed guards were posted at the edge of the pier. They let Kirut and the rest through, yet eyed the dogs especially closely. For all his size, Guppik remained surprisingly close and took up a lot less space than Yumi anticipated. It seemed the new scents and sounds were enough that Tam kept his head down, although he did stare or snarl at a few of the local dogs, all much smaller than him.

They continued along the boardwalk over the beach and into the largest part of the island: the head of the turtle. The foliage here was dense, with an abundant diversity of fig, laurel, gourd, and citrus trees and a verdant fern understory.

The great lodge of Hollow Turtle Island dwarfed the lodge back home. With a hall that could comfortably seat several hundred, it had been the largest structure she had ever seen until she joined her brother as a mercenary serving the Imperial general. The wonder she once felt for this place had been long eclipsed by the striking mainlander cities that the Imperials built into their mountains or the Pakardiant towns grown from the very trees they dwelled in, but the lodge of Hollow Turtle Island was still quite impressive, with its entryway framed by the lower jaw of a sun whale on either side and the upper jaw of a grandmother shark at its peak. The shark it was said had been killed singlehandedly by their first chief, Mokano, although others said it had been a gift from the gods, washed into the lagoon in a storm. Whatever its origins, it was sacred to the people of the island, and the many rows of hand-sized teeth raking from above was a clear display of their might.

The interior of the great lodge had two stories, with an open center where any point in the lodge could see the coral throne atop an elevated platform at the far end.

The throne was now empty. A crowd was gathered around a table to the left of the platform.

"Matron? Chief?" said the young man. "Guests from the Guardian Atolls."

Matron Jonka, a tall woman with a hard build, looked up from her table. Her weathered face wrinkled into a smile beaming with relief. "Welcome, Yumichin and Bruhechin."

Chief Tonko, Matron Jonka's eldest son, loomed behind her. He was an enormous man, almost as tall as Yano, broad yet toned, with mottling of grey through his beard and temples. A kind and honorable man by reputation, but not one to be crossed. He gave Yumi a warm smile.

Before Yumi could muster a response, a familiar black-haired head peered around Chief Tonko.

"Uru!"

Her cousin stumbled around Chief Tonko and charged to Yumi. She met him halfway and the pair clashed in an embrace. Yumi didn't care that all eyes were surely upon them. It wasn't until she held him close, smelled his scent of earthy sand with a hint of bitterness and brine from all the salted olives he liked to eat, that Yumi realized she assumed her only living family was Bruhe and her fellow mercenaries on the other side of the known world.

Yumi gripped him close, elated that she had been wrong.

"I'm glad to see you too, cousin, but you're suffocating me."

Yumi released him slightly. "Apologies."

She stepped back and took him in. Last she saw, Uru had only just come of age, was only slightly taller than her, and a bit lanky. In the two years since, he had filled out and hardened, growing at least another two hands taller now that he was regularly skin-changing. This sort of second growth spurt after coming of age was typical of male skin-changers. She remembered when Yano went from slightly shorter than their tallest uncle to the tallest man in the atolls by a hand in a matter of a single year after he came of age.

She also smelled a witch on him, and with such consistency that she could only guess it was an intimate partner. It was not a scent she recognized, and she thought she knew of most of the witches in the region.

Bruhe clasped arms with Uru. "Warms my heart to see you, little cousin. Ogao and my sister?"

Uru's expression fell. "Ogao fell when we were attacked. Jadhe and I were both injured by the creature. My injuries were minor, but she was bitten fiercely on the neck. I brought her to Black Sand Island, and we were rescued by a ship from one of the western islands fishing on a southern guyot. They were kind enough to take us in. By the time I recovered, we heard our home was attacked. The people I was with came to Hollow Turtle because they were afraid of being the next target. I've been helping them scout and bringing in refugees since we arrived. Shortly after I got here, two boats from Guardian Atolls arrived who had been out fishing the night of the attack. The people of Hollow Turtle have been generous.

Their witch is having much more success helping Jadhe heal than she was on her own, and the fever has passed, but the infection was powerful and she is not yet on her feet."

"What- what happened?"

"Best slow down and hear the whole tale," said Matron Jonka, holding out a hand. "First, who are your friends?"

"This is Kirut Modekesh. He is an Akanuk whaler who has in years past fought and defeated the creatures who have been terrorizing our waters. He has come here to kill the beasts. His companion Haruin is a..."

Haruin grinned and spread his arms. "Merchant, smuggler, pirate, or liberator depending on who you ask. I have no vow of vengeance, and my blood is from the Ring, not these waters, but these are dark times and dark creatures. This is all of our fight."

"We spotted the creatures approaching on our way from Fallen Stars," said Kirut. "A fog of ice we passed shortly after departing at a hand past noon. I do not know their speed, but they might arrive some time tonight. We should not delay."

Matron Jonka held out a hand. "I appreciate that, but we need as much information as possible. This is not a foe we have any experience against, save for what we've pieced together from survivor reports and scouting what they leave behind, and it sounds like you do. If we are to coordinate a defense, I need you to tell us everything you know, and we will tell you what we know of their current movements. You know their methods in the previous attack. We know their current tactics. I am glad you approach this with urgency, but my son and I know our home and how best to defend it."

"Let's get some drinks for our new friends," said Chief Tonko, his steady baritone a remedy for the tension in the room. "Here. We keep these barrels of Qadanith lager in the cellar. Keeps them cool."

"Golden," said Haruin, clapping Kirut on the back.

Bruhe put his hand on Yumi's shoulder and indicated for her to go before looking to Matron Jonka. "I appreciate your efforts here and hospitality more than I can say, but I must see my sister."

"Of course," said the matron. "Down the boardwalk and to your left will take you to the healing house. We will have breakfast, and you may join us for discussion after seeing to her. Please do hurry. There is much to discuss, and I fear we have little time."

***

Kirut liked the pale lager far more than the spiced ale Haruin had gotten in the Ring.

The matron, chief, three of their elders, Yumi and her cousin Uru, Haruin, and Kirut sat in one of the rooms built off the side of the main hall. The dogs were both given water and a bowl of walrus meat and shredded taro. Kirut thought it might be offensive to the walrus skin-changers in their company, but both ate the smoked meat as Chief Tonko passed it around, so he assumed it must be of another type of walrus than whatever they took the form of. In his travels Kirut had seen four different species, and then realized he had no idea which of the four Yumi and her cousin could trans-form into, or if there might even be different walruses this far east. Legend back home said that skin-changers needed the skin of the beast they transformed into, but the only hide the two wore was spotted sealskin boots and a wolf pelt Uru wore over his shoulders, so that story was evidently false.

Bruhe returned looking resolved. Chief Tonko passed him a horn of lager as he took the seat beside Yumi.

"It seems prudent to start from the beginning," said Matron Jonka. "Kirut, if you would be so kind as to tell us your story. We will then say what we have seen, and with our threads combined, hopefully we can see the full quilt."

Kirut nodded. "My family, my people, make our livelihood as whalers. Especially when hunting the mighty cachalot, this can be dangerous. Seven years ago, a diver cachalot we wounded in a previous hunt struck the side of our ship and we were run aground. Because I was on watch and did not see it in time, and my cousin Tamuk struck the blow which injured the beast, we were charged with securing aid from the island on which we landed. My aunt Shaku joined us, as did my large friend Guppik over there.

"The settlement on that island was Huu Taukit. They were in a panic as neighboring settlements had been wiped out by an unknown foe. Amongst their people, warriors do not remain with their mother's village, they are sent to join an order of warriors called the Blackfish Cult. The order only sent one man to defend the village, and they were afraid he would not be enough.

"Their young matron and her sister, Mia, asked that my family help defend the settlement. Although some argued that we should wait for the Blackfish, we set to work. It wasn't much, but we managed to get most of those who could not fight in the temple, archers on buildings, and other such conventions.

"The first attack was not of the creatures themselves, but of their puppets: through their magical venom they animated the corpses of the villagers who fled to inland settlements. They sent these corpses, mostly children, to strike both morale and injure our forces. A man they had infected earlier and we presumed was only injured attacked those in the temple, wounding the matron and killing their priest."

Uru held out a hand. Kirut saw his face had gone pale. "You said their venom controls their bodies?"

"Yes," said Kirut. "It made them as puppets, with the creatures both casting light and making them dance. The puppets themselves only fought. They did not spread as an infection or control others like the hezuki could."

"What is it?" said Yumi, interlacing her fingers in Uru's.

"Jadhe was bitten by the creatures, as were a few of the refugees we've brought in."

Kirut's jaw clenched. He hated how quickly his thoughts turned to a dark pragmatism.

"We will discuss that once the story is fully before us, but I assure you we will not rush to anything or make any decisions without your consent," said Matron Jonka. "Kirut, please continue."

"The living dead, or at least some were dead, were resilient but could be vanquished by conventional means. Although it took more effort than slaying a mortal man, they can be killed by conventional methods. None of those who attacked Huu Taukit were living dead, or if they were they were so fresh as to not decompose, but I expect the living dead like we encountered in Yumi and Bruhe's home would be no different than the puppets I fought in Huu Taukit. The demons themselves, however, proved almost immune to mundane steel. The Tsu Henjin call them hezuki. Are you familiar with xuul?"

"Yes," said Chief Tonko. "Said to be a hybrid of penguins and panther seals. Rare in these waters, but we know of them."

"They are closer in relation to jackal birds, and like them, have potent venom. These creatures, though, are not mundane xuul. As our people have witches and skin-changers, it seems xuul have hezuki. They have spells that control weather, bringing frost and snow, along with using their venom to inject magic to command the minds of their victims. When the hezuki finally engaged, it was clear that we were outmatched. It's very breath shattered my spear, and my axe slid off its skin like I was trying to chop into steel. The demon only fled when Mia hit it with fire. The other villagers managed to drive away the hezuki outside.

"That was when the Blackfish told us the truth of his mission: to ensure that we did not fight them. Hezuki are cowards, but also ever hungry. They must constantly feed, but also avoid direct confrontation. They may be resilient, but they are afraid of being harmed, likely because witch hunters and others armed with enchanted weapons have slain them in the past when they got too bold. Fire also killed them, and with sufficient forces, they could be overwhelmed, so they prefer prey that doesn't fight back. He told us he had been sent to make sure Huu Taukit was a massive easy meal, then the Blackfish militia would come in and finish them off. In fighting them, we may have saved Huu Taukit, but had condemned many smaller settlements to a horrible fate.

"So we drew them back. I rode to the beach and found the hezuki speaking with a great white beast. A giant of their kind who I believe was their leader and creator. Their mother. I cut open the body of a child they had slain to attract them with the scent of blood, then rode back to town.

"Fortunately they followed. While I was gone, the others had set a trap. As the hezuki came before the temple, they lit a ring of flames.

"We set upon them, and this time there was no escape. Although mortal weapons could not kill them, they could be subdued enough for me to finish them off with Nyrannuk, the enchanted harpoon blessed by a witch of my bloodline. Magic is the only thing that can truly kill them.

"Although we killed the grey hezuki, the white beast escaped. I failed. I am sorry for that failure for many reasons, not the least of which is that now your lands have been plagued and ravaged by the creature and her new pack. Her tactics are different now. They struck Guardian Atolls I believe to eliminate a threat. Yumi told me that when she arrived, several skin-changers died in grapple with hezuki they killed. That means the two of you can kill these beasts. I not only bring with me Nyrannuk, Haruin here acquired for me this enchanted Pakardiant throwing knife, and the bronze sword at his waist is also magical. This gives us a lot more tools to work with."

"My brother and the other skin-changers in our company might be on their way," said Yumi. "I sent word to them by pigeon as soon as Bruhe and I arrived home."

Uru slumped back. "I am so glad to hear it. Hollow Turtle Island does not have any pigeons linked to the Pakardiant, much less to the general. I kept meaning to sail back, but there are always more refugees to guide back."

"We don't know how long they will take, or even if they are coming," said Yumi. "I sent the pigeon five days ago, so it has probably arrived by now, but if they come, I doubt it would be for at least another few days, and that's being quite optimistic. If they do, that will be another twenty-nine skin-changers."

Uru almost leaped out of his seat as an idea struck him. "One of the refugees from Iron Line Archipelago is a young witch named Sam. She has a buck tern familiar! She's been helping me with much of the scouting. Sam might be able to find Yano and the rest on their way in and guide them to wherever the fight is happening."

Matron Jonka nodded. "We might explore that, although I think presently her scouting might be better served in keeping an eye on this ice cloud. Regardless, knowing that some reinforcements might be coming is a reassurance. We have been sending messengers to tell locals to come here if they can, and requesting others from the eastern islands send warriors and supplies to our aid, but so far no word has come back. The closest large islands are at least two days away, and I would not be surprised if they decide to fortify or flee rather than send aid. I hate to say it, but I believe we are on our own in this fight. The three of you is more of a blessing than I've seen in some time, and you of course will have everything we can offer you."

"What are our numbers? Our defenses?" asked Kirut. "Fire is a reliable deterrent and can be used to fight them even for those not armed with magic, so we should conserve any oils you have. I did bring four barrels of cachalot oil with us, but we need warriors to use it."

"Our numbers of warriors is unfortunately far surpassed by the numbers of injured, sick, and generally unable to fight," said Chief Tonko. "Normally Hollow Turtle Island is home to around eighty families. Twelve hundred or so people, and of them one or two warriors per family. Our current numbers may have doubled, with some from the southwestern isles, others from Krakenstone and Iron Line Archipelago, but these refugees have not doubled our fighting forces."

"Iron Line was attacked?" said Kirut.

"Yes. The attack came in the night five days ago, and most at Iron Line Archipelago were killed. Even some of the ships that departed were iced over and scuttled. Half the hundred or so refugees we've taken in from their ships have been frostbitten. Many had bites. We separated those bitten, but mostly to make sure they got more urgent care, and our healers are at their limit. Many of those bitten have died, and were returned to the sea."

"Where they joined the army of the living dead," said Haruin.

Kirut sighed. "It's possible. Going forward, any who die should be burned. I know this is a difficult decision. Burning the bodies does not return them to The Goddess and may seem like a defile-ment, but-"

"So does the notion of their bodies used as puppets to kill their kin," said Chief Tonko. "One should not cling to the wheel as the ship sinks. Their ashes shall be returned to The Goddess. This will ensure their spirits are reborn."

Matron Jonka nodded. "We will see it done."

"What is our defense strategy?" asked Kirut. "If Iron Line was slaughtered, based on what we've seen, a significant portion were likely added to the army of the dead."

Chief Tonko stood. "Come, my friends. Best look at a map for this."

Kirut and the rest stood and followed him to the table the group had been at when Kirut and the rest first arrived.

Chief Tonko waved a hand over the map. In general form, the great atoll was indeed shaped like a turtle from above, with an outline of beach, a few larger islands that could be interpreted as flippers, and the great island to the southeast its head. "The seaward side of the head is fortified with surge walls, as is the northern shell where we need storm protection, so those are our strongest points. They come from below the waves, and it seems reasonable to assume they will come into the lagoon from the ship mouth here."

"Are we going to have an enchanted weapon at each of the fortified points?" asked Haruin.

"I think not," said Chief Tonko. "This would spread what forces we have. I think we should concentrate our defenses here. Once they are sighted, bring the civilians into the lodge. There are four entrances, but the boardwalk is the only reliable way to get in, so we can set up a defensive position there. It has worked in the past when fending off mainland slavers, and from what I understand, they will fundamentally work the same: attack from the sea and come inland. We will have our scouts out patrolling, something which will be far more efficient with both Yumi and Uru, although I think it best for us to try and keep the fight on land where we have our strength."

Beside the map of Hollow Turtle Island, Kirut saw another map, this one of the region. Guardian Atolls was at the bottom, Fallen Stars at its center, and Hollow Turtle on the west. Iron Line Archipelago and a dozen small islands to the south formed the end of what Kirut assumed was a mountain range continuing from Hollow Turtle through Fallen Stars. Another large island was situated to the north, with its own chain of smaller islands. "All these outlying islands to the north there and there... have their peoples all assembled with us here?”

Matron Jonka frowned. “No, that is Krakenstone. Tonko’s father was their chief before Mosdin, so they are his kin. I sent word for them to assemble here, but our messenger was turned away. Some of their people joined us against Chief Mosdin’s orders, but mostly they remained. Their warriors are numerous and mighty, having much experience repelling raiders from the Free-States, but they are not large enough to support all the refugees we have. Krakenstone might be larger than the head of the turtle, but our lagoon will provide far more food.”

“Also, they do have an enchanted weapon,” said Chief Tonko. “Sunset Cleaver is a relic of their first chief, an old war club, and is said to have an ancient enchantment. It may not be potent, but their tradition is to leave it exposed to the sun but covered from rain, and I expect the magic still holds. For their own safety and for reinforcements, I wished before that they had joined us. Now that desire is doubled.”

Kirut nodded. “With our new information, do you think they might reconsider? Their addition of warriors and another artifact could be invaluable.”

Chief Tonko frowned. “I doubt it. Chief Mosdin is a proud man, and their matron has been unsound of mind for some time. Mosdin is fully in control of the island. His nephew Jardin is much more reasonable, a young and ambitious man who initially expressed an interest in joining forces and resources, but as my mother said, Chief Mosdin declined our emissary. I will send a pigeon to ask for their aid, but if we are the next target, I imagine Mosdin will be happy to remain distant and fortify. If we fall, he will be the next logical target, after all.”

Uru raised a hand. "I will check in with Sam and see if she can send her familiar to keep an eye on the progress of this ice cloud Yumi mentioned."

"Good," said Chief Tonko. "Please do so. Bruhe, if they were moving slower than your boat, do you anticipate an arrival in two days or so?"

"Perhaps, but it's difficult to say. They appear to attack in the night, so I'm not sure if we want to go to sleep until Uru's witch friend confirms it for us."

"We will have scouts keep a close eye to the east. Facing this foe exhausted will do us no favors. I suggest we send Sam's familiar, and the rest of us try and get some rest during the day before the coming storm."

Kirut nodded. "Where shall we make rest?"

"The upper floor of the lodge," said Chief Tonko. "You are free to use any of the beds in the side chambers."

"You have my thanks."

"As you have mine," said Tonko, clasping Kirut's forearm. "Truly. I do not take your arrival or efforts lightly. Rest while you can, my friends."

After bidding the chief and matron luck with their own rest, Kirut called the dogs in from the other room. Haruin was by his side, while Yumi was leaving the group with her cousin. Kirut was happy that at least one of her family had survived. She already had a lightness to her step and animation to her expression being with her kin for a few moments.

Despite resting on the boat, Kirut was asleep moments after he removed his kit and slumped on the bed between his hounds.

***

"Is this witch the one I smell on you?" said Yumi, nudging her cousin's shoulder.

Uru looked down, a slight smile dancing across his features. "Yes. I was cautious at first. Neither of us had matrons to approve, but… it's been comforting to have each other."

"None of my unions had matron approval, and neither have Yanochin's," said Yumi, waving him off. "Perhaps that mattered long ago, but no one cares for such things, especially with all that has occurred. I am fairly certain Amyi is with child from an Imperial father. If you bring each other happiness, that's all that matters."

Uru brought her to the upper floor of the lodge, opposite the side she saw Kirut, Haruin, and the dogs making their way to. The room Uru led her inside was partially shielded by a wooden standing door with a striking creature illustration burned into it.

Seated in the middle of the chamber, atop the bed deep in a book, was a young woman in a pretty if disheveled blue and silver dress. Her dark curls were tied overhead, and several feathers tucked in where they would stay. Resting its head on her lap was a large buck tern: a skin-winged seabird around the size of a dog. As Uru entered the room she looked up excitedly, looked momentarily downcast that he wasn't alone, but smiled warmly in polite greeting.

"Sam? This is Yumi, my cousin."

"A pleasure to meet you! I would stand, but Arix is sleeping and I don't want to wake him."

As Uru informed Sam of the situation, of the identity of the monsters that had plagued their waters, Yumi couldn't help but feel joy at the tenderness of their exchanges. Although they spoke of dark and terrible things, Yumi only saw their caring attention to each other.

"I can send Arix to keep watch on this cloud. He's faster than a wild tern, and I can see through his eyes," said Sam, holding out her arm. It looked to be some sort of command, but the tern barely opened lightning blue eyes before squinting in open annoyance and shifting to a new resting position. "Apologies. I think he knows I'm about to ask him to go out again."

"Please tell him I'm sorry," said Yumi. "No one else is equipped to do this."

"He certainly knows his importance," said Sam, grinning and scratching along his feathered jaw. "Come on, baby boy. Let's go."

With a heavy sigh, Arix gripped the bed post with the hand of his wing, which had two clawed fingers and a thumb. As the claws dug into the wood, the bird pulled himself to a standing position. The pronged yellow crest atop his head, similar in profile to the stags on larger islands, was impressive from the side, but so flat from the front that it looked like a blade. Arix yawned, flashing the hook at the end of his upper beak and slicing tip of his lower jaw, and stretched open membranous wings in front of his witch, which spread nearly twice Yumi's arm span. He may look like a conventional bird with his wings folded, but spread as they were, with skin stretched from the tip of his elongated finger down to his ankles, it was clear that his kind were far from conventional.

As he folded his wings back in, with the membrane retracted so that it was covered by the silver and blue feathers on his back, Arix crawled on his hands and feet over to the window. Without so much as a glance back to Sam, Arix planted his clawed fingers on the sill and used them to climb out the window and upward.

"He needs to take off from the roof because of the nearby trees," said Sam as Yumi watched in confusion and wonder. "It's an easy enough climb. He's being dramatic."

"Did he need to eat before taking off?" asked Yumi, thinking back on how much Kirut's dogs ate.

"He ate after getting back from his last scout."

"Very well. I'm going to find something to eat myself, then maybe get some rest. You two want anything?"

Sam and Uru glanced to each other.

"I'll leave you alone, then," said Yumi, chuckling before kissing her cousin on the forehead, punching his shoulder, and leaving the two young lovers to whatever excitement they could steal in this calm before the storm.

After filling up on leftover taro and smoked walrus, Yumi got directions to the healing house where Jadhe was resting. If anyone could have shrugged off hezuki venom by now, it was Jadhe.

Guards were posted outside, two of whom Yumi saw walking from the lodge to join the rest. They were armed with rubberhead polearms, but she noted the metal blades at their waists. There were also a lot more of them than Yumi anticipated. It seemed Chief Tonko had taken the threat of those bitten by the hezuki to heart.

Many of those in bed were strapped there, speaking to additional precautions. It was practical, and most seemed content with their restraints, but it made Yumi nervous if for no other reason than it reminded her of what was to come.

Separated from the rest was Jadhe, her arms loosely restrained. Her foot was bandaged, but aside from that, she seemed in good health. The attack had been nearly twenty days ago. It was odd that she had not yet recovered, but then again, the venom was likely fighting Jadhe's skin-changer magic, so her body likely couldn't recover at its usual pace.

Jadhe's face ignited when she spotted Yumi. She couldn't move, but Yumi closed the distance and took her in. Her scent was her own, but there was a new smell, one that Yumi realized saturated the air in the longhouse:

Brine and rotting flesh.

"Bruhe said you were here, but I wasn't sure how much of his visit was a dream. Are the others with you?" Jadhe asked. Her hands had just enough mobility to grab both of Yumi's in her own. Jadhe's hands were cold, an unexpected contrast to her damp forehead and fevered trembling. Her hair had always been ivory, but her skin used to be more typical tawny brown, and now was several shades lighter and drained of color.

Yumi pursed her lips. "No. It's just me and Bruhe, although I do come with a man who has experience killing these creatures, and I sent word to Yanochin. I hope he and the rest are on their way, but I don't yet know."

Jadhe nodded sadly, her hands shaking slightly. "If nothing else, maybe they will be too far away and might survive. That is good."

"We're going to survive. As I said, I'm here with someone who has killed many. He calls them hezuki. They can be slain with magic, and he and his friend have many artifacts to do the killing."

"Yumi... are you sure about him? Uru and I only managed to escape because we were only focused on flight while Ogao fought them off. They are fast, agile, and powerful. They strike with the speed and power of a sea serpent. All of my fortitude has been devoted to fending off a single bite, and the healers aren't saying much, but they've been told to restrain all those bitten. I didn't have the strength to stop them, but I wanted to. I'm feeling well. Fine. I'm ready to fight. Just get me to the ocean. Help me shift."

Yumi bit back a swell of emotion. She freed one of her hands and ran it through Jadhe's damp hair. "It's alright. Here. Drink more water. Shifting is the last thing you should do right now. It will just move the poisoned blood through your heart and strain your breath. Just let your body keep healing."

"Don't trust him, Yumi."

"What?"

Jadhe strained against her bonds, grabbing Yumi's suspender and leaning closer. Her eyes were wide, unfocused. A cold crept through her hand and into Yumi's chest. "Don't trust him, this stranger. Pretty face and pretty words. He will try to earn your trust. Don't fall for the trick. Trust will get you killed."

"You have my word," said Yumi, putting a gentle hand on the one gripping her clothes. "I don't trust him. You have nothing to worry about."

"Good. You always were perceptive," said Jadhe, releasing her grasp and slumping back on the bed. "I'll take that water now, if you will."

Yumi helped her cousin drink. As soon as she had more water in her, Jadhe immediately slumped back and showed all the signs of slumber.

Yumi rushed out of the longhouse. It wasn't until she got back toward the beach, up the stairs to the boardwalk, and into the great lodge that she felt her breath returning to her.

Although she did not take Jadhe's words to heart, assuming them the words of the hezuki through their venom, the notion that even they could be controlled was challenging to face. Witch magic does not work on skin-changers. Such was wisdom she had known all her life. She had nothing to fear from curses or other malicious spells. If the hezuki could control a skin-changer, then Kirut had if anything underestimated their power.

Yumi drank another full horn of lager to drown her anxiety. Frustrated by it not having much effect, she downed another along with some whiskey she found. As her thoughts finally began to haze, she wished there was a pretty girl she could take to bed, but that would mean leaving the lodge.

In her stupor she noticed Haruin also had entered the room. He said something about drinks. By any metric she gauged from those who liked men, he was handsome, in a rugged sort of way. He wouldn't be a bad last sail, if that was indeed in her future, but she knew it wouldn't be satisfying, and she liked him well enough not to put him through that.

"Haruin, have you seen any pretty girls in our time here? I find myself in need of intimacy."

Haruin laughed, a jolly sound that echoed through the small chamber they were in.

"Don't mock me. I am fierce with my bite."

"I appreciate that, and normally I'm just the sort of scoundrel you'd want as an ally if you're looking for partners in intimacy, but I've been around long enough to know when a friend needs a bed for romping and a bed for resting. You, my friend, are in need of a bed for resting."

Yumi frowned. "That's not the answer I was hoping for, and we're not friends. I've known you for three days."

"You wound me! These have been three particularly eventful days, and I've made close friends in half the time. Someday I will take you to a distant port and show you all I've learned about wooing exciting strangers, but not tonight."

"What sort of pirate are you?"

"The sort that is going to walk you up to bed."

Yumi rolled her eyes, but didn't stop as Haruin traded her whiskey for water and guided her upstairs.

As they passed Uru and Sam's room, the sounds and smells of their lovemaking filled the hall.

Haruin sighed. "Maybe you can sleep on the other side of the lodge with me and Kirut."

Yumi finished her water and nodded.

She only had a few threads of awareness as Haruin lay her down, and in a moment, she was asleep.

Chapter 4

"Yumi! Come! Sam has seen something!"

Kirut jolted up.

Both hounds were awake, their tails wagging frantically. A quick glance confirmed that Haruin and Yumi were in other beds in the chamber. The first streaks of pink light marked sunrise. Haruin was already reaching for his sword despite wearing nothing but his trousers, but Yumi snored away.

Kirut felt a wave of exhaustion amidst the building panic. He stood and stretched, gulping down some water to clear his throat. Guppik was holding Nyrannuk patiently. Kirut had no idea where Tam had run off to.

The origin of the call was on the other side of the balcony. Kirut took a deep breath. He took up the lance and scratched Guppik behind the ears.

"Let Yumi sleep," said Haruin, still shirtless but securing his weapon belt. "She had a night. Let's go see what the witch spotted."

Kirut and Haruin hurried around to the room that Yumi's cousin had called out of.

Uru beckoned them in. A beautiful young woman was sitting up, gripping his hand so her knuckles went white. If the grasp hurt, Uru showed no sign of it. Cool brown eyes were glossed over. Kirut had never known a witch with sufficient connection to see through their familiar's eyes, but it made sense that she could not see through her own during the trance.

"What do you see?" asked Kirut.

"The cloud is not coming this way," said Sam. "It billows north toward Krakenstone. Arix almost missed them, for they were so far from where he was looking. His night vision is not strong, so it took a while to find as it was."

"How far are they from Krakenstone?"

"I haven't got a good sense of their precise location. I just found them. Apologies, I would have expected an ice cloud to be easier to find based on what Uru described." A long moment passed of Sam looking about the room, as though it were the sea before her. "He can see the southernmost island near Krakenstone to the north, but it is far away. It was not long ago that he was able to see Fallen Stars. I would guess the cloud is near halfway between, but in an arc if that makes sense. Not directly between."

"We need to wake the chief," said Haruin. "I'll get Yumi. Meet us at the map."

"Gratitude for your help, Sam," said Kirut before running to the stairs, nearly tripping over Guppik and Tam as they followed with tails wagging furiously.

Once the leaders were assembled, all in differing stages of awareness, Uru and Kirut worked to estimate where the cloud was.

"Here would you say?" asked Uru.

"I think so," said Sam, nodding. "Again it is hard to say with certainty, the sea does not look like a map from the sky, and I am not the most skilled navigator, but based on the stars above and where he could see the different islands, I would say it was around there."

Kirut took a deep breath. He set a finger on the map just west of Fallen Stars. "This is where we saw the ice in the water. I assumed they were coming here, to Hollow Turtle Island. Is there any reason to think they might instead be moving to attack Krakenstone instead?"

"Wouldn't they have just gone north?" said Haruin. "Seems an indirect route to come a third of the way west then cut north."

Chief Tonko rubbed his face with his hand and scrunched his features before looking at the map again. "If they're traveling below the waves, it might actually be the most direct route. There is a great underwater valley between the islands from here to Iron Line Archipelago and those surrounding Krakenstone. There is, however, a bridge of sorts along here. A series of guyots called Crab Bridge. Not only does it make the waters on this side of the guyots still, separated from the currents to the east, it also forms a flat space on which we have excellent fishing and crabbing opportunities, and that extends all the way to the northern islands in this arc here."

"How would they know about that?" asked Haruin.

"If the dead can communicate with their puppet masters, any of them with any local fishing experience would know that."

"So what, are their armies of the dead walking on the bottom rather than swimming?" asked Uru.

"I saw nothing in the water, just the cloud of chill wafting from the surf," said Sam. "I can try to get estimates of their movement and numbers once there is more light. I asked Arix to keep his distance but remain in sight."

"Didn't you say these poor sods at Krakenstone had an enchanted artifact?" asked Haruin.

"Sunset Cleaver, yes," said Matron Jonka.

"Well, if the dead knew about Crab Bridge as you called it, they probably also know about the artifact. They attacked the Guardian Atolls first thing when they reached these waters. Knew they were a threat. Sunset Cleaver is the only threat to them, at least in the eyes of their dead. I suppose it could make sense for the hezuki to take them out first. They don't know we have several enchanted artifacts here."

Kirut turned up to Chief Tonko. "If we go to help them fight, to face the hezuki at Krakenstone, we lose all the advantages we have here. They don't know how many artifacts we have, so there's an element of surprise. Here, we can lure them into the lagoon, close it off, and butcher them in a contained space. Some might escape, but I think we stand a good chance of setting up a trap and finishing them permanently. The white beast is unlikely to join in the assault. She didn't in Huu Taukit, but perhaps our skin-changers can find her while the rest of us fight. Killing her is critical to ending this scourge, and I think that can only be reliably done here."

"The notion of abandoning them to their fate sits like a stone in my chest," said Chief Tonko. "We offered them shelter and a shared roof, and while Chief Mosdin refused, the people of Krakenstone should not suffer for their chief's arrogance. You are right, though: I fear rushing to their aid not only robs us of our strategy and defenses, we abandon our own people. You said they are not following the strategy they have in the past. What if some of them are attacking Krakenstone and others strike at us? So far they move as one, but I will not risk the safety of my people, nor those who came to us with the promise that we would do everything we could to protect them, all on assuming their tactics will remain the same. It would disrespect the warriors who died so their families would escape and be safe here. This nemesis of yours, the Great White Death, she seems just the sort of clever to lure out our forces and have over a thousand defenseless meals at her disposal."

"So we let the people of Krakenstone get butchered?" said Haruin. "Is that our plan?"

Kirut rested his palms against the table. He glared at the map, willing a better plan to come to him.

Yumi raised a hand, drawing all eyes at the table. "The hezuki might know that Kirut is here."

"How? I haven't faced them?"

"When I spoke with Jadhe last night, I told her that we had a stranger come who had experience killing them. I said it to reassure her, but it was not long after that I realized she might not be herself.

That there seemed to be someone else in her body, if that makes sense. I apologize, I know it was irresponsible, but I thought she could use some comfort."

Kirut cocked his head. "That could prove useful."

"How so?" asked Chief Tonko.

"If the Great White Death is truly able to influence or even see through the minds of those her children have bitten, we could provide her with false information or goad her into a fight."

Haruin was grinning. "I like that. She knows you have the lance, and knows that at least two skin-changers are here, but doesn't know about the rest."

"I did mention that Yanochin and the other mercenaries were coming, but that it probably be too late."

"If that's the case, she will be acting quickly," said Kirut. "Likely trying to take out Krakenstone and bulking up on them before coming here with as much of their village amongst the dead as possible, hoping to clear out the area before Yanochin arrives. If we go now, meet her with as much of a surprise force as we can muster, we might be able to forge a victory from this, while also protecting the innocent of Krakenstone."

Bruhe crossed his arms. "She is our matron, and I cannot abandon her. I will tell her that Uru and Yumi cannot visit her as they will be scouting, and do my best to make her believe we all remained here."

"Beautiful," said Haruin. "What say you, Chief?"

Chief Tonko frowned. "I say you're building a tower on sand. Our foundation for this plan is hope and conjecture. I have no command over you and yours, but I will not break my vow to those who came seeking shelter in my home, nor my duty to those in my village who call me chief. I will stay and keep a wall of defense. It sounds like you take all the means of killing the demons with you, so of course I will pray for your success, but I cannot in good conscience commit fighters to this cause."

"I appreciate your position and respect your decision," said Kirut, offering a hand. "We must leave at once if we are to reach the island before the hezuki arrive."

Chief Tonko frowned and met Kirut's grasp. "May the shark bite through your spears, the turtle guard through your shields, and by the coldest storm and cries of the first babe: cast the frosted remains of this wretched creature into the abyss."

Kirut shook Chief Tonko's hand. "Much appreciated. Everyone who is going to Krakenstone: pack in a good meal and fortify yourselves. We meet at the Sea Badger on the docks as soon as possible."

***

Yumi ate quickly and ran to meet with Jadhe.

"You're back!" said Jadhe, her smile wide and genuine. "I wasn't sure if I dreamt of you when last we spoke. This sickness has muddied my thoughts and memories."

"It's alright, I'm here."

"When you first had the dreams, did you feel as though you shared your body with another being? During my first shifts, it was like I had someone else with me, and I let them make the transformation. These days it's just a part of me, but it really felt like a separate entity back then."

"I suppose," said Yumi. Jadhe was always a shifter with talent that Yumi aspired to. All her life she'd wanted nothing more than to have these sorts of conversations, but now she had to measure every word carefully. How much was she saying to her matron, and how much to the Great White Death? "I don't know, it always felt like the form, the sea, it was all part of my body and spirit. Like swimming or running, it was just another way of moving my body."

"They say it is different for everyone," said Jadhe. "This venom, whatever it is, feels the same. As though my mind is sharing space. Well, not the same. What I'm sharing my body and mind with doesn't feel like it's here to keep me safe. Sea Badger is my protector. My teacher. My closest companion. This presence has its own agenda. Its desires. When the fever spikes, I feel lost, like I'm on the brink of drowning, and the fire in my lungs would rather be quenched by the sea than endure another moment of heat."

Yumi pet back Jadhe's white hair. She took up the cup of water beside her cousin's table. "The best thing you can do is let your body rest. Our magic is strong. As you said, Sea Badger has blessed us and will protect you. I'm going to be patrolling often. Uru and I are probably going to see if there are any survivors back home. Bruhe will be with you the whole time. I will stop in when I can. Be sure you rest and drink as much as you can while I'm gone."

Jadhe nodded. A shiver rolled through her, and the grip on Yumi's hand went suddenly cold. When she looked up at Yumi, her normally cool grey eyes had frosted over with blue. "I remember watching you being born. It's odd, having you of all people take care of me. You were ever sick as a little girl. Always taking the healers time and attention. Ever the smallest. The weakest. Everyone took care of you, though. Protected cute little Yumi. Held your hand and told you that you were strong. Why Sea Badger gave you His blessing I will never understand, but I suppose there is use for the small and the covert. You would have been more useful if you were downcast, though. Easier to be overlooked if you were used to sneaking about. Now you're small and weak, but used to being told you're mighty. Amusing that you are the aid that Yano sent. It's as if your brother just wanted to be rid of you. A sad legacy for our people, but I suppose even the brightest sun sets at the end of the day. When my son is finished with Krakenstone, you and your friends will have quite the guests in your harbor. I hope you show them proper hospitality."

Yumi was in shock, unable to speak as Jadhe doubled over in a fit of coughs.

After the worst of it had passed, Jadhe slumped back, her eyes having returned to grey and expression one of confusion. She was damp with sweat.

Yumi inhaled slowly. She took a cool cloth from the bowl on Jadhe's bedside and dabbed it across her cousin's brow. Already she was warming to the touch, but there was a chill to Jadhe's fingertips.

Bruhe had come into the healing house. Although he could not wish Yumi luck, not surrounded by the ears of the enemy, she saw it in the intensity of his brief stare and nod. They briefly gripped hands.

With a kiss to Jadhe's forehead, Yumi stood and left the hospital.

She jogged back to the boardwalk and went to the Sea Badger. Checking over the shurugen and making the craft ready took little time.

Kirut and Haruin weren't far behind, packed with as many provisions as they could carry. Uru walked with them, wearing a simple tunic and suspended trousers that he could easily cast off, and holding a large basket presumably packed with rations.

"We really going to need all this food?" asked Haruin as Kirut got in the boat first. Kirut held the plank steady and Haruin the top so Guppik could carefully make his way onto the boat. "Although the wind isn't really in our favor, I expect we'll make it by midday tomorrow. Surely it's going to just weigh us down."

"Skin-changing takes a lot of energy," said Uru, passing his large basket to Kirut. "We need to eat about twice as much as you. Normally Yumi and I would just shift and fish, but I assumed we didn't have that kind of time. Also, we have two beautiful boys here." Uru gave Tam a pat and scratch on the side. "They need their share too."

"I suppose," said Haruin. "They do pack it in, especially Tam. I swear he's grown in the near twenty days I've known him."

"You should have seen Guppik when he was that age," said Kirut, grabbing the great hound and kissing his forehead. "Never seen a beast grow so quick. Your turn, Tam!"

Tam barely set foot on the plank before leaping into Kirut's arms. Yumi had to steady him as the boat tilted.

"Have room for a few more?"

Chief Tonko and three men, all carrying their own kits of shields, sharkskin armor, and spears, marched down the boardwalk. The armor Chief Tonko carried was styled like mainlander plates but was blue sharkskin on a gilded metal base. The center of his cuirass sported the massive tooth of a grandmother shark.

"I thought you were staying to protect your home?" said Kirut, a wry smile on his face.

Tonko nodded. "I'm acting in defense of my people, yes, and taking the fight to these creatures seems our best chance at doing so. My mother has defended this village before, and she can do so again, but I would feel quite the coward bellowing from the shore when there are threats in the waves. If you will have me and mine on your crew, I would be grateful for it."

"Will be a bit tight," said Yumi. "But it would be our honor."

All four boarded the craft. Haruin and Uru climbed in, and Kirut withdrew the plank. Each man took up an oar, and they rowed away from the pier.

Once they were in open water, they withdrew the oars. Haruin cranked down and rotated the sails to take on as much wind as possible, aiming the prow a half turn to port from the strongest winds. At Tonko's suggestion, rather than trying to tack back and forth to the island, he sailed west then would loop around once they passed Krakenstone. This would have the wind at their backs for the last stretch and skirt around their incoming foes.

One of Tonko's men scaled the mast to take first watch.

Once they captured building winds, Yumi took a deep breath, taking in whatever peace she could.

***

Although it was a bit of a puzzle fitting eight people, four barrels of whale oil, and two large dogs, Kirut had far more in less space, and with Guppik in the middle of the boat to keep it steady, they cut smoothly through the waves despite exceeding the intended capacity of the craft.

Kirut's heel drummed the hull of the boat. There was a building chill in the air. It may have been imagined, since their cold foes were downwind, and none of the others on the boat showed any sign of feeling it. Tam pressed his side against Kirut's shins. The warmth was welcome.

"What is the plan now?" said Haruin. "We're going to this chief and telling him to, what… clench and hope?"

Kirut chuckled in spite of the tension. "My friend, I think we left our plan back on Hollow Turtle."

"My cousin, Chief Mosdin, needs to feel as though he's in control of the situation," said Chief Tonko. "We cannot tell him how to defend his people."

"So we need to hold his hand through the whole fight?" said Haruin with a grin. "Should we have checked the beach before we left for any pretty shells to reward his ideas that we feed him?"

"I'm only saying we need to be tactful. Believe me; I hold him in no great respect. None of this need have happened had they not joined us at Hollow Turtle, but if we are to secure any sort of victory, we will need his cooperation. Do it for his people. He's stubborn and proud, but he cares deeply for his image, and if we are smart, we can use that to steer him toward success."

"Dealing with his nephew would be a lot easier," said Uru. "I've met him a few times. He's a good man."

"Indeed he is," said Tonko. "He would be far easier to negotiate with, but if it were up to Jardin, I doubt we would be in this situation to begin with. Unfortunately we must roll the stones we are given."

Haruin raised his hands. "This game is yours, Chief. I would not face you in the dance of politics."

Chief Tonko lounged back with a laugh. "The moves are easy once you figure them out. Just need to get over the initial frustration that you cannot speak directly."

Kirut scratched Tam behind the ear. "How many fighters did you say he had again?"

"Eighty I can say with confidence, but most will take up a spear when their lives are in danger. We can reasonably think to be joined by at least twice that, if not more. I would not count on those common fighters being armed with better than fishing kit, but it sounds like we can fight the dead at least."

"The most important part is to lure them to come onto land," said Kirut. "They're less mobile, and we might be able to surround them. I'll need to see the island, but we can likely make some target to draw them in. Fishermen armed with harpoons and nets not only could draw them in thinking it will be an easy fight, but nets could prove quite useful in restraining them and slowing them down so those of us with enchanted weapons can finish them off."

"When we get there, what say you survey the island, try and find a good place to lure them, while I speak with Chief Mosdin?"

Guppik's tail shook furiously, interrupting Kirut's thought of a reply, and Tam whined loudly as he crawled under Kirut's seat.

Kirut stood, looking about.

No cloud in sight, and certainly not one of frost.

Chief Tonko's man up on watch didn't seem to be concerned by anything.

"What is it?" asked Yumi, standing with him.

Kirut gestured to his hounds. Guppik pointed behind them over the starboard bow. Kirut moved to the rail to investigate.

"Loto!" Tonko called up to the man on watch. "See anything to starboard?"

Loto held up a hand to shield glare from the sun. After a moment he tensed.

"What is it?" Uru shouted.

"Grandmother shark! Half hand from the rudder and closing in."

"Closing in?" Haruin all but shrieked, looking back.

"Do you see the fin?" Tonko shouted, since from his angle he could not see.

Loto paused. "Yes, just cutting the surface!"

Tonko nodded. "Haruin, draw in the sails, outrigger, and rudder as well if you can."

"Chief, that… how will any of that make us faster?"

"It won't. Even this shurugen won't outpace a charger, and if they are on the surface, they're just curious. Slow us as much as you can."

Kirut balked. "A curious whaler shark will still bite through a hull."

"With respect, not in these waters."

Kirut's mind was dominated by a memory of a whaler shark harassing their ship for most of an afternoon and damaging their hull such that they had to make land for three days of unexpected repairs. That was a full ship with a crew of over a hundred. A whaler shark could sunder the Sea Badger in a single bite.

Despite open reservations, Haruin pulled a few levers, and the shurugen all but folded in on itself as the sails and outriggers drew in. Haruin turned the sloop hard to port so they were against the wind and rapidly slowing. Finally he took in the rudder. With this last act they continued forward at a pace still exceeding any boat Kirut had sailed on, but eventually the Sea Badger stalled to a casual drift.

Over the port side, Kirut saw a great black fin slice through the water before disappearing behind the stern.

A moment passed, and a dark silhouette circled around to the starboard side, striking against the turquoise water below. The fin was now below the waves as it was slightly deeper. Although this was nowhere near the size of the shark that nearly sank Kirut and his fellow whalers four years earlier, it was still a massive god of the sea, slightly longer than the Sea Badger at a little over six span. While the shurugen had slowed considerably, the shark continued at a rapid clip, circling around the prow. Once it reached the other side the shark was beginning to slow.

A surge of its tail sent a splash two span into the air in a dive.

"They strike from below, yes?" said Haruin.

Tonko held out a hand. "Hold."

As Kirut looked back over the starboard side, he raised Nyran-nuk, its point toward the water.

"Kirut..." Chief Tonko's tone was gentle but firm. Kirut knew injuring a curious beast could provoke it, and provocation at this size could be cataclysmic, but he wasn't going to sit idle while their boat was torn apart in open water. Movement under Kirut made him start, but he stayed his hand.

The pointed head of the great shark eased into view. Angled slightly to the side so it could look up, the shark's eye seemed to meet Kirut's gaze. It was at least a span below the surface, but Kirut was astonished by its size. Contrary to his other close encounters with whaler sharks, this one made no moves of aggression, appearing to only be investigating.

With an undulation the mighty shark continued under the boat, breaking the surface two span from the starboard rail, maintaining its position so one eye could look at the boat as its head fully emerged in a spyhop.

Unlike the great whites he was used to seeing more frequently in the western waters, the colors of this colossal shark were much more striking. The back above its eyes was black, with sides of a rich silvery blue, and white on its lower jaw and belly. The black speckled past its line in spots throughout the blue.

"Aren't you beautiful," said Tonko, his voice higher and soft as one speaking to a child or pup. "Sorry if we startled you. I'm sure you've seen boats before, just never one so fast."

The shark looked to Tonko, then back to Kirut. Although Kirut had remembered their eyes as white while attacking and black voids at peace, likening them akin to the demons of Huu Taukit, with the late morning sun illuminating it, he saw the eyes of this shark were far more natural, with a dark pupil surrounded by an iris blue as the sky above. Not a human eye, but not one of demonic origin either.

Kirut lowered Nyrannuk.

With a shift of the tail, the shark turned back into the water, rolling along the surface on its side before righting itself. It circled back around, fin breaking the surface to show it was not diving. As it swam around to the other side, its head was partially above the surface, the whaler shark kept its attention on the boat.

Once it rounded back to the starboard side, the shark opened its jaws, yet the eyes were still a calm blue.

As it bumped the side of the Sea Badger, Kirut's heart sprang into acceleration. The shark snarled slightly and trailed its upper teeth along the hull. Each of its front teeth was as large as Kirut's hand. Although it applied barely enough force to leave a mark, Kirut felt the scrape in his joints as the hit vibrated through the shurugen.

The shark carried along the side of the boat, shoving its breadth against the hull. Against his wiser judgement, as the tall fin passed by, Kirut brushed the tips of his fingers against its rough hide.

After circling the Sea Badger three more times, the whaler shark turned west and returned to a more rapid cruising speed, sinking below the waves.

***

Later that evening a buck tern, white wings spanning wide and forward, soared toward them from the east. Based on its larger size than usual birds of this species, Yumi assumed it was Arix, Sam's familiar, which was confirmed by Uru standing when he saw it.

After gliding down toward the craft, the great creature folded its wings and made land, its fingers grasping the rail of the Sea Badger. Kirut's dogs both watched it suspiciously, and Tam's lip curled up when the bird stared directly back and inflated the white feathers of his broad chest.

"Hello, Arix," said Uru, diffusing the tension with a pair of ironside snappers, which Sam's familiar happily snapped up. "Anything to report?"

"Can it talk?" asked one of Tonko's men. Moko, from what Yumi remembered.

"No, but he understands us, and can give me yes and no answers."

After an audible snarl from Tam, Kirut gave commands for the dogs to calm. It was not unusual for Tam to snap and bark, but for Guppik to glare caught her attention.

"They really don't seem to like him," said Yumi.

Kirut nodded. "Banshee gulls and elk terns are much more common back home, and both are dangerous. A banshee gull attacked our village last year, when Tam was just a little yapper, and killed two of our hounds and injured three others after they grounded it.

I imagine he remembers it quite clearly. Guppik was the one who killed that bird. Buck terns like that are only a threat to pups, but I'm sure it smells the same."

Yumi noticed Tam's ears were back, and he looked more frightened than angry, but that wouldn't make him any less dangerous. Guppik had stood with ears forward and, despite Kirut's additional command, looked ready to spring.

"Alright boys, to Haruin with you both," said Kirut, and the hounds obeyed, albeit reluctantly. Kirut then raised a hand, showing a long scar. "That blade on the beak's lower jaw? A buck tern got me here while I was unloading fish just after Huu Taukit. I didn't see it on my left. I've no love for those birds, and I'm sure the boys sense as much. I certainly appreciate his value, but I'll not be petting him."

Uru was speaking to the bird. It croaked at him in reply, clacking its menacing beak several times. Uru thanked Arix, tossing the buck tern another snapper.

Yumi stood to meet with him "What does your lover's bird say?"

"He says at their pace, the cloud will arrive at Krakenstone tomorrow."

"Good," said Tonko, looking to Kirut. "This means we will arrive first, since you said they attack at night, yes?"

Kirut nodded. "Although I still don't want to count on that. We should prepare for their attack as soon as we arrive. Go in wearing our armor."

"Agreed," said Tonko. "If we can convince them to leave, we may be able to circumvent the demons, but I expect we should be prepared to stay and fight."

Yumi looked at the buck tern and cocked her head. "Uru, do you think Arix could find a ship out at sea if he knew an estimate of their location?"

Uru shrugged. "Perhaps."

"While it would no doubt be useful for him to watch the fog, what if he went to see if he could find Yano and the rest? If they left right away, and General Tikah loaned them a clipper, they might be home in a few days. Krakenstone is two days north. He could certainly get there sooner and with the wind at his back if he knew."

Tonko nodded. "Excellent. Can he do it?"

Uru looked back at the buck tern. "He does have thumbs, but I'm not sure how well he could hold it while flying. Maybe I can make him a collar and purse? Would you mind that?"

Yumi didn't think a creature without expression could show contempt, but Arix's deadpan stare gave off the distinct impression. However, he did not protest as Uru began making a necklace of his coin purse while Yumi wrote out a missive for their kin.

While Arix hadn't perched with a pleasant disposition, he barely held back a hiss as the purse was secured around his neck. He vaulted into the sky with what Yumi could swear was a grumble of curses.

***

Kirut struggled to drift to sleep that night. A chill hung in the air.

For the first time since he fought in Huu Taukit, warmth spread from the Lance of the Corpse Whale into his fingertips.

Demons were close, and Nyrannuk was hungry.

Chapter 5

Yumi had taken over steering for the later half of the night while Haruin slept, but he was quick to take over with sunrise. She wasn't tired, so sat beside him in silence while the rest slumbered.

A beautiful morning of warm winds turned to an afternoon of chill as Haruin turned the boat south to ride the strongest winds the rest of the way to Krakenstone. She withdrew the headsail and let free the great yellow spinnaker. This massive sail hadn't been much use to her since getting the craft as she had spent most of her time against the winds, but as they were now at her back, Yumi forgot the troubles ahead for a little while, relishing in a speed far outpacing any she had sailed before.

Uru, who was taking a rotation in the nest, called for land.

At his notice, Haruin passed off the wheel so he and the rest of the men aside from Uru could assemble their armor.

Chief Tonko wore a cuirass and great plates over his shoulders with layers of gilded bronze and sharkskin as its outer surface. Especially after their encounter with the grandmother shark, the great tooth on his chest was a striking centerpiece.

Haruin barely wore armor, although he did strap on a goggled helmet and carry a round boss shield with a pair of nude dancers on its face, same as the sail of his boat back in the Guardian Atolls.

The armor Kirut strapped on was primarily lacquered baleen lamellar with highlights of cachalot ivory. It was styled much like the full plate of mainland knights, but the material was lighter and more mobile. His teardrop shield was tall and made of a single seal pelt over baked leather.

Both dogs were also outfitted with vests and helmets of lacquered baleen. Yumi wondered if it might benefit her and Uru to have some sort of armor to defend from the venomous bites of the hezuki, but she knew armor would only slow them down while swimming. Agility was their best chance of survival in fur.

The lagoons of Krakenstone were to the south through the maze of small islands, so she veered slightly starboard to catch a last surge of momentum before cranking in the spinnaker and turning hard to port. Already the air had taken a chill. She couldn't see any clouds of frost to the south, but the same bite in the air welcomed her to the island as had greeted her when she first arrived back home.

Yumi had been to Krakenstone once in her youth. Far from the trees and sand of most islands in the region, it was defined by a hundred dark basalt tentacles fused together in a looming tower. According to their stories, this island had once been several great volcanos, but the mountains had crumbled into the sea, leaving only a few basalt towers behind. The rest of the main island was the common sandy beaches and forest of fig, palm, and rubber trees, but the mighty tower of a hundred fused columns on the far eastern corner of the island gave Krakenstone a distinguished grandeur. Several of the small islands throughout the shallows inside the reef had columns too, but none matched the great tower of Krakenstone.

With aid of the oars, they rowed into the deeper lagoon, skirting through the channels carved through the banks and small islands on either side.

Right away, Yumi spotted many men on the docks and along the tree line. In line with Chief Tonko's prediction, there were easily a hundred men on the docks and beach in armor, while those in the tree line were a mix of women, elders, and youth. Everyone who could hold a spear did so. Aside from a few posturing faces everyone looked terrified, as though the drop of a coconut might send the lot of them running, but to their credit, they were present and ready to defend their home.

Although the wind was broken up by the trees, Yumi still caught the scents of those on shore: fear was the strongest, but she also picked up the faintest hint of death.

Chief Tonko stood, making his way to the prow as Yumi steered them to an open space on the largest pier.

"Halt!" called a large fellow carrying a bronze longaxe with a blade shaped like the tail of a whale.

Chief Tonko stepped onto the dock, standing his full height a hand taller than the man.

"Oh! Chief Tonko!" he said quickly, taking a step back. "We got no word of your visit."

"I didn't send one. Fudol, yes?" The man nodded, his shoulders losing some of their stiffness. "Good. Where is my cousin? I do not see Chief Mosdin here among your forces."

"He is with his family and guards in the upper lodge, Chief. Do you wish to have audience with him?"

"I do," said Tonko. "This western fellow, here? The Akanuk and his hounds? Treat them as you would me. Kirut has experience with the monsters that bring the chill you feel in the air. He is here to help us kill them."

The man named Fudol nodded, his initial posturing and aggression calmed to a grateful but still sturdy demeanor. He still smelled afraid, and looked on edge, but happy to see a familiar face. Yumi wondered if he had been given any instruction at all from their chief. "Narmo will take you to Chief Mosdin. I'll talk strategy with Kirut here. Thank you for coming, Chief. Do you bring more ships?"

"Unfortunately not," said Tonko. "But I think you'll find what we did bring will make a good bit of difference."

Fudol gave a final nod, then introduced himself to Kirut.

"Should we go with Kirut or you?" asked Yumi.

Chief Tonko took a deep breath, looking up to the basalt tower and lodge built atop it. His next words were hushed. "If his family and best warriors are up there, I may need a lot more support. I may be his cousin, but blood has not stayed his hand before."

"Then we're with you, Chief," said Haruin.

Narmo, a young man who couldn't be more than a few years past coming of age, led them down the pier, through the forest, and to a winding stairway carved into the stones.

"Watch your step," said Narmo. "I'm not used to it being this precarious outside of the occasional summer gale. The chill has made everything, well…"

"We're alright," said Chief Tonko. "Lead the way, son."

Although the tower wasn't nearly as tall as some of the stairways to Imperial forts, maybe ten span to the top, it felt far less secure than the meticulous carving and rails on Telmede mountain stairs.

Once they reached the top, they were greeted by the upper lodge of Krakenstone.

A balcony at their current standing level wrapped around the lodge. It was not nearly as grand as the lodge at Hollow Turtle, being much closer in overall size to the lodge back home, but it was built into the columns so they acted as a shield against any winds from the northwest, and made the structure look like it was only a single story. Two spires grew from the roof: one was the chimney, and the other the reliquary home of Sunset Cleaver.

Standing before the door at the end of the boardwalk was a pair of guards who closed ranks as young Narmo approached. The youth's spear shook slightly in his hand as he approached.

"Chief Tonko requests an audience with Chief Mosdin."

The guards were stiff, and did not move, their spears still barring the path. Their eyes had a faint crimson shine through the goggled holes of their helmets. Although the wind was at her back at first, Yumi was finally close enough that she could pick out their scent:

Brine and rotten flesh.

Yumi grabbed Chief Tonko's hand while the guards looked at Narmo. He didn't speak, but tilted his head down slightly.

"The guards have been bitten."

***

Kirut stood on the beach, looking out to the waters beyond the small lagoon. Several towers of basalt protruded from the waves. He couldn't see any sign of the snowstorm yet, but his joints were stiff and the old scar that blinded his left eye felt hot.

"Chief Tonko said you know what's out there?" asked Fudol, his voice a whisper. "We heard some horrid stories from Chief Tonko's emissaries when he first invited us to Hollow Turtle. Sounded too outlandish. Too fantastical to believe, especially from the ship we took in from Iron Line Archipelago. Walking corpses? Ice monsters? Babes biting their mothers and skeletons crawling from their bodies? Even the greatest witches before the dark ages didn't have that sort of power. I know we should have taken Chief Tonko's offer, but it seemed foolish to throw our lives ass over canoe because of a story. Just seemed like the sorts of tales that get talked all to piss because everyone's scared and no one has a clear head. You seem like you have a clear head. Surely it's not anything so fantastical."

Kirut tried to muster some words of comfort, but the mere thought made it hard to inhale. He looked up to Fudol. The man was barely keeping his composure, and he was the most collected of the lot. This poor man was desperate for reassurance, but Kirut didn't have it in him to lie. Not when the lie would be proven false the moment the sun set.

Kirut looked back out to sea.

It might be a trick of the light, but he was certain he spotted a white cloud at the furthest horizon.

Guppik whined at Kirut's left.

"You should have accepted Tonko's offer."

***

"You may enter, but weapons stay outside."

The guard who spoke in a parched voice indicated the bench at the door. Tonko set down his spears, bladed club, and shield without hesitation. His men followed suit. Yumi and Uru set aside their knives and spears. Yumi wasn't sure why Tonko was so at ease disarming himself when he must have heard her warning. She and Uru could defend themselves well enough. Tonko was a respected wrestler. Perhaps that was enough in his mind.

Haruin was quite casual in unfastening his weapon belt, setting it on the bench. He withdrew his throwing knife from its scabbard on the belt, but Yumi noted he kept the bracer on.

Narmo looked back, gave the least reassuring smile Yumi had ever seen, and led them into the lodge.

They were faced with a wall painted with many legends of old victories over beasts of the sea. The hall went in either direction. Narmo went right, guiding them down the stairs to the main hall of the lodge.

This chamber was far larger than it appeared from the outside. A fire had already been lit, with fragrances of clove and nutmeg added to make a pleasant if a bit overpowering aroma to the room. It was warm, and at first Yumi felt it a pleasant comfort, but consideration of the fact that these people intended to keep warm while their villagers fought in the coming frost below made her own temperature rise.

The main room was crowded. On the balcony above, several guards were posted with throwing spears. They may not have been readied, but held point down and could be thrown at the slightest provocation.

Their matron was not present, likely resting in her personal chambers. A handful of older men were in the seats around the lodge. Four young women were seated around the throne, two seemed to have been talking, and one reading, and the other on Chief Mosdin's lap.

In the corner sat a man with unkempt black hair playing with a young child. Yumi had met Jardin a few times, and knew he had a little sister. Their mother, who would have been matron when her and Chief Mosdin's mother stepped down or was deemed unfit, had fallen off the tower a few years earlier. Rumor was she had been pushed by Chief Mosdin, who did not wish to surrender the power he had enjoyed since their mother's health declined.

Chief Mosdin was a large man, his torso a barrel and arms each trunks of a palm tree, and took up all the more space as he sprawled across his throne. Unlike most men, who shaved their mouths and chins and only grew beards on their cheeks, he let his auburn beard grow full and in many braids. His brow glistened with sweat from the heat trapped in the insulated lodge. The hands that gripped his drinking horn and waist of the girl on his lap both tightened when Chief Tonko entered the room, but he put on a grin all the same.

"Tonko! It has been too long, young cousin."

"It has indeed, Chief Mosdin."

Chief Mosdin raised his drinking horn. "I didn't know you were coming! I would have had warmer hospitality prepared. Please, have a seat."

One of the men of Mosdin's got up and moved so Chief Tonko, Haruin, Uru, and Yumi could all sit together across from the chief of Krakenstone. Tonko's men stood behind their chief, tall and at attention.

"We come to speak with you regarding the enemy who has plagued our seas for the past moon. They are demons of ice and famine. They can turn men they bite into puppets. Although frightening, we have with us a young man who possesses a spear that is capable of slaying them. They are on their way here, across the Crab Bridge, and will be on your shores this night."

Chief Mosdin leaned back, nodding to Haruin. "Is this the young man?"

"Not me, Chief. I'm but a humble pirate, and a few years past young. My friend Kirut is the one you're looking for. He's down on the beach assessing your defenses, such as they are."

Chief Tonko's eye twitched, and he stepped in quickly. "Kirut is indeed seeing where we might be able to best engage with these creatures. He's the only one who can kill them and has experience fighting them, so that's what he's directed his attention toward."

"So you come into my home, seeking to tell me how to defend my people?"

"I was hoping that you and he might be able to work together. He knows the enemy, but no one knows your island better than you. His guidance informed how I set up my defenses. I am so confident in his suggestions that I came here, after all, so I might be able to persuade you to trust in his experience. In addition, with the Sunset Cleaver, you yourself will be able to vanquish them as efficiently as he will."

"You sure you aren't here to tell me to come with you? To sail to your home so you control the situation?"

"Mosdin, I have no desire to take control from you. All I seek to do is bring you the information that was brought to me, that you might protect your people with the same knowledge that I have."

Chief Mosdin leaned back. "This is quite interesting. You come with information, and you may think it valuable intelligence, but you are mistaken. You see, my nephew here has already faced and vanquished one of these creatures. He and his ship encountered them while out seeking refugees, and with his own hands, throttled the monster so it crumbled into ice."

At this, Jardin set down his little sister Myra and stood. For the grandeur of his uncle's statement, he looked humble as ever. "What he says is true. I did slay the beast, although it was no act of heroism. I was saved by my armor as it clawed into me. I do not know how my hands were able to slay it. I assumed they were vulnerable to our touch. To the warm touch of the living. One of my men killed another with a harpoon. Mundane weapons are sufficient for the task."

Chief Mosdin laughed, pushing the girl off his lap. "You see? I dare say you have been taken for a fool, my friend. You knelt to the fear of these strange creatures, frightening though they may be, and found yourself trapped in a grift. His accomplice here even admits he's a pirate! These creatures must be fought, but they are yet beasts, and can be slain accordingly. Your great uncle slaughtered the shark you wear on your cuirass. A shame that such might and fortitude was diluted into the swindled mark I see before me."

Chief Tonko looked down at his hands. His brows were knotted in thought. After a long moment of uncomfortable silence, he let out a heavy sigh then turned to Jardin. "You may have killed the creature with your hands, but they would be more easily slain by Sunset Cleaver." He then turned to Chief Mosdin. "You should wield it tonight as you defend your people."

Chief Mosdin's jaw clenched. "Jardin! Go get the cleaver. You will fight with it. Tonko is right: it will be an inspiring sight to our people."

"Surely you should carry it, uncle," said Jardin, a hint of a smile curling through his composure. "As Chief Tonko says: it is the weapon of a chief. I would not presume to take up your mantle in such a way."

"Your people will understand that you are acting on behalf of your uncle, Jardin," said Chief Tonko. "It would be no insult to act on his behalf."

"Indeed," said Chief Mosdin, looking a bit taken aback by the support but nodding to Chief Tonko. "A good chief is not only a strong warrior, but should also have a tactical mind. I will be up here observing the fight so I can properly direct our forces, but my friend is right: the cleaver is a symbol of our ancestors and their claim of this island. It should be on the front lines."

"If you give me the cleaver, it will be seen as a surrender of your influence," said Jardin, standing taller. "If you submit it to me, you relinquish command of the island."

"No need to make such bold assumptions of your people," said Tonko quickly. "They will understand that you are acting as an ally to your chief. As his heir, it is reasonable for you to assume the position as your chief monitors from this vantage point."

Jardin shot Chief Tonko a scowl. "I think it would be a far stronger message for you to carry it, uncle."

"What's gotten into you?" said Chief Mosdin with a snarl. "Get the cursed club, boy. I'll not ask again."

Jardin pursed his lips, looking ready to retaliate, but instead turned and marched to the stairway on the left, which Yumi assumed led up to the tower.

"I'll go with him," said Tonko. "With your permission, of course. Try and talk some sense into the lad."

"Good luck. Fool has been irritable ever since killing that ice beast," said Chief Mosdin, pushing himself to stand. "Oh, and apologies for what I said before, Tonko. I spoke out of turn."

"Forgiven and forgotten," said Tonko. "You are under a great deal of pressure, cousin, and had every right to be defensive. I'll speak to the boy. Alright if I take Yumi and Haruin with me? They know of these creatures."

"Of course," said Chief Mosdin, waving his hand.

Chief Tonko stood, motioning for Yumi and Haruin to follow.

The stairs were tight and spiraling. Yumi felt a building tension with each step, especially leaving her cousin alone in a room with what she assumed were at least a few puppets. The scent of clove, nutmeg, and flames followed Jardin up the stairwell. Maybe it was just her fear and tension, but she smelled a hint of rot and salt carrying up from the main hall.

The top of the tower was a wide balcony, built in a circle around a central altar. Set upon the altar was a beautiful club, nearly as long as Yumi was tall, with one edge lined with teeth carved from the red juniper wood itself, and the other honed with arcs of dark obsidian. The scent of its crisp, sweet magic filled Yumi's nose. Jardin leaned against the outer wall, arms crossed and glaring at the weapon.

"I hate him," said Jardin, his thumb tapping his bicep rapidly.

"I had to do a lot of easing his pride, but believe me when I say you are who should be holding this cleaver," said Chief Tonko, his baritone soft but audible even over the winds at Yumi's back. "Your people deserve a leader in their midst. They're ready to fight, to die, to defend your home, but they're scared. All they have is rumor. You must know how inspiring it would be for them to see you amongst them? You've already killed one of these monsters that has slaughtered thousands of our people this past moon. You belong on the front lines, not hiding in this tower, and this cleaver belongs in your hands."

"If I take that cleaver, I don't care what he says; the village will see me as chief. I don't know if I'm ready, but I know he isn't fit for the throne."

"Are you going to challenge him for the title?" asked Haruin. Chief Tonko looked back at him, a long brow raised. "We don't have chiefs in the Ring, but I've still heard the stories."

"He deserves nothing less," said Jardin, his fist tightening.

Chief Tonko put a reassuring hand on Jardin's shoulder. "Then take the cleaver and save your people. He can sit in his tower. There's no use challenging him now. You know better than most he likes to be underestimated. If you fight him, he will not face you with honor, and you are likely to sustain injury. Let him think he has won, and we can resolve this matter after the encounter with the monsters."

Jardin looked up at Chief Tonko, took a deep breath, and nodded.

At Chief Tonko's indication, Jardin reached his port hand to the cleaver. Yumi noticed his starboard hand open and move back around Tonko.

In the setting sun, Yumi saw a flash of red in Jardin's brown eyes-

Yumi hopped onto the altar in a crouch, stepped over the cleaver, and kicked with her other foot against Jardin's chest.

***

Kirut and Fudol completed a brief survey of the island.

A stone and plaster wall had been erected and maintained around the perimeter of the island. Even the beach had a wall. These people had certainly fortified well against human invaders, and this would be a boon in fending off whatever living dead were part of the attack. The wall was along the tree line. Kirut and Fudol were now on the beach.

"You expect all of them to come through here?"

Kirut frowned. "I'm of two minds. This is too wide a space. Even with your walls, I think there will be too many points of access for creatures that can swim. Covering all the possible access points will be challenging, and any one of our defenses could be overwhelmed. I also don't like how much space is between the beach and the wall, but I don't know how much we could do about that."

"Should we fortify the lower lodge, then? Just plan on facing them there? It's where we've fallen back during some raids, and over on that side of the wall is a tunnel that will take us to the cellar. The ditches shouldn't take much work to get back to-"

Cold seemed to be closing in around him.

Although Fudol kept talking, looking out to sea too, Kirut noticed figures on the edge of his vision.

Kirut barely managed to raise his shield in time to catch the first thrown spear. Fudol shouted, but had to raise his own as the next javelin went his way, punching through and stopping a thumb's width from his nose.

Kirut called for Tam and Guppik to fall back down the beach.

Panicked cries rang through the crowd as the majority of the fighters scattered.

Four men in sea cow leather armor and large shields stood on the wall, sending a barrage of javelins toward Kirut. Fudol quickly dropped his protesting cries, instead falling back with Kirut to a lower section of beach that afforded a bit of cover.

"I haven't the fucking notion what they are-"

"Bitten by the hezuki, I expect," said Kirut, drawing his javelins and taking them in his shield hand. "Mind control, turns them into puppets. Seems they aren't using children anymore."

"Can we save them? Fellow with the turtle on his shield is my little brother."

Kirut groaned, pain shooting through his arm as a javelin scraped and broke against the boss of his shield. They continued to fall back, and the next two javelins could not reach them. "by the first song...I would like to think so? If they aren't dead, perhaps. They didn't crawl out of the ocean, so they are among the living. I can't exactly promise nonlethal force all things considered, but I'll do what I can."

"Appreciated," said Fudol, tossing aside his cachalot-tail axe and drawing a rubberhead club. The four men hopped off the wall, enduring the drop of over a span and clearing the ditch to the sand. Without breaking stride, the warriors continued. "Charge or let them come to us?"

"They're spreading out rather than closing in, so we may just have to go back to back and hope they-"

Absent command, Tam barreled toward the nearest fighter.

Kirut threw a javelin of his own, aiming for the face so the man had to raise his shield.

Tam leaped, latched onto the fighter's arm, and yanked him down onto the sand.

Kirut elbowed Fudol and pointed toward the three still standing. "New plan: charge."

***

Jardin had recovered his footing by the time Yumi landed in front of him. His hand snapped forward with blinding speed, and she only managed to evade by dropping.

His next viper-quick strike was interrupted as Chief Tonko caught him in the face with an open-handed slap that should have snapped his neck back with the force of the blow, but Jardin absorbed the blow with barely a jolt. Tonko's next blow was a punch across his jaw, and Yumi kicked out his leg in the same motion. She was strong for her size, enhanced by her magic, but already she could tell that Jardin was far stronger than a common man of his stature. Now that they brawled and she was aware of it, Yumi smelled the stink of briny rot through the fragrance he was clever enough to disguise himself with.

As Yumi dodged his next swing, she grabbed his wrist and arm with both hands, checked his hips with her own, and threw him headfirst into the altar. Before Jardin could get his bearings, Chief Tonko had his arms clamped behind his back, and Haruin stepped in with a small length of rope.

An inhuman hiss echoed from a far deeper chest than Jardin had before.

Just as Haruin began to tie off their foe's arms, Jardin gnashed and tried to bite his leg. Haruin yelped and stepped back. As Jardin turned up to him, he let out a feral yell which was accompanied by a blast of cold that frosted over Haruin's port arm. As Haruin stumbled back, Jardin contorted to try and bite Tonko. The chief grabbed him by his hair and held the frothing head away.

With a roar, Jardin freed a hand and raked it across Tonko's face, leaving several lacerations of blood and ice. Chief Tonko released the grip on Jardin's hair and landed a punch across his jaw. At first Yumi assumed the resounding crunch was from Jardin's broken jaw, but the young man seemed at worst a bit dazed, while Tonko growled and gripped what she feared was a broken hand. Jardin roared and kicked Tonko in the chest, and the big man crumpled against the wall.

Yumi grabbed the handle of Sunset Cleaver in both hands. A pulse of magic seared up her arms, lighting her skin in flames of agony. With a scream she struck Jardin across the face with the flat of the club. As she hoped, he recoiled from the impact, the entire right side of his face scorched in a hideous rash.

As Yumi raised the cleaver for another strike, the pain in her arms became too great, and she had to drop it. When she looked down, Yumi saw a rash had spread from her hands up most of her forearms.

Jardin hissed, a cloud of cold fog emanating through fangs he now sported. He had grown slightly, or perhaps Yumi was simply frightened and disarmed. Jardin's skin had faded from the normal tawny brown to a desaturated grey with mottled black spots. Much of his face was an opaque white, save for the rash still burning across his features. His eyes were now an icy blue, fixed on her with predatory focus.

Yumi scrambled back, trapped against the wall by the enclosed space they were in. Her hands still burned too hot to touch the ground or help her stand.

Tonko was on her starboard side, straining to catch his breath. Haruin was to her port. Despite his wounded left hand, the pirate did not cower, instead reaching his uninjured hand out over the rail of the tower. What he was reaching for, Yumi did not know.

Her gaze fixed on his bracer…

Knowing she needed to buy him time, Yumi turned back to Jardin.

"You're not Jardin," she hissed.

The creature in Jardin's body grinned. "How very perceptive."

"Are you what is controlling my cousin?"

"No, that would be my mother. I am one of her children. A son in mortal form. Her best work, if I might be so bold. Controlling all the pieces was more than she could undertake on her own. I've now infected and infiltrated many peoples. I wish I could take credit for how perfect it will be for me to use Tonko as my next host, but the praise really must go to him, all but leaping into a trap I hadn't even set!" Jardin turned a grinning visage to Tonko. "When I drain this girl in front of you, know her blood will be a drink of celebration for your and my coming partnership. You as a mortal man nearly bested this form! With a body like yours, I will be formidable. What wonders we will accomplish together."

***

Kirut moved his shield in an arc as he charged the nearest attacker, hoping the motion would prevent the next throw from penetrating too deep. His effort paid off: the spear barely broke through the last layer of leather. Although Kirut didn't have a weapon suited for this task of not inflicting lethal harm on their foes, he compromised by not aiming for vitals.

The warrior parried his thrust to the man's leg with his own shield, a great oval with a turtle painted on its face with the scales of sea turtle shells along its edge. Fudol's brother. Although the man had been throwing javelins before, he now held a long bladed club with a spearhead at its tip.

Fudol was engaged with the man furthest down the beach, Tam was still grappling with his foe. The fourth warrior was to Kirut's right, some five paces off, and looked to be readying his next spear throw.

Keeping his focus between the two men, Kirut stepped back so as to give himself as much chance as possible of using his shield to fend off both lines of attack.

As the next spear was thrown, Fudol's brother attacked.

Rather than try to catch the spear, Kirut ducked and rolled, keeping his shield toward Fudol's brother. The man advanced, trying to quickly close the distance to accommodate his shorter weapon, but Kirut was quick to reposition. As he took a sturdy crouched stance, Kirut redirected the swing of the club with his shield, flipped its grip to the right to keep the club swinging away rather than meet its force. As Fudol's brother stumbled, Kirut swung Nyrannuk under his shield arm and, while still keeping the shield flipped to guard, thrust the lance into the man's rawhide skirt just above the knee.

The warrior howled in pain and swung back in retaliation. Kirut's shield prevented any momentum in the strike, and he withdrew the tip of his lance.

As Kirut anticipated, the magic of his lance held such potent effect against this mind-controlled warrior. Even the thrust, which a mortal man could have endured, had him staggering aside, hissing in pain and fury.

Another javelin narrowly missing Kirut's own thigh reminded him that there was another opponent.

Before he could make sure Fudol's brother was really out of the engagement, the other man had reached him. This man had a large bronze axe which he swung in one hand. Knowing it would cut through all four layers of his shield, Kirut circled his shield about and redirected it.

With astonishing speed the man swung the blade around and back for another strike. Kirut tried to thrust for his leg, but the man's shield got in the way.

Kirut and the man continued trading blows, first moving back toward shore then up the beach as Kirut pressed with a series of rapid thrusts. Horrid screams rang out from his right. Out of the edge of his vision Kirut saw that Tam's wrestling had progressed to mauling, and once his foe had lost his shield and spear hand torn off, the hound silenced him with a bite to the throat.

After deflecting another strike, Kirut whistled, and Tam rushed to his aid. As Kirut pressed the attack, keeping his opponent's weapon occupied with the hook of his lance, Tam circled about and grabbed the man's axe arm, tackling him to the ground.

A monumental force struck Kirut, taking him off his feet and knocking the wind from his lungs.

He crashed into the sand, dazed and gasping for breath, barely able to raise his shield as the sun went out as a figure loomed above.

The turtle shield of Fudol's brother came crashing down upon Kirut, first as a flat disorienting blow, then in several jabs. Kirut's armor absorbed the few strikes that his shield failed to take, he knew it was a matter of time before an attack struck his knee or-

As quickly and unexpected as the man appeared, he was jerked from Kirut's view.

Kirut looked around his shield to see Guppik had the man by the ankle and was thrashing him about like a pup with a length of rope. The whale hound wasn't trained to fight people, in fact explicitly trained not to cause harm. His acts didn't have lethal intent, but Kirut heard a sickening crunch as the man's leg was snapped to the side at the knee, Guppik's size simply too great to bring down an armed man without harm.

Before Kirut could even get up to try and restrain the man, a red-stained Tam had already fallen upon Fudol's brother, his long wolf-like snout finding its target around the man's throat and tearing it open with a swift jerk.

Kirut looked to see Fudol on top of his own foe, looking to have few injuries but blood on his opponent's own bladed club as he chopped down on the man's head, howling and weeping as he continued to strike past reason.

For all the blood and agony, despite the stench of death now steeping in the air, Kirut could only muster a tired sigh as he looked out toward the distant cloud backed by a radiant blue sky.

Amidst the panicked cries of those on the beach, Kirut barely heard the sound of fighting up on the tower above.

He looked up and saw a few silhouettes in the highest point of the lodge.

Of course he was not the only target of the hezuki's puppets.

Kirut pushed himself to his feet, called his hounds from Fudol's dead brother, grabbed the massive turtle shield and Nyrannuk, and sprinted toward the looming tower of Krakenstone.

⁎⁎

Yumi hissed through the pain, clenched her hands, and pushed herself to standing.

The Son turned Jardin's body toward her. He grinned in an unnaturally wide arc, showing fangs more as a threat than expression of joy. "My brothers and sisters enjoyed slaughtering your family. It was a pragmatic elimination of threats, but I must say their bravery made the kills all the sweeter. I know Mother prefers easy kills, but I like a good fight. Hope makes prey far more engaging and interesti-"

A streak of bronze slashed across Jardin's neck, and his hand snapped to the spot. Before he could recover, the throwing knife was spinning back toward Haruin's outstretched hand. The Son barely managed to kneel and evade the returning strike, which landed hard in Haruin's palm with sufficient force to make him nearly lose his footing.

Yumi launched herself at The Son. He buckled before her impact: Chief Tonko kicked his knee. As Yumi tackled Jardin's body against the wall, she pressed her arm to raise his jaw and bit onto the meat of his throat where Haruin's enchanted blade had cut him.

A swell of rage elongated her jaws as she sank growing fangs into the cursed body. She had never shifted in the throes of combat, something ever advised against by her mentors, but she knew this was the only way she could kill this wretched monster that had slaughtered her family. Her heart pounded wildly. Her vision blurred, but she carried on with singular purpose. As she chewed and shook, Yumi felt her own magic killing his, the monster's fortitude waning with each clench of her jaws.

The demon's rage was now fully replaced by fear, and that panic gave it the strength to shove her off.

Yumi collapsed, her breaths short and heart strained from the effort of shifting in such a state.

Haruin's next throw slashed across Jardin's shoulder. The Son hissed, scrambling to its feet.

With gasps to still her body, letting it return to mortal form, Yumi saw Chief Tonko stand, Sunset Cleaver in hand.

The chief's swing was barely evaded.

Before he could return with a backswing, The Son launched over the rail.

Haruin caught his knife just in time to throw again, but his stream of curses told Yumi the throw failed to make contact. He started to climb over, reaching to catch the returning blade, but Chief Tonko caught him by the tunic and pulled him back.

"It's over the edge, lad," said Tonko, patting Haruin's shoulder. "We won't survive the fall."

Sounds of fighting down the stairway reminded Yumi that they weren't the only one dealing with puppets.

"You alright?" asked Haruin, a bit out of breath as he took in both Chief Tonko and Yumi.

"Which one of us are you asking?" said Yumi.

Chief Tonko gave a tired chuckle, flexing the fingers of the hand with which he punched The Son. "No one's doing well, and it won't get better. Let's go."

****

Kirut kept the massive turtle shield high as he advanced up the stairs.

Several javelins had been thrown from above, but fortunately this shield was made of more layers than his own. It was a heavy beast of a shield and he wouldn't want it in normal combat, but with the strength granted by Nyrannuk it wasn't as cumbersome as it would be with his own strength, and the size made it so he and Tam were covered. With how many strikes he was enduring, Kirut was glad he told Guppik to remain at the base of the tower and not let anyone else come up.

The moment he reached the top, Kirut was charged by one of the men. Tam raced between Kirut's legs and clamped onto the shin of the charger. Kirut caught the falling man against the shield, ordered Tam to release, then spun to hurl the guard off the tower.

As he was spinning, the other guard threw a javelin. It sank into Kirut's pauldron with force enough to nearly lose his footing, although his momentum was such that the angle of the spear didn't reach his skin.

Before the man could ready his next throw, Kirut threw Nyrannuk. The lance took the guard off his feet, crashing into the lodge.

After confirming that Tam was alright, Kirut ran forward and withdrew Nyrannuk. He gathered what he could hold of his friends weapons in his shield hand. After a moment of searching he saw no sign of Haruin's throwing knife. He cursed, hoping his friend had managed to sneak in the weapon, as it would be quite potent against their foes.

Ordering Tam to keep at his heels, Kirut advanced into the lodge, leading with his shield.

The lighting inside the lodge was dim, only illuminated by a lantern, and it took a moment to realize that a large chair had been shoved against the base of the stairs. As Kirut looked around the turtle shield, a figure peered about with a log in hand. Kirut held his thrust when he recognized Uru.

"I take it the audience with Chief Mosdin ran into complications?"

Uru nodded. "They've injured one of Tonko's men, and Jardin, Tonko, Yumi, and Haruin are trapped up in the reliquary."

Kirut stepped over the chair with Uru's help. Tonko's three companions were hunkered behind a wall of couches and chairs, and several javelins were imbedded in the nearby wall and furniture barricade. He looked over their fortification to see at least three men up on the balcony. Within the lodge itself, many were clustered in the back corner under the balcony, and two had been felled with spears from above.

Tam growled at Kirut's side, but he silenced the hound with a click.

"How many?" Kirut asked.

"At least seven," one of Tonko's men replied. "Some on both balconies. We were waiting patiently, all was well, then they just started throwing."

"I was attacked on the beach," said Kirut. "Also no warning. All were puppets as far as I could tell, and I presume that's the same with these men here, all attacking at once. Probably seeking to eliminate skin-changers and those armed with enchanted weapons." Kirut began passing out the javelins he had grabbed from the weapons piled beside the lodge door. "These people can be killed with conventional means, but we don't have many spears. There are a few more up there if we run out, but still, strike true. Their armor is generally thorough, but a good throw should pierce. Is there any way for us to get up to the balconies from down here?"

"Not on this side of the lodge," said Uru. "Set up to be defensible from a frontal assault. There are side doors, but I assume they are locked."

Kirut nodded.

The balcony was too high to reach, even jumping from the low platform on which the throne was built. The rail of the balcony was solid and high enough for them to crouch out of range.

Kirut's gaze drifted back up the stairs to the lantern.

"No…" whispered Uru.

"Have a better idea?"

Uru frowned.

Kirut passed him the turtle shield and jogged back up the stairs. He plucked the lantern carefully off the wall platform. Although there was no way Tam could possibly know what was happening, he waited at the base of the stairs with paws spread and tail wagging: a pup excited for mischief.

"I think I'm a bad influence on you," Kirut said in Akanuk before turning to Uru and Tonko's men. "Who is best at throwing?"

Both of Tonko's men pointed to Loto, the fellow who had done most of the steering and was currently applying pressure to the javelin in his thigh.

Kirut sighed. "Of those presently able to throw?"

"Moko doesn't have the best eyes," said the tallest of the men, nodding to the redhead.

"My eyes are fine you dry-"

"You throw this one," said Kirut, passing the lantern in the hands of Tonko's tallest man. "You cover him. Uru, you're with me, and bring that shield. We're going to the other side. When you all hear Tam here bark, throw to that balcony. Understood?"

Both men nodded. "Understood."

"Excellent. I will try to have everyone go out from that side so you don't need to take down the fortification. I assume they will jump off rather than endure the flames, so I'm probably going to need to engage in the main hall there. I would appreciate as many javelins as you can throw in my support."

After getting confirmation, Kirut led Tam and Uru up the stairs. He grabbed the remaining javelins, along with a few from the guards and one of their shields. After passing some to Uru, they descended down the other side. Kirut took the other lantern as he went.

From this angle, the carnage inside was far more grim.

Several more bodies could be seen, including at least two who had tried to reach the stairs. It seemed one or two people within the crowd had been puppets, for several bodies in the middle of the lodge appeared to have knife wounds. Chief Mosdin was slumped back on his throne with several open punctures in his chest and no sign of breathing.

Most horrid was a babe, barely able to toddle, seated in the middle of the lodge. Four bodies had been slain by javelin as they tried to get to the center and save him. The babe looked about, as confused as he looked frightened.

Tam snarled, snapping his jaws as he stared at the babe.

As the child turned to look their way, Kirut noticed his eyes flash red, and a hint of a smile crossed the babe's face before it started crying again, reaching for the adults hunkered under their own bunker safe for the moment from the javelins up above.

"Good boy," Kirut said to Tam, then nodded to Uru. "Go."

"Should I throw it?" asked Uru, indicating Kirut's eye patch.

Kirut smiled. "I only have one, but it does the duty of two well enough. I need you to keep hold of the tower shield so I can use Nyrannuk to fight them in case they come down."

Uru nodded then advanced a few paces. Kirut told Tam to stay. He followed close behind Uru.

At his whistle, Tam barked furiously.

With his own shield held high, Kirut threw his lantern up in an arc. It landed on the other side of the balcony, and he heard a satisfying shatter. Tonko's men hurled their own lantern up, which also landed in the balcony above Kirut.

"Go," said Kirut, keeping the guard's shield high. "Start bringing those folks over there so we can get them out."

Uru did as requested.

With the massive turtle shield, Uru was able to endure the javelin thrown at him while the other guards worked to put out the fire. Kirut had assumed it wouldn't spread fast, but the air in the lodge was surprisingly dry, and already he saw smoke heavy from the balcony across from him. As one of the men was in view trying to frantically stamp it out, Kirut threw one of his javelins. The spear struck true, sinking into his armpit as his arm was raised. The man slumped out of view.

Uru got three people over to Kirut. They were cautious about the hound, but Tam let them by without a second glance.

Good boy. None were puppets.

Kirut threw another javelin as a man on the balcony popped into view. The throw missed, but if nothing else it prevented that puppet from making another throw.

Two men came into view, their shields preventing Kirut from striking them as they hurled spears down to a hall out of his view.

"That's the hall up to their enchanted cleaver," said Uru as he brought over another batch. "That's Yumi and the rest."

"Unarmed I assume?" said Kirut. "Shit. I'll draw their attention as best I can."

***

Yumi danced back, barely dodging the javelin that sank into the stair where her foot had been before.

"Fantastic," said Chief Tonko. "I would trade my ships and title for a shield."

"Do you smell smoke?" Haruin asked.

Yumi nodded. "Smells strongest through these cracks in the wall here."

"What's the plan?"

"None so far," said Chief Tonko, raising his foot off a creaking stair. "If we step out there, we die. That door behind you - does it lock from our side?"

Haruin shook it twice. "No. Their side."

"Gull shit. Alright. How well can you angle that weird knife of yours?"

Haruin laughed. "I need to see my target. Don't think it will work out for me to just fling it into the room, although that would be quite an exciting weapon."

Yumi inhaled, and a sickening pulse rolled through her. "I do smell Chief Moslin's blood, and I'm pretty sure he's still in his throne. Many others are slain. I can't tell numbers by scent, but I fear most might be dead."

Haruin and Chief Tonko fell into a somber quiet. Tonko rested Sunset Cleaver against the wall, knelt down, and ripped the creaking stair off the floor.

"Your hand looks better," said Haruin.

"I could have sworn it was broken, but evidently not."

"My bond with this knife heals me. Not that quickly though, I must say."

Chief Tonko nodded to Yumi. "Your hands, kid?"

"I can't hold your stair," said Yumi. "As soon as I'm able to shift I will be fine. Being in the sea will help, if we can just make it that long."

"By the first gods I swear: I will get you to that ocean."

"Let's not call in any divine favors just yet, Chief."

Haruin scoffed. "Now seems an appropriate time. Here, pass me the stair. I can throw and hold."

"Appreciated, but I can manage both. I want your throwing unhindered. I'll go first, and the two of you stay behind me. We head straight for the stairs, then out the front door."

Chief Tonko stepped around Yumi, holding the stair in both hands and the cleaver pressed against it.

"Let's go," he said, and rushed forward.

***

Kirut hurled more javelins at the puppets. The smoke spread through the balcony, and it seemed they failed to contain the flames.

Chief Tonko, Yumi, and Haruin ran into view. Tonko instantly took a javelin through his makeshift shield. Before the thrower could dive, Kirut had sent a javelin against his helmet, knocking him out of view.

"Jardin was a demon who bit these people," Tonko said to Kirut as they closed ranks. "I thought you said the puppets couldn't do that."

"Clearly there have been developments since Huu Taukit."

Three of the men leaped off the balcony and charged Tonko as the last man on the balcony threw another javelin.

"Don't let them bite you!" shouted Tonko.

Kirut hurled his own spear up at the man, took his lance in hand, and charged.

The nearest puppet, who was focused on Tonko, Kirut caught in the hip with Nyrannuk. The man tumbled forward, and Chief Tonko swung about a great toothed club and cut him down. Kirut lunged at the next, running him through in the armpit of his cuirass, which immediately prompted his fall. Tonko circled back and killed the last, while Haruin threw his knife up at the last man on the starboard balcony, arcing around his shield and sinking into his helmet, killing him instantly.

A sickening sound cut through the air as Haruin called the knife back to him, a trail of blood streaking down and spattering onto the floor.

Kirut and his friends fell back, making sure to stay below the range of any that might be above. As he suspected, two men leaped over the balcony. Kirut gave point to the closest before he even hit the ground. The other was struck back by an upward cut from Chief Tonko with such force that he was sent spiraling to land some three paces away.

Behind Kirut, Tam was snarling.

Kirut looked to where his hound was pointing.

A girl dressed in fine robes was holding the babe he had seen before. One of the young women was urging her to follow them out, but the girl and babe both stared at Kirut with dazed eyes.

An elder woman stepped into the main hall. Her silver hair matched the pale finery of her dress. She walked with a cane of the same elegant wood as the club Tonko held. She stood beside the fireplace, brown eyes staring at Kirut with the same dull gloss.

Kirut took a deep breath.

"Go. All of you. There may be more circling around to kill those who have escaped outside. Make sure they are safe."

"Are you sure?" asked Tonko, looking between Kirut and the three puppets.

"Positive. I'll see you all out there."

Chief Tonko nodded and ushered the rest upstairs.

Once they had the lodge to themselves, Kirut clicked, and Tam fell silent, coming to attention beside Kirut.

"You can hear me, yes?" asked Kirut, looking between the girl, the babe, and the old woman who he assumed was the body of Krakenstone's matron.

"Yes, I can hear you," all three said in unison. "I am glad you came."

"Your trap failed."

"Did it? I sent my son to give them hope then break their spirits. I think he has accomplished this quite efficiently. You killed more of my bodies than I anticipated, and I'll admit I am disappointed none of you with poison claws were slain, but the dead will feed my children either way."

"We put up a fight, though. You have no interest in conflict."

All three; babe, girl, and elder, shared in a discordant laugh. "We both know the other has grown colder and wiser since our last meeting. Do not insult either of us by feigning ignorance."

"So you still come to Krakenstone?"

"Of course. I am touched to hear you missed me so."

Kirut's grip tightened on Nyrannuk. "Why do you feed on beings? You don't like fighting, don't want to risk your own injury, and you get far more from an elk than a man, let alone a child. Why risk fighting things that can kill you with fire and magic?"

All three grinned. "Best think of me as magic. As a mystery. If mortals wanted to understand us, that knowledge would be passed down, yet they ever prefer to let us fade into myth. The more you understand, the more tangible I become, and I anticipate you will find no comfort or satisfaction in the answers you so desperately seek."

"I don't seek to understand you to sate some ill-minded desire or satisfy an idle curiosity." Kirut jabbed Nyrannuk toward the babe. "I seek to understand so I might end you permanently, that you may never again infect the mind and body of my people."

They cocked their heads to the side. "You still have noble aspirations. Still see this conflict as external. As a calling greater than your own hunger for vengeance. Pity. I thought you had grown past such lies, but it seems you have yet more to break."

Before Kirut could process a reply, the matron of Krakenstone reached her hand into the fire place, enduring the searing burns of the flames, and withdrew a log. As though her hand were not now scorched, she tossed the log onto the furniture barricade at the base of the other stairs.

Her dress caught fire, and she began to ignite, but not before taking one of the oil lamps beside the fireplace and dashing it upon the floor. The little girl set down the babe and followed suit, taking a lantern from the corner and spilling its oil onto the wooden floor. The babe looked up at Kirut, the gloss leaving his eyes as his expression became one of confusion.

"You could save him if you must," said the little girl as she dropped the lantern on the oil and watched its flames spread. "The girl too. She's heir to this sad pile of sand. Both will try and bite you, so you can probably only save one unless you wish to risk infection yourself, and that would be a most disappointing way for your story to end. You may save one. The choice is yours."

Kirut set down his lance and advanced.

***

Yumi didn't smell any rotting or brine amongst those gathered outside. While prudent to not race down the precarious stairway, she still disliked their proximity to the lodge as smoke trickled through gaps in the lower roof.

"What is the meaning of all this?" asked one of the elders. The surviving members of his court cleared away.

"Jardin was one of the puppets of the ice demon," said Chief Tonko. "He attacked us, just as his fellow puppets attacked you in your hall. He was never going to touch the cleaver, for it would have scorched his hands and been his doom."

"Did Chief Mosdin survive?" asked another elder, this one with an unfocused gaze.

The first elder who spoke put a hand on the old woman's shoulder. "No. When Pachin turned, the chief was his first target."

All eyes turned to the lodge. Yumi smelled burning flesh wafting out of the main door.

"Kirut's still in there," said Haruin. "I'll get him."

***

Using his sash, Kirut restrained the girl, using his knife to cut a gag.

Tam snarled behind him, but it was Haruin who stumbled into view.

"What's taking you so-" Haruin stopped, taking in the scene.

"She said we could only take one. She's the heir. If Krakenstone survives, they will need a matron."

"Fine, well you take her," said Haruin. "I'll get the boy."

Kirut considered expressing his doubt, but Haruin already moved in.

"Make sure it can't bite you," said Kirut.

"He's a child, Kirut, not a creature."

"A child infected by a demon. I don't know if she has made them capable of spreading the venom. I don't want to have your body at the end of my lance, Haruin. Be sure to gag him."

Haruin did so as Kirut lifted the girl, who's expression was dazed.

The moment Haruin picked up the babe in tender arms, a series of sickening cracks rolled through the body. Every possible joint strained or twisted. Before Haruin could even scream, the babe locked in a knot of impossible turns, and his skin rapidly frosted over. The cold was so great that Haruin dropped the lifeless form, which landed with a metallic thud on the floor.

Haruin stared at the body, his own eyes almost bulged from his skull. He stood immobile as the babe he held a moment before.

The babe's eye twitched.

Kirut thrust Nyrannuk into its torso, shaking Haruin from his trance.

"This is what we are hunting, Haruin," said Kirut, withdrawing the lance. "Let's go before this lodge smokes us out."

***

Yumi was about to rush in to help when she heard people walking up the stairs.

Haruin and Kirut stumbled out amidst a cloud of smoke, a girl in Kirut's arms. Tam was between them, snarling at the girl.

The child was restrained, albeit not tightly. Haruin looked to Kirut with brows knotted in worry. Kirut's hold was firm on both child and lance.

Kirut advanced wordlessly through the crowd.

The roof of the great lodge finally ignited, the flames rapidly spreading along the rubber-coated shingles and sending black smoke into the clear afternoon sky.

Even so close to the flames, Yumi felt a chill in the air.

It grew colder with their descent.

Chapter 6

With the setting of the sun, snow fell for the first time in Krakenstone in nearly a century.

Although many had advocated for piling into ships and fleeing, Kirut had convinced most to stay. They might avoid the army of the dead, but in open water their boats and ships would be easily outpaced and scuttled by the hezuki. A few families insisted on returning to their outlying island homes, and others had gone to Hollow Turtle Island. Kirut wished they had all stayed, and knew they were likely fleeing to nothing but a quicker end, but if a few could escape, they had his blessing.

Many of the nearby islands and outcroppings had fires and lanterns lit and covered to fend off the elements, but Kirut could barely see the closest of these flames amidst the dense snowfall.

Using spare baleen scales, Kirut had repaired his shield after removing the javelins. The hide was easy enough to stitch. He had considered using the turtle shield, as its great size could be useful, but he liked that his own shield was nimble enough to be used with the lance. Besides, Fudol seemed enthusiastic to use the shield in his avenging fight against the monsters that took his brother's mind.

The lower lodge had been fortified and the people inside were busy preparing as many javelins as they could. Kirut didn't know how efficient throwing spears would be against the dead, but puppets could be killed by mortal weapons, and he would much rather put down as many as possible at a distance.

Amidst the air that got colder by the moment, Kirut was thankful to have a warm hound on either side.

Boots on sand-covered stone alerted Kirut of someone approaching. Someone he knew, based on the wagging of both tails.

"Do you really think we'll get the chance to end this?" said Yumi, scratching Tam's neck as she stood to Kirut's right.

"I hope so. I assume you'll want the final blow?"

Yumi scoffed. "I don't care how she dies. I just want her dead."

Kirut wasn't optimistic about their chances of defending from the wall. He wondered if perhaps they should have invested all defense on the lower lodge. It would be easier to maneuver their defenders in that space, but they would surely overwhelm the space with everyone packed in.

"Think we'll be lucky and sharks will have picked off most of the marching dead?" Kirut said as Chief Tonko appeared on his left. With what little light remained in the sky to the west, the skies only got more opaque as the cloud overtook them. Even Kirut felt the cold, and Chief Tonko had gone back to Yumi's boat to wrap a large seal skin over his shoulders. Yumi looked indifferent to the temperature, in fact she looked as warm as the hounds: all three emanated mist from their forms as much as their breath.

"I see no harm in indulging a bit of optimism" said Tonko, tapping the hand-sized tooth at the center of his cuirass. "A grandmother shark feeds only on the finest of whales, sea cattle, and walruses, but I've seen greater striped sharks consume armored men, much of a rubber shipment, and even the hull of a canoe. They're common around Crab Bridge. Doesn't seem an unreasonable comfort to assume."

"How fares your hand? Yumi said it got injured in your fight with Jardin."

Tonko flexed the hand. "In truth? I have never felt healthier. Faster. Stronger. Bonding with this enchantment is quite the rush."

"Just be careful. In Haruin and my studies of enchanted artifacts, they can be dangerous. Nyrannuk here is bound to my bloodline. It wants to keep me safe. You and Haruin are just hosts. Be careful it doesn't take control."

"Once this fight is over, if all goes as I hope, I will return it to young Myra. Poor girl. Feels cold to tie her up in her own home, but I understand the predicament."

"She will have much to learn about leadership if she survives this," said Kirut, crossing his arms.

"Indeed she will. Let's see that she has the opportunity."

Voices drew Kirut's attention behind him: Haruin and Uru were coming up the nearest stairs to join them.

"Mind your steps," said Chief Tonko. "I almost got a whole new set of features a moment ago. Frost has set in fast."

"Any sign of them?" asked Uru.

"Nothing but the snow," said Kirut. "At least some aspects of their attack are predictable. I expect the attack will be soon."

"We're as ready as we can be," said Haruin. "Had the children do another run of sand along the wall if we need to run to one of the reef gates, but filling the entrances in with stone should slow them down enough for us to meet them if that truly is their point of attack."

Kirut nodded. "I expect they will have some attack from all sides, but most from the front. It's ultimately our weakest, and I am confident they know that. Will be hard to funnel them, even with our trenches and barricades on the shore."

"We should go take fur, then," said Uru. "Good luck on the beach."

"Gods be with you," said Chief Tonko as Uru and Yumi clasped arms with him, Haruin, and Kirut.

The cousins descended the stairs. Despite the cold, Uru and Yumi stripped off their clothes and stepped into the water.

As they hunkered down, both began to change.

Yumi's transformation was almost instantaneous. In short order her limbs shortened into flippers, torso bulked out and elongated, and her features stretched into a face not unlike Tam's, especially the gnashing fangs. Her fur was in patches of dark brown, white, and golden blond, much like her own hair. She looked a bit larger than she had been before, although it could simply be added bulk from her dense fur.

In contrast, Uru had at least doubled in size. It was as though each wave of icy water rolling in washed into his form and added to his mass. His body was so warm that mist wafted from him. Unlike the patches of different colored fur that Yumi's walrus form boasted, Uru's fur was a uniform black save for a streak of white on his chest. He was massive in contrast, perhaps as large as Guppik. Larger than a hezuki, as massive as the Great White Death if not as long, and with the magic in their bite both he and Yumi could slay one of the monsters in the waves. Yumi had remarked on the boat that her cousin was not notably large for their kind, and her brother Yano was at least a third larger.

Kirut whispered a prayer into the wind that Sam's familiar found them and that Yanochin might arrive to something other than the frosted bones of his cousin and little sister.

Once both were transformed, Yumi and Uru galloped with surprising proficiency up the stairs and along the wall to their respective posts by the two gates.

Chief Tonko wished Kirut and Haruin good fortune, then walked down the wall to take his position with the central unit on the beach, where most of their fighters would be positioned.

"I think some part of me wanted it all to be a fantasy," said Haruin, his tone barely audible over the building winds. "I've always loved a good adventure story. Heroics. Bravery. I've had my share of adventures myself. Some made me feel like a good man. Others sit in my chest to this day. This sounded like a true fable. The sort of thing I expect mainland lords to hear ballads about from bards in centuries to come. I imagine they'll leave out… most of what I've actually experienced so far. Demons infecting infants doesn't make a pleasant or inspiring fable."

"If we win, none of the mainland lords will hear of a conflict this small, regardless of how fitting of a legend it may seem. If we lose, and the armies grow and spread north, the stories will be of the mainland champions. No one's going to sing about us, Haruin."

Haruin patted Kirut on the shoulder. "I bet you're wrong, and I look forward to proving it so."

Kirut mustered a tired smile. The two clasped arms, then looked back out to the dimming waves.

"I'll get to my tower," said Haruin, drawing his knife. "Take care you three."

"Haruin?"

"Aye?"

"Thank you for joining me on this adventure."

Haruin chuckled. "What sort of pirate would I be if I didn't?"

Guppik raised up onto the rail of the wall, pointing out to the south as his tail wagged vigorously.

Kirut sighed and scratched Guppik's neck. "I feel it too."

With a click, Kirut lead his hounds along the wall toward the section closer overlooking the beach.

***

Scent is far more potent in fur.

Yumi sniffs the wind, taking in the beings around her.

Hundreds of unique scents on the island. Back on the beach she could smell them all. Now that she is upwind, only the dozen or so people around her have scents that she can pick up.

Only three of them are of proper fighting age and stature.

All stink of terror.

Yumi does not blame them. She would be afraid too were she not so hungry for a fight.

For all the salt in the air, Yumi notes the brine from the infected was different. Saturated with rot. Yumi crawls forward and stands to the best of her ability, putting her front flippers on the wall before she falls.

That scent is ripe.

Yumi spots a shape moving in the small lagoon, just below the surface.

A growl builds in her chest. She wants to leap down upon it. A surprise catch like this, before it knows it has been spotted, might grant her an early kill, but perhaps it wishes to lure her into a trap. There could be others. If her uncle, a far more accomplished fighter, had been killed by these creatures, she knows she would be wise to face them in a more favorable context.

With this in mind, Yumi breathes slow to calm her accelerating heart, and keeps focus on the waves in case these creatures seek to launch a surprise attack.

✳✳✳

Kirut's focus had been on a fire dancing on a nearby outcropping for longer than he could confidently say. His hounds had been on edge the entire night, but now even Tam was silent, his snout pointing out into the lagoon. Most of the men and women around Kirut were shivering. The fires they had lit blew out to sea, and it seemed little warmth cut the chill. It was foolish to demand the villagers keep hands on their javelins if it meant their fingers would freeze off, but he didn't like that they weren't prepared for immediate combat. The hezuki would attack soon. They could not afford a prolonged siege. That might suit them better: they could feed off the sea and freeze out the morale of Krakenstone, but they knew that Yumi's brother would be there soon, or so all on the island hoped, so Kirut assumed they wouldn't waste time.

Yet it was now well past sunset. He could feel them all around. Waiting. Hungry.

A while longer passed. He guessed it was near midnight when women and children came from the lower lodge, bringing not only the javelins they were making inside, but a bowl of warm yam and otter stew with a hunk of mainland bread. The pretty woman who brought food for him and the dogs stood looking out to the water. Kirut didn't like seeing her shiver. Assuming she was waiting to take his dishes when he was finished, Kirut ate as quickly as possible.

"There, have a seat beside Guppik," said Kirut. "He's frightful to look upon, but I assure you he won't do you harm, and he's the warmest thing on this island."

Although she said nothing, the woman took him up on his offer.

Kirut swallowed. "Apologies. I'm almost finished."

"You've killed them. These creatures. This is what the locals are saying."

Kirut's brow furrowed. "Yes. I take it you are not from Krakenstone?"

"No. Iron Line Archipelago."

Kirut nodded. "I've killed several myself, but their mother escaped. I have no intention of letting her escape a second time. This lance, Nyrannuk, can kill the hezuki, and the dead can be killed with conventional weapons, although fire worked on the demons and I imagine the dead are the same."

"What is your name?"

"Kirut."

"My family is among the dead, Kirut. I saw them killed on the docks, and I watched them stand and walk back to the interior of the island to finish off any of my kin who didn't escape. I say this not to garner sympathy, but that you understand my urgency when I tell you to kill them all. Use your artifact to pierce every demon. Every corpse. My family is gone. I don't want to see them tonight or ever again."

Before Kirut could think of what to say, she stood.

Having lost his appetite, Kirut let Tam clean out his bowl, then passed the dishes to the young woman. Perhaps not so young. Once she looked his way, he guessed she was his senior by at least a few years. Kirut pushed down thoughts of attraction once he realized she was waiting, and he still held his spoon.

"Thank you, ah-"

"Danwe."

Kirut watched Danwe go back down the stairs.

Chief Tonko was leaning against the wall when Kirut looked back out to the beach.

"A man your size shouldn't be quiet enough to sneak about," Kirut said after calming from his start.

Tonko chuckled. "Maybe you should keep your mind on the battle and you won't be so surprised. Can't say I blame you. She's quite a beauty."

"I don't think that was on her mind," said Kirut. "Nor should it be on mine either. If I survive the night, there's a delightful woman with my twin sons I was going to visit before I heard about these attacks."

"You Westerners are monogamists?"

Kirut smiled and pulled his necklace from under his armor, his thumb gently brushing the pearl. "Most aren't, but she and I are."

"I respect that."

"That woman I spoke with? Danwe? She was from Iron Line Archipelago."

Tonko's brow knotted. "Poor thing. From what I heard, it was... Such a thing should not be endured once, let alone twice."

"So let's end it tonight."

A steady drum echoed through the storm.

Kirut stood beside Tonko, both looking out to the beach.

Shadows against the white storm was their first sign, mostly submerged in the shallows. More bodies arose than Kirut could count.

The first figure to arise from the waves was clad in rubber-coated lamellar, advancing with jerking strides. His form was wrinkled in parts and bloated in others, blistered all over with a mottled greenish-black hue accented by frost. Other figures emerged: one quite bloated and still having a golden-tawny hue, another emaciated and rotted dark. A child was among them, her tiny body frosted in most places. In the light of the flames, eyes flashed crimson as many gazes fixed on Kirut.

"By the mother of the sea..." Tonko managed.

A grim smile crossed Kirut's lips. "Remember what you said, Chief: indulge a bit of optimism."

Kirut threw his first javelin.

The spear sank hard into the armored man's shoulder. He stepped back, his torso cracking as it turned from the impact, but the corpse turned his gaze back to Kirut and continued advancing.

Rather than waste more spears on the armored individual, Kirut threw his next spear at the child, assuming others would struggle piercing such a foe. The girl was knocked off her feet from the throw, falling backward into the water, but by the time Kirut readied his next spear, she had stood.

Kirut kept throwing, hindering the slow but unyielding advance of the dead.

Several of the villagers were frozen in terror. He couldn't blame them. He was glad the sight of walking corpses was unnerving to him as well. It was a reminder of basic mortal instincts, and an oddly comforting notion that some part of him wanted to run.

One of the more decayed bodies reached the ditch first.

Kirut took the lance from his shield hand and thrust it into the dead man's torso.

The corrupted body did not immediately halt, much to Kirut's dismay, but it did slump back and collapse against the bags of sand the villagers had set to support the shape of the ditch.

Snow fell harder as wind howled about. It was hard to see more than a dozen paces, and even that was not with much clarity. The stink of salt and death was the only thing Kirut could smell through his frozen nose.

More of the dead marched up the beach. It seemed for each body Kirut put down, three more crawled out of the sea.

***

Yumi hears fighting on the beach. Screams. Hollers of glory. Pain. Grief. It is downwind, yet she can still smell the rancid affair.

Where she is now?

Quiet.

She waits on the wall still, waiting to ambush a foe that may never come.

Finally! Yumi sees movement.

Their scent is of a corpse, yet the figures are moving. It can be difficult to concentrate in fur, but she thinks there are at least a dozen.

Bellows of Uru to the northeast confirm he has opponents too.

The warriors with her throw their spears. These weapons seem to have little impact, yet some are... killed is not the right term. There may be a better word to kill the dead, but Yumi cannot think of it.

Although Yumi wanted to wait to attack until the demons came into range, as the dead crawl over the wall and begin engaging with the villagers, she knows waiting is no longer an option.

Yumi launches herself upon the nearest dead. He is effortlessly tackled down, and her jaws tear into him. She wretches from the taste: he has been bloated for over a week, and his taste bites her like a hot knife. The magic animating his body is vanquished with a bite, though, so there is comfort that she will not need to strain herself in this encounter.

Sputtering and trying not to vomit, Yumi lopes to the next closest dead, grabs her leg out from under her, and lunges for the kill.

***

Although Kirut saw Haruin kill some dead from his tower, it seemed quickly evident that a majority were attacking from the lagoon itself rather than scaling the wall, so he rushed to join the fray on the southern stretch of the beach. Most throws of his knife dropped the dead it struck, but as Kirut was experiencing himself, it seemed any progress was matched by new bodies.

Chief Tonko had made clear his section, but dead passed through the ditch around him and Kirut. The villagers generally vanquished the dead in single encounters, but it took many more blows to put the dead to rest than it did to hinder and slay the living, and the dead army seemed in endless supply. Many of them had arrows and javelins in their forms before any of the villagers took their throws: some of these bodies had been used to attack earlier villages and had continued fighting. Fortunately the dead seemed incapable of the coordination necessary for their own ranged weapons, but their patinaed or rusted knives and algaed spears were devastating in melee.

After Kirut added another body to the growing pile in the trench before him, Kirut quickly assessed the engagement at large.

They started with fifty fighters on the beach. Already they were down at least a dozen. A few who had sustained injury were pulled back, but at least two had pressed on through their wounds into the trenches to add their bodies to the pit rather than retreat.

Kirut blew his conch.

To the far end of the beach, young Narmo ran to the side and, with the help of two young women, lifted one of Kirut's barrels of whale oil.

As the defenders of Krakenstone fell back, letting the dead crawl into the ditch and hurling javelins to add to the pile, Narmo and his companions left a long trail of whale oil down below. Another team ran with a barrel from the opposing side of the beach, moving around so as not to ignite the planks leading to the main docks.

Once both barrels met in the middle, the teams threw them into the ditch. Haruin and another on the opposite end hurled torches, and upon impact, a mighty flame burst and spread along the trail. Kirut and the rest thrust into any dead trying to crawl through the flames. Others threw logs and more oil, and soon the whole trench was a wall of fire.

Cries drew Kirut's attention north.

"The demons are here! North beach!"

Keeping their focus south with the dead while the hezuki slaughtered from the north was a reasonable tactic for the demons to take.

As their own forces added to the fire, Kirut, Haruin, and Chief Tonko ran down the stairs and into the forested village, Kirut's hounds close behind.

***

Yumi tore asunder another of the dead.

Twice their blades pierced her skin, one leaving a painful slash along her side, but as she rips open the one now pinned beneath her, their section of the wall is still.

Six of her companions have been slain. She wonders if she should bite those bodies so they are not added to the dead, but knows she cannot do so while their family is so close. They will not understand.

There is quiet.

She calls out to Uru.

His response takes longer than she would like, but he seems to confirm that there were no foes in the area.

A man calls from inland. Words can be challenging to discern, but Yumi hears 'demons' and 'north', and charges toward the sound.

When she closes in, she picks up a familiar scent.

It's not Jardin, the smell of the body is different. Perhaps a different host. However, the magic of The Son is the same.

Not seeking to face him alone, Yumi slows her advance and keeps to the yellow fern thickets throughout the village.

The figure stands a nearby clearing, looking south.

Barking and shouts prelude other arrivals. Yumi decides to wait for their distraction to launch from an ambush.

Yumi notices Uru's scent.

She cannot see him, but assumes he has a similar plan if he's also upwind.

Can the being smell her and her cousin? With the winds as chaotic and swirling as they are, she must assume so.

Not much she can do but wait and hope he somehow hasn't noticed them. The rusted sword in his hand would do considerable damage especially when combined with his strength, so she has to be careful.

✳✳✳

The hounds barreled past Kirut to the north.

He called them back, not wanting them to face the hezuki alone, but only Guppik slowed and looked back.

The circling winds picked up, and biting cold seemed to cut off sound around them.

Kirut sprinted.

He knew he left Haruin and Tonko behind, but didn't care.

With Guppik at his heels, Kirut raced around a residential hut to an open common area, and nearly slid on ice when he halted and held out a hand for Guppik to do the same.

A tall figure with mottled grey skin and bone-white features and throat was holding Tam by the scruff, lifting the entire hound casually in one arm. In the other he held a rusty iron sword, aimed at Tam's torso. The hound snarled and snapped, but was immobilized.

"So this is the one who bested my mother," said the demon Kirut assumed was The Son. From what his friends said, Jardin's body had been severely damaged after their duel. There was no evidence of any damage in the man now before him.

Kirut clicked for Tam to be calm, and the hound begrudgingly complied.

"I must admit I'm a bit disappointed," said The Son, flashing a fang-toothed grin. "Your knife throwing companion is taller, and have you seen Chief Tonko? I certainly hope he survives. I cannot conceive of a better body to conquer Hollow Turtle in, then who knows? He might last for the next leg of our journey."

Haruin and Tonko had caught up, but slowed when Kirut held out his hand.

"That's quite close enough," said the demon, touching his sword to Tam's chest at the arm hole of his gambeson. "I had to get this new body after our last dance, and acclimating can be disquieting."

"We wouldn't want to compromise your comfort," said Haruin with a slight bow as he and Chief Tonko fanned out slightly on either side of Kirut.

"What is it you desire?" asked Chief Tonko. "You have a hostage. You're talking with us. I assume you want to negotiate. You know well what we want: you to leave our waters. Is there something you have come to offer in discussion?"

The Son's brow furrowed. "You just want us to leave your waters? Not kill us? I assumed being champions you wouldn't want to make us another region's problem. Did I misjudge you?"

Chief Tonko shrugged, taking another wide step. "In truth, I take my duty to my people quite personally. They are my priority. If you would accept such an accord, and the cost not so steep, I would allow it."

The demon grinned. "As much as such a bargain would delight me, Chief, I've already accomplished my ambitions here. I know you're only stalling to set up a favorable strike. The irony is that I'm also stalling, but unlike you, I've already made my attack."

Screams echoed. It was difficult to discern their origin in the howling winds, but Kirut thought it was from back toward the beach.

"So will you fight me, knowing your men are being slaughtered and are not equipped to face my kin, or will you pass this opportunity to face me so you might spare a few lives? We share a stomach, and I can tell you this: my brothers and sisters are already eating well this night."

Kirut's grip tightened on Nyrannuk. The demon's sword was still pressed against Tam's armpit, and a simple thrust could be lethal.

Two pairs of yellow eyes glows caught Kirut's attention: one to the demon's right and the other further back on the other side.

"Go," said Kirut. "Save who you can. You too, Uru."

Haruin and Chief Tonko both looked primed to argue, but fell back. There were yet more screams at the beach, and their weapons would make all the difference in that conflict.

The massive black form that was Uru in fur didn't fully come into the clearing, but he did gallop around and toward the beach.

The other eyes, which he assumed belonged to Yumi, remained.

Once they were gone, the demon smirked at Kirut. His sword remained primed to thrust into Tam's torso.

"I thought I smelled a skin-changer. So what is your plan? Mother holds your cunning in high regard."

Any throw Kirut made would be obvious enough that the demon would kill Tam before his blow made contact. The lance to the demon's chest would slay it, but not before Tam was killed.

"You truly love these hounds," said the demon, raising Tam higher. The dog whined. "I cannot understand. The dead are my pets, but I would have thrown that spear by now. Your attachment to them is one of your many shortcomings."

"A trade: I drop the lance that can kill you. Toss it away, and you set down my dog."

The demon pursed his lips and nodded. "We have an accord."

Kirut let Nyrannuk fall, turning his wrist so it clattered aside a pace away.

As soon as it was free of his grasp, the demon exhaled, and a cerulean mist wafted from under his fangs. The cloud seeped free of its body, which collapsed, and was immediately set upon by Tam.

The swarm of blue fog spread, many tendrils calling to mind a clawed hand, and lunged at Kirut.

Cold pierced his face as the cloud lashed its way into his mouth, nostrils, and remaining eye.

The world went black.

***

As soon as the magic enters Kirut's body, he collapses.

Yumi gallops out of the brush. She was prepared to fight the demon in its new body, but even if she thought she could muster the fortitude to rip out Kirut's throat and kill the demon while it was in a new host, she doubts his two hounds would allow her to get close enough to try. As it is, both stand over their master with tails wagging and tongues licking frozen features.

With a snarl and no shortage of reluctance, Yumi takes Kirut's enchanted lance in her jaws.

Immediately a cool burn spreads through her mouth. It is not as potent or painful as the cleaver, yet still unpleasant.

Yumi crawls over. Tam snaps and snarls at her, but Guppik recognizes her right away.

Kirut is now thrashing about. He's gripping his hair and screaming. Amidst whatever fight is happening in his body, he thrashes against anything in the area. It's hard to guess how much damage the lance might cause his form if he is being possessed by the demon, but it's the only way Yumi thinks she might help expel the magic.

She can't aim well, and her jaws are searing as the magic in the lance combats the spirit of Sea Badger. With a growl Yumi sinks the lance into Kirut's lower leg, piercing down through armor and meat.

Kirut lets out a harrowed, cutting scream. As his gloved hand grabs the lance to withdraw, Yumi keeps the point in his form despite the pain cutting through her jaws.

Tam tackles Yumi, his jaws clamping around her neck. She shakes him off without much trouble, but he's the same size and much more proficient on land. Although she's generally able to keep him from landing any particularly harmful blows by turning about and snarling back, she doesn't want to hurt him. He's just trying to protect Kirut.

Guppik leaps over Kirut.

Fending off the whale hound is another prospect entirely.

Although she expects to flee, it's Tam that Guppik grapples to the ground. He doesn't bite, simply putting his mass on the much smaller hound. While he gives a deep-chested bark to Yumi that makes her start, especially running hot with her brawl against Tam, she doesn't fear he will attack.

Kirut coughs and his uncovered eye snaps open. He coughs again. As he does, his grip on the lance tightens, and a cloud of violet blue expels into the night air.

With a deep gasp, Kirut slumps back.

✳✳✳

With each breath, Kirut's vision came back into focus. Wet, hot licks on either side of his face and a stench most foul brought further awareness. He laughed and thanked both hounds for their attention.

As soon as he shifted his leg, Kirut roared in pain.

After catching his breath, Kirut cautiously raised up to inspect his right leg.

Nyrannuk was thrust into the meat of his calf, breaking the lamellar and looking to be halfway through his leg.

Once Tam and Guppik finished their inspection, Kirut looked about.

The body that had once been the form used by the demon was slumped and dead a few paces away. Snow fell hard, and there was around half a hand's width stuck on the ground. Yumi was finishing a transformation to mortal form to his right.

"Are you alright?" Kirut asked. "Did we kill it?"

"No," said Yumi, gasping herself as she wriggled her fingers as though back into place. "I think we hurt it though? Looked like you were fighting it, and the lance in your leg made it flee."

Kirut assumed the first of the barbs would have hooked into his shin, but the area around the wound was so burnt and blackened that it seemed almost loose within. Normally he wouldn't dare withdrawing a weapon from an open injury, but there was little blood to be seen, and the lance only hurt when he moved.

With a deep breath he pulled the lance free.

Yumi looked up from collecting herself after skin changing and gasped. "Wait, did-"

Kirut dropped the lance and leaned in to check the injury.

As soon as Nyrannuk was out of his hands, agony swelled from his leg with such intensity that he nearly went blind. He grabbed the lance, and the pain subsided, at least for the most part.

"I think I will pass out if I'm not holding this," Kirut said as Yumi rushed to his side. "Maybe this wound is worse than I thought."

"I dare say it is," said Yumi. "Let's get you back to the lodge, then I'll... oh, I don't know. Our friends haven't returned, so I assume they got tied down at the wall, so I should go back them up."

Kirut nodded. "I'm sure I can find someone who can dress it."

Yumi helped him to his feet.

Even with Nyrannuk numbing the pain, each step sent a dull throb. If nothing else, he was reassured that he could still move the foot. Progress was slow, but with Yumi holding him on one side and Guppik on the other, they reached the lower lodge.

A low wall and ditch surrounded the large wooden structure. A balcony encircled the second floor, reaching near the wall. It wasn't a fortress to repel a mainlander army, but it was suitable shelter for the two hundred who could not fight. A few youth and elders were posted on the balcony. The two guards posted before the door were both women. Kirut recognized Danwe as one of them, who promptly rushed over. She stopped, her brow suddenly knotting, then aimed her spear forward. Tam growled, but Kirut soothed him with a click.

"We're not possessed," said Kirut, waving Nyrannuk from behind Yumi. "I appreciate your concern."

Danwe lowered her spear and got under Kirut's shield arm. Her fellow guard was openly staring at Yumi, only gaining her composure when they got closer and jogged up to knock and have the door opened from the inside. Kirut hadn't much noticed Yumi's nudity, but the young guard clearly had.

Once they set Kirut on one of the elevated cots quartered off by hanging tapestries, Yumi turned to Danwe. "Can you treat wounds?"

"I have some experience."

"Good," said Yumi. "I'm needed at the wall. He's yours. That lance is going to help heal him, so do what you can to get him back on his feet."

Danwe nodded, looking down as Yumi left, then relaxing slightly. She knelt before Kirut. Her grimace upon inspecting the wound wasn't reassuring.

"I'll clean it as best I can, but that tusk spear of yours must have potent magic if she thinks it's actually getting you to walk in the next… month."

Kirut shrugged.

"I'll gather bandages and alcohol. Might find something in the kitchen to use as a splint. Don't try to take the boot off until I get back."

"Thank you, Danwe."

Danwe looked into his eyes for the first time and smiled slightly. Although likely trying to distract himself from the coming pain, for a moment he was lost in their warm sienna hue. "I expect this will hurt like repeatedly dunking your foot in hot oil. Thank me when it's done."

After she helped Kirut pull off his armor, Danwe left to gather supplies. A sore pulse rippled across his chest.

While keeping his shield hand on Nyrannuk, Kirut opened his tunic.

Mia's necklace had flipped and her pearl was darkened on its face, with a matching burn on his sternum.

Although worried it may have been destroyed, a simple brush across the pearl cleared the char, and a soothing warmth spread through his hand at its touch.

***

After gulping down a full gourd of water, grabbing a melee spear, and pulling on a robe, Yumi stepped outside.

Sounds of fighting rang out to the southeast.

Yumi set off at as fast a sprint as she dared in the snow.

The fire in the trench before the wall yet glowed, but the dead still came. Tonko stood out atop the wall, sweeping Sunset Cleaver at the dead climbing over. Yumi spotted Haruin not far from Tonko, throwing his knife with a fury. Uru was on the other side, still in fur, tearing into one of the dead that had cleared the wall. A few of their warriors had fallen, but for the most part, it seemed they were holding their own. She did spot movement down the wall along the island's edge, but by the sound of it, most of the action was on the beach front.

Yumi hopped onto the wall beside her cousin. Although she used the spear to check a corpse back into the fire, she noticed it was dying down. For all the logs they had thrown along with most of Kirut's whale oil, the amount of snow falling into the flames was taking its toll, and the fact that the dead were all bloated with sea-water was making matters worse. As it was, all the water melted on the whale oil flame spat so much smoke that it was barely possible to see more than a span out onto the beach. Fortunately the wind blew away from them, but it meant there was no reliable prediction of where their opponents were until they had already leaped for the wall.

"Where's Kirut?" Tonko shouted after a long sweep of his club.

"Recovering in the lower lodge. He was injured."

Tonko's next words were silenced by a harrowing scream down the wall near Uru.

Yumi turned to see an armored man tackled off the wall to the cleared area behind. His attacker was much like a penguin in basic form, yet emaciated, with a serpentine neck, legs pronounced, and flipper wings ending in butcher's hook talons. The hide of this creature was naked of feathers, and had a slickness as though it were partly encased in ice. Its long jaws were clamped on the man's shield, and a swift jerk, cast it aside.

With blinding speed the creature snapped forward, grabbed the man's face, and planted the hooked talon on its foot under the man's jaw.

As the talon withdrew, the creature's snake-like neck twisted so the head glared to Yumi, its eyes catching the dwindling firelight in a flash of red.

Yumi threw her spear. Although it shattered the ice of the creature's shoulder, she saw no sign of measurable injury, and her spear fell useless into a nearby snow bank.

A roar with such force that Yumi started cut through the cold air, though not from the hezuki.

Uru launched himself off the wall and onto the creature. Although it hopped out of the way, Uru's jaws caught the demon's leg. Uru wasted no time in thrashing it to the side. With a shriek it curled in on itself, the toothed jaws snapping shut as Uru drew back. The talon hooked into Uru's neck. He shrugged it off thanks to the thick fat and fur protecting him, but a better pierce could easily be his end.

Yumi leaped off the wall and took up the axe and shield of a fallen warrior and started back toward her cousin.

A flash of spinning bronze left a shattering gash across the hezuki's leg, tripping it.

As Haruin's knife returned, Uru took advantage and grabbed the back of its neck in his jaws. Enduring the beating of its clawed wing and thrust of its talon, Uru gave a hard twist. His attack was lethal, and by the time Yumi reached them, the demon crumpled dead into the snow.

Uru let out a soft groan.

Although he shook his head, shrugging her off, Yumi checked his starboard side where the claws seemed to have struck him. Ice encased the several scratches and punctures he had taken. Thankfully she didn't see any indication that he had been bitten.

The dead fell quiet.

The few remaining near the wall slumped, suddenly acting as mundane cadavers and falling to the cuts and cudgels of the living.

A chilling silence spread along the wall. The only sound was heavy breathing as their surviving forces collected themselves.

Far out to sea, a resounding cackle built in volume, sounding as a rush toward the shore. The laugh carried on, rising to a scream of such volume and discordant pitch that Yumi felt it in the joints between every bone.

A chorus of similar cries rang out from the west. The south. More out to sea, then finally amidst the fog billowing up from the remains of their trench fire.

A flash of ice and blood all but erupted above Yumi as a creature grappled one of the warriors off the wall in an arc, landing amidst the foliage behind her and Uru. With no supernatural defenses, the poor woman was torn apart before Yumi could process what had happened.

Like a great wave, warriors were tackled off the wall on all sides. Each impact seemed a kill. Blood was cast in arcs. Lines of red in the snow. A few villagers abandoned the wall, and in their flight, hezuki set upon them. Every time Yumi thought to move and assist, another scream or wretch caught her attention.

Haruin had already leaped off the wall and was running backward into the woods, throwing his knife to the hezuki in his sights.

Beside her, Uru leaped upon another hezuki, tearing it apart.

Although Chief Tonko cleft through one of the demons in a cut of Sunset Cleaver that sent a wash of red slush to his starboard, he could not bring his club back to defend the next hezuki, which grappled him in a blinding pounce that sent both crashing into the snow below.

Yumi only completed two strides before Tonko's body was swarmed by two more demons.

His cries were silenced.

Sunset Cleaver had been cast aside in the grapple. It was only a span away.

As one of the hezuki on the fallen chief looked up to Yumi, she dived for the ancient cleaver. Enduring the heat of the club in her arms, the wild swing kept the demon at bay. She backed up a few paces, swinging at any that came close.

Uru was far to her port, busy battling his own pair of demons and allowing a few villagers behind him to fall back into the village. As they closed in he backed up, roaring with a fury as other hezuki nearby finished off their warriors and circled toward Uru. Yumi lost sight of Haruin.

By her reckoning, she and her cousin were the only living things near the wall.

Her hands trembling from the heat of Sunset Cleaver, Yumi backed up closer to Uru.

Just as the hezuki closed in, they all slowed, turning their attention back to the wall.

The storm winds accelerated. A bitter cold pulsed from the sea. The few remaining fires on the beach were snuffed as if their very heat was sucked out in the drop in temperature.

A silhouette arose from the other side of the wall. At first it seemed human, with broad shoulders and a round head, but as it climbed, the length of the neck increased with an undulating motion. Her hands ended in three great claws. The foot that hooked into the wall to pull her fully into view was armed with a curved sabre of a talon. As the great demon stood to her full height, the empty sockets of her eyes glared down to Uru and Yumi with a chilling blue glow behind the smoke that emanated from within.

For her ungainly proportions, the Great White Death stood with a calm dignity.

She turned slowly to Chief Tonko's body.

Yumi nearly cried out as a soft blue mist seeped into his mouth.

Tonko gasped.

The Great White Death looked back to Yumi. Although her features were static, the curve of her long snout and jagged teeth as her scale-lipped jaws opened struck a petrifying grin.

All around, the other hezuki mirrored the expression.

The Great White Death spread her clawed wings, and Chief Tonko's body stood. His motions were no longer of feline grace and power. There was still a smoothness to his motions, but it was with quickness between still positions like she had seen with Jardin. When Tonko's eyes opened, now pale blue, they wrinkled as a grin spread far too wide across his features.

Although Yumi and Uru both tensed for a fight, the motion of the hezuki was them lunging upon the bodies around them. Yumi had assumed most were dead, but the few muffled screams as the demons began their feast proved some had lived.

Sunset Cleaver burned in her hands. The rash had spread up her forearms. Yumi knew she couldn't hold it much longer.

While keeping his eyes locked on Yumi, Tonko stepped toward the nearest body. Yumi recognized it as Narmo, the young man who had first guided them to the upper lodge. The youth tried to move, but his legs did not respond: his back must have broken in being thrown from the wall.

A resonant series of clicks echoed from deep within the Great White Death.

Tonko's head cocked to the side, then he looked back to Yumi and Uru. His grin remained, showing the fangs that had replaced his mortal teeth. He knelt down and took a fistful of Narmo's hair, all while still looking at Yumi.

"Mother says you two are free to go," he said, his voice still his own yet with a slightly higher tone and sharp edges to each consonant. "With your combined magic she thinks you will harm and even kill some of us before we bring you down. I expect you will want to accept her offer. We are hungry, and I doubt you will want to stick around for what happens next."

Although Yumi wanted nothing more than to cut Tonko down, Sunset Cleaver fought her magic and body with increasing fury.

Uru looked ready to fight, but he had sustained many wounds, and Yumi knew he would be killed quickly if the whole flock were to attack at once.

Narmo looked up to her, pleading in his wet eyes.

Anger made Yumi's grip tighten, which made Sunset Cleaver burn her skin all the hotter. She had to get the weapon to someone who could use it if they were ever to have a chance of killing these monsters.

Yumi backed into the foliage. Uru growled, but followed suit.

Screams echoed from the beach as Yumi and Uru fled the cursed feast.

Chapter 7

Danwe's efforts of cleaning, treating, and bandaging Kirut's leg were painful, even while holding Nyrannuk, but once she was done and the splint was set, he felt the lance focus on healing. Mia's pearl sitting on his chest also helped. It was a soothing process. He lost focus on where he was.

Just as he felt himself drifting to a tranquil slumber, the door to the lodge was thrown open, sparking both hounds to spring to alertness.

A dozen warriors stumbled into the lodge. Some were injured and all were petrified. The three wounded were set down unceremoniously, while the rest scattered. Haruin was the last in the door, slumping against the wall and sliding down, brown eyes focused on a distant nothing. Kirut pushed himself to sitting.

"You four to the balcony!" called Fudol, pointing hard to the nearest stairs. "You two with me. You as well. We need as many hands as possible to fill in the trench with oil and logs and light it! Go!"

Several youth and elders left with Fudol. Just before the door was closed, Yumi and Uru stumbled in, with Uru still a great black walrus. Yumi threw Sunset Cleaver on the ground. The act drew Kirut's attention to her hands, which were covered in welts and a striking rash up to her elbows.

She stumbled over to Kirut's cot. He reached up to help her sit, but she barely made it to his arms before she collapsed. Guppik prevented her from hitting the floor. She hissed slightly, raising her hands as Tam inspected them with a few less-than-helpful licks. Once she had settled against Kirut's chest her body began to shudder. At first Kirut feared she might be going into shock, but he quickly realized Yumi was sobbing.

Kirut held her close.

***

Yumi lost time in her tears. At one point she lay down with Kirut. Although she could tell that he had fallen asleep behind her, his embrace was still firm and supportive. It helped to have the hounds, even if Tam was a bit too insistent on checking on her. Perhaps he felt bad for attacking her before, she wasn't sure.

When she knew she wasn't going to fall asleep herself, she carefully slipped out from his embrace and made sure Kirut's lance was close so he could continue healing.

Her own hands were improved, but she wouldn't be able to touch sea water to heal anytime soon. She did get some soup and water, which helped. Kirut's pretty friend Danwe served it to her to spare Yumi's hands, for which she was grateful. Danwe also applied a salve and bandages to Yumi's hands. She was not used to needing first aid for anything short of open wounds, but holding an artifact designed to kill beings with magic for as long as she had left a harsh toll.

Although the locals were cautious around her and Uru, no doubt due to the superstitious reverence many in their waters showed the skin-changers, it seemed Uru warmed them up to him quickly. Knowing there would be fighting soon, he stayed in fur, but his charisma was infectious even as a beast larger than Guppik, loping around and making silly faces for the frightened children and letting them pet his fur.

Although she was happy for both the children and for Uru having something to direct his mind to, Haruin was much more where Yumi's spirits were at.

Haruin was still by the door, not having moved since she and Uru got back. She got a pair of liquor gourds and went to sit beside him. Wordlessly Yumi set the gourd in his hand. For a while he did nothing, but eventually he uncorked the bottle and took a long drink. When he finally set it down, at least some color had returned to his face.

"I ran."

Yumi raised an eyebrow. "You ran from demons made of ice and hatred that killed sixty people in less time than it takes to draw in a line. I suppose you had best swaddle yourself and sit by the fire with the other babes. Haruin, you were wise to run. If you had stayed, you would be dead too, and that would be one less artifact now."

Haruin took another drink.

"I did very little even though I stayed. I could do nothing as Uru was nearly killed, and I couldn't stop them from infecting Tonko."

Finally Haruin expressed, his brow furrowing. "They bit him?"

"Worse. He's now The Son's body."

Haruin knocked his head against the wall behind them. "Fuck."

Yumi tapped her gourd against his and took a sip.

"I knew I was in over my head, but I didn't think I would run at the first sign of them."

"You killed a lot of the dead with that knife, and you're the reason The Son didn't win the first fight. That's not for nothing."

Haruin sighed. "Thank you for the drink and kind words. Now how do we turn those frigid deranged penguins into slush? The few I cut barely missed a step."

"Kirut seems to think we can defeat them with fire and the artifacts. They did wait to attack until the fire died, although they could have attacked from any other point on the wall. I think they wanted to inspire fear."

"Consider that goal achieved."

"Right. Well I think our priority now is killing The Son for good. When Kirut was possessed, he fought it off, but it had to leave when I stabbed him with the artifact."

"So we, what… stab it with Nyrannuk, or do you think it has to be an artifact the body is attuned to? His body took to Sunset Cleaver quickly. Lineage and all that. Maybe we need to restrain him and put the club in his hands?"

"Then it just leaves the body. We must somehow prevent it from escaping."

"So we hold him down, cover his mouth and nose, and hope holding the cleaver does its job of purging him?"

Yumi nodded. "As close to a plan as I have."

"And in this plan of yours, it is quite considerate of the other demons to sit by and let us set up this elaborate grapple and extermination," said Haruin with a tired grin.

"I'll admit I don't have it all figured out, but that's what I'm starting with. Better a mad plan then no plan, right?"

Haruin laughed and tapped his gourd to hers. After a sip, his brow furrowed, looking across the room. "That little girl? The child who will be matron if this all works? She's still infected, yes?"

Yumi nodded.

"If her blood is also bonded with the club, maybe we can test your theory on her."

"And if we kill her?" said Yumi as he stood then helped her carefully to her feet.

"Like Tonko said; let's indulge a bit of optimism."

Haruin carefully picked up Sunset Cleaver. It didn't burn his hand, but did seem significantly heavier in his hand than it had in Tonko's, and his grimace suggested it wasn't particularly comfortable.

"I don't think my knife likes sharing," he remarked.

"What's wrong?"

Yumi hadn't noticed Danwe come over.

"We're going to try to clear the hezuki magic from Myra. If we put it in her hands, it will fight the demon's magic inside her. Her body should attune to the cleaver and it might protect her."

"*Might?*" said Danwe, crossing her arms. "You're going to risk killing a child as an experiment? You don't know what that might do to her."

"Can you take this?" asked Haruin, offering the club. "I think my enchanted knife is getting jealous."

Danwe took the club absent thought. She looked a bit surprised by its weight, holding it in one hand where Haruin had been struggling with two.

Haruin waited a moment, nodded, then turned to Yumi. "She's right, we shouldn't risk the girl."

Danwe raised an eyebrow. "You seemed quite ready to try a moment ago."

"You made a good point, and you also proved that you're not infected. For a moment I thought you only suggested as much because you didn't want us to expel the girl."

"Apologies," said Yumi. "This element of mind control has us all paranoid."

"I appreciate that," said Danwe. "But we can't experiment on children."

Haruin put up his hands. "I said we're casting that plan overboard."

The door opened. Fudol and two warriors came in, each helping a wounded warrior.

"From the beach?" asked Yumi.

Fudol shook his head. "No, from the north wall."

"Any sign of the hezuki?"

"No, Guardian. They seem to still be… feasting on the beach."

"Hold," said Haruin, drawing his knife. "Each of you must touch this knife."

Each did, and none showed sign of rash on contact. Haruin looked a bit deflated as they took the wounded to cots near Kirut.

"You're upset they aren't infected?" asked Danwe, a wry smile on her face.

Yumi smirked. "Would have meant he could test his theory."

Haruin returned his knife to its scabbard. "Forgive me if I want to test and see if we can save Tonko while still killing the demon. Kirut can just stick him like a boar, but if he can be saved by putting the cleaver in his hand, I would very much like to try."

Yumi and Danwe sobered.

After seeing his wounded to cots, Fudol returned to them, resting slightly on his whale-tail axe.

"I've lit the trenches, and we have enough whale oil from Kirut and logs from our stores to keep the whole monster of a fire burning until morning, although I can't count on that given the snow. All our fighters are on the balcony with javelins and slings or have spears and axes on the wall. We haven't seen the dead or demons, but there's plenty of glowing eyes out in the village around us, so I expect they're waiting. For what I cannot say."

"How many fighting men have we left?" asked Haruin.

"Of our original hundred and seventy? Thirty eight, and seven are injured to a point that I can't count on their aid. Twenty on a given post, so at least some can get a blink here and there."

A chill rolled through Yumi at his frankness. She pulled her robe closer. Of course many had died, but she didn't realize the attack had been so devastating.

"Me and six of those on the beach are only alive because of Uru over there," said Fudol, nodding to Yumi's cousin blowing raspberries for the young children of the village, sparking a chorus of laughter. "You be sure to thank him for me, Guardian?"

Yumi nodded. "Of course."

"Good. I'm going back out there. I'll be on the ground near the door if you need anything."

With that, Fudol took a sealskin poncho from a pile by the door, pulled it overhead, and stepped out into the snow.

"What should I do with the club?" said Danwe, raising the club. "Should we have seen if Fudol wanted it? He may not be heir, but he is chief as far as I can see."

"Keep it for now," said Haruin. "It seems comfortable with you, and that could prove useful. If we end up trying to catch Tonko, that may mean leaving the lodge, and Fudol should stay here. How would you feel about joining us for such an adventure?"

Danwe's lips pursed. She looked to the floor, then the club in her hands.

"I will do everything I can."

"Good," said Haruin, patting her shoulder. "Welcome to the crew."

Yumi wanted to act now, but she knew they all should take advantage of any rest they could.

Danwe glanced back to Kirut, who was difficult to see fully with the tapestry in the way. "I should see if he needs anything, then sleep while I can. You should too."

Danwe nodded, holding the club carefully as she crossed the room. She set it down beside the bed near Guppik, then sat beside Kirut. He didn't stir, being deep in slumber. As Danwe curled up beside him, Yumi turned to Haruin, who had turned his attention back to his gourd of liquor.

"Want to go find a pretty girl to fall asleep in your arms?" asked Haruin, looking up from his drink.

Yumi chuckled, tapping his arm. "You do owe me a pretty girl in a strange port, but tonight I think I'd be happier drinking with a friend."

"Well aren't we depressing," said Haruin with a grin.

***

Kirut awoke to someone sleeping at his left who was not Guppik or Tam. At first he assumed it must be a dream of Mia, but Mia's hair was dyed white ever since she became matron of Huu Taukit. He then thought of Yumi, having been by his side when Kirut fell asleep, but this woman instead had black hair.

As he shifted, Danwe stirred and turned.

"Apologies," she whispered, sitting quickly and fixing her hair. "I fell asleep."

"You're alright," said Kirut, rising up on his elbows. Although he wasn't holding Nyrannuk, his ankle still felt alright while immobile. "Things are quiet."

"We have a fire around the lodge. Guards posted. They see eyes out in the village, but no sign of attack just yet. How's your foot?"

"Feels well now, although I assume the moment I put weight on it or remove your bandages, I will be singing a different song if I'm not holding Nyrannuk."

"Good," said Danwe. "Can I get you anything?"

Kirut shook his head. "In truth, just lying with you was comforting."

Danwe nodded and smiled. "It was for me, too."

She nestled down back beside him. With Guppik on his other side and Tam on Danwe's other side, they quickly drifted back to warm slumber.

Yumi and Haruin sat together, glaring out into the night. Although Yumi was fine in the chill, Haruin had long since leaned against her for warmth, and she rested her head on his shoulder. Yumi lost count of the glowing eyes of the dead somewhere in the hundreds. Their stench saturated the air. Powdered snow fell at a steady pace, and on the nearest of the dead it went halfway to their knees.

Fudol and his companions down below scattered logs and dry bark over the stretch of fire. They emptied the last of the whale oil in the last rotation. A trench of flames all the way around the lodge was astonishingly demanding in fuel, and Yumi noticed some furniture in this round of fire, but it emanated such heat that the snow mostly evaporated.

"What are they waiting for?" asked Haruin. "Is it truly just the fire? They could clear the flames, I'm sure of it. Both fire and wall are lower here than on the beach."

"The Great White Death said we could go so she and her children could eat. That Uru and I would kill some of them before we were slain."

"So they're eating?"

Yumi nodded.

Haruin frowned. His face fell with a slump of his entire body, then he frantically stood.

"What?"

"They're eating, and their puppets are keeping us here. We're investing everything in our defense, and they're keeping us surrounded. Here is where they want us! Once they're done eating, they'll leave for Hollow Turtle. You saw those creatures fight: they don't need the dead, at least not all of them, to slaughter people with no magic. Tonko will open the doors, and if we're hunkered down in dread with every weapon that can hurt this side of the Crab Bridge, Hollow Turtle will be a feast that will make Iron Line Archipelago look like an appetizer. If we're going to free Tonko and kill the Great White Death, we need to attack. Now!"

***

"Kirut!"

Kirut awoke with a start. He tried to still, but Danwe went from asleep on his arm to up and alert.

"Apologies," said Yumi. "Keep quiet. Kirut, do you think you can walk? Fight?"

After a deep breath, Kirut looked at his splinted foot. He couldn't see the wound, but movement felt fine. "I imagine Nyrannuk is lying to spare my feelings, but it doesn't hurt."

"Good. Get on your armor, and keep quiet. Meet us outside and act like you're going to take a guard shift. Danwe, be sure to bring that club."

Once Yumi was gone, Kirut sat up carefully.

After helping Kirut into his armor, Danwe went to find some protection for herself. Kirut shifted about on his foot. He knew his leg was damaged, but it barely ached when he shifted. For the time being, he decided to trust he was alright, and not let go of Nyrannuk.

Danwe returned with a leather cuirass, padded jacket, and helmet that was all entirely too large for her, but Kirut assumed she had been limited to whatever armor had been on the wounded men. She held Sunset Cleaver with both hands, a slight tremble in its grip, and no shortage of worry on her face.

Kirut shouldered his shield, took her hand, and stepped outside with Tam and Guppik close behind.

Outside Yumi, Haruin, and Uru still in fur were speaking with Fudol in hushed tones. Four of Fudol's men were there too, along with Tonko's last man Moko. Haruin closed the door behind them.

"Foot is good?" asked Fudol in a hushed tone.

Kirut shrugged. "As good as I can hope for. So what's the plan?"

"We need to get back to the beach," said Haruin. "I think the dead surround us to keep us and our enchanted artifacts occupied. They feast on the hundred men and women we lost on the wall, then they take Tonko's body, which is now host to The Son, to open the doors of Hollow Turtle and slaughter the thousands who have taken refuge there. Yes they have some witches, but all are healers save for Sam, who's I assume still in a trance to find and guide Yumi's brother, so will be defenseless against demons impervious to mortal weapons and can make more puppets as they go. We need to deal with them here and now. My hope is that we can save Tonko, use the cleaver's attunement to purge the demon from his body, so when we charge we need to keep formation around Danwe and get her to Tonko."

"What will stop from the demon simply leaving his body and finding a new host? Also what will we do about the other hezuki? They will be lethargic after feeding, but they are still demons."

"We fight as best we can, and as you said, they will be easier to battle now than they were before. From what Yumi said, the demon goes in and out of the host's mouth." Haruin drew a rubber coated fishing glove from his belt. "Best I could do. Once he's pinned and the club is in hand, I'll hold this over his mouth and nose."

Kirut inhaled sharply at the thought. "So we're killing him?"

Haruin offered a cautious shrug as he returned the glove. "I've revived drowned men by pressing their chest. If you all can keep the demons off me, I imagine I could get air back in his lungs."

"How do we get to the beach with all the dead?" Danwe asked, glancing over Yumi's shoulder to the swarm of crimson orbs reflecting at the edge of the firelight. "Our small group will surely be overwhelmed. Also how does killing a few of them save the people of Hollow Turtle? If we injure them, surely they will wipe out the people in the lodge once we're killed off."

"The lodge has a tunnel that leads to the wall," said Fudol. "We barred it so the dead could not get to us even if they had memories of it in life, but you will have no trouble opening the doors from within."

"To the rest of your points, all I can say is we must do our best," said Haruin. "Get to Tonko, free him, and kill as many of the hezuki as we are able."

"If I see the Great White Death, I will try to kill her," said Kirut. "She is the blood and breath of this threat. Everything comes back to her."

"We must be united on the goal," said Haruin. "I know killing her will end this as a whole, but if we don't free Tonko, she could break his body. You know she can."

"Honorable though he may be, one man cannot be our priority. The thousands who have perished in these waters would yet breathe if the white death was killed at Huu Taukit. Slaying her should be our focus."

"He's not just a good man, Kirut. Tonko's body is her main weapon, her son, and he's weaker than the white death. If we focus on her, all the others will pin us down. At least taking care of Tonko will make it easier to kill her."

Kirut scowled but nodded. "I disagree, but I will follow the plan. As soon as Tonko is free, my focus is on her."

Haruin nodded.

"If we're ready, I'll take us through the tunnels," said one of Fudol's men.

"I'll take fur," said Yumi, taking off her robe. "Then lead the way."

"Gods guide you all," said Fudol.

Once Yumi completes her transformation, she joins the group surrounding Danwe.

Fudol's man takes them to a small building built out of the lodge. As they go, Yumi looks out to the village. She sees glowing eyes against countless silhouettes. Some of the dead meander, but most stand motionless as they watch the lodge, waiting for the flames obstructing them to finally attack.

The team descends into a tunnel below the lodge.

It is a cellar. Many goods are stored here. She smells salt, food, lumber, and other supplies. Furs catch her nose too.

Several people light torches. They then proceed into a tunnel going south. Yumi is disoriented down here. The tunnel is wide enough for two in skin to walk side by side, but she and Uru take up the whole space as the group proceeds. It winds and turns.

Finally they reach a larger chamber. There are crates to the side, and Yumi smells a few more supplies, along with seeing spare fishing gear. It smells musty. Most of the regularly used goods must be in the boathouse.

The door above them is barred by a pair of long planks. Fudol's men carefully remove them, step out, and beckon the group on.

The stench of death hits Yumi's nose like a hammer.

As she crawls out, she realizes they are on the inland side of the wall on the eastern end. Skeletal forms are scattered about. The hezuki completely stripped every bone of flesh, and many of the larger bones are sawed into so the marrow could be extracted. The consumption was thorough: Yumi doesn't see a single corpse out of the dozens before her that have any remaining flesh.

Tam is growling at the scene, but falls quiet when Kirut clicks at him. On Kirut's other side, Guppil wags his tail frantically side to side. His ears are erect and body stiff. Although quiet, his mane and hackles are raised, and an uncharacteristic snarl reveals massive fangs.

Yumi can smell that the hezuki have been here, and recently, but she doesn't smell them immediately.

She crawls up to Kirut. He looks down, a quizzical expression on his face. Yumi holds out her flipper, touches her chest, then points her snout up to the wall.

Kirut nods.

Uru crawls near the wall so Yumi can use his form to climb.

There is yet more death out on the beach, and she spots the hezuki lounging about in the snow. Their bellies look full, although their skin is still stretched tight over the rest of their forms. Both Tonko's body and the Great White Death are present.

The winds blow at her back, southeast toward the hezuki. They aren't in the line of wind yet, but the slightest shift will give away their position.

Besides, The Son is closer to the waterline.

Yumi climbs back down. She crawls east, jerking her head for them to follow.

The march around the wall is long and over uneven terrain, but not only does it position them closer to The Son, they are also downwind. Although the stink is nauseating, Yumi is reassured when the scent of the hezuki rolls over the team.

They crest the furthest section of the wall. The hezuki remain down below, still sleeping off their meal as far as Yumi can tell, including Mother and Son. The drop into the trench, which is long since doused of fire, is further than the full reach of their arms, but the drop is survivable.

Surely it would be a challenge to endure without making any noise, but Yumi isn't aware of an alternative.

Haruin is the first down. He lowers himself carefully. A half span remains, and he lands in a muffled crouch. Haruin then guides two of Fudol's men and Koto. Kirut tells the hounds something in his native language, and both hunker down on the wall. Koto then helps Kirut down so he doesn't land hard. The man then reaches up to assist Danwe in her own descent.

A shrill call building to a scream draws Yumi's attention back to the beach: one of the hezuki spotted them and let out a wretched cry to awaken the rest.

So much for surprise.

***

The hezuki collectively stood, using their snouts to push themselves up. Their movements were sluggish, no doubt strained by the fullness of their bellies, but Kirut knew they could strike as lightning when engaged.

"Hold formation!" Kirut shouted, keeping his shield high. The others gathered about. Behind him, Kirut heard both skin-changers leap off the wall into the snow on the beach side of the trench. He clicked to call the hounds down too.

Kirut kept Nyrannuk at its furthest reach, keeping the hezuki back. The demons spread out. He hadn't realized just how many of them were present: many hands of demons, ranging in size from a large child up to half again as tall as Kirut. A far greater range than he recalled from Huu Taukit. Fudol's men and Koto made a shield wall with Kirut as the hounds, skin-changers, Haruin, and Danwe all gathered behind. The hezuki continued to encircle them, with some stepping into the waves and turning the waters around them to slush.

Kirut's eyes locked on the Great White Death. She loomed behind her swarm of children, at the far range of Kirut's vision in the swelling storm. All he could really see was the dim blue lights of her empty eyes.

The Son was nearby, Tonko's body looming tall. He grinned, holding a rusted sword in one hand and a cracked femur in the other.

"We all know the goal," said Haruin. "Charge!"

Kirut rushed forward, lashing out with Nyrannuk. The closest hezuki evaded his thrust, but he wasn't really looking to engage. Fudol's men repelled the first few attacks with their shields, yet one was quickly overwhelmed by a pounce. Danwe fended off the hezuki, but the man had fallen, and the formation pressed on.

Although Kirut wasn't sure if The Son knew he was the target, he didn't back down as the team made for him.

Guppik charged past the group, yet he made his way around The Son, sprinting toward the foe Kirut knew he should be facing.

Before he could see if Guppik even reached her amidst the kicked up snow, Kirut dived with a thrust for Tonko's leg.

Kirut wasn't sure if he was glad Tonko parried with his rusted sabre or not. He withdrew the strike and gave point again. A throw from Haruin's knife made The Son take a knee, which Kirut nearly caught with another thrust before Tonko parried.

Although Kirut hoped for some support, it was quickly evident that the rest were occupied with other hezuki. A quick glance to the side showed Koto grappled into the snow, a spatter of red staining the white snow before his body was hurled many paces away and fallen upon by more hezuki. Yumi was grappling with one of the smaller hezuki while Danwe swung Sunset Cleaver to keep another pair back. Haruin was out of view, but his blade spun about in an arc than made several hezuki dodge. Kirut didn't dare look back further, but a scream heralded what he presumed to be another death.

A pained yelp drew Kirut's eye to Guppik. The massive hound had made impact and was beating her back, but for all his strength, the whale hound could do her no harm. He evaded her riposte, but if he got into a proper grapple, he would be dead in a single blow.

"I'm a bit insulted that I don't even seem to have your attention," said Chief Tonko.

Kirut took a low stance. "Then cease your dance and do something worthy of my focus."

Before Kirut could prepare his next attack, a hezuki pounced from his right. He barely flipped his shield before the demon impacted. A talon pierced his thigh as the creature scrambled to bring him down. Although Kirut stumbled, it was a small enough demon that he held it off.

Tonko raced in while he was occupied, but Kirut had used his shield to block the demon in anticipation of this.

Nyrannuk was still placed for a thrust.

Kirut caught Tonko's thigh with the point of the lance, stopping him in his tracks. With a yell, Kirut shoved the demon off his shield, withdrew the Lance of the Corpse Whale, and slashed its blade at the neck of the hezuki. It was not a decapitating blow, but the creature did stagger back with a sputter.

Before seeing if the blow was fatal, Kirut thrust again at Chief Tonko's form.

Another yelp cut through Kirut. As the blizzard around them picked up, he couldn't see more than shadows behind Tonko. He couldn't take his focus off the task at hand, although the thought of Guppik facing the real threat alone lit a fire in Kirut's chest, and he screamed as he pressed the attack.

With each thrust Kirut changed the angle. He had trained with a focus to face demons, not men, but was thankful for all the sparring he had done with Haruin. Even with his supernatural speed and strength, Tonko was losing ground, ever on the defensive in parrying Kirut's strikes.

It seemed he recognized this, for The Son cast aside the sword that gave him little advantage, sprang claws from his hands, and leaped at Kirut. Although Kirut cut him with the blade of Nyrannuk, cleaving through the sharkskin cuirass he still wore, The Son endured the pain of both slice and touch of the lance as he grabbed it to shove aside. He roared in pain, but still closed in.

A swipe of his clawed hand demanded Kirut reposition his shield. Tonko's talons punched through the many layers of hide and baleen, and pushed nearly to Kirut's face. Once his claws established a hold, Tonko cast the shield aside.

Kirut switched to a two-handed grip on Nyrannuk, parrying the next strike of Tonko's hands with its pommel.

Tonko grabbed the haft of the lance with both hands. The demon's hands burned, audibly sizzling as he leaned in on Kirut. Pain shot through Kirut's foot. The lance's magic must be focused on combating The Son, for each moment sapped whatever numbness Kirut had enjoyed before.

With a final pulse of agony through his shin, Kirut buckled.

The Son cried out as red fully seared his once-opaque hands, but once he had pushed Kirut down, he jerked Nyrannuk from his hands and cast it aside. Although his hands were burnt horridly, the demon grinned in triumph.

Once the lance was out of hand, the pain in his leg became blinding. Kirut felt as though the wound opened raw, sending more pain with each beat of his heart.

As his vision faded to white, Kirut barely heard the furious bark of a guardian hound.

***

Yumi tears into the neck of another hezuki, relishing the quenching of its magic under the force of her jaws. The icy claws on both wings and feet pierce her hide, and some part of her knows any wild strike could be lethal, but she is now in the throughs of combat, and any pain only increases her fury. Hones her strength. Spurs her to slaughter more of these wretched creatures.

Many of her allies are slain. She struggles to remember their names. The word Haruin passes through her mind as a body a few paces away is taken down, holding back a vicious bite with a hand as he slashes it with his knife. Before Yumi can reach him, his cut strikes true, but Haruin's hand in the creature's jaws is slashed and iced from its serrated teeth, and he cries out in agony.

Behind her, one of their companions is mobbed by several demons. They are cowards on their own, especially wary to strike a skin-changer or one armed with magic, but the beings with no supernatural defenses draw the focus of overwhelming numbers.

Uru is holding off many, and has three of their bodies before him, but Yumi knows the sheer numbers now gathered around him will be too much.

A memory of their objective passes through her mind.

Kirut is engaged with Tonko's body, but his lance is cast aside.

Tam abandons the hezuki he was facing, rushing to help his master. The hezuki starts to give chase, but Yumi catches it by the leg. Before it can face her, Danwe chops into it with the great Sunset Cleaver, turning its chest to a mess of crumbled red ice.

Before The Son can raise his hand to strike Kirut down, Tam leaps, grabs the demon's hand, and swings about with such force that Tonko is taken back into the snow.

Kirut wastes no time in grabbing Nyrannuk. His motions may be dragged as he all but falls on his lance, but as The Son reaches to throw Tam off, Kirut catches that hand with the back hook.

Yumi roars up at Danwe, then gallops through the snow toward The Son.

Before Tonko's body can kick off hound or whaler, Yumi leaps on top of him.

For a moment, rage is the only expression on the demon's face. It gnashes, trying to bite her, but a hint of fear crosses The Son's face as Yumi only replies with a snarl.

A rumbling bellow echoes around as Uru gallops nearby, chasing off a few hezuki that were getting too inquisitive. Haruin's knife spins about on the other side, cutting a demon that was nearing Tam, who diligently holds down The Son's hand.

Danwe all but collapses next to Kirut, planting Sunset Cleaver in Tonko's scorched hands.

A growl builds in Yumi's chest.

Before the demon can scream, Yumi lunges forward and envelops his mouth and nose in her jaws.

***

Kirut had no notion of how long the exorcism would take. Yumi said it was a brief but violent moment when she used Nyrannuk to clear the demon from his body, but it had only a moment to infect him, while Tonko had been its host for half the night.

Although the bellows of Uru defending one side and cries of Haruin on the other rang out over the howls of the cold winds, Kirut heard nothing more from Guppik.

His hands trembled. Hot tears filled Kirut's eyes, knowing he could not dare disengage. Not when they were this close to freeing Tonko's body from The Son.

After what seemed an eternity, Tonko stopped struggling. His skin was still pallid, but the welts looked quite human in their imperfections. Blood flowed from where Nyrannuk's back spike had pierced his wrist.

Yumi disengaged. After snorting out a puff of heat, she sniffed the chief.

The moment Tonko gasped, she turned to Kirut and gave a nod.

Kirut withdrew the spike of his lance, prompting a human cry of agony from Tonko. His hands were still scorched from holding Nyrannuk, but as he held Sunset Cleaver, it seemed a hint of strength pulsed through him.

With a click, Tam released Tonko's hand. The wolfdog still glared at the chief suspiciously, but let Tonko's broken body curl in on the cleaver.

A rippling cry of some distant seabird broke through the steady wail of the storm.

Kirut pushed himself to stand. Holding Nyrannuk in both hands, he glared out to the hezuki now surrounding them.

His friends had done some damage, but the numbers were still insurmountable. As he surveyed the hezuki, all circling and seeking an opening now closing as Kirut, Yumi, and Uru fanned out, Kirut surveyed his friends.

Yumi and Uru had their share of injuries. Each had several slashing bites and punctures. Uru in particular was riddled with them, although Kirut couldn't say what of the blood drenching his mouth and chest was his own and what was of the hezuki he had killed.

Haruin's entire left hand was a mangled mess. He still threw his knife, but the spinning blade had yet to hit a target that Kirut had seen since they had purged Tonko. If nothing else, it was keeping the hezuki in the waters from getting too close, and that itself was a boon. Even with the knife's healing, Haruin's face was drained pale, and it was surely only the magic in his bracer that kept him standing.

Danwe was curled up beside Tonko. At some point in the fight her leg had been bitten, torn into by the serrated jaws. It was a wonder she had been able to walk to set the cleaver in the chief's hand. Likely through the same magics which kept Kirut moving now. Without the magic protecting and strengthening her, she looked on the verge of passing out.

Tam had a slight limp, but crawled through the snow to Kirut's side. The wolfdog whimpered, his ears were erect and gaze locked on the nearest hezuki.

When Kirut's gaze turned back to the demons, his heart sank as he saw countless silhouettes back against the wall. The dead crawled over the fortifications and were filling in the ranks of the hezuki. Unlike their demon makers, the dead would attack without reservation, and they would be overwhelmed.

In the conflict, Kirut hadn't noticed the first traces of yellow in the sky. Even through the gale, a warm hue spread through the fog.

With a deep breath, Tonko pushed himself to a knee. His footing was weak, and he trembled, but his grip on Sunset Cleaver was firm. Already the damage to his hands were mending, although his consciousness was likely due to the same lies that Haruin and Kirut's weapons were telling them. Tonko helped Danwe to her feet. Out of the corner of his eye, Kirut saw the chief offer the rusted sword he had held before. Danwe took the blade, locked wide eyes with Kirut, and nodded.

The shrill cry of a hezuki slain cut through cold silence, far down the beach to the east.

A great golden beast, with ivory fangs and a billowing mane, carved through the snow like a ship at sea. Although it did not roar, the very breaths were as a rumbling growl as it galloped toward Kirut and the rest. Many other creatures, spotted and solid, in gold, black, grey, and white, spread out along the snow-covered beach.

They fell upon the hezuki and the dead without challenge or resistance. Some of the hezuki fled, but were outpaced by the charge. The dead who were not trampled in the charge were torn asunder. Most of the great walruses were around Uru's size, but the great golden chief was easily twice his mass, and barely slowed as he shoved and mauled his way across the beach.

The skin-changers were as a surge preluding a storm, clearing all in their path.

As soon as it was evident that the walruses had shifted the conflict in their favor, Kirut sprinted to the west where he last heard Guppik. Despite his limp, Tam was by his side.

After what felt an eternity, Kirut saw a massive white and black form in the snow.

No sign of the white beast in sight.

Kirut skidded to a stop before Guppik.

Red stained his fur. His vest had been punctured by great talons, then frozen over. The marks of a bite on his neck drew Kirut's terror, although perhaps for his mane there was not much blood. It was not until Kirut saw the deep puncture where Guppik's neck met his shoulder that Kirut realized the extent of his injuries.

For all these wounds, the mighty hound drew in a breath.

It was weak, but weak was better than absent.

Kirut dropped his lance and placed a gentle hand on Guppik's chest. Hot tears welled, and Kirut lost sight.

"I'm here, boy. I'm here. I'm so sorry."

Tam licked several of the wounds. After getting as close to a frustrated growl as Guppik could muster, Tam settled in on Guppik's other side.

Kirut set Nyrannuk on Guppik's shoulder. If he had been infected by the bite to his neck, being possessed by the Great White Death was the last thing Kirut wanted for him. Thankfully, the point of contact did not burn.

Although Guppik at first shrank from its touch, he quickly eased, his breathing becoming slowed. Despite Kirut's initial worry, it seemed his level breathing was not in passing, but in slight recovery. Kirut wasn't sure if the lance was healing him as it did Kirut, but he decided to indulge that hope. Guppik was, after all, of Clan Modekesh.

Snow was still thick on the ground, but the wind and snowfall had settled down to the point that he could see with greater clarity.

Death permeated the beach. It seemed there was more blood and bodies than white ice. The skin-changers were still hard at work dismembering any of the dead that may have endured. His friends remained in their cluster. None had moved save for Uru and Yumi joining their kin in the slaughter. Another rippling cry rang out as a shadow passed overhead. Tam growled up at Sam's buck tern familiar.

Kirut looked out to sea.

Although the storm had calmed on Krakenstone, a cloud of mist trailed southwest.

With a slow exhale, Kirut glared after the beast as she fled once again toward the distant polar sea.

Chapter 8

Of the two-hundred and ninety-four people on Krakenstone the night of the hezuki attack, only eighty-six were accounted for in the morning.

When Yumi and her friends had attacked the beach, several people attacked those inside. Myra had been tied up so could not participate. It was later surmised that they had been bitten by The Son and kept their infection hidden until the attack. Some of the dead had fallen upon the lodge, but most rushed to the beach to defend their creators. Fudol and his men successfully defended the lodge from the outside, but much blood was shed inside before those infected were restrained. When the Great White Death fled, she killed several of the bodies she possessed, each contorted and frozen in agony. Myra was among those who survived, although she had not yet awakened from the subsequent coma. The few infected who endured the White Death's attack were also unconscious, and kept tied up in separate cots.

The living dead ceased attack after the white beast broke her bond to them. They ambled about, and none fought back as the skin-changers finished them off.

Along with the remains of the living dead, the contorted bodies were burned on the beach, letting their ashes wash out to sea with the melting snow. Yano and his fellow mercenaries worked tirelessly to clear out the bodies, gather food, and tend to the wounded as best they could.

Two days later, three ships came from Hollow Turtle Island.

Yumi's hands, throat, and chest were scarred from the battle, but she was able to help unload the ship. Uru was in the same condition, with a puncture to his neck that barely missed his windpipe. Although it healed during his return to skin, his voice was strained. He seemed as well as could be hoped for.

Most of their friends had not been so fortunate.

Tonko's wrists had both been severely wounded, not to mention several scorched thrusts from Nyrannuk, as had Danwe's leg from a hezuki bite, but between their bond with Sunset Cleaver and as much medical attention as they could be given, the worst of their wounds healed. Tonko's port hand, which had been hooked by Nyrannuk, might never properly grip. At first they had discussed having to remove Danwe's leg, but although she would likely always have a limp, she could keep the leg.

So it was with Kirut.

His steps were labored and he felt an ache when he wasn't holding Nyrannuk, but it appeared Kirut was generally able to walk. His starboard leg had a horrid black scar, and Yumi felt a pang of guilt any time it was exposed for cleaning and dressing. Tam's injuries were thankfully minor. Guppik's fever had broken and it seemed the worst had passed, but he still struggled to move his starboard front paw.

Haruin was not so fortunate. The bite on his port hand was beyond repair, and he accepted its removal. They had done so quickly and with much liquor, but with how many were injured and also needed such treatment, he forewent the use of their pain relief tea, instead insisting the knife would do the task so those without enchantments could have relief.

Now that the ship from Hollow Turtle had arrived, he could have all the tea he desired.

Yumi recognized one of the witches from the healing house leading several sailors with medical supplies. Fudol met with her and escorted her to the lodge.

Sam was on the same ship, her buck tern familiar circling above. After kissing and embracing Uru, she greeted Yumi as well.

"Thank you and your familiar for guiding my brother," said Yumi. "We would all be dead were it not for their arrival. Is Jadhe well? The infected here were all..."

Sam took Yumi's hand. "Your cousin is alright. I think it was her magic, the protection of you guardians, which spared her the grim fate of many others we had restrained in the healing house. She said she felt the demon try to attack her, but her magic fought off this last use of power. From then she felt her mind was clear. Most of our bitten people lived, though. I don't know how only a few perished unless this demon's magic wore thin. The other two witches think their magic was able to purge any remaining magic from their bodies."

"Maybe killing her children made the White Death weaker?" offered Uru.

"I hope so," said Yumi. "She fled after Kirut fought her before, then came back stronger. I don't think we can count on her current weakness being indefinite."

Sam took a slow breath. "Perhaps, but I think we must focus on healing. Speaking of which, I should help Aya. If nothing else, I can use my magic to enhance her healing spells."

"Again, thank you," said Yumi, and she got to work helping unload the ships.

Later that evening, as Yumi sat on a few rocks on the southern-most corner of the island looking out to sea, she heard someone walking through the scrub grass behind her, and smelled the ripe scent of her brother.

"You should really hop in the water," said Yumi with a grin. "Your scent could kill a hog."

"I've earned this sweat, thank you." Yano passed down a bottle of chilled ale.

Her hands, which were yet sore and her grip weak, welcomed the cold touch of the drink, and it was of exceptional flavor. "Are you sure we should be drinking the general's entire stores?"

"General Tikah oversaw the clipper being loaded," he replied after a long drink. "She knew exactly what was going on, and made sure to include the ice box. I imagine she felt guilty she could not come herself."

"She has helped far more than her obligations demand, and I never thought I would say this, but now that the frost is melted, I appreciate a cold drink."

For a long moment the two sat on the stone, their feet dangling off just above the water line.

"I am sorry I did not come sooner," said Yano. "I should have sailed with you."

"You made the right decision with the information at hand."

"You should not have had to return our family to the sea on your own."

Yumi looked down to her bottle. So much had happened that coming upon the slaughter of their family felt a long-distant memory. It truth it had only been nine days.

"What now?" asked Yumi.

"It ultimately falls to Jadhe to decide, as she is now our matron, but I'm of two minds. The general will need both her clipper and sloop returned. Uru says some of our people now reside as refugees at Hollow Turtle. I wish to help rebuild our home. Make it safe for us to start anew. That said, I wish to honor our contract with Tikah, and other Klaeg have been sighted on the eastern islands. Having us with her as scouts will be invaluable. Likely we will all go home, then after we repair what requires many hands to fix, I will take half our company back to the general. You need not decide now if you wish to rebuild or come with me, but I wished for you to know the plan, at least as I will present it to Jadhe."

Yumi looked back out to the sea. "I think Jadhe will need to heal. You should do as you deem appropriate. You lead our warriors, and as far as anyone will say, you are our chosen chief."

Yano shrugged. "In times of strife, many appreciate the comfort of familiar structure. We will see how Jadhe has come out from her own battle, but I expect she will emerge hardened and ready to lead our people. She has never shied from her duties, and I doubt she endured a demon sculpting her mind only to surrender after the danger is passed."

Yumi did not feel the danger had passed, but kept such thoughts to herself.

As the sun set on their starboard side, Yumi sat beside her brother in silence, her thoughts on the demon to the south. Although Yano no doubt assumed as much, he simply sat beside her. His presence was a comfort.

✳✳✳

After another few days of recovery, Kirut and the rest were brought to Hollow Turtle Island.

He passed the time in a haze. Many celebrated, especially those reunited with their loved ones, but Kirut had no mind or heart for festivities.

Although Tam had made a full recovery, Guppik struggled with tasks that once gave him no trouble. His front right paw was permanently curled up and could not support any weight. Kirut was attentive in cleaning the wound and ensuring he got plenty of pain relief. Nyrannuk also seemed to aid in his healing, but it was clear to Kirut that Guppik must retire once they returned home.

Chief Tonko and Danwe had become close in the days of their healing, no doubt in part because their shared bond with Sunset Cleaver had aided both of their recoveries. Kirut was happy to see they both took comfort with each other.

Fudol, who had been named chief by the survivors, never let Myra out of his sight, guarding over his new matron with a ferocious eye toward any stranger who got too close.

After she was guided to alertness by the healers of Hollow Turtle Island, Myra was given the enchanted club, which attuned to her and guided her to a striking recovery. She had not yet spoken a word, and none could blame her. At one point she took Kirut's hand, squeezing it tightly. It was about as close as he imagined she could muster to a connection so soon after the attack. Kirut wondered how much she remembered of her possession. His mind went blank when The Son took over, but the whole time his lingering bond with Nyrannuk was protecting him. Had Myra been a spectator to the whole thing?

Kirut squeezed her hand back, knowing no words could properly express his thoughts nor console her mind.

Far from the broken man Kirut was prepared for, Haruin took his lost hand in stride, speculating on the matter during a dinner Tonko's mother hosted.

"Do you think I should have a hook, or perhaps a buckler? A simple cap of iron sounds most dreadful."

"One of General Tikah's son's has a mechanical sword hand custom for him by the smiths of Trist," said Captain Yanochin, wiggling the fingers of his massive hand. He was seated between Yumi and Tonko, and it was strange to see someone who made the chief look small.

"You wound me with prospects far outside my means," said Haruin with a grin.

"I think a hook would be practical," said Yumi. "You could steer a ship, fight with it, and I imagine the intimidation would be of use."

"Did you not tell us of a notorious pirate in the Crescent Sea who had a hook on both hands?" said Uru. His voice had a gravel from the hezuki claw that, from what Kirut could tell, would be permanent change in cadence.

"That I did," said Yanochin with a grin. "Gold-plated hooks, if memory serves. Calls himself The Gilded Butcher."

Haruin laughed. "I've no use of a reputation so lavish or ferocious, but as Yumi says, I do think a hook could be useful in many aspects. I shall give it strong consideration."

After dinner, Haruin and Chief Tonko came to Kirut, leaning on the rail of the boardwalk on either side. Tam was with Kirut, while Guppik remained inside the lodge with Nyrannuk. Kirut's leg ached with greater ferocity than it had before, and while he regretted leaving the Lance of the Corpse Whale inside, Guppik needed it more, and he should get used to the reality of his capabilities.

"So, are you returning to the life of a smuggler?" asked Kirut.

Haruin frowned. "I have not yet decided where my life goes next. The mundane arts of smuggling now seem so trivial. I fear I would get terribly bored."

"Lot to be said for the simple joys of a boring life." Kirut nudged Tonko. "You and Danwe have been inseparable. Looking forward to a bit of boring together?"

Tonko chuckled. "I certainly wouldn't mind some excitement less supernatural, although there is much I must do to rebuild all the homes that were lost. What is next for you?"

Kirut sighed. "I go back to the way it was before: whaling voyages, raising hounds. I owe Mia a visit, something I look forward to, and I wish to see my sons again."

"Do you want me to let you know if I hear rumor of... her," asked Haruin. "Or would you rather I only visit as a friend, and never speak of monsters again? I would not hold it against you."

Kirut put his hand on Haruin's shoulder. "I have not decided yet." He then looked up to Tonko. "You are both of course welcome to Modegk Island if for some strange reason you find yourself that far west."

"If you do, I hope you like a lot of kisses from hounds bigger than you," said Haruin. Tam's ears perked up as if he knew Haruin spoke of play.

"I certainly would enjoy such a thing," said Tonko, clapping Kirut on the back. "Alright, I'm going to enjoy the rest of this evening without responsibility. May the winds fill both your sails."

Kirut and Haruin remained on the pier, watching the setting sun and bantering of mindless nothings. Kirut sat up on the rail to fully take pressure off his leg, then helped Haruin up as well.

"I want to move forward," said Kirut. "I want to live a simple life. By the stars and might of the moon: I would love to spend the rest of my days in Mia's bed and teaching my sons how to fight, to dance, to fish. I should want that. Part of me does."

"I think you should listen to that part of you."

"And when she kills again?"

Haruin took a deep breath. "It might be in another seven years before she returns. Maybe thirty. Perhaps a century. Kirut, you cannot build your life around the possibility of misfortune. I say we should go to the Guardian Atolls, help them rebuild, take what we left, then get you home. Get you to your beloved. You will go mad standing on the shore watching for a storm that may never come. As your friend, I cannot allow that. Let's give you that simple life, my friend."

Kirut nodded. "I like the sound of that. Thank you, Haruin."

Haruin waved him off. "Of course. As we say in the Ring: good friends join you for the adventure, and make sure you return safe at the end of the night."

"I like that."

"You should. I know the Ring is loud and busy, and you clearly hated it, but there are gems of wisdom in those muddy streets."

"I'll take your word for it."

"Good. Now we should find our beds. We have many long voyages ahead."

***

In his dream, Kirut is a wolf.

He sprints through the forest after a white hare. The creature is looking away, attentive to something ahead.

At every turn he nearly captures his prey, and with each attempt, his efforts end in empty jaws. The creature always waits just out of reach, only dashing away when he gets close. He has yet to see its face.

The stink of blood seeps into the mud underfoot, yet still Kirut runs. It is all he can do.

Soon he is trudging through mud, stalling as the metallic sludge rises. Roots catch on his feet. Brambles slash his face.

The white hare is just ahead, striking against the dark thicket.

As Kirut closes in, the hare is no longer moving, yet it still seems to shrink in the distance the harder he presses on.

Eventually Kirut is swimming. His fur is matted, thick with blood.

The hare is waiting on a patch above the mire.

Kirut struggles up the muddy island, his claws digging into the soil. He looms over the hare, his lips drawn back and ready for the kill.

The hare turns.

It is his own face he sees, just as he has seen it in reflections.

Although he tries to stop, Kirut cannot halt his jaws.

The impact is cold. So chilling that it is like heat shoots up the roots of his teeth. With each shake of the hare, relishing the crackling of its fragile bones, more of Kirut becomes ice. His own body breaks as he mauls the tiny beast, but he cannot stop, and soon both bodies are crumpled on the muddy bank.

The black and red forest has frozen over in white. Kirut is frozen in place, his awareness both gripping a hare in his jaws and trapped in the maw of an enormous wolf.

A chorus of three voices speaks in the fragments of his consciousness.

"By your choice, both live. By your decision, both die. You chose life, as did I. Perhaps we understand one another after all."

Kirut snapped awake.

Tam was already on top of him, frantically licking Kirut's face. Although Guppik was on the floor, with a cushion set to help his recovery, he also pushed himself up to check on Kirut. Kirut reassured both with pets and soft words, slumping back once they had calmed.

He held Mia's necklace tight.

For the rest of the night Kirut was locked in consciousness, fixated on the ceiling of the great lodge of Hollow Turtle.

***

The following day, Yumi, Kirut, Haruin, the hounds, and the other peoples of the Guardian Atolls all said their farewells to their friends on Hollow Turtle Island, and sailed south to her family's home. Sam travelled with them. Without any living family, she accepted Uru's invitation. It was unusual for a woman to live in the home of a man, but these were unusual times.

Arix the buck tern glided overhead, keeping a watchful eye on the horizon for dangers which, thankfully, gave their ships a respite.

With the eleven people who had been fishing when the attack happened and were taken in as refugees along with thirty-two skin-changers, the Guardian Atolls felt empty even with all accounted for.

They made do as best they could. After the voyage got them home by nightfall with the wind at their backs, they steered through the maze and unloaded into the boathouse and lodge.

Yumi had forgotten about Bari.

The corpse was still restrained in the wood shed. Parts of his body had been picked at, and after twenty days his skin was loose and torso emptied of organs. The stench was unbearable. Even so, he was still animated, and whatever magic still held his body together did so despite its decomposition. Although he had sought to attack Yumi and Kirut before, now Bari leaned passively against his restraints, staring idly out to sea.

Jadhe was carrying a cart of fresh water to the lodge. When she saw Yumi standing upwind of the body, she set down her things. Although her breaths were labored since her infection, Jadhe stood taller than before. Yumi was glad her brother had been right about her: she had taken the title with quick resolve.

"Poor boy," Jadhe whispered. "He loved collecting shells. Always showed me when he found an ammonite because one time I lit up when he showed me. He wanted nothing but to see people smile."

Yumi's heart tightened. She barely knew Bari's name. He had always seemed kind, but she never spent much time with him. Yumi hadn't spent much time with her family. She was ever quick to follow her brother's path.

"I wonder if he remembers. If any part of his spirit is still in that body, or if our bodies truly are just a host."

"Do you remember?" asked Yumi before she realized it was likely too soon. "Apologies, I-"

Jadhe placed a hand on Yumi's arm. "You need not apologize. I remember stronger now that my mind is my own once more. There were times that I could see through her, and in those times it was as if I was seeing through a thousand eyes. At the time I thought it was madness, but now I think I was seeing through the strings of her many puppets, as Uru called them. I tried to warn you about what I saw through Jardin in a way that would not make her exert too much influence over me."

"I didn't understand at the time, but maybe it helped me act quickly before he did too much harm to Tonko."

"I wish I could have spoken with more clarity. Having her occupy my body, make me move and speak... I do not wish that upon any-one." Jadhe looked back to Bari. Her chest sank, and she looked on the verge of tears. "I wonder if he's there too. If he's been trapped this whole time. See how he looks to the water? It was little things that kept my mind my own, even at the height of her strength. My love for my family. My hope that Uru survive the fight. Even my desire for the taste of cawfruit in my tea now and then. I know you all killing her creations broke her hold, but happy memories carried me through. Just some familiar comforts. Do you think he's trying to find shells? Seeking some little passion he can hold onto?"

Yumi followed Bari's dead gaze. True it went to the sea, but not the closest shore. There were nearby shells in the sand, but he com-pletely overlooked them. Jadhe picked up a scallop and held it out.

Bari looked down to the shell briefly, then back up to Jadhe. Un-like before, there was no sign of aggression. Just a blank nothing.

After looking briefly at the shell, he looked back out to sea.

No.

He was looking southwest.

***

"Kirut!"

As Haruin had only one hand. Kirut had offered to inspect the hull of his boat and touch up the wax. Haruin was still there, throwing a stick for Tam to chase. Yumi sprinted through the boat house, nearly stumbling onto the pier.

"What is it?" said Kirut, her urgency prompting a reflexive reach for Nyrannuk over by Guppik.

"Here," she said, helping him to his feet and supporting his arm as he picked up his lance. "Come."

Kirut and Haruin followed, the hounds at their heels.

They stopped at the remains of her distant cousin Bari. In the escalation of Krakenstone, Kirut had completely forgotten about the dead boy they left behind. Many had gathered before the lodge, hearing the excitement. Uru and Sam, Bruhe, Yano, and several of his fellow skin-changers. Their new matron Jadhe, Bruhe's elder sister, looked to Yumi with open confusion.

Yumi pointed to the little corpse. "Where is he looking?"

"To the sea?" said Uru.

"Southwest," said Haruin, confusion trailing to realization.

"He's looking to his mother," said Kirut. "He's looking to go home."

Kirut advanced toward the dead boy, slowly kneeling to fully interrupt the corpse's focus. At first it tried to look around him, then generally taking him in with an innocent expression. Once their eyes finally connected, though, he went still. A snarl twisted what remained of his features.

A dull blue glow passed behind blank eyes.

Kirut leaned in, ignoring the pain that shot through his leg.

"I don't know if you can hear me. I hope you can. I'm done waiting for you to come and pick us off. Trying to anticipate, prepare, and react to your every move. My people will no longer be your prey. Now I am the predator. You can run, hide, or fight: I care not. Make peace with what you must. I am coming, and I won't stop until you are reduced to a disappointing memory. The hunt begins now. I'll see you soon."

Kirut, Yumi, Haruin,
and the Great White Death
will return in the
next anthology,

WHISPERS FROM BEYOND
THE KNOWN WORLD.

Tempered in Ash and Blood

6

Tempered in Ash and Blood

Tempered in Ash and Blood

The hunt begins.

Matriarch has taken us to the southern shores of a land far from our home. I am fourteen years old, but have only been here twice. Matriarch only takes us north when there is little food where we usually hunt. There is usually plenty of food back home during the winter, even though summer is when there is abundance, but this year was different. Matriarch knew that even though there was some food, we should go north, because what little food could be found would not be enough.

There are more dangers in the north than we are used to back home. This much I remember.

Matriarch has decided we will hunt beaked whales today. They are hunters like us, but they eat squid deep in the abyss. There are beaked whales back home. I have eaten them before. They are... they're fine. I don't like the tang. Baleen whales have far more pleasant texture. I don't know if beaked whales are different as they do because they eat squid or because they hunt so much deeper and the heavy water makes their meat tough and have an odd edge to it. Whatever the reason, I would prefer other game.

But it is Matriarch's decision.

We spread out. Normally we send out clicks to keep track of each other on a hunt, but that only works for hunting seals or walruses. Clicks when hunting other whales can alert them of our presence, so we can't make a sound when setting up an ambush like this.

We are spread far. It is difficult to see more than basic silhouettes. I can see Mother on my left. To my right is Gran, the eldest daughter of Matriarch. She is not my grandmother. My mother is the granddaughter of Matriarch's sister. Everyone in the pod except for me and Mother is descended from Matriarch. It means we are usually the last to eat. Gran doesn't like to share with us, and her lineage show us little affection or welcome, but Matriarch insists that we are family, so they do not openly antagonize us. I sometimes wonder why Mother and I don't just leave. Yes, the ocean is treacherous, but surely we could get more food for ourselves if it were just the two of us. If we were our own pod.

Mother said it is too dangerous. That her mother was killed by a whale eater. I do not know what that is, but she does not like to talk about it.

So we live our lives on the edge of the pod. Not family enough to be welcome, but unable to leave.

I wonder sometimes if it is because of my father that we are so unwelcome.

Mother says he was a pointed blackfish that she met in a northern migration much like we are on now. They are similar to our kind, but their snouts are not as round. Some of the pod say that pointed blackfish are dumber than us and their heads are pointed because they have smaller brains, but when I first met a pointed blackfish, a simple click-stream confirmed their brains are the same size. They have smaller melons, smaller jaws, and more but smaller teeth, but their mind is shaped and sized the same. Their language sounded just as complicated as ours, even though I couldn't understand them.

They are much larger, though, a trait which I inherited. Even though I am not quite a bull, I am the largest member of our pod. Even Champion, Matriarch's eldest son and the lead bull, is no longer bigger than I am. He is not unkind, but not interested in training me either, and his two nephews harass me at every opportunity. I do worry what might happen if Champion were no longer the lead bull. Whoever of his nephews became lead bull would surely treat me with even less than Champion's indifference.

I begin to hear the droning clicks of the beaked whales. They are coming up for air. Their clicks are different than those of beaked whales back home. Deeper. Longer. Ending in sharper notes. Not as loud as a diver cachalot, but close. These must be larger.

The beaked whales back home are already a bit larger than us. Are we still planning to attack?

We must follow Matriarch's lead. If she thinks we should still attack, then attack we will.

I turn a bit to the side, trying to see them. All I can see is darkness below. Back home, most of the waters are shallow enough that I can see the bottom. I am not fond of this view.

Movement! There are several shapes moving below us, swimming up into the center of our massive ring, just like Matriarch said they would. I can't make out their forms. They are swimming straight up so all I can see is spheres. It takes all my willpower to not send clicks.

The shapes keep coming up. Swimming into view. I think there are five of them, but without sending clicks, it's a little hard to discern.

Anticipation builds faster. A click is hot at the base of my head, but I know I must be patient.

Too late I realize that the rest of the pod has begun to charge, intercepting them before they can take a breath like we planned. I was too busy watching the prey.

I launch, flukes propelling me forward.

As soon as I hear Matriarch's yip, I know the pod is close enough that we can see what we're up against.

I send out a blast of clicks.

The nearest beaked whale is massive. Nearly twice my length and many times heavier. His belly is full of squid, their menacing beaks most notable in the clicks. I raise my head to comprehend his features.

His jaws support a pair of massive tusks. Male beaked whales back home have tusks, but nothing like these. These tusks are as long as my entire jaw! His body is also covered in scars. I wonder how many are from predators, how many from the squids he eats, and what are from fights with other whales.

The other beaked whales panic, but the bull closest to me looks unafraid.

In fact quite the opposite.

His jaws open, and my clicks are drawn to the size and curve of his tusks.

The bull charges at me.

I swim up as he comes toward me. He is larger and faster, but I am much more maneuverable. Especially now that I can click, I'm able to predict where he will go and evade accordingly.

"Stop playing!" I hear. I think it is in Gran's voice.

I don't want the bull catching a breath, so I dive. It is hard to see behind me, but my clicks carry enough to see that he is in pursuit, so I continue.

The other beaked whales are smaller and do not try and fight. As I turn I send another click stream to see how that fight is going.

One of the smaller beaked whales, still larger than us but not as big as the bull pursuing me, has several members of the pod holding her tail. Matriarch has bitten her blowhole, and she will drown soon. Another beaked whale has been caught by the tail by Hero, one of Champion's nephews, but Hero is struggling to hold on.

The distress calls of the cows have drawn the bull beaked whale's attention, and he turns to charge Hero and his prey. He's so long that the arc gives plenty of time, and I can probably catch up.

Hero is focused on maintaining his bite, and doesn't notice.

I call out in warning, but he ignores me.

Although the beaked whale bull is faster, he's taken so long to turn that I can probably intercept.

Before I can make contact, Champion crashes into the bull, knocking it off course. He sends a series of warning yowls at Hero, who lets go. The cow is injured at the base of her tail from Hero's teeth, but manages to swim away as Hero backs off.

The bull turns off. Maybe he can see that the base of her tail is broken, and he's given up on her. Hero and Champion are keeping their distance but sending warning blasts to the bull.

He dives.

Now the cow is swimming up, hoping to catch a breath.

I see an opening. Her blowhole is facing me, and as I've seen Matriarch do this countless times.

I charge.

My impact is swift and with such force that she is launched forward. The bite doesn't sink in, but she's too shaken to evade, and my next strike lands true. With a flex of my jaws, I feel her blowhole forced open, and her lungs take on water with a satisfying rush.

Rather than join me, Hero and Champion are keeping their distance. Their calls are still of warning to the bull to stay away. They haven't come to help me.

Before I can wonder why, a click of my own picks up movement below.

I disengage from the cow, turning left. Another click confirms that the bull has charged me. Clearly he hasn't given up on his mate as I presumed.

His bite barely misses my fluke. I swim fast away from his mate, but again I can sense him in pursuit.

I dodge right, but his bite catches me at the base of my tail. Agony surges through my torso as his left tusk plunges into my side.

Once he has a bite of his own, he dives.

I panic. Any struggle I make just seems to embed his tusk deeper into my side. I had gotten a breath right before we set up our ambush, but I will need another soon. The bull has been in the abyss for over an hour, but clearly has sufficient energy to hold fast.

I send out a drum of distress yips.

There is no response.

The waters around me darken as we go deeper.

Finally Champion's warning calls get closer.

Mother's are also getting louder.

The bull releases his bite. Another pulse of agony ripples through me. I swim away, but my clicks confirm he's swimming away. Diving deeper to join his pod.

I try to swim, but each stroke of my tail shoots more pain from the bite wounds.

I'm sinking, rather than rising, from the effort.

Mother's head presses into my chest, and she swims upward. My contributions amount to nothing. Did the bite do more damage than I anticipated? A wide click gives me the faint outline of flukes, so my tail is still intact, at least. A small comfort considering I can't swim on my own.

Mother is elevating me towards the surface but we are making slow progress. I strain to advance, but my effort amounts to little progress, and all I'm doing is burning through what little remains of my energy. I need another breath. Fast.

Although her help is invaluable, Mother is straining too.

Another head under my pectoral fins is identified as Champion when I hear his hums of reassurance.

The next moments seem to drag on, my chest burning with the need for new breath amidst all the excitement.

I gasp as soon as we break the surface. After a pause I exhale again, taking in fresh air and the strength that comes with it.

Following a third breath, Champion lets go to take a breath of his own before diving to join the feast. I thank him for his help, as does Mother, but he does not reply.

I look down and send a click stream to take in the scene.

We have killed two beaked whales. Now that the action has subsided, Matriarch sends a distance pulse north, calling in the young and their guardians from the shallower waters to feed. I know that Mother and I will eat last, so I take the time to catch my breath.

"Is it bad?" I ask Mother.

She relinquishes her support of my chest, which I reassure her I will be fine with, and sends a click stream followed by a steady boom to fully assess my injury.

"Tusk pierced deep, but no organs. The tusk just missed your intestines. You are lucky. The wound is deep and you have lost much blood. If you do not strain, I think you will heal, but it will take time before you can swim well."

I thank her before trying to rise for another breath. Mother helps me break the surface. I hold my flippers out so she can take a breath of her own. She has not breathed since we began the hunt.

The young and their protectors have arrived. Our pod is large, and there are seventeen calves too young to help in a hunt. Mother has not had a calf since her daughter after me was killed while we were on a hunt. She will probably not have another. I have asked her before if she intends to have another calf, but she never answers.

The adults below make sure the older calves get the lips, tongue, and tender parts of the underside. I cannot help but feel a pang of jealousy. I remember when I was little, I was never allowed to eat these parts. I was told that I ate too much and was growing too large for my age, and would have to eat the tougher meat with the adults.

Mother and I recouperate on the surface, waiting for the rest of the pod to have their fill before we can indulge in whatever remains.

***

Three months have passed since the beaked whale hunt.

I have almost recovered, although it still hurts to swim fast. Mother says it is an intimidating scar. I cannot see it, but I assume she is being kind. It doesn't feel intimidating or a mark of pride. It causes pain and reminds me of the position I am now in.

I cannot hunt anymore. I tried when we last hunted, but couldn't keep up with the pod, much less catch one of the seals we were hunting.

Now I am a defender of the calves.

I don't mind terribly. It's not like I was getting any advantages out of participating in the hunt. Mother and I still ate last. She has been making sure I eat as much as possible at the expense of her own meals. I worry about her. She is getting thinner. She says the waters are warmer up north so she is losing blubber, but I know much of it is from not getting enough to eat.

I think soon we should go off on our own. As soon as I am able to hunt, I will take care of her better if it was just the two of us. As long as we aren't tackling large and dangerous game, working together will be enough and we can get all the best parts.

I just need a bit more time to recover.

My thoughts are interrupted by Questions.

He is the eldest son of Heir, Matriarch's granddaughter. One day he will take the role of Champion and be the pod's great defender. For now he is a calf of only seven years. He has a long way to go before he is ready to defend anything.

Questions knows this though, which is refreshing compared to some of the male calves, who often harass me to prove to the others that they aren't afraid. Questions doesn't try to posture at me.

He did, however, earn his name.

I give his stream of queries single yip answers. Most of my attention is on sending clicks out into the water. The other two calf defenders are also vigilant. It is our duty to look out for them while the rest of the pod hunts.

"Who do you think would win in a fight: a corpse serpent or a diver cachalot bull?"

"Cachalot bull," I reply, still clicking for any threats out towards the deeper waters.

"Corpse serpents are really agile. And they have nasty teeth!"

"And a cachalot bull is much larger. You have seen diver cachalot bulls. Even their cows are bigger than I am. Their bulls make a corpse serpent look like a calf."

"I haven't seen them next to each other. What about a cachalot bull versus an abyssal serpent?"

This carries on for a while, but I don't really notice the rest of his questions. The waves above are moving with increasing speed. It has been darkening for a while. The water is getting hotter. I don't really know what it means, but the other two guardians seem unfazed.

"When will they be back?"

I turn my attention to Princess, Questions's younger sister. Princess is four years old. She will one day be the Matriarch, and is used to everyone doing as she says and answering her every query. Not all the calves respect her, though, and one of her older cousins bit her flukes the other day. He got scolded, and the injury wasn't terrible, but her flukes are still in recovery.

"Matriarch saw diver cachalot. Diver cachalot can hold their breath for a long time. It may be a while until they even come up to breathe."

"Like the beaked whales that bit your tail?" she asks.

The question doesn't sound like a blow, but feels like one. I am suddenly aware of how sensitive the base of my tail is. I consider bringing up her own injured tail in some capacity, but set those thoughts aside. "Yes, like that."

Questions and Princess continue their conversation, thankfully not feeling a need to include me.

A rumble echoes from back towards land.

I roll about and send a series of distance pulses towards shore. It's hard to know what I'm looking at. Sound bounces strange in coastal waters under good conditions, even without the waves suddenly building up.

Waves going… in the wrong direction.

I turn up and spyhop above the surface.

The weather is worse than I thought. A dark cloud has overtaken the sky inland. It is spreading, and although it is hard to perceive distance without clicks, I think the clouds are getting closer. The air is also hot. Too hot. I'm used to storms bringing cold air and snow. The snow I see falling from the inland cloud is black, not white. At least I think that is what I am seeing.

With an upward pull of my flippers, I submerge.

I send a distress call to the other two guardians. One, the eldest named Grappler, sends a low grunt of annoyance that I am disturbing the calves, but the other, a distant cousin named Gentle, spyhops too. I join her.

The cloud hasn't advanced from what I can tell. Although we can feel its heat and the rumble of its thunder makes the waves roll away from shore, it is still far away. Its moving slowly, and I think we can swim faster than it rolls, but I don't want to find out what being in black snow feels like on my skin or as I breathe.

Gentle seems to agree.

I ask if she has seen anything like this. She says no. She is only a few years older than me so it makes sense. This is unlike any storm either of us have ever seen. Storms are cold, come from the sea not the land, can be felt for hours beforehand. This came with little warning and contradicts all either of us know about storms.

Storms can be avoided either by finding shallows with tall coasts that block storms. There are many islands inland, and Gentle suggests we look to them for cover. When she proposes this, Grappler and several calves spyhop to investigate for themselves.

Panic has set into the calves. They are squeaking questions towards all three of us guardians in too rapid a succession for any of us to answer.

"We should go out to sea," clicks Grappler. "If the storm comes from inland, its most dangerous inland, and we should be in open water."

Gentle and I agree. We make a wide triangle formation, with Grappler as the eldest taking point, calling for all the calves to check in and remain within the formation.

I slow my swimming to make sure Princess is accounted for. She isn't the youngest, that would be Gentle's own son, but her injured fluke is clearly preventing her from remaining in formation. Questions is quickly by her side, acting as a shadow and making sure she is kept on course.

Although we make good time out to sea, the waves pick up rapidly. I spyhop now and then, and the cloud is spreading fast.

My tail begins to ache from the strain. I was a fool to think I was ready to be on my own.

I can keep up with Questions and Princess, but the others are quickly outpacing us.

When I next spyhop, at least the air is cooler. We seem to be beating the storm at least.

Something below catches my attention. Something massive.

I pulse click in rapid succession.

A diver cachalot bull.

He is massive. Not the largest I have ever seen, but close.

And he is swimming straight for the cluster.

I have not known diver cachalot to hunt our kind. Whales of his kind usually hunt squid, much like beaked whales. Killer cachalot hunt blackfish, but they are smaller than diver cachalot. Maybe diver cachalot in these northern waters are different.

He is coming at us with great speed.

I take a deep breath before diving to intercept.

I unleash a stream of warning clicks. If he hears them, he pays them no mind.

Just when I prepare to engage with a whale more than five times my size, he veers and levels out, seeming to finally notice my clicks. His speed and trajectory is still aimed up, but no longer pointed to the pod. Was it just a coincidence?

I swerve to the side and let him pass. He breaks the surface and spouts. His own clicks are deep, but I wonder if it might be the distress call of his own language. I don't speak the language of the cachalot. I always assumed they only had a few words at most. His clicks now are highly dynamic. Maybe they are more intelligent than I anticipated.

Regardless, it seems clear he is no longer a threat to my pod.

Who, in the panic, appear to have scattered.

I close the distance between myself and the nearest pair of calves. I call out to them.

Questions and Princess quickly swim to my side. I can sense their panic and tell them to spout.

Once they have a fresh breath, I call out to the others.

They are silhouettes at the far end of my echolocation range. I think there's two of them. Two groups? It's hard to tell at this distance.

So many other distress calls sound throughout the sea. I recognize the calls of some, like beaked whales, blackfish strangers, and other diver cachalot. Others I do not know, like high pitched squeaks or low rumbles. Although I don't know them all, the panic is clear in every cry.

A call of agony rings from inland, followed by many more. Each scream is silenced before it can complete. I try not to think about what they must be going through, gasping for air only for the very act of taking a life-sustaining breath to be their end.

The cachalot exhales again then swims hard west. His next clicks sound very much like my own warning call. So close it sounds like he is mimicking me. Is he trying to tell me to go west? It seems foolish, considering the wind is blowing hard southeast. He is a much slower swimmer than we are. Maybe he can endure, being an abyssal hunter, but we will need to breathe much more often. We should try to outpace the storm.

He mimics my call again.

I never considered trying to communicate with a cachalot. Does he know our pod is out hunting his kind? His effort is thoughtful, and I do feel a pulse of guilt at his compassion, but-

I spyhop, and am daunted by the speed of the approaching cloud.

The wind has carried much of the black clouds our way, and the dark snow is falling fast. More screams echo from inland, but they are getting fewer. Most who fled to the islands for cover will soon be dead.

The sperm whale clicks again.

At a loss, I heed the warning of the cachalot.

I tell Questions and Princess to take two breaths each, then swim west, keeping as far under the surface as we dare.

The diver cachalot is built for endurance. We are not. For fear of the hot snow, I spyhop before taking a breath. At first I can see it isn't safe. On my second surface, the immediate area is clear to spout, so I call Questions and Princess to come up for air before we go under again. Princess is struggling, so Questions and I flank her to carry her forward. When I spyhop a third time, the smoke is so thick and hot that I feel several burns on my back.

We hold our breaths as long as we can after that.

After a stretch of swimming that feels like an eternity, I spyhop again and am relieved to see that the skies above are mostly clear. I spout, calling on the calves to do the same.

The storm is confounding. I spyhop to be certain, but now I am confident: it is coming from inland. From the mountains if I understand correctly. Is it a volcano? I have heard stories of the mountains of the abyss breathing out heat and smoke. Perhaps I should not find the notion of surface volcanoes to be so bizarre.

The world above the surface is a strange place indeed.

Following another moment to catch my breath, I realize the cachalot saved our lives. Considering the injuries of Princess's flukes and where my tail meets my core, we might not have been able to swim faster than the clouds went, but he knew based on the wind that if we could just make it west, we could avoid its surge.

I hear more distress calls all around. Pods of different whales trying to reunite with their kin. Many that would normally be prey seem to trust that I have no intention or energy to hunt. We're all just trying to make sure our families are safe.

I send a click stream back east, followed by my longest range of deep pulses. I cannot find the cachalot who saved our lives.

Cachalot are slow swimmers, but can hold their breath for almost two hours. I must hope he's still under the threat, slowly making his way to safety.

I cannot worry about him.

I have two calves depending on me.

Although the cloud of volcanic ash is mostly spreading southeast with the wind, it still spreads in our direction, and we cannot afford to linger. With several clicks, I tell Questions to flank Princess so she will have one of us on either side, and we continue swimming west.

***

Eventually we will try to find our pod, but first we must let the ash pass, and in the interim, the calves and I need to sleep.

I push them for a while longer. Perhaps longer than I need to, but I want to be sure the cloud doesn't reach us in the night.

Although I consider finding shallows to rest in, as we often do back home, I don't like the notion of how busy reefs can get, especially since the waters are busy this evening from all the creatures displaced by the smoke and ash. We swim slow and steady as we sleep, keeping to open water. I don't know if I should have my left sleep while my right watches the calves or if my sleeping half should face out. Eventually I decide that both watching them and keeping watch are important, and I'm too exhausted to decide which should have priority, so I try to keep the calves on whichever side I'm looking at so I can see if something is approaching them and shield them from whatever I can't see.

This carries us through much of the night. I can feel the air is still hot. Now that I have calmed, I feel the burns along my back, and several times in my partial sleep, I fully awaken in a panic. It takes focus to return to sleep.

I hope Mother is alright. The pod was further out in open water. I have to believe they spotted it early and outpaced the storm. Might they have come back for the calves? Possibly. If they did, hopefully Gentle and Grappler got to the pod and told them to flee.

"When can we start swimming back?" asks Questions.

I wish I could offer him some comfort or reassurance, but I have no idea. I'm no matriarch. I have known only a few bad storms, and none were from a volcano. I heard what happened to whales that breathed in the cloud. I can still feel heat in the wind even though the cloud is far behind us. My lungs hurt, and we didn't even breathe ash, just warm air.

"I miss Mother," Princess clicks sleepily.

"Me too," groans Questions.

I hum an agreement, wishing my own mother was here to tell us what to do.

***

In the morning, the calves thoughts have switched from sleep to hunger. We didn't get to enjoy the meal that Matriarch and the rest of the pod were hunting. I'm hungry, and a few clicks to their bellies show Questions and Princess are too. They don't complain or say anything on the matter, but I know we need food. Soon.

I send several booming pulses to get as wide an impression of the area as possible.

No game in the immediate area. The water is too deep to see the bottom even though I can see the land nearby when I spyhop.

With a few whistles, I urge us to turn inland. There isn't much in the way of shallows. Back home, shallow waters extend for hours of swimming before it drops off. Sometimes half a day. Here it is astonishingly close to shore. I can see the beach from the dropping point, and the shallows are so exposed to the ocean currents that no reefs can grow. Back where we waited before the volcano erupted, at least there was a long stretch of shallows and islands before the shore, and there would be some game to be found. Out here there is nothing.

I keep sending long, generic pulses to find any potential prey.

Something catches my attention. I take a deep breath and dive to investigate.

With more clicks, I see it's an octopus. Not of a sort I'm used to back home. There aren't many places for it to hide out here. It's just crawling along the edge of the dropoff. I imagine it might be like us, displaced by the volcano and making its way in this confusing new context.

I've never liked octopus, but I need to get food for the calves.

I charge, sending a focused pulse of sound at the octopus. It darts to the side, perhaps looking for a hiding place that won't be found here. Although it launches up, trying to stick with the current, my clicks have disoriented it enough that it's a fairly easy catch.

It is not much, but will tide them over.

After I call, the two come to feed. Princess eats first, eagerly tucking in with some of the arms. Although I can tell he's very hungry, Questions waits for her sister to have her fill. I think he might be emulating me as a protector, since he's usually one of the first to feed. It's good he is being patient and taking this seriously.

I give him an approving click, then nod to the head of the octopus.

Questions digs in, ripping it apart and sparing nothing.

The octopus was a blessing, but it's not a sufficient meal for either, and I still haven't eaten in two days now.

Questions is cruising against the current, sending a wave of clicks. All I saw was rocks, but upon inspection, I see that there are many snails, barnacles, and mussels scattered throughout.

"We don't eat those-" I begin to say, but Questions has already grabbed a large snail in his jaws. His first tug doesn't even dislodge it, which is a bit shocking, but it does come loose when he twists. The snail promptly closes its door, sealing off the meat he is surely going for.

Undaunted, Questions uses his tongue to flip it around. He then spits out a jet, pushing the snail's door along his tooth line, then bites gently enough that the door is opened. From there, he quickly bites and shakes, cracking along the base of the shell before a click of his tongue against the roof of his mouth sucks the snail out and he swallows, giving a satisfied whistle.

"When did you learn to do that?" I ask after an approving hum.

"In the shallows while we waited for the grownups to finish hunting," he replies. "I saw walruses doing it, and wanted to try it myself. They usually do it with clams and mussels, but I find it's a lot easier with snails. I'll show you!"

With that, Questions shows me and Princess his walrus technique. With my much larger jaws it's hard to get the placement right. Questions and Princess each get a substantial amount of meat from the method. I worry I will just end up cracking the shells and hurt my throat or teeth, but at least they're pretty close to satisfied, and I'll take that as a victory.

I must eat soon if I am to defend them, though. Just because we haven't yet seen any predators in these comparatively barren waters doesn't mean it's a safe place for us to wait to try and return to the pod. There is no cover here. We're just as exposed to danger as the octopus, and I know we will be just as easy to pick off if something comes along and I'm not strong enough to defend us.

Luckily, this bounty of shellfish disguised amongst the rocks has drawn things I might actually get a meal out of.

My passive clicks pick up a walrus further down the shelf. There's not much on the way of beaches to speak of, so it must have traveled a long way. The plethora of food only a walrus (or evidently Questions) would be excited by seems to have made the journey worthwhile.

I tell Questions and Princess to stay here. Remain amongst the dark rocks where seeing predators will have trouble spotting them. Once they both offer a whistle of confirmation, I turn and dive off the shelf.

With care I swim along the edge. Walruses have decent vision and their whiskers mean they can feel danger approaching, often in time to get to shore before we can launch an attack.

There isn't much of a beach, but I still want a quick kill.

I pop above the shelf and send a series of clicks. It's smaller than the walruses back home in the colder seas, but at a third my size, more than large enough to fill me and the calves. It has tusks. My side pulses with a reminder of the beaked whale's tusks, but the walrus isn't armed with nearly that level of weaponry.

I must still be careful. The last thing I need is to get another injury.

I duck under and close the distance.

When I launch over the edge, the walrus is facing away, and barely reacts by the time I've grappled him with a bite at the base of the neck.

He twists, shoving against the bedrock and trying to roll and strike with his tusks. His skin is loose and he does turn enough to nearly catch my flipper. I surge forward, overpowering him and landing a more secure bite.

Once I have the hold, I clamp my jaws as hard as I can. My teeth have dug deep into his hide, and a set of cracks confirms I have broken his neck. My next click confirms the spinal cord is snapped in several places, and his lungs have taken on water.

I disengage my bite and call the calves over. By the time they arrive, I've opened the walruses throat and pass the tongue to Princess. She takes it in her jaws, but doesn't swallow.

"Is it alright?" I ask. "Something wrong?"

She swims closer and tilts her head up. "You eat it. We need you to be strong."

Questions lets out a 'woo' of agreement.

I pause for a moment before taking the offering. Even when I catch prey, I always surrender the tongue and lips. I needed such a bulk of food to account for my rapid growth that the elders said I had to make up for it by eating the bulk of scraps. I've often considered sneaking, but the other youngsters were always a step behind even if I caught prey before we were allowed to join the hunts.

After thanking them, I gulp it down.

The meat is tender and rich. I can certainly see the appeal.

I do insist they have the lips. It should top them off.

Once they are finished, I dig into the fat of the neck and muscles of its shoulders. I'm very happy that the calves are full, but I cannot deny a swell of pride getting to eat the prime meat of something I killed myself.

Princess sends out a squeal of alarm.

I look up and see a familiar silhouette above. A click stream confirms it.

A corpse serpent.

These great reptiles are common back home. In basic form they resemble a sea lion or turtle, with four broad flippers, a tail fluked like a shark, and a thick, muscular neck so long that it doubles their length, but the head is where the monstrosity truly lies.

Save for an enormous lump of muscle on either temple and the back of the jaws, its head conforms close to the skull. The head looks the way our skulls do inside all our skin and muscle, and the appearance of a skull nearly exposed is truly frightening to consider.

Their teeth are huge, with the longest fangs three times the size of mine even though the skull is only slightly larger. Their brains are small, but Matriarch says this is deceiving: they are more clever than we would expect, and with reptiles, brain size is not as reliable an indication of intelligence as it is with whales and seals.

Also horrid is the placement of their eyes at the top of their skull, meaning both eyes are focused in the same direction. They do not make noise when they hunt, instead relying on taste like a shark or using their strange eyes. They are limited in vision with this placement, which is why this creature now circles above us upside down, leering with massive eyes trained on me.

I send a stream of clicks to assess its condition. I see no signs of recent injury, but there is a kink in its left hind flipper and an old scar on its neck that suggests a rather significant injury much earlier in life. It hasn't fed recently, but there is something in the serpent's barrel torso that catches my attention.

A baby serpent is curled up inside.

This is a pregnant mother.

My next clicks confirm her lungs are full. She must have taken a breath right before flipping over. I have not breathed in a while, and given that she's only five lengths away, I certainly don't have time to surface. She's moving slow now, investigating more than anything, but I've seen how fast and agile serpents can be at close range.

Maybe she just wants the walrus.

I could eat more, but I've had a substantial meal, and it's not worth the injuries that fighting a serpent her size would surely inflict. I think I outweigh her, but not by much, and she would almost certainly land a bite or two before I could close the distance.

With a slow, steady hum, I tell Questions and Princess to back up. "Don't turn and flee. That will only trigger her instinct to chase."

We give way, swimming backwards and letting the remains of the walrus entice her on.

Once we're a few lengths back, the serpent rolls over. A long barbed tongue pushes out of her jaws, touching the corpse. Although she tests the meal, her eyes are both locked on me. Above her head she keeps her back to me. Clicks illuminate the many bony plates under her hide. Piercing her torso would be impossible. The bold pattern on her shoulders and fins mirrors the shape and intense focus of her gaze. It's a bit unnerving to my eyes. I imagine it is terrifying to a creature that can only see.

Just when my heart rate begins to ease, I hear a surge of water behind me. The realization that serpents often live in groups crosses my mind. I turn, ready to fight, but my passive clicks confirms it is Princess.

Her lungs are empty. In the panic she must have exhaled and now she needs air.

The movement had the effect I feared it would.

With a twist, the corpse serpent launches forward, rolling about all while keeping her eyes locked on Princess.

I release a torrent of warning calls and charge.

As I predicted, the serpent turns and strikes with speed. Greater than I anticipated. Before I can land a bite of my own, she plunges down, turns her armored back facing me, then arcs under to strike at my torso.

Although she impacts, a dozen teeth raking across my chest, my momentum carries me forward and I collide with her back, shoving her down. The downward stroke of my tail buffets her neck before she can retaliate. I carry on, putting distance between us before turning around.

She has already rotated to face me. Her agility is astonishing. I feel the wounds along my chest. They aren't deep, but I know that was luck and my momentum at play. If she lands a proper bite, it could pierce organs. The corpse serpents I've seen back home can go from motionless to rapid strikes with blinding speed, and a well-placed bite to the blowhole would end me swiftly.

For all her advantages, I am much faster.

Although she is focused on me, I panic when I see Questions charging from the other side for an attack on her belly. With her eyes on me, she cannot perceive his incoming attack.

I know a direct assault robs me of my advantage in speed, but I cannot let him engage alone.

I'm close enough to the surface that I am able to grab a breath.

With the renewed strength it affords, I charge.

Right before I impact, I spin. As I hoped, this motion prevents her from landing an initial strike. Although I wasn't planning on attacking, her right rear flipper is in range, and I bite hard and fast, letting my teeth deal an impact and letting go rather than trying to tear.

Her second strike as I release her flipper and pass above does sink where my flukes meet my tail. On the downstroke she holds on. Pain sears through my tail. The flexibility afforded by her neck is infuriating. She shakes, keeping her hold as I try to buffet away.

Questions lands a strike of his own, his bite sharp where her rear left flipper meets hips.

It must be painful, for she lets go.

And rounds on him.

Luckily it takes a full rotation for her to get into a striking position. I call for Questions to flee, and he does so, able to turn much more readily than I could. Although I was worried that she might have done serious damage to my tail, I'm advancing with typical speed, and soon we are both clear of her strike range.

Princess is waiting, and promptly takes off as her brother and I reach her.

The serpent does pursue us for a few lengths, but now that we are swimming in the open, my broad clicks suggest she's losing ground.

By the time I feel safe to turn, I can see that she has rounded back and begun feeding on the walrus. Rather than targeting the tender portions like I was, she establishes a hold on the belly and twists, tearing it open before thrusting her tongue inside to withdraw the organs.

Once we have put distance between us, I realize we are swimming east, back towards the volcano.

I spyhop to check the cloud.

The dark smoke is still in the distance. My vision is not terribly keen above water, but I think it is getting closer. The wind has shifted slightly, and the cloud could certainly start coming more southwest.

"We cannot go much further in this direction. Even with the wind going generally south, it will get hard to breathe."

Princess and Questions send whistles and chirps of understanding. I feel them both sending clicks at my tail and chest. They aren't saying anything, but I can tell that they are checking. Although it makes me insecure, I can't blame them. The wound in my chest is longer, but luckily it isn't terribly deep. I will heal within a day. My tail is more concerning. Each stroke of my tail hurts: downstroke as the wound opens, upswing as it is forced closed.

"I'm alright. It's not deep," I remark after taking a deep breath.

They spout too, but don't respond.

"I know it's day, but I will feel better if we rested for a bit, alright? Once I'm well, we will swim around her and continue swimming west."
"She was scary," says Princess.

I whistle in agreement. "Are you two alright?"

"I am," says Questions. Princess echoes him.

"Good."

"I think she could have beaten a cachalot bull," whispers Questions.

I whistle in amusement, remembering our conversation back before the volcano erupted. "Gratitude, Questions."

"Her tooth is stuck in your tail," cooed Princess quietly.

I curl in so I can catch the end of my tail at the edge of a focused click stream.

As she said, there is a tooth lodged in the lump of meat and muscle at the base of my flukes. There are many punctures, and a lot of blood, but the tooth crown is stuck fast. If it stays in, it will delay healing and likely get infected.

"Would you like me to take it out?" asks Questions.

I whistle and grunt in affirmation.

As I straighten my torso, he cautiously advances. I feel his clicks against my tail as he makes sure he has the angle right. I try to calm myself. Any sudden movements could hurt him or lodge it deeper.

I feel his tongue curl around the tooth and dislodge it slightly. I clench my jaw but remain still. After another steady pulse, he clicks his tongue against the roof of his mouth then spits out the tooth.

"Thanks again, Questions," I call out.

He sends a proud call, and Princess bumps against him.

We put more distance between us and the corpse serpent, just in case she decides to investigate, then rest for a while.

Once I have had time to digest and feel some strength returning, we swim out into the open ocean to make our way around the serpent and continue swimming west.

***

The next six days see us steadily swim along the coast. We don't want to get too far, since we hope to be in range of the pod if they come in range, but the ash cloud continues to expand out, so we need to keep moving.

Most of our days are spent with me watching over the calves as they forage. With his tutelage, Princess is getting proficient with Question's walrus method, and they both get most of what they need from the plethora of massive snails feasting on algae along the shelf. There aren't many walruses, but there are enough that I'm able to get enough food.

The corpse serpent has become our frustrating but tolerable companion. I've begun to think of her as Hungry Shadow considering she is always lurking nearby. She seems to have figured out that I'm willing to fight her, but we both eat different parts of the walrus, with me preferring the lips, tongue, shoulder muscles, and neck skin and her targeting the organs, so the truce of sorts works out a lot better than I would have anticipated. We also both have young that we not only need to provide for, but stay healthy to defend, so she doesn't seem as aggressive as she was the first day. I'm aware of her presence once I've made a kill, but she doesn't make any effort to move in until I've had my fill.

Something approaching sympathy sparks in me when I realize on the third day that Hungry Shadow likely has, like us, been displaced from our usually abundant waters in the south. She is a mother with someone to care for. Her kind are usually social. Perhaps they were separated by the volcano too, just like us. Now she's lost and alone in a strange land. It doesn't make me trust her, and I keep my guard up, but I find myself at ease around her, trusting that she would rather scavenge my kills than threaten the calves.

Also, she's from home, and with as many strange new things as we've seen, even an ancient enemy comes with a twisted element of comfort. At least the threat is familiar and I know how to share space with her.

On my morning hunt, I find a female walrus feasting on snails further south.

As I have now done many times, I sink low below the edge of the shallows, making sure I'm low enough that my tall dorsal fin won't give me away.

When I launch over the ledge, I realize I underestimated the distance.

There's a good four lengths between my ambush and where she was feeding. The walrus abandons the mollusk she was positioning and swims fast to shore.

I'm faster and close the distance, but she got enough of a head start that she has reached the pebbled shore that is too shallow to swim. I attempt something I've seen Hero do plenty of times in a hunt but never tried myself outside of play.

I pursue the walrus, beaching myself with a surge of water.

There's enough beach that the walrus clambers out of reach and continues west. Once she's confident she is out of harm's way, the walrus rounds about and grunts. I can't use my sonar out of water, but I can see her with my right eye. Maybe it's just my disappointment and hunger, but she looks awfully pleased with herself.

I snort and shuffle back into water deep enough to swim. The effort is arduous and takes an embarrassing amount of time. Through the whole process, the walrus watches me with her bugged out, unfocused, silly eyes.

I take out my frustration on a flounder I catch for longer than I care to admit, then resume the hunt.

After a while I find a large crab seal. This hunt is successful. Seals are much less pleasant to eat than walruses. Walruses don't have fur and their skin is delicious. It takes a lot of effort to get to the good parts of a seal, but at least this bull is big enough to provide a sufficient meal.

Princess and Questions don't say anything, but I can tell they aren't enjoying the tenders of the seal as much as a walrus. I'm certainly disappointed by the pathetic amount of shoulder muscles this seal has to offer. His neck meat isn't much to speak of either. I am near the end of my meal when a distress call out in the open ocean catches my attention.

I look to the calves, clicking to see if they hear it.

"I don't recognize them," says Questions. "Sounds like calves, but it's too far away and I don't recognize the voices."

"Are you sure?" says Princess. "That one sounds a bit like Singer."

I listen closely. If it isn't our pod, there are other young blackfish in danger. They sound terrified.

Maybe they aren't our pod, but perhaps they are lost and separated just as we are.

One call does sound remarkably like Pebbles. The same notes trilling up and down whenever he was frightened, which was a regular occurrence. It matches his cadence, but something sounds slightly off.

Maybe they sound off because they're hungry. If it's just Grappler and Gentle hunting for them, feeding over a dozen mouths can't be easy.

I send out a steady pulse stream, maximizing my range out into the open water to let them know we're here.

Hungry Shadow is waiting on the surface around ten lengths away. I don't think serpents have particularly keen hearing, but she's definitely noticed that I'm not eating anymore. Normally I have my fill and immediately give ground, then let her close in. Although there's more I could eat, I don't want to leave the distress calls unanswered, so lead Questions and Princess away so Hungry Shadow can dig in. She won't be interested in the shoulder meat still left anyway, and I can come back for it if all goes well.

We swim out into the open ocean, sending clicks as we go. Although I still hear the distress calls, it almost sounds like they're getting further away. It's difficult to identify where exactly they are coming from. Maybe they're farther away than I anticipated. It could account for why the sounds are so distorted.

"I don't like open water," hums Princess quietly.

"Me neither," I reply.

If they're far away, maybe I've been aiming my distance pulses in the wrong direction.

After taking a breath at the surface, I unleash a torrent of response signals in varying directions. Eventually they should hear them.

Although I don't get direct replies, and still hear the distress calls in the distance, I do pick up some distant shapes approaching fast from the east. They're shaped much like blackfish calves, but I don't sense any adults. Now that I'm paying attention in that direction, I can hear that seems to be the origin of the distress calls, but they still bounce around the coast and are distorted by open water, so I'm not certain.

"Is that Pebbles?" asks Questions.

"Certainly sounds like him," I say.

The silhouettes come into clearer focus. I'm pretty certain that these are young blackfish, but there's no sign of Grappler or Gentle. How long have they been alone?

I charge, trying to close the distance.

As their voices and forms become more clear, I slow to a halt.

I don't know what they are, but they are not young blackfish.

The distress calls are convincing mimicry. As they close in it no longer sounds much like the young blackfish of our pod, but the general sounds are spot on.

The creatures themselves are also close mimics of calves. As the twelve forms close in and spread out, I see that their bodies are sleek, in some ways more resembling a dolphin than a young blackfish as I first presumed. In profile they seem most similar to the squid-eater dolphins. Their skulls, however, are quite like ours: their teeth are deep-rooted and curved for tearing flesh.

As the calf-mimics circle us, they continue to cry out in distress, but now I know it is a ruse. A trick.

The formation they assume is familiar to me.

They are hunting.

Princess and Questions stay close, clicking nervously. I reassure them, but I've never seen creatures like these. I can confidently kill one of them, possibly several, but that would require charging which would leave the calves vulnerable.

"Help, please!" calls one of the calf mimics, her voice so close to Princess's that I have to confirm she's still by my side.

"Save us!" another calls, matching Question's tone.

At this, Questions sends out an angry warning call. He is almost as large as the calf-mimics. I know he isn't a fighter by nature, much more interested in solving puzzles, but I am impressed by the ferocity of his clicks.

He and I flank Princess. I would rather one of them on either side of me, but at least this way Princess isn't exposed.

I steadily rise in the water, and my wide clicks confirm Princess and Questions are staying close. It may leave us vulnerable to an attack from below, but the last thing I want is for us to have to break formation to breathe. Although I know I should display, I don't want to draw attention to the serpent's wound in my tail. It isn't debilitating, but could be a weakness for them to exploit. My turns will be ever so slightly delayed, and that could make all the difference.

I do feel their clicks, and it's a matter of time before they know I'm slightly impaired, if they don't already know.

One of them rushes from below. Questions turns down, but I tell him to remain in formation: the full pack will charge when they want to make a kill. This mock charge is just to test or separate us.

As I suspected, the calf-mimic arcs down just before impact.

"Help, I'm frightened!" she calls before rejoining the circling pack.

They test our resolve with several more charges. I know my turns to face them with open jaws only exposes my impairment. I also am familiar with their tactics as I've used them myself, but the reaction is involuntary. Some part of me knows the situation is dire, that at best they find my efforts amusing, but I have to try and intimidate them. If I can just get one of them close enough to land a bite, perhaps I can kill one. Show them that they should find easier prey. I know this is a foolish hope. These mock charges won't be close enough to put them in danger. All I'm doing is reacting and showing them where they need to strike. I'm doing their work for them. I am prey, but I can't seem to stop.

We need to get to shore. If we had something at our backs, I could face the calf-mimics with greater confidence, but exposed as we are, I cannot mount a strong defense.

As I click to the nearest calf-mimic, I see the bones of a flipper in his belly. It might be from a dolphin, but they are of the exact dimensions as Princess's flipper...

"It hurts! Help me! Make it stop!"

The voice is a perfect match for Singer.

As rage burns through my chest, I charge. The calf-mimic anticipated me and darts away, letting out a cackle of clicks.

Now that I've moved away from Questions and Princess, the pack all charge in unison.

I feel several bites nearly land, but twisting about helps fend most of them off. My flukes buffet hard against one of their sides. One of them does land a bite at the base of my tail, but their jaws aren't strong enough to punch deep. All around me I hear distress calls as the calf-mimics continue to cry out in mockery.

I see an opening in one of the calf mimics, a female, seemingly dazed. She might be the one I hit with my tail. Although I feel another sharp bite at my flukes, I swat it away and charge the dazed female.

I catch her back in my jaws. Lower on the back than would be ideal, but she's caught.

With the calf-mimic in my jaws, I charge towards the surface and breach. I fully clear the surface in an arc. My hold loosens in the jump, and I am denied the satisfaction of breaking her back as we impact, but she still looks shaken.

I round about for another attack, hoping to finish her off before taking another in my jaws.

The calf mimics continue to cry out, but I realize some of the cries might be Princess and Questions.

Although a few of the calf-mimics are on me, most are swarming Princess and Questions. Questions bleeds from several injuries as they target his flukes and head. They haven't managed to catch his blowhole, but it's a matter of time. He keeps Princess above him, enduring their assault with furious calls.

I charge, but two of the calf-mimics grab hold of my flukes. Their teeth tear into me, not fully ripping apart my flukes, but it slows me. Some part of me knows I should ignore them, that they are only harrying me so their pack can kill Questions and Princess, but I still round about and shake them off. The other two calf-mimics on me hit with a series of nips. I keep trying to remind myself to ignore their attacks and get back to Questions, but their bites keep demanding my focus.

Princess cries out: a large male has her by the tail and is dragging her away from Questions. Questions cries out, but the three on him are boxing him off, and one from further back lands a charge that spins him aside. All the while, the calf-mimics are crying out with perfect matches of Princess and Questions's distress calls, and it's disorienting to figure out where the real calves are amidst the chaos.

A massive form collides with the male calf-mimic that is dragging Princess away.

Hungry Shadow has him in her jaws.

The calf-mimic releases Princess. The cry of pain and terror is completely alien to the calls they made before: his true voice is revealed.

With the base of his tail firmly in her grasp, Hungry Shadow launches upwards. She raises the full length of her muscular neck out of the water, taking the calf-mimic fully out of view.

Two lengths away, the calf-mimic is struck against the surface with a crack like thunder.

The commotion has freed me, and I charge at Questions. His harassers are confused and disoriented, and I catch the closest in an upward charge.

This time my bite holds true, and my victim's back breaks when we plunge back into the ocean.

I call out to Princess once I've cleared Questions.

She is crying out, scared and confused on the other side of Hungry Shadow.

The serpent has grabbed another calf-mimic, and I am elated to see her give wide shakes of her long neck, the sheer force of the arc shredding it apart.

As the pack scatters, Princess swims around our murderous savior. Her tail is hurt, but she's making good time.

I turn back to Questions, and my heart falls.

He is covered in bite marks, and a cloud of blood floats around him. His chest, flukes, and side all have horrid wounds. Worst perhaps is his dorsal fin, the top half of which was fully torn off in the brawl. He tries to swim up, but can't quite close the length of distance.

I close in, offering consoling calls. Princess is soon by her brother's side too. I click quickly at her and confirm that the bite to her tail isn't impairing her too much, then raise Questions for a breath.

He takes it, but the inhalation is weak, and there's a coughing struggle. I can't tell if his lungs took on water in the impact I sense has bruised much of his side or if one of their bites punctured one of his lungs, but his breaths are strained.

At my call, Princess and I switch sides so I'm not pressing against his bruise. As I get a better view of him in the rotation, my clicks don't show any punctures in his lungs. A small comfort considering his condition, but a comfort nonetheless.

With Questions leaning as much as he can on me, we begin to swim back to shore.

I glance back as we advance.

Hungry Shadow is happily tearing into one of the four calf-mimics we killed.

I hope she has a satisfying feast.

***

Three days have passed, and Questions is able to swim on his own for the first time since our encounter with the calf-mimics.

It isn't far, and soon he needs me to bolster him, but it is a promise of recovery.

After he survived the first night, I was more confident he would make it. He still needs to be fed and brought to the surface to breathe, but he's recovering. His dorsal fin has been halved, but there's enough to keep him stable, and I imagine once he matures and his fin grows fully erect, he will gain at least a bit more length to it.

Luckily it seems the damage was mostly superficial. My experience was the same: from what Princess describes of my appearance, I will have many scars, and my flukes are scraped quite substantially, but nothing deeply damaging.

Princess has now perfected her brother's snail hunting method, and brings him several snails wrestled from their shells every day, and the steady supply of food is helping his strength return.

Hungry Shadow brought a walrus she killed to us on the second day. She had already eaten the organs and much of the torso meat, but I was still surprised and moved by the gesture. Since I can't leave Questions for long enough to hunt, it was a gift I know likely saved us, or at least made it so I could be more attentive to Questions.

I never would have thought a corpse serpent, ancient enemy of our kind, would be our savior, but the strange times has made for unlikely allies, and I am grateful for her presence.

Since my attention is focused on Questions, Princess has been doing a lot of scouting and calls for the pod. I ask her not to stray far, and she always keeps close enough that I can close the distance in cases of danger. Several times a day she calls for our family out into the open waters. I'm worried that it will draw in the calf-mimics, but I admire that she still holds hope. That she's still trying. That her spirit isn't broken.

She will make a strong leader one day.

That evening, she calls out nervously. Hungry Shadow is out hunting. I take Questions up for a breath, then go to investigate.

"What is that?" Princess asks.

I send a click stream after hers.

A form is swimming up from the depths, its motions slow and meticulous. The creature is around a dozen lengths away. It is around the size of a cachalot. The head is massive, flat and wide. It's skin is pale and wrinkled. The fins are broad, and it has four like a serpent or turtle, but it swims with a lateral stroke like a shark. I've seen these creatures a few times before on hunts, but only in deep oceans, and never this close.

I call out to Questions, encouraging him to come see. He does so on his own. Although he swims slow, he can do it alone, and he seems proud to do so. I am elated to hear the coo of wonder he made all the time before the volcano.

"What is it?" he whispers.

"That is a Steward of the Abyss. Although some call them a fish, Matriarch says they are between fish and creatures like mammals and reptiles. Like a sleeper shark, stewards spend their days deep in the abyss, where whales go when they die, and light and clicks cannot reach. When night comes, they rise to the surface to breathe. They may be frightening, but they feed on the dead and the rotting, so perform an invaluable service in keeping the oceans clean. Matriarch says that without them, the ocean would be filled with death and nothing new could be born."

Princess and Questions both make whistles of amazement.

"We shouldn't get close, but it's not dangerous unless we bother it."

For a long time we watch the creature. Slowly it rises up to the surface. Like us, the steward breathes with a spout, but Matriarch said they can also breathe water, so only need to surface for air a few times every night. I can see the gills under its astonishingly powerful jaws with a steady click stream. I tell the calves that this creature can breathe both air and water, and point out its gills. This further captures their wonder.

Its teeth are sturdy but have a cutting edge. In addition, it's lips have hardened like another row of teeth, with tiny serrations along its edge. Questions asks why they have teeth both inside and out. I wish I could answer him. I can only guess.

"Is it to help clean the dead?" Princess asks. "Those weird lips can scrape off gross bits?"

"That would make sense. Maybe the teeth are to crush and the lips help pick off meat?" Questions suggests. "Those jaws are huge, like a grandmother shark. I think it can break a whale's bones with those jaws."

"I think you're both right. Matriarch says they can eat anything. It makes sense that they would need more than just teeth to do that. Looks like they have another set of teeth on the roof of their mouth too."

"And I think another set of jaws?" Questions adds after a stream of clicks.

"Its so weird," Princess whispers. "I love it."

After another few breaths, the enormous creature empties its strange single lung and sinks back into the abyss whence it came.

Later that evening, Hungry Shadow swims towards us, a walrus cow in her jaws. This time she hasn't even had her portion yet. She sets the corpse down in the shallows around three lengths from me and Questions before digging in.

I notice her movements are sluggish. She seemed a bit slow last time she brought food to us, but it is exaggerated now. Was she injured in the calf-mimic encounter? It didn't seem to be the case at the time. She seemed to have no trouble throwing them about like toys.

Once she has fed, she backs up, something she is able to do a lot more smoothly than our kind given her four highly flexible fins. She doesn't back up more than a length. A few days ago that would still have me on edge, but it looks like she doesn't have it in her to go much further. The hunt appears to have exhausted her.

I send out a click stream, trying to see if she may have been injured in the encounter with the walrus. She was a bit sluggish before, so that wouldn't really make sense, and I see no sign of any injuries. Most of her hide is too thick and tough for a walrus to pierce anyway, especially a cow with smaller tusks like she brought.

Once I confirm it's safe, Questions and Princess begin to feed on the lips. Princess opens its throat with a bit of a struggle and offers Questions the tongue. He takes it with a click and whistle of gratitude. Once they've had their fill, I help Questions up for air, although thankfully he can do it mostly by himself.

I then take my usual portions. As I'm feeding on the neck hide, I notice Hungry Shadow is struggling to rise for breath. I glance back to Princess and Questions. They are a safe distance back, clicking at me nervously. Willing myself to be calm, I advance slowly towards Hungry Shadow.

She arcs towards me, jaws agape. It's just a threat, but the warning is received. Even so, she needs to breathe. Whatever's happening to her, she can't go without air much longer.

Although her jaws are still open, she doesn't make a motion to strike as I continue a slow approach.

Once I'm within range, I start to turn, letting my body face her broadside so my jaws aren't facing her.

A tense moment passes. Finally my wide clicks pick up that her jaws have closed. I shift a bit closer. Slowly I lower my head under her massive pectoral fin and lift.

With my help, she gets up for a breath. I feel her torso expand, and strength returns to her flipper. After I feel her take a second inhalation, I lower her back down. I need a breath of my own. Once I've gotten another breath, I help her up for a third.

As I go up to spout again, I see why she has been strained.

A swell of blood erupts behind her, and I see a pale serpent unfurl from the cloud. Hungry Shadow curls down and nudges the large-headed creature. It twists. I've seen enough births to know it needs a breath, just like our kind.

I consider approaching, but having helped Hungry Shadow catch a few breaths, I may have given her all the assistance she needs, and I don't want to risk her wrath in approaching the newborn.

She dips her head under the calf's chest and lifts its pale form up to the surface. After a few breaths, the little serpent begins to squirm about, testing its flexibility in limbs and neck.

Leaving him on the surface, Hungry Shadow dives back down and voraciously digs into the walrus. It seems after giving birth, her priority has shifted quickly to replenishing her strength.

Like our kind, corpse serpents usually live in groups. I wonder if she was expecting to give birth with her family. It would explain why she was so lethargic and willing to cooperate with us over the past few days. I'm honored that she trusted us to be her pod for such an event. A few months ago and a few months from now we will be enemies, but in this moment, I am thankful for this bond of conditional trust and respect.

After consuming the organs and much more of the skin than she usually feeds on, Hungry Shadow rises to the surface and checks her child over, making sure it catches several new breaths. Already the calf is curious. Its head is much more round than its mother's, and the massive eyes face out rather than both up, sacrificing focus for a wider field of vision. Its snout is blunt and, unlike orca calves, its jaws are already lined with plenty of sharp teeth.

Hungry Shadow and her offspring relax on the surface for a while. Eventually she regurgitates some of the walrus, and Little Shadow feeds with a ferocity and enthusiasm that must make its mother proud.

***

Another four days drift by. Little Shadow and Princess have become playmates, seemingly indifferent to what adults of our respective kinds think our relationship should be. Although she makes few sounds, I'm beginning to perceive elements of Hungry Shadow's body language. I can at least glean general emotions from her. She seems relaxed around us and makes no signs of aggression.

Princess has taught Little Shadow how to evict snails from their shells. He picked up on it surprisingly quickly, although he hasn't seemed to figure out how to eat them after. So far he always takes it back to Hungry Shadow, expecting her to eat it then regurgitate. She doesn't seem interested, but he hasn't given up.

Questions continues his recovery. I'm happy to see him making progress. He is now reliably able to swim and breathe on his own.

"It's weird without my fin," he tells me after my latest check. "I think I've figured it out, though."

Hungry Shadow and I take turns hunting while the other watches the young. In the last few hunts I've taken Questions with me. Although in the pod he wouldn't be expected to hunt for another few years, he's old enough that he's able to help, and I think it's good practice for getting used to swimming without most of his top fin. His impairment coupled with inexperience does mean that one walrus manages to get to shore, but I reassure him that the purpose of him joining the hunt is to practice, and practice does not mean immediate success.

"I was eleven when I made my first seal kill," I whistle and hum. "You are seven. Now is a time to learn."

On one afternoon as Hungry Shadow returns with a walrus, I wonder if she and I might make a good hunting team. I'm faster than her once I've built up speed, but she is more agile, faster in bursts, and has wide reach. If I could drive game towards her, there's little chance of escape. I don't know how I might coordinate such an attack. If I can figure out how to communicate the idea to her, we could be hunting with a lot less effort.

Thoughts of how I might coordinate with her carry me into the evening. I attempt to convey things to her. At first she seems confused, but it's hard to read her body language. I try the groan I've heard her use now and then to beckon Little Shadow, but she ignores me. Eventually she yawns at me. There's no effort in a threat behind it, but even I pick up on her lack of interest in continuing the conversation.

Questions clicks out a warning about strange forms approaching.

I bolt up to spout before meeting him at the edge of the shallows. Hungry Shadow is close behind. I send out a long-range pulse.

At this range I can tell that they are a range of sizes, with most around my size. There are six forms. They move with four flippers.

Corpse serpents.

As they close in, Hungry Shadow swims out to meet them.

I'm now familiar enough with her body language to register that she moves with more enthusiasm than I've ever seen. Normally stoic, she rolls about playfully, much like Little Shadow does with Princess. Now that I'm seeing her with others of her kind, I realize Hungry Shadow is not particularly large. The smallest of the adults. I assumed she was in her prime, but maybe she's not much older than I am. This was likely her first time as a mother, and she had to take the first days without her pod.

Little Shadow lingers back with us. These may be his family, but he doesn't know them. He hasn't done much swimming in the open ocean, and remains between me and Princess.

Hungry Shadow circles back. When she sees her son remaining behind, she closes the distance. Her family remains behind, for which I am thankful. I have grown to trust her, but I doubt she would defend us if they decided to attack, especially since she no longer relies on our strange partnership for the survival of her son.

She emits a low groan, one of the few sounds I've heard her make, when she wants to beckon Little Shadow.

He doesn't come.

Hungry Shadow swims a bit closer, letting out another groan.

Princess nudges Little Shadow and swims out towards his mother. He reluctantly follows.

They close the distance, and Hungry Shadow nudges his snout with hers. She then repeats the gesture to Princess, who lets out a steady drum of sad clicks. Princes nudges Little Shadow once more, then swims back to me and Questions.

Although it looks like Little Shadow might swim back with her, as his mother turns, he follows out to the serpent pod.

They all gather around to meet their newest member of the family. Serpents don't make much sound, but they communicate with a lot more touch than I ever noticed in my previous inter-actions. There is a lot more affection than I would have guessed. They clearly care deeply for one another, even if they show it much differently than our kind.

I never would have thought I would feel sad to see a corpse serpent leave, but my chest feels tight as I watch the pod of now eight individuals swimming west, against the current.

I wish them a happy journey.

Princess cries long into the night.

***

We had only known Little Shadow for four days, and Hungry Shadow nine before that, but our little group feels quite empty in their absence. We don't talk much. The day after the serpents left is quiet. To pass the time, Questions and I idly hunt, but it's only after a while that we find a pair of walruses and catch one.

The following day, Questions doesn't feel like hunting. I strike out alone.

After searching most of the morning, a ways in either direction, I don't find any walruses. It seems the bounty of our sanctuary may finally have become depleted, or at least the walruses and crabeater seals are being more cautious.

I do spot a sea otter as I'm swimming west, but they are mostly fur and surprisingly, frustratingly lean. Not much of a meal to be had. I don't feel an urge to spend energy on something with such a miserable return.

If I don't find anything, I won't be so inclined to turn down an otter.

It begins to rain. A steady drum on the surface of the water. It's not raining hard enough to significantly interfere with my echolocation, but the constant and steady impacts do make shapes at a distance a bit blurred.

I carry on, sending pulses far and wide to find anything worth pursuing. I'm sure my mood isn't helping. Normally I would have been patrolling for a while longer before feeling this defeated. I'm glad that Hungry Shadow and her son found their pod. They should be with their family, but it's been a stark reminder that we still haven't found ours, and we can no longer distract from that grief and loneliness with their company, strange though it may have been.

After spouting, which I hate doing in the rain, I dive off the shallows and search along the cliff. I'm not optimistic. I'm not looking for any food in particular. More curious than anything else.

My wide pulses down do pick up some movement. Mostly fish. Perhaps some squid far below, but it's hard to make out more than vague shapes that far down. There's something bigger further out. Perhaps a beaked whale, but more likely a shark or fish that simply looks larger at that depth and wide range of my pulses.

I continue west, pulsing out as I go.

There is something out in the open ocean near the surface. I focus my clicks. It's massive. The general shape is that of a whale. It is enormous, around the size of the cachalot bull that rescued us, if a bit shorter.

It might be a cachalot. It's hard to tell at this distance, especially as the rain is picking up.

The notion that it might be the same cachalot sets my thoughts wild in excitement, and I take off into the open water.

As I close the distance, my pulses begin to clarify the image.

I slow my approach.

Before, when it was facing me, the shape reminded me of a cachalot. Perhaps a killer cachalot, with a bulky torso and broad fins. The rain and distance made it blurred, and I suppose I saw what I wanted to see.

It has turned slightly to the side, and I can now more clearly discern its profile.

The head is quite like that of a blackfish in shape. It's snout is pointed, but a lump is elevated over its forehead. Although in profile it resembles a melon, I can see it is a wedge-shaped structure to raise its blowhole. As it raises its head to spout, the left eye remains locked on me, and I can see why it's nostrils would need to be raised that way. Its teeth, though encased in lips, are serrated, robust, and long: clearly built to compromise between crushing and cutting.

The flippers are broad, shaped like those of a male blackfish more than any other creature. The chest is massive, and it uses its pectoral fins to power as well as steer, flexing the fins to advance slightly as it drifts along. It has two dorsal fins like a shark, one large and one small, and indeed a pair of pelvic fins. Also like a shark, its tail is vertical instead of horizontal like mine, although the longer lobe is the lower of the two.

This is not a whale. It is a reptile, like Hungry Shadow. His hide is thick and covered in tiny, sharp scales. I do not think I could break the skin, even on his flippers.

With focused clicks I see into his massive torso. In his belly I see bones. Most are crushed, chewed into pieces by his massive jaws, but some are still intact. Much like I saw in the calf-mimics, these are bones of blackfish, but these bones belong to adult blackfish.

Terror sets in as I realize what this creature is.

A whale eater.

He dwarfs me. Twice my length and many times my size. I feel like a terrified calf in his presence. As I take in his form, I realize there are no obvious vulnerabilities to exploit. Although I know I can't pierce his hide, I can see others have tried: several raking bites of a megatooth shark, a bite on his back that I'm fairly certain is from a cachalot, and I think the rake under his eye is from the barnacles on the snout of a fighting whale. This is an ancient beast with a long history of battles, and although he has plenty of scars, it all looks surface level. Each stroke of his tail is smooth. Fluid. Effortless.

His tail is broad where it meets his flukes, a trait in strong swimmers. He moves slowly now, but he is built for speed. I imagine I might be more maneuverable, but although it is nothing like Hungry Shadow's, he has a neck nearly as long as his skull, and he's probably more agile than he first appears.

With a single lazy stroke of his tail, he's already two lengths closer to me. His size and the casual motion of his tail masks the speed at which he is cruising.

He may have bones in his belly, but a beast like this might never be satisfied.

I cannot lead him back to the calves.

I turn and swim west, keeping a broad pulse so I might know if he is following me. His form is still there. I spout, keeping my pace casual, and turn back slightly before clicking back his way.

He's now fully facing me. Still at a leisurely pace, but aimed in my direction. A pronged tongue flicks out. His eyes face forward, gaze locked on me. I'm a good ten lengths away, but he has proven more than capable of closing distance much faster than I anticipate.

If he charges properly, I may not be able to escape.

I still don't move with my full speed, hoping to not trigger a predator response. If he hasn't charged yet, perhaps he's just curious, but running would only prompt him to chase.

I spout, taking on fresh breath.

He spouts as well, the force of which echoes along the surface.

I see the coast up ahead. How did I get this far out? Perhaps it only feels a greater distance because I'm moving slowly.

A familiar call to the east sinks in my core.

Questions and Princess are coming closer.

"Stay quiet!" I click in their direction. I don't know how well the whale eater can hear. As I turn, he's still following me.

I see the vague silhouettes of Princess and Questions on the coast. They're some twenty lengths away, but if I can spot them, surely he can too.

"Go east. Silent. Slow."

They begin to swim east.

I turn and click back. The whale eater has turned towards them.

I charge towards the coast, headed west away from the calves. With my full effort on speed, I can't risk looking back to confirm. I have to trust that the whale eater will follow me now that I'm fleeing.

Once I've reached the shallows, I glance back and click.

He's closing fast.

I can't fight him. If I'm going to survive, I have to think like prey.

Like the walruses that evaded me, I launch myself onto the pebbled beach. As I do so, I turn before impact so my tail sweeps further up on shore and I can still see. Rain pounds hard around me, irritating my skin as much as the rough stones on my chest.

The waves are carved in half as the whale eater launches towards me. His bulk prevents him from swimming much further, but to my horror, his massive pectoral fins enable him to crawl forward. I remember the colossal size of his chest and now see his shoulders flex as he pulls himself closer to me. His long tongue flicks out, the prongs alternating before it withdraws. His front-facing gaze is locked on me, each pull of his pectoral fins closing the distance.

I wriggle backwards, trying to get away. I send out a click stream to see if his lungs can endure the weight, but as nothing comes back, I feel foolish in the attempt since I know echolocation doesn't work on land. He's now only two lengths away from me, and actually making more progress than I am despite much greater mass.

In my panic, I shift between moving further onto the pebble beach or turning back into the surf. I thought this would be safe. This should be a sanctuary. At his mass he should be trapped and defenseless, yet still he crawls, carving his flippers into the rocks and hauling his bulk ever closer.

Amidst the rain, wind howls around us.

The whale eater is silent, advancing ever closer.

Eventually he will catch up to me. His progress is too great. I turn towards the sea and haul myself into the waves, exerting everything I can into pushing myself into the water. At first I barely move, but I manage to dig where my flukes meet my tail and use that as an anchor to push myself into the water.

As I feel the water envelop me in a cool comforting embrace, I know I must keep moving. The effort has exhausted me, but now is no time for rest.

I continue west, staying in waters shallow enough for me to swim but I think will slow him down. If he's in open water he is a bit faster than me. I might be able to lose him if he's constantly struggling with the shallows.

It isn't long before I hear him get into the water behind me.

The surge of his tail launching him into the surf is chilling.

I remember Champion once telling me that corpse serpents and other reptiles must taste the water to find you, so it can help to stay downstream of the current so your scent isn't being washed towards them. It is also helpful when hunting reptiles, and sharks for that matter, to be downstream of them too. I'm now swimming against the current, so will be easy for him to follow. I should return east. However, if I try to turn back and the whale eater sees me, I'll be luring him towards the calves.

My breath is short. I can't continue sprinting much longer, not after hauling myself onto shore and off again. Turning back may be a risk I have to take.

A possible solution occurs to me.

I catch a breath and swim as hard as I can against the current. Exerting myself to get a bit ahead. Once I've gotten as much distance as I dare, I spout again, turn hard towards the open water, and dive.

As soon as I'm below the line of the cliff, about a length underwater, I come to a halt and hug the cliff edge.

A moment passes in complete silence. Nothing happens. More time draws along. All I hear are the waves and steady drum of a thousand rain drops on the surface. Did he already pass me by?

What sun still pierces the clouds overhead goes suddenly dark.

I dare not click. Know I can't look up. A single glance could be my end. All I can do is wait. Hope. Devote my entire focus to remaining still and silent.

A rumbling growl, almost too deep for me to hear, pulses through the water.

I can hear and feel his movement above me.

Just when I think I have no choice but to dive, to give myself away, I feel him move further upstream. The force of his tail sends a swell towards me, and I move just enough to keep steady. As he continues along, I still can't bring myself to click, but I do glance up and see his flukes disappear back over the wall.

I wait as long as I can endure. Finally I must go up for air.

As I do, I send a careful click steam out in a full circle.

Nothing.

After catching a breath, then taking another, I let out long range pulses. I even spyhop after the horrifying thought of him lurking on the shore occurs to me. Irrational of course, but I must confirm.

No sign of him.

I continue breathing and searching for any sign of him. I'm glad for his absence, but some part of me is nervous that I can't see him. It looked like he was swimming west, which is ideal and the whole purpose of hiding, but I need to know for certain.

Finally I accept he is gone, and make my way slowly east, my heart still pounding against my chest.

***

Once I return to what has become our territory, I begin to call out.

Princess and Questions quickly swim out of the shallows and greet me. I can feel Questions scanning my body for injury, and hear his relief when he confirms I am alright. Although I know I should hunt, I am too exhausted and tired from my encounter with the whale eater. I spend the rest of the afternoon sleeping and recuperating.

Questions awakens me with a warning click. I told them to keep quiet since we didn't know if it was safe, if the whale eater might be drawn to the sound, so I trust that it's important.

It isn't long after I join him and Princess at the edge that I hear it too.

The songs of our kind.

It is not words we know or voices that are familiar, but it is the sorts of clicks and whistles at a complexity only found amongst blackfish. After our encounter with the calf-mimics I find myself reluctant to engage. I'm sure Princess and Questions do too, for they haven't made a sound since they called me over.

The pod of strangers is getting closer.

Princess and Questions look to me.

The choice is mine.

I tell them to stay back. Once they both acknowledge, I swim out and call to the incoming strangers.

At first I only hear their replies. Eventually my long range pulses pick up several vague shapes. Then more. Soon I identify at least twenty individuals. As the first few come within ten lengths or so, I can tell that they are pointed blackfish. Mother said she met my father when they interacted with a pod of northern pointed black-fish. Although I have no reason to believe my father is a member of this pod, the thought does endear me to them.

I cannot identify any words in their clicks and whistles, but I can tell the tone is friendly. They slow at a distance that I think is meant to be respectful: they don't want me to feel frightened. Even their cows are the size of Champion, and one of the three bulls up front with their matriarch is even larger than me. He has a long, cracked-looking scar across his eyes spot.

The matriarch greets me with a stream of pulses. It's much more rapid and dynamic than the greeting I'm used to. More high notes trailing to low, with a few jittering waves of song. The others all assess me with quieter pulses. Mother said that mixed children like me can only be born of our kind, and that we cannot have children of our own. I might be the first blackfish of two sorts they have ever met.

With a drumming under a swirl of notes, the matriarch seems to be trying to ask me something. Her tone is curious. A bit sympathetic. I wish I knew their language. So silly of me to have ever believed Hero and the others when they said pointed blackfish had simple dialects.

Her next words are a series of yips, which her three bulls echo. Scar whistles to me.

Rather abruptly, the pod turns west.

I tread for a moment, confused. After they have swum a few lengths, the matriarch turns and clicks at me. It is a question.

I think she wants me to follow.

Suspicions at the many dangers we have encountered prompts me to send a click stream to assess her and Scar. Although it feels rude to do to a stranger, I cannot risk putting the calves in danger again, and I won't leave them behind.

Both the matriarch and Scar seem to know what I'm doing, and actually swim closer before turning to the side so I can get a clear view of what they have eaten. Not much solid, but I do recognize a few salmon bones.

They are safe.

I thank them for their reassurance, even though I know they cannot understand my words. Unlike the neighboring pods back home, with whom we share at least a few words, nothing I say seems to get a reaction. Their clicks, whistles, and pulses all sound random. Our tones seem consistent, so at least they can comprehend my gratitude.

I turn to shore and send a steady pulse of clicks back to the calves.

After a moment, I see Princess and Questions swim out of the cover of the pebbled shore and meet us in the open water. The pointed blackfish greet them with the same chorus they did to me. I can tell that Questions is reluctant, but Princess replies with a happy greeting.

Again in a way that feels abrupt, the matriarch turns west and leads us on. The six calves of the pod are towards the middle and the bulls have formed ranks around them, with the matriarch at the front. Scar is towards the back and beckons me and the calves onward.

I lead Questions and Princess in a spout, and we follow the pod.

It doesn't take long for the initial excitement at swimming with my father's kind to be overshadowed by the realization we are swimming in the same direction as when I saw the whale eater this morning.

I click a warning call to Scar. He slows, and gives me his full attention. I wish I could speak their language. Although I appreciate wherever they are trying to guide us, I cannot let them take us towards danger. They did come from the same direction, so perhaps they know?

The pod has stopped. Their matriarch swims closer. Like Scar, who I assume is her son, she waits patiently for me to speak.

If there isn't a way for me to tell them directly, perhaps I can get my general thoughts across?

I send a steady warning of danger. I get a few uneasy clicks in reply, so I imagine this is generally understood, even if the vocabulary isn't universal. I try to imagine how I might convey the threat to them.

As I continue warning clicks, I point towards the shore. I stick out my tongue to emulate the way the whale eater sensed the water. No reaction. I swim with a twist in my body while trying to have my flukes vertical. Again, they just seem confused. Eventually I give up.

Of all things they seem to understand this, sending me sympathetic and reassuring clicks before continuing west.

All the while, I send distance pulses towards shore and out to sea, seeking any sign of the whale eater.

I hear calls down below, and when I focus my clicks, I can just make out the shapes of cachalot deep below us. They are hunting squid. I recognize the steady pulses they send when trying to find prey.

My pulses pick up a huge form directly below us: a sleeper shark. It is around my length. I have seen some double my mass back home, but this is still an impressive creature. They spend their days in the abyss and come up as the sun goes down and hunt on the surface overnight. Although too slow to catch us, Matriarch says they can kill a blackfish if we let them get too close, and the one time I caught one its flesh was the most disgusting meat I had ever tasted. I'm not worried by its presence, but I am happy that we keep moving.

A shoal of salmon pass closer to shore. They aren't old enough to be swimming up towards the river, at least compared to the same type of salmon back home. I had always assumed all salmon went upriver back home, but it makes sense that some kinds would go upriver to reproduce here in the north. The pod we are swimming with are salmon eaters. They likely fed recently, or maybe they pass over the potential meal out of the urgency of wherever they are taking us.

Concern draws my focus back out, seeking that now-familiar silhouette in the far reaches of my sonar. I send a few pulses behind us too. We're swimming up the current, so if it catches our scent, it will be at our backs.

Nothing of consequence.

Questions gives an excited yelp, and clicks out to the south.

I follow his stream and see a steward of the abyss. The great pale beast advances as before: slow and meticulous. It might be the same one we saw a few days ago. At its pace, we will be long gone by the time it reaches to the surface to catch its breath. Last time we saw the steward, the creature appeared just before Little Shadow was born. I hope this sighting signals hope for future life, or at least some safety ahead.

I resume my distance pulses in a wide arc.

Nothing.

For a while we continue on. My vigilance drawing my focus back means I constantly have to catch up, but I would rather be aware and a bit exerted than just focus on keeping up.

A distance pulse behind us catches a large form. It's at the edge of my range, hovering out of reach. I send more pulses.

Something is definitely there.

I send a warning. At first they ignore me. I must seem paranoid. I pulse again, and see the vague shape of the whale eater comes into sharper focus.

He's around ten lengths away and closing fast.

My warning calls finally get replies, but I know there's little time. We're too far from the coast to use it for cover. He's built up momentum and now there's little chance of us outpacing him. The pod might escape, but Princess is much too slow at her age and Questions is still in the final stages of recovery.

"Get to the coast," I tell Princess and Questions.

Knowing it is a hopeless challenge, I catch a breath and charge.

With as much force as I can muster, I send claps of sound in focused pulses aimed at Whale Eater's eyes. He doesn't hunt by sound, so it won't be as disorienting as it would be to a whale, but it hopefully causes discomfort.

After another spout, I dive.

He is fast straight ahead, and his powerful tail in the lateral stroke means he can turn faster than I could ever hope to, but in a vertical plane, the shape of my tail provides me the advantage.

I feel him turn down to bite. He misses, but the clap of his jaws shudders through me.

Hungry Shadow's strength was in her agility. Whale Eater does not share that talent. As I turn and click, he turns with grace, but it is a wide and time-consuming arc.

I can't keep this up for long, but I can occupy him long enough for the calves to get to shore.

I dive, keen to stay out of range. Once I've circled around, I launch up and land a bite on a pelvic fin. A rumbling hiss pulses through the water. The hard tiny scales of his fin scrape against my teeth. Like my own flippers, his have bone cores, and there's little my twisting does. However, his torso is inflexible enough that as I hold on, I'm dragged behind him and it's pretty easy to stay out of reach.

Although I'm safe for the moment, I don't want to count on him not being able to find a position to arc around. As he struggles, I give his fin a hard twist, prompting another hiss of anger and pain before releasing him and darting to the other side.

Not a moment too soon, as I feel his jaws snap at my tail.

A bellow pulses through the water like thunder. As he turns, the water displaced by his massive flukes sends me spiraling a bit and it takes a moment to reorient myself. By the time I do, I realize the stroke of his tail was to turn his body about, and I barely evade his next strike.

Another rumbling hiss ripples through me, followed by several more. I dart away, knowing he is surely right at my tail.

When I turn to face my end with a bite, I realize Whale Eater is back where we tousled before.

Scar and two of his kin are swimming away from Whale Eater, who turns after them. Their trajectory looks like they rammed his side as he was turned towards me. Another bull impacts his belly as Whale Eater tries to turn after the initial assault. He's so large and heavily armored that their ramming lacks the debilitation it would against a whale, but it's rattling and distracting him, and that's a victory in its own right.

I spout and join the fray.

Whale Eater is turned down and swimming after the bull that struck his belly, and I turn just before impact, throwing my full weight into his side.

Rather than try and score another hit, I swim up and away, following the example of the pointed blackfish. This is a predator of their waters, and they seem to be dealing with him confidently.

The next sequence of impacts are on his back, pushing Whale Eater lower into the water. They only charge after he has been hit on the other side. Although I go in for two more strikes, I have to abandon one as he's already rounded and I fear he will catch me before I can land a blow.

Although he initially tried to catch us, he has changed his aim, and is now in flight. As soon as he begins to swim off, Scar calls off the attack. A part of me wants to press on. The impacts emptied much of his lungs, and he might be close to drowning if we persist, but I choose to trust their evident experience. Perhaps once he has transitioned to flight, he will be more likely to target one of us, and if he focuses like that, I doubt we will get away. Also pushing him under will increase the chances of getting caught in his bite. With the size and power of his jaws, a single bite would almost certainly be a killing blow.

After he has put a few lengths of distance between us, Whale Eater surfaces and lets out an explosive spout. As he inhales, my clicks sense a strain.

He'll live, but hopefully we have bruised and battered him enough that he thinks twice before attacking blackfish ever again.

Following a spout of my own, I return with Scar and his companions back to the pod.

***

As we continue through the evening, I make sure to check behind us now and then, but I do not pick up any sign that Whale Eater is in pursuit.

At my side, Questions sends an excited whistle.

I pulse where he starts swimming, and see six forms ahead of the pointed blackfish pod.

Their songs are familiar.

With a nudge to Princess, she and I follow Questions through the pointed blackfish pod towards our family.

Champion is among them, as is my mother. It is not our whole pod, but I am too elated to ask for more.

Mother and I circle one another, singing a song of greeting. We both check each other for injury. She notes where Hungry Shadow bit me and I remark on a strain in her lungs. She tells me that she was among those who went searching for me in the cloud, and breathed in some of the horrid ash. Thanks to Champion's care, she has mostly recovered, and thinks she will be alright as long as she does not strain herself.

Champion and the rest dote on Princess and Questions. Questions is rapidly telling them of our adventures, although Champion simply seems happy we were found. Although I expect all attention to be on the calves, Champion crosses the water and sends a stream of grateful clicks.

"Is the rest of the family well?" I ask both.

"Many others were injured in the ash," says Mother. "But we went east to avoid the smoke. It followed us, so we had to swim far, and it is still blowing, though not as strong, and two days ago we were able to swim under."

Champion clicks in agreement. "I am glad we found you all. The rest remained west, not wanting to pass under the cloud. We will let the calves recover a short time longer, but then we should return to the family."

"Oh!" I say, turning back to the pointed blackfish pod. "Thanks to them, we evaded Whale Eater. We must be careful in our return. He might attack our smaller group, but I think we have the numbers to fend him off, especially with the injuries the pointed blackfish and I inflicted upon him."

Mother and Champion agree that we should be careful and hug the coast.

Before we depart, I thank Scar and their matriarch. Questions and Princess say their goodbyes too. Although they do not know my words, the pointed blackfish seem to understand my meaning, and sing a song I take to mean farewell as they continue west.

Singing a song of our own, our small pod begins the journey east with the current.

With my mother on one side, Princess and Questions on the other, others in our family surrounding us and Champion leading the way, I feel I can finally relax. Mother has always been family, and with Questions, Princess, Hungry Shadow and her son, we became our own pack, but this feels different. Relishing the song and adding my voice to the tune, I feel for the first time I can remember that I am part of the pod.

As our song carries through the currents, our family begins the long voyage east.

Cast of Characters

A Legacy Stolen, Uncovered, and Forged

The Hunters:

NASIRI: Pakardiant hunter who specializes in man-eaters

ZHEHAN: Nasiri's first apprentice, an Imperial scholar.

RUKIRHA: Pakardiant hunter of the Yellow Panther Clan who seeks out Nasiri as an apprentice.

BORUS: Qajarith hunter from a village Nasiri helped save from Vaskalamaldus the Raven King.

The Librarians:

RA MASLANI: scholar from the Acquisitions Department of the Great Library specialized in artifacts of the First Age, when the first wild magic was domesticated.

HELANA: apprentice of Ra Maslani.

The Rogues:

LOREGUS: bastard son of a Qajarith noblewoman who has turned to a life of crime to support his lavish preferences, being talented in acting and persuasion.

JARAN: facilitator of the Shards, a widespread criminal organization.

TOYATE: Kentarim thief skilled in lock-picking.

MULUK: Akanuk rogue who excels in a wide range of martial arts.

SHIN: Trist smith who knows a great deal about the strengths and weaknesses of magic.

Where Sea Meets Shore

ARGUNITE: Kentarim pirate caught by Pakardiant while on a smuggling job.

EMAHARI: Pakardiant princess with much to prove.

UTANI: Emahari's agichi, a sacred bodyguard.

ROLANIX: Emahari's elder brother and heir to being champion of the confederacy.

JOHANI: Rolanix's agichi.

KATINARI: Rolanix's twin sister and heir to being queen of the Pakardiant Confederacy.

YURAI: commodore in the fleet of Koban the Pirate-King.

Grandmother's Roots

WILD HEART: a Maku who, when an army arrives, flees into the marshes with her daughter and grandchildren to avoid conscription.

CHERRY BLOSSOM: gentle mother of three children and daughter of Wild Heart.

REED WHISTLE: eldest son of Cherry Blossom, struggles with focus and wishes to protect his family at all costs.

OWL EYES: highly inquisitive daughter of Cherry Blossom.

NETTLE TOP: youngest child of Cherry Blossom.

THE SKIN-CHANGER: a shapeshifter from the north who seeks to punish the deserters.

Tides of Restoration

YESI: a Kentarim who hears the call of the sea and wishes to become one of the Khalorim, or merfolk.

CORAL UNDER MOON: a young dolphin Khalorim who is Yesi's lover and introduces her to the other merfolk to undergo the transformation.

HEMI: Yesi's cousin who encourages her to listen to the call of the sea.

CLARITY IN FOG: a Khalorim with the aspect of Rose Shark.

The Reaper's Choice

KIRUT: an Akanuk whaler who has dedicated his life to seeking out and slaying the Great White Death, the demonic creator of the hezuki.

YUMICHIN: a young skin-changer who seeks revenge against the demons that slaughtered her family.

HARUIN: an Eskadin smuggler who has been Kirut's source of information on the whereabouts of the hezuki.

TONKO: an honorable giant of a man and chief of Hollow Turtle Island.

URU: Yumi's cousin, also a skin-changer able to assume the form of a great black sea badger.

DANWE: a refugee of Iron Line Archipelago.

SAM: a witch with a buck tern familiar who was forced to flee her home when the hezuki attacked.

BRUHECHIN: Yumi's cousin and chief of the Chin Atolls.

YANOCHIN: leader of the Chin Guardians, a mercenary company currently overseas in service of an imperial general.

FUDOL: a warrior of Krakenstone who has assumed the role of their leader once their chief retreats to the tower.

THE GREAT WHITE DEATH: the prime hezuki, an ancient demon of frost and famine.

THE SON: a demon created by the Great White Death to inhabit human bodies, yet in all other ways function as a hezuki.

Tempered in Ash and Blood

GOLIATH: an orca/polar blackfish hybrid

QUESTIONS: seven year old elder brother and guardian of Princess.

PRINCESS: a four year old calf and heir to the title of matriarch.

HUNGRY SHADOW: a female zanitel, a species of elasmosaur 'sea serpent' and rival predator of the polar blackfish.

LITTLE SHADOW: son of hungry shadow and playmate of Princess.

MOTHER: Goliath's mother and a descendant of Matriarch's sister, making her and her son of a distinct lineage compared to the rest of the pod, all of whom descend from Matriarch.

CHAMPION: Matriarch's eldest son and defender of the pod.

HEIR: Matriarch's granddaughter and mother to Princess and Questions.

MATRIARCH: the leader of Goliath's pod.

WHALE EATER: a large male motomazor, a species of mosasaur and one of the top predators in the warmer waters of the inland sea.

SCAR: an orca that helps Goliath face Whale Eater.

Glossary

Kaimere:

Kaimere is a distant planet much like Earth in size and climate, but with an ecosystem influenced by waves of life taken from our world and replicated to evolve independently in this new context, integrating with the indigenous life. This native life is microscopic yet interconnected and intelligent. It is often described as magic by the humans who have now colonized the region around the portal that they call The Known World. This 'magic' often bonds with animals and plants, which are then thought of as witches, demons, and magical creatures. It is this native magic that first created a portal linking Earth to Kaimere with the intent of populating their planet with flora and fauna.

Peoples of Kaimere:

Kaimerans

Kaimerans are a subspecies of *Homo sapiens* who were brought to Kaimere around 250,000 years ago. At some point in their history, kaimerans were symbiotically bound with magic native to the world. This magic slightly altered a few features, but the most dramatic change was the slowing of kaimeran's life cycles: adulthood is reached around 80 years of age, and many kaimerans live well into their fifth or sixth centuries. This has made for slow population growth, and despite significant technological advancement and innovation, they are still centuries behind their counterparts on Earth, and their civilizations have not expanded beyond a fairly small region of the planet that they call The Known World. There are five major ethnicities of kaimeran peoples:

Khalin: Children of the Sea

A seafaring nomadic people, the Khalin are the most widespread kaimeran ethnic group. The Kentarim can be found on islands north of Qajar, the Tsuu Henjin live in the west and regularly sail beyond the 'known world', the reclusive To Katon dwell in the southern seas, the Akanuk are common along the western Khalin islands, while the mercantile Eskadin dominate the east and have diaspora in every port city of the known world. Many will go years while barely setting foot on land. They are a diverse people, but generally share an appreciation for freedom and a love for travel.

Pakardiant: Children of the Forest

The Children of the Forest claim to be the first humans of Kaimere, and the ancestors of all other kaimerans. They revere the forest of the vast island, indeed the largest island of the known world, and are the only kaimeran people to live among the drakes instead of fortifying in walls, although their villages are often dwellings suspended in trees. During recent centuries a united group of tribes has grown into the Pakardiant Confederacy, which now controls the northern half of their island home.

Qadanith: Children of the Stars

In the creation myth of the Qadanith, they fell from the stars, while other kaimerans are made of clay from this world. The islanders of the Free-States, one of the two major Qadanith factions, are responsible for opening the portal device made by the fallen First Children civilization and trading not only with humans for a time on the other side in the 'Plaguelands' but also uniting the known world of Kaimere in a vast trade network. Their tongue is spoken by all ethnic groups as a trade language. Their mainland cousins, the Qajarith, are a much more isolated and traditionalist people. The past few centuries has seen a shift from independent fiefs to a consolidated republic of lords, although not all parties are happy with this transition, especially since it was put in place by oligarchs from the Free-States who have positioned themselves in roles of great influence in this republic.

Shu: Children of the Sun

For millennia the Shu were a nomadic people isolated from other kaimerans in the houze prairie. Many lived in a verdant river valley, until years of drought forced their civilization to emigrate. They were led on this journey by a messiah who claimed to be an avatar of the sun. The people of the valley joined many tribes of their kin, the Dolani horsemen, and these people became the Cha'Khati, the Children of the Sun. The Cha'Khati reached the crescent and, using cavalry and tactics the locals were not accustomed to, consolidated the largest empire in kaimeran history. The Cha'Khat Empire now dominates the Crescent.

Telmede: Children of the Mountains

Throughout the Crescent are a diverse ethnicity of people who call themselves the Telmede. The Children of the Mountains are a proud people who hold tradition close to their heart. For millennia the people of the Crescent Sea would war with each other, although none established a longstanding Empire. Once the Cha'Khati invaded from the north and consolidated them in a united Empire, most of the Telmede, such as the Zardic, Tristir, Unkubmitir, and Bolondakir, are content with the economic benefits of a united trade empire. The Serid, people of the eastern hills and wetlands, are most outspoken against Imperial subjugation, although so far, every revolution has failed.

The First Children

The First Children are an extinct civilization of diminutive humanoids, likely descended from *Homo erectus*, said to have been technologically advanced and attuned to the innate magic of Kaimere, even domesticating it to create homunculi. The device that controls when the portal opens or closes, along with allowing travel both ways instead of just from Earth to Kaimere, was built by them. The collapse of the First Children civilization is the source of much interest to kaimeran scholars.

The Maku: Children of the Ocean-Walkers

Called Klaeg by the Pakardiant, the Maku are peoples descended from H. erectus that were brought to Kaimere in the middle Pleistocene, the Maku were enhanced by the First Children to be the perfect soldiers, with superior endurance and fanged jaws. They were driven from their home by kaimerans at the conclusion of the Second Age, now residing on the White Coast of Kairul east of the Known World, and seek to return to their home by voyaging back across the Abyss.

Enchanted Creatures/Demons/Homunculi

It is not unusual for hives of Kaimeran magic to bond with a host. Normally these enchantments have little impact on the host, at most making them slightly healthier as the magic seeks to preserve their home. Sometimes the impacts are more significant, and some hives are aggressive and malicious, turning their host into powerful and aggressive demons that seek to spread the magic like a virus. When the First Children domesticated many strains of magic during the First Age, they used these controlled hives to make homunculi, bodies specifically made for these more potent and aggressive hives. Early homunculi were simply beings with some alterations (which is thought by some scholars to be the origin of Kaimerans long lives, although this is not discussed in polite company), but later forms were astonishingly sophisticated, able to endure decapitation, immolation, and even mimicking mortals.

The Plaguelands

The term for Earth used by most kaimerans. Interaction with humans from Earth has been minimal after trade for livestock inadvertently brought several devastating plagues, which kaimerans attributed to humans. The portal was then closed to all but occasional and critical transit, sometimes going years without opening.

Fauna of Kaimere and the Realms Beyond

Drakes: Dinosaurs

DIRE HERON: long-snouted fish-hunting dromaeosaur.

INDRAKAI: the great trickster of Pakardia. Largest of the firebirds.

KURAJAKU: largest of the megaraptoran drakes, often called crocodile drakes.

XUUL: aquatic dromaeosaur, ecologically similar to a leopard seal.

Sky Titans: Pterosaurs

BANSHEE GULL: giant coastal scavenger, so called for their harrowing cry.

BUCK TERN: a marine tapejarid known for long migrations and great speed.

ELK TERN: larger cousin of the buck tern, sporting a massive pronged crest.

TITAN CROW: robust tapejarid with black filaments and macropredatory inclinations.

Beasts: Mammals of Kaimere

BILYUK: the 'fighting whale', a large aggressive cetothere that feeds on tiny prey in the sediment of shallow seas.

BOAR-CAMEL: also called the katoblepas, large marsh camelids of Kairul.

BOKODU: 'god of the hoofed beasts', a multi-ton entelodont of Kairul.

COMMON BLACKFISH: small species of *Orcinus* common in the tropical waters of the known world. A social hunter and frequent hunter of dolphins and seals.

COMMON BEAKED WHALE: called the boar whale by Kaimeran whalers, a large whale with long tusks.

COMMON DOLPHIN: dolphin especially common in the tropical waters around the Kentarim islands.

COMMON WALRUS: second largest pinniped in Kaimere, this species sports four tusks and has tough grey hide.

COMMON WHALE: medium-sized cetothere, most common whale of the known world.

DIVER CACHALOT: tall-finned sperm whale in the same genus as the species of Earth.

KILLER CACHALOT: giant predatory sperm whale descended from *Acrophyseter*.

KOMATU: the 'dire hare' of Kairul, a large multituberculate predator.

MARSH PANTHER: a leopard-sized nimravid.

NEROTAN WARCAT: a lion domesticated by House Nerotok of the western Qajarith peninsula.

POINTED BLACKFISH: *Orcinus orca*, the same species of killer whale on Earth today.

POLAR BLACKFISH: species of *Orcinus* specialized in marine mammals.

RIVER SEAL: an aquatic hyaenodont, one of the top predators of Kairul's western wetlands.

SEA BADGER: a small walrus common in the inland sea which hunt fish and small marine mammals, and look much more like sea lions than walruses of Earth.

SPUR RAT: a multituberculate analogous to a muskrat.

Other Natural Creatures

ELK CRAB: a large marine scorpion common on the Kentarim reefs.

KATABO: serpentine mosasaur and the top predator of the reefs of the known world.

KRAKEN: clade of squid, with some growing as large as a whale.

MOØRKUTLOT: the Silent Ones, mysterious heterothermic predators of the polar continent.

MOTOMAZOR: largest mosasaur in Kaimere, top predator of the warmer oceans of Kaimere.

ROSE SHARK: pink shark common in the reefs of the known world.

STEWARD OF THE ABYSS: a massive temnospondyl that resides in the deep oceans south of the known world.

WHALER SHARK: the mighty megalodon, apex predator of all Kaimeran oceans.

ZANITEL: macropredatory elasmosaur

Magical Creatures, Beings, and Demons

FAMILIAR: animal companion of a witch that shares their magic hive.

HEZUKI: demons with an affinity for cold inhabiting the bodies of xuul.

KHALORIM: merfolk with aspects of a specific marine animal, such as sharks, mosasaurs, and dolphins.

WITCH: generic term for a kaimeran with magical abilities.

Illustrated Menagerie

Beasts Featured in

TALES OF KAIMERE: SONGS OF THE INLAND SEA

Beasts of Kairul

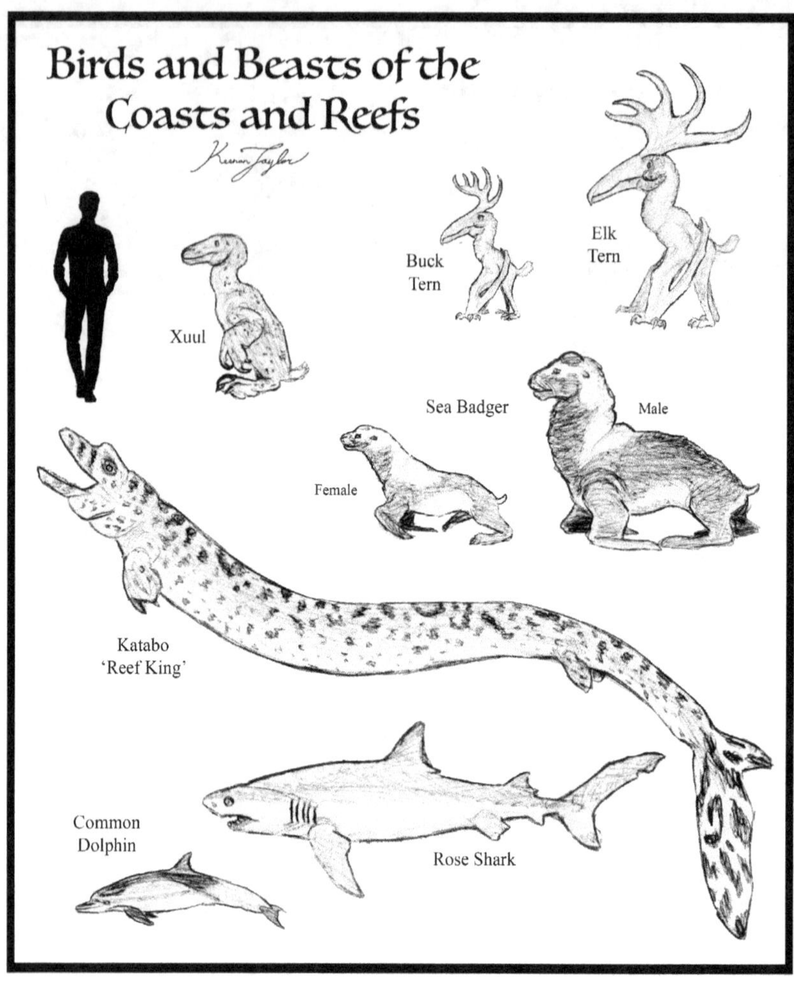

Birds and Beasts of the
Coasts and Reefs

Xuul

Buck
Tern

Elk
Tern

Sea Badger

Female

Male

Katabo
'Reef King'

Common
Dolphin

Rose Shark

Marine Beasts
Boar Whale
Common Walrus
Zanitel
Orca
Polar Blackfish
Motomazor
'Whale Eater'
Common Blackfish

Ocean Giants

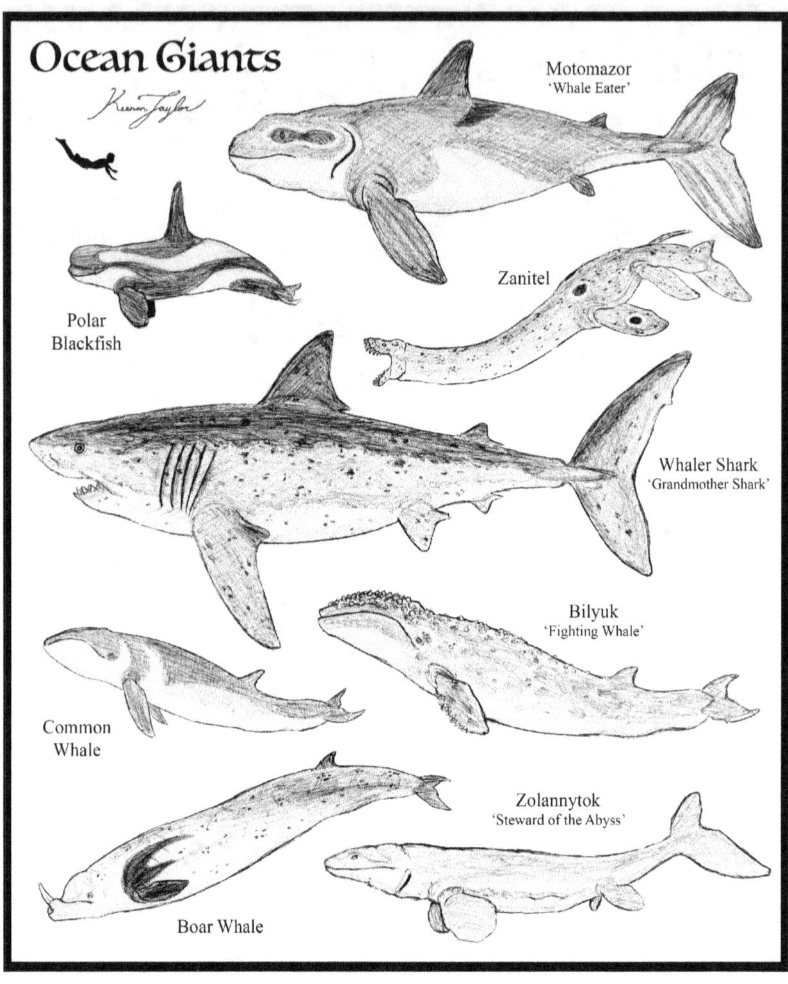

Moørkutlot

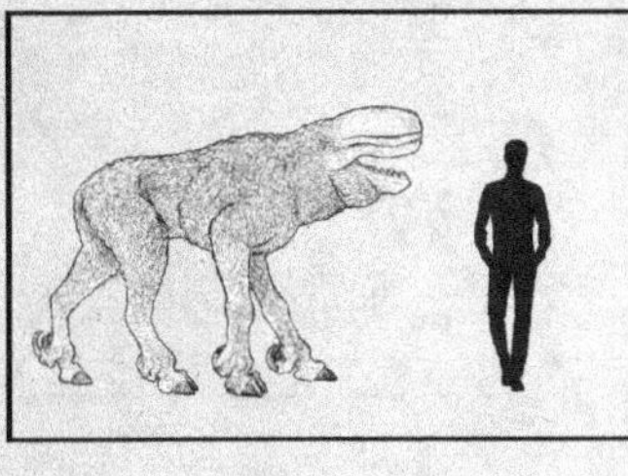

The Silent Ones

"Through Death They Create Silence"
Length: 6-8 feet long
Height: 5-6 feet tall
Mass: 600-1,100 pounds

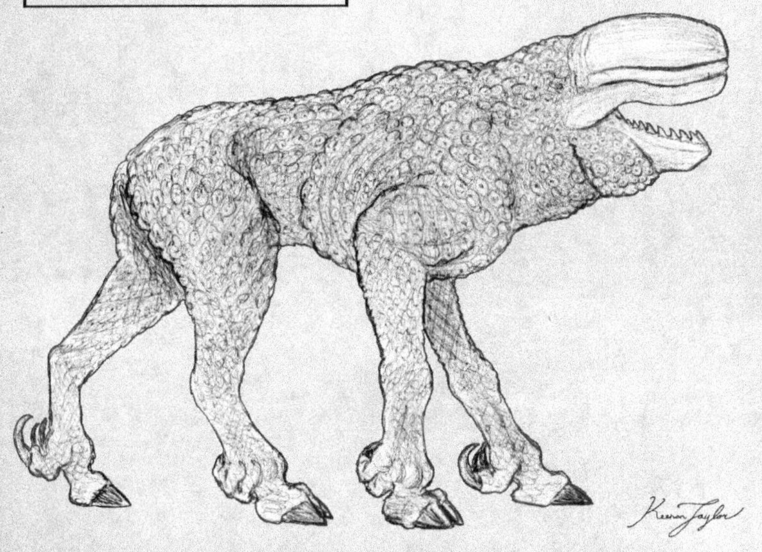

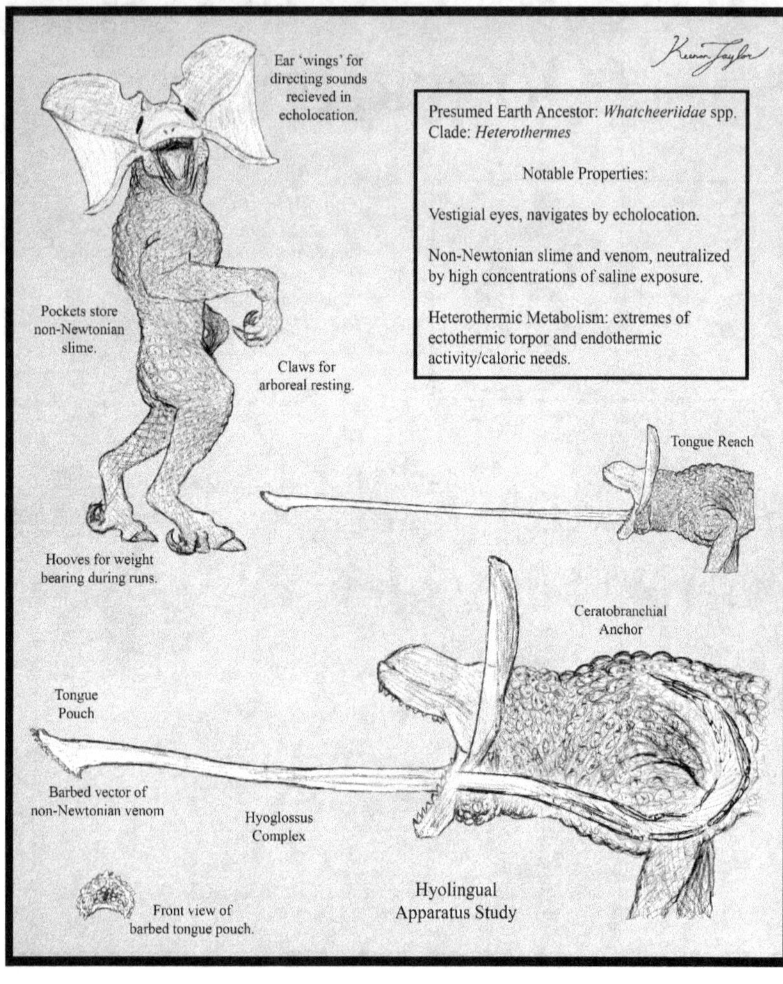

Ear 'wings' for directing sounds recieved in echolocation.
Pockets store non-Newtonian slime.
Claws for arboreal resting.
Hooves for weight bearing during runs.
Tongue Pouch
Barbed vector of non-Newtonian venom
Hyoglossus Complex
Front view of barbed tongue pouch.
Tongue Reach
Ceratobranchial Anchor
Hyolingual Apparatus Study
Presumed Earth Ancestor: Whatcheeriidae spp.
Clade: Heterothermes
Notable Properties:
Vestigial eyes, navigates by echolocation.
Non-Newtonian slime and venom, neutralized by high concentrations of saline exposure.
Heterothermic Metabolism: extremes of ectothermic torpor and endothermic activity/caloric needs.

Contact and Social Media

My writing would be incomplete without my art, and my illustrations are often inspired by my work as an author. Together the two are my driving passions, and Kaimere simply wouldn't exist as an idea without both. If you enjoyed my writing, or wish to learn more about the setting and creatures, I invite you to follow me on social media. It is on platforms like Instagram (@illustrated_menagerie) and Twitter (@taylor_menagerie) that much of my world is developed for all to see. Patreon (Illustrated Menagerie) is also a way to both support my work and get early insight into my worldbuilding, drawing, and writing projects.

I have a youtube channel, Keenan Taylor's Tales of Kaimere, where I discuss worldbuilding for this project. I mostly focus on animals, but there are plenty of episodes on ecology, cultures, and the natural sciences of this setting if you want to know more!

If you wish to contact me, any of these platforms work, and I am also available by email at talesofkaimere@gmail.com with any questions.

Cheers, folks!

Acknowledgments

There are many people to whom acknowledgement is due for helping me bring these stories from ideas in my head to the book you now hold:

- Endless appreciation to Christy for your support, feedback, scheduling, editing, and cheerleading, without which this book could never have been completed. You have been my lighthouse and my compass.
- To our three cats, who added their share of joys and complications to the project.
- Thanks to my alpha and beta readers Christine, Douglas, Heather, Kevin, Liam, Peter, and the Spec Council.
- Gratitude to my family for indulging my insatiable curiosity and nurturing a sense of wonder, ambition, and creativity.
- Thanks to my many incredible friends who endured hours of character, plot, dialogue, craft, and world-building discussions. Special shoutout to Heather and Johannah for enduring my many unhinged requests of your medical expertise, and I hope you never have to perform any of the procedures that this book inspired me to propose.
- To Gage for taking that wonderful picture of me at the helm.
- Cheers to my Patreon patrons Alex K, Alex Mastodon, Anthony, Armando, Brin, Brandon, Cai, Chris, CJ, Connor, Crow, David, EJ, Gage, Hayden, Inaki, Joe, Kai, Kevin, Leandra, Link, Lucas, Martaugh, Michael, Otter God, Segg Way,

Stonebone, Sunny, Toros, and Zach. Also to my YouTube episode sponsors. By your support I have been able to make worldbuilding, illustration, and writing my career. This has been a dream come true.

- My sincerest appreciation to Dr. Welker for her expertise in human evolution, Dr. Judkins for his inspiration in the myths and fantastical elements of Kaimere, Mr. Cuffy for his lessons in perseverance and patience, Miss Tina for encouraging me to build from my missteps, and Miss Ann for showing me the importance of optimism and integrity.
- Last, but certainly not least; cheers to the late Dr. Denice Szafran, with whom I spent many an office hour developing cultural and linguistic ideas for the people of Kaimere.